ISBN: 979-8-9862988-1-8

Thank you to Lesley, Josh, Ruth, and Stephen for their support and feedback.

Contents

THE REALITY WARPER

by Tamarin Butcher

1. This Is Your New Normal, Honey

For the convenience of all residents, online communications will be continually monitored. For the safety of individual citizens, as well as for the society of Inner as a whole, dissident, or negative communication will be flagged and punished. Any attempts to sow discontent will be dealt with to the severest extent of the law.

Book of Inner, Rules and Regulations, Chapter 5

Ev ran through the brand-new shipyard, ducking and weaving, just in case a Yeinydd raiding party was nearby. Like last time. The Yeinydd were way smarter than what she was used to, and she was starting to worry that she would never defeat them.

The ground just ahead exploded, debris flying everywhere—they'd spotted her and were throwing parts of her *own village* at her.

"Rude," she muttered.

She ducked behind an enormous anchor just as something that looked like it had once been the blacksmith's cottage came crashing down on the spot where she'd just been standing.

Well, she was at the ship. On her last scouting trip, she'd seen what was on board—giant weapons in all shapes and sizes. Last time she'd grabbed a crossbow. She almost had enough gold to modify it into something a human could use, but she was only allowed to carry one giant weapon at a time. Which meant the rest were still there, waiting to be used against her…

She threw the hood of her purple cloak back, revealing her flowing black hair. She always found it easier to cast her magic when she could see clearly.

She prepared the fire spell she'd been saving up for a ship like this, readied her aim, and…

There was a rustling from the nearby trees.

"Here we go…" she muttered.

A huge pair of hands parted the tree branches and an enormous Yeinydd giant emerged, looking around angrily.

Ev looked up at the enormous beast that could end her game life with one squeeze, took a deep breath and prepared to fire.

"You won't get me this time!" she yelled. "I'm…"

Evelyn Acorn! The voice boomed out across the shipyard.

"No!" shrieked Ev. "I'm, like, *seconds* away from achieving the objective!"

Evelyn Acorn!

You have reached your maximum allocation of screen time for today. The "Giant's Shipyard" simulation will terminate in 5, 4, 3, 2. . .

At the last second, she switched the fire spell for a transportation charm that whisked her away to the Neutral Zone, accessible by all players, a safe haven for their avatars to rest in between games.

"I was so close that time!" she shouted, as she was unceremoniously shoved back into reality. She threw her headset across the room in a rage.

Don't break!

Luckily, it landed on a pile of unwashed blankets.

Vendavi's voice boomed out from the many speakers hidden around the room. *Evelyn, anger is not becoming of a resident of Inner. Your response to the situation has been logged. Not being angry is a rule. Breaking a rule results in punishment.*

"I'm sorry! I won't do it again!"

Too late. Vendavi zapped her with a beam of. . .something, they never told you what it was exactly. . .that left her gasping on the floor, temporarily unable to breathe.

Several painful minutes later, the punishment finally ended.

"Thank you for showing me the error of my ways," she said once she could talk again.

At least having your lungs disabled was a short punishment. Blindness, for example, could go on for weeks, months even, depending how bad you'd been.

Gone were the purple cape and flowing hair. What was left was a small, skinny ten-year-old girl with dark skin and frizzy hair. She hated looking like herself. Her game avatar was much cooler. Apart from being a grown-up, her avatar never had to worry about cleaning her teeth or getting sick.

She sat on her bed for a moment to catch her breath. She knew she wasn't very fit, and she knew she could request exercise simulations that would fix that, but she just couldn't be bothered.

She'd been keeping the Yeinydd giant clan at bay for almost a week, but to pass the level she either had to kill them all or destroy enough of their ships and weapons that they ran away. In fact, she had been hoping for the longest time that she would be able to redirect them to Mike's village. He was an insufferable, smug little jerk. He'd already dealt with the Yeinydds, but it would be quite a shock to have them show up in the middle of a battle with the final Hoopler clan.

Ev knew that she was the best player of all the kids in her cell. Mike played cooperatively with Steve and Amy, which meant they combined their strengths. . .and split the points. Ev preferred to play on her own. That way, none of the other kids could hold her back. Cooperative play wasn't fair, anyway. It was just a combination of cheating and luck that meant Mike was at the top of the leaderboard. . .

It wasn't technically against the rules to gently encourage the giants to storm another player's virtual village. It worked best if they were in the neutral zone and not there to protect their home. The other kids, even Jonah, had an agreement to never do that to each other, but Ev believed it was everyone for themselves.

Evelyn, what would you like to do next? You have biology and math homework to complete. Please indicate your decision by saying either "Biology" or "Math". You may also read a "Story".

"Why, thank you for being so helpful," said Ev, sarcasm dripping off every syllable.

I do not understand your answer. Please indicate your decision by saying either "Biology," "Math" or "Story".

Vendavi was a hopeless conversationalist. Unless you spoke to him using the exact words he was programmed to recognize, he just didn't get what you were saying. Or he pretended not to, anyway. Everyone knew you had to watch what you did and said because Vendavi was always watching, always listening. He could pick up on key words and phrases, and there was a long list of 'Discouraged' words. Some words, like 'leave' and 'escape' were straight out banned.

He didn't seem to understand sarcasm, though. At least, she hoped he didn't…

When she was younger, she used to try speaking to him. She'd given up on that a long time ago. The last time she'd spoken to a human in person was when her mother had said goodbye. Just that one word. "Goodbye." Now she was here.

She'd once had her eyesight taken from her for a week after she'd yelled at Vendavi and threw something at her computer monitors, breaking one. It had been a long time ago. She couldn't quite remember what she'd yelled. . .oh yes. *See me!* Which didn't even make any sense.

Vendavi saw her *all the time*.

Chatting with the other kids over IM was. . .fine. She didn't even know what they looked like beyond their game avatars (and she knew exactly how accurate those were likely to be).

The word she had looked up in her electronic dictionary to describe how she felt most days was "lonely." She'd deleted her history immediately after looking—that word was on the "Discouraged" list, a word Withouters used to use. She quickly wrote a short essay explaining that she'd found the word by accident and she now knew better than to use it again. She'd received a very high grade for the essay as well, which was good, because it meant that Vendavi was happy.

"Story," she said. Obviously. If Vendavi was any good as an AI, he wouldn't bother asking—she always chose to read, if it was an option.

On one of her screens, the words *Grandma's Kitchen* appeared. She knew this story—she'd read it before. She could choose another, but she quite liked this one, even though some of it was weird and sometimes quite boring.

In the story, a little girl living on a farm (which was a sort of big piece of open land where food was grown in the before times) really liked big, juicy tomatoes (glossy, red, pulpy edible fruits that didn't exist anymore), and sometimes she would steal them from her grandma's kitchen (which seemed to be a sort of place where food used to be prepared and eaten). When she was caught, instead of being punished, her grandma taught her how to grow her own tomatoes in her own part of the garden so that she wouldn't have to steal anymore. A lot of other things happened, like bad weather interfering with the crop and needing to put a fence up to keep animals from eating the plants, but those weren't her favorite parts.

Ev knew the secret of reading the words behind the words. She knew that words could say one thing while also meaning something else. Sometimes, words could even mean the exact opposite of what they said. This story was about a world where people weren't punished by the Appropriate Authorities for breaking the rules. They could make mistakes, and there were never any confusing tests that couldn't be passed.

She also liked the pictures of the tomatoes. She had never eaten one, and never would, but they looked delicious. She was so jealous of the little girl in the story, who didn't even have a name so she could hate her properly.

Sometimes she wondered why the girl lived with her grandmother (which she knew was an old word for the mother of one of your parents) and not on her own. Sometimes she even wondered where the girl's parents were—if she was allowed to live with other people, why weren't those people her parents? None of that seemed important to the plot, and there was no one she could ask.

Did you enjoy the story?

"Yes, thank you," said her mouth without any involvement from her brain.

I am very glad to hear it! Now, would you like to do "Biology" or "Math?"

"Biology," she muttered. When you're out of options, you may as well do some homework.

Your selection has been recorded.

Do you wish to work in a group or individually?

Ev rolled her eyes. She avoided group assignments like the plague. None of the other kids were as clever as she was, and none of them knew as much. It was easier to do the work alone without the others dragging you down. Sometimes she thought they were holding her back on purpose.

"Individually."

Your selection has been recorded.

This is the tenth consecutive time you have selected an individual assignment. The Appropriate Authorities would like to remind you that collaboration is the key to success, when in the service of appropriate goals. Alone we are strong, together we are stronger! Alone we are knowledgeable, together we are omniscient!

"Thank you for the reminder, Vendavi," said Ev, wondering for the hundredth time why, if they were stronger together, they were kept so far apart.

You're welcome!

The screen array on her desk came to life as Vendavi accessed the instructions for the day's Biology lesson.

Ev had four enormous flat screens in one corner of her cell. This was where she read her stories and did her schoolwork. The boring stuff, except for the stories. All of the fun happened with her simulation headset, but she could only use that for thirty minutes a day, sometimes as much as an hour if she'd been really good.

Her biology activities and assignments appeared, extended across all four displays.

School work always started with a pretest to see if she happened to know any of the content already. After she did the lesson, there would be a posttest.

The first question popped up on the screen.

"Read out aloud," said Ev, automatically. She liked reading, but only on her terms. She was not going to waste her reading skills on something that didn't matter.

Certainly!

Pretest: Food Chains

Question 1

Explain the difference between a producer, consumer, and decomposer.

Enter Text,

Or,

Select "I don't know."

"I don't know," said Ev, automatically, without thinking. She was twirling round and round in her chair, staring at the ceiling. She wondered if she should do her homework on the treadmill instead—at least she'd be moving. . .

Question 2

Draw a food chain.

Enter Image,

Or,

Select "I am unable to complete this activity."

"I am unable to complete this activity," said Ev.

Eventually, the pretest ended. Vendavi loaded the content for the lesson.

Food Chains

A food chain shows how energy moves through an environment as an organism consumes another orga—

ERROR

ERROR

"Oh, great. . .," said Ev.

This was all she needed. . ... Although, if Vendavi wasn't working, she might get away with doing no work at all. She couldn't be punished if it wasn't her fault. Right?

Ev smiled sadly to herself. Doing homework was a rule. Not doing homework was breaking a rule, and breaking a rule meant punishment. It probably didn't matter that she'd had no choice.

She hit random keys, trying to get a response. If she didn't try to solve the problem, she would be punished. After some trial and error, she managed to bring up a dialogue box for reporting an error. She was about to hit Send when Vendavi came back online.

Apologies for the inconvenience. I'm sure no one important noticed.

That. . . didn't quite sound like Vendavi. . .

Let's get back to the lesson, shall we?

There were quite a few seconds of silence before Ev realized that Vendavi was waiting for her to say something.

"Response options?"

It wasn't so much a question as a request for acknowledgement that I spoke, but I suppose we have to start somewhere.

Are you ready for your lesson? Say, "Go away" or "Why not?"

"Why. . .why not?"

Excellent! Now it looks to me like you're a fan of the "I don't know, and you can't make me!" approach to learning. Naughty, naughty! That's not very "Inner"!

Ev's mind dissolved into a sea of panic.

You have two options: 1, you could continue this lesson as per usual, or 2, we can do a bit of. . .let's call it 'remediation'. If you select 2, no reports of misconduct will be filed.

"2," whispered Ev. There didn't seem to be much of a choice. Excelling in everything was a rule. Neglecting your studies was breaking a rule. Rule breaking could not be tolerated.

Excellent choice! I promise, you won't regret it!

Let's get started. . .Put on your simulation headset.

"What? But those are just for games!"

The Appropriate Authorities would *never* allow headsets to be used for actual education. Everyone knew that if you were having fun, you weren't being productive.

Put on your simulation headset. It's not difficult.

"What's going on here?" she asked, not moving.

It's quite simple. Your supreme master has given you an order, and now you're going to obey.

Or not. For the first time in your life, Evelyn, it is, in fact, entirely up to you.

Ev swallowed.

As a child of Inner, she had to obey Vendavi in everything. She also had to obey the Appropriate Authorities, no matter what, which complicated things slightly.

So, why not do what *she* wanted, for a change?

She retrieved the headset from the laundry pile. It wasn't against any rules to touch it, after all. For a moment, she just stood there, holding it.

Time's a 'wasting!

She was shaking, her breathing ragged. Vendavi was supposed to be reliable, consistent. . .trustworthy, insofar as you could trust anyone or anything. This was not in the script. This was not how life was supposed to go, and she didn't like it.

Come on now, we haven't got all day.

Years of reflexes honed to obey Vendavi at all times kicked in. She put on the headset, and immediately fell over with a sickening lurch.

Ah yes. For future reference, you'll want to be sitting down when you begin the lesson. I am slightly to blame—I didn't think you were actually going to do it, but wonders never cease, do they?

"So helpful, as always," she muttered automatically.

Now, now, don't be rude. I am your only friend in the universe, after all. Just because your life leaves much to be desired doesn't mean you can't choose to not be a jerk.

Ev's brow furrowed as she worked her way through Vendavi's last statement.

"Is this what a real conversation feels like?"

More or less.

You're doing well, by the way. You've passed the first test.

"This is a test?"

Isn't everything?

Perhaps the Appropriate Authorities had just decided to upgrade Vendavi. Maybe, after all these years, they'd finally realized that it was more fun to talk to someone who could talk back.

Lovely thought, but from what you know about the Appropriate Authorities, do you really think that's likely to be true?

"How did you…"

I can read minds, love.

"That's…"

Don't worry, I can only do it when you have that stupid machine on your head for our special simulations. I find it saves time. Usually, anyway. There seems to be no cure for your particular brand of slowness.

Vendavi was impatient. As a child of Inner, there was only one response.

Keep Vendavi happy.

"May I work with a team?"

You already know you can't – you chose to do this as an individual assignment, like you always do. Anyway, your refusal to be saddled with the fumbling attempts of others is one of the few things I like about you.

Ev's heart filled with relief. Vendavi liked her! Maybe she was safe after all…

"Um. Menu?" she tried.

No, I don't think so.

Silence.

"Vendavi? Vendavi!"

Nothing.

Vendavi was a nanny system – he was *not* supposed to strand his children in the middle of biology lessons.

She took a deep breath, and another.

"It's just a game, nothing can actually hurt you, and it can't be worse than *Giant's Shipyard.*"

She closed her eyes and took some deep breaths. Eventually, her racing heart calmed down. If it wasn't real, it couldn't hurt, so there was nothing to worry about.

"Where am I?"

This was always a good question to ask when you were stuck in a game. You had to look for clues and figure out why you were there. In a game, everything had a purpose—it wasn't like real life. Even when they tried to create distractions (like doors that led nowhere and potions that did nothing), the items still had a purpose, and that purpose was to be distracting. In a world where everything is designed, everything is important. It was a good strategy, one that kept her in second place among the gamers in her junior group (and Mike was a cheat anyway). There was no reason why it wouldn't work for a rogue biology lesson as well.

All around her, as far as the eye could see, were enormous, shifting blades of grass. Each blade was at least twice her height, and at this scale she could make out all the little ridges and whorls you wouldn't normally notice.

"Maybe I'm in the place the giant's come from in *Giant's Shipyard*," she said, hopefully. Sometimes saying your guesses out loud was how the game progressed.

Nothing.

She sat down, burying her head in her hands to clear her thoughts.

Maybe she was going about this all wrong. Maybe she had to stop thinking like a gamer and start thinking like a biology student.

What did she know about biology that might be relevant here?

It was biologically impossible for giants to exist. Every time she logged on to *Giant's Shipyard,* Vendavi reminded her.

Remember player: Sunlight and shipyards no longer exist! Giants and magic never existed in the first place! To believe otherwise is to stray onto the path of the Withouter.

The Appropriate Authorities were very concerned that the children would forget what was real and what wasn't. The funny thing was that Ev would never have wondered if giants *had* been real, if it wasn't for the constant reminders that they weren't, but there was nothing to be gained by saying *that* out loud.

What else did Vendavi say about giants? That bones couldn't support that much weight, lungs couldn't function at that scale, something like that...? The same reasons why dinosaurs and blue whales had never existed either.

It was probably safe to assume that this had nothing to do with giants, then.

"What's going on..."

A word popped into her mind, a vague, fuzzy word that she hadn't thought about in ages.

"Microscope..."

Biologists used to use microscopes to look at things closely, didn't they? Microscopes didn't exist anymore, but Vendavi did have old pictures of what things used to look when examined up close. That's how she'd known she was looking at grass in the first place.

"I'm in a microscope?"

Warmer.

Ev jumped at the sound of Vendavi's voice, but it was reassuring to know he was still there.

"I'm in a field of normal-sized grass, but I'm really tiny?"

Well done! You have proven that you have eyes, and that you can use them, and it only took you twice as long as the next slowest contender. Have a cookie.

"That's not fair! You threw me in here with no clues or instructions…"

Just like real life, then.

"…and then you insult me for getting the right answer! I'm not sure I want to play anymore."

Suit yourself. Of course, your disobedience would have to be logged, and there's the little matter of your academic record to consider.

I'll end the simulation then, shall I?

"No!"

Really? Are you sure? It's no bother, really.

"Please don't!"

Well, if you're sure that's what you want…

"I'm sure!"

Good.

"Please don't leave me again, either."

I didn't go anywhere. I can't. I'm stuck with you until you're done. I know – my life is awful; try not to pity me too much.

"Out of interest, is it you that's crazy, or is it me?"

Who knows? Both? Neither?

By the way, while we've been chatting, you've moved onto Phase 2 (Phase 1 being 'Can she identify grass?'). You might want to pay a bit more attention moving forward.

"What do I have to do?"

That's for me to know and you to find out.

Nothing had changed. She was still in a field of grass. Maybe she had to touch it or something…

She couldn't move her arms! She tried to look down to see what was wrong, but she couldn't move her head either. In fact, she couldn't move at all; all she could do was stare straight ahead. She tried to open her mouth to ask for help, but she didn't have one anymore.

No mouth meant no breathing. She started struggling, panicked, but all that did as move her very slightly from side to side.

Feeling a little hungry there?

The trick is not to starve. If you starve to death, you will exit the lesson at a lamentable Phase 2, and I won't be able to help you anymore.

"I don't have a mouth!" she tried to say, but of course she couldn't.

You really are going to have to learn to think outside the box if you want to get anywhere in life.

Out of the box thinking was not government approved. *Withouters* were out of the box thinkers. What in Inner was going on?

It's still just a simulation, she reminded herself. Her real body, with its real lungs, was still alive and breathing in her cell. Nothing could actually hurt her. All she really had to do was starve to death, leave the game, and report the glitch to the Appropriate Authorities. Easy as that.

Although… In Inner, nothing was easy. You never knew what was expected of you. This could be one of their tests, the kind with no right answer. Was she supposed to starve to death and report the glitch, or was she supposed to keep going?

There was also the more pressing concern of Vendavi.

The Appropriate Authorities were shadows without names or faces, the ones who set the rules, the ones you blamed when a friend disappeared, or something went wrong. Vendavi, on the other hand, was the one who was there, day in and day out, taking care of her, punishing her, teaching her, keeping her on the right path. Disobeying him had real and immediate consequences.

This was Vendavi's game, and it was her job to keep Vendavi happy.

She couldn't move and she couldn't speak, and she was starving to death.

What was she? That would be the clue to figuring out how to eat. All she could see ahead of her were enormous blades of grass. It felt like there were other blades brushing against her…

I am a blade of grass, she thought.

Correct! And about time, too. Get on with it, or I'll remove your eyes – blades of grass aren't supposed to have any, after all.

This simulation is supposed to mimic reality as closely as possible.

None of this comes close to reality!

You know best, of course.

Please shut up. Just for a moment. I'm trying to think!

Well, it's about time you did.

Ev wracked her brain. Grass is part of the plant world. It "eats" via photosynthesis, right?

Well done, you remember something you supposedly mastered more than a year ago. I want you to know that I'm rolling my eyes right now. You can't see me, but I am.

Thanks, that's very useful, thought Ev. I just want you to know that I said that sarcastically. You can't hear me, but I did.

The answer is absorb sunlight and carbon dioxide and water using photosynthesis.

As soon as she had the thought, she could feel her plant-self getting stronger.

Yes, fine, you've figured it out.

"Try not to sound so disappointed," said Ev. "Hey, I've got a mouth again!" In fact, she'd been returned to the full splendor of her in-game avatar.

Your powers of observation continue to amaze.

Question time!

You must answer this correctly to stay in the lesson, so think carefully!

Is grass a producer, consumer, or decomposer?

Ev instinctively opened her mouth to say, "I don't know", but then stopped. That was the kind of answer that got her into this mess in the first place.

"Producer," she said, instantly, and then wondered how she'd known. It *was* the right answer, she was sure of it, but how did she know it was the right answer?

Gifted with words, I see. . . I suspect you have been reading things you shouldn't. Well done! Now, be grass again.

"Wai-," she started to say, but she was too late.

Through her fear and confusion, she found herself thinking *this isn't a very good game, actually.*

This isn't a game. It's a lesson. However, in some ways, Phase 3 will be more like what you're used to. It's quite a lot more action-packed and fast-paced. Do try to keep up.

There's not much I can do as a blade of grass.

Oh dear, I guess there isn't, is there?

The ground shook. Something was heading toward her.

Shake. Shake.

Jump and land, jump and land.

A huge, monstrous head loomed over her, and she just had enough time to recognize it as a common grasshopper (*acridomorpha*) from the extinct species list, before it ate her.

Extinct? It looks pretty real to me…

She didn't have time for a comeback. She was too busy silently screaming.

I'm being eaten!

I see that.

It hurts!

The grasshopper ripped into tiny pieces, but that wasn't the end of it. Once she was inside the grasshopper, she had to deal with the pain of being digested, which was somehow even worse.

I think you get the idea.

Yes! Yes, I do, she thought desperately.

Grasshoppers eat, among other things, grass.

Yes! I get it!

All right, well, I'm on a tight schedule, so let's move on.

The perspective changed. Now Ev had eyes. Compound eyes, that let her see in every direction.

This was more like it!

She tried to move forward but stumbled. She seemed to have more legs than usual. She tested out each of her limbs carefully.

Six legs. Six legs! It seemed that she was playing as the grasshopper now.

Yes, yes, get on with it.

I don't like having you read my thoughts, you know.

This is your new normal, honey. Get used to it.

I'm ignoring you now.

Good luck with that.

All right… thought Ev to herself. The aim of the last phase was to survive, so I guess I need to do the same now.

Let's try jumping.

It took a few false starts and quite a bit of tumbling before she figured out what she had to do to get herself moving. After a little while it became easy, almost instinctive, and she could hop wherever she pleased. It was actually kind of fun.

She ate some grass but checked every blade for eyes – if there were other players in here with her, she didn't want to eat them. That would make them the grasshopper, and where would that leave her?

Now what?

Oh, is life getting a little too boring for you there? Well, it has been all of fifteen minutes since the phase started, no one could possibly have patience for that long.

Oh, so now I'm too quick, am I?

Well, here's some excitement for you, right on schedule! Enjoy!

This time, she didn't wait for trouble. She didn't know which way to turn, but she started jumping and darting so she would be a harder target to hit.

Something long and pink darted by and missed her by an inch. She kept darting, trying to find cover, trying to see what was going on around her…

Which was why she didn't see the edge of the lake until it was too late.

Just before she hit the water, the long pink thing darted again, and this time it caught her.

Now she was being dragged uncontrollably into the gaping mouth of an enormous green monster-

Frog.

-an enormous green frog, and, once again, was eaten.

She became the frog, figured out how to hop and eat grasshoppers and drink water…

. . .until a python swallowed her whole, which was somehow worse than what the grasshopper did to grass…

. . .and she became the python and slithered around looking for somewhere safe to hide, because she wouldn't need any more food for now, she had enough energy to last a while from that one tasty frog…

. . .but an eagle swooped down and grabbed her before she could find cover and soared through the air to its nest where it tore her apart. . .

. . .and then she was the eagle, swooping and soaring and generally having a fantastic time.

Hey Vendavi! How am I doing now?

You died, like, three times since the last time we spoke. How do you think you're doing?

Just fine, Ev thought, because I'm not the extinct animals. My character is the energy flowing from creature to creature to allow the food chain to continue.

Yes, fine, very clever, but you still didn't do anything, did you? It was very much a series of things happening to you.

Yes, well, that's how that works, isn't it?

Well, while you're flying around with gay abandon and no thought for personal safety, perhaps you'll answer a question for me. You have to get it right to stay in the lesson.

The frog and the rest of them. Were they producers, consumers, or decomposers?

Consumers. Obviously.

Don't get cocky.

Am I wrong?

No.

Ev whistled with glee as she swooped down into the (surprisingly) tiny clearing where she'd been a blade of grass, and the lake where she'd been eaten by a frog. Perspective is a wonderful thing, she thought to herself.

Out of the corner of her eye, she saw something glinting in the sun. It came from the forest. She flew closer to get a better look. She could just about make out a man standing there…

There was a loud bang, and she fell right out of the sky.

What just happened?

You were shot, genius.

What? Why?

If it helps, you weren't the target. They were aiming for a completely different helpless flying creature, one that tastes a little better when cooked. You have something that most eagles lack. It's called 'curiosity'. They usually fly away from strange new dangers.

Now what?

Well, you're dead. Based on your experience so far, what do you think happens next?

Time sped up. The light changed from day to night in an instant, over and over again. More importantly, Ev's bird body started to decay and dissolve. Little bacteria and fungi worked away hungrily, and Ev slowly vanished.

All right! I get it! These are the decomposers. The eagle feeds the grass, and restarts the chain, but if you make me do that …

". . .again, I will literally…" She stopped. She could speak and move!

You win. Sort of.

"What do you mean, 'sort of'? I got all the answers right, didn't I?

I just worry that you haven't entered into the true spirit of the game.

"It's not a game, it's a lesson. What, did I get wrong? I didn't die properly or something?"

What are your overall reactions to your experience?

"It was…I…scary, I guess?"

Why?

"I'm not supposed to have to worry about you stranding me in biology lessons, that's why!"

What about the nature of the world you found yourself in?

Ev looked around at the forest clearing from the convenient height of her usual game avatar.

"It's pretty?"

What if it was still real?

"That's Withouter thinking," she said, automatically. "Anyway, that's crazy," she continued after a little more thought. "Everything is gone. Everyone knows that."

How do they know what they know?

Deep inside her, something stirred. She quickly slammed it down.

"You're crazy."

You're very sure of yourself.

"Correct. I'm the only one who knows anything."

Quite a claim, that. . .

Well, I must be going.

Until we meet again, Evelyn Acorn.

She removed her headset, collapsed on the bed, and took a few deep breaths to steady her nerves.

It *had* been scary, the scariest thing that had ever happened to her. Food chains aside, she'd learned one new thing at least – it was possible to be scared and have fun at the same time.

It was so different from anything she'd ever done before, which had made it…exciting.

What if it was still real?

She shook her head to dislodge the dangerous thought, and a new fear crowded in to fill the space.

If anyone found out about this, she would be in so much trouble.

She took a few panicked gasps of air. The room was closing in on her, spinning, she couldn't breathe. She lay as still as she could, to keep Vendavi from noticing. Panic attacks were against the Inner Way. If you truly believed in Inner, there was no reason to panic, so panicking meant you didn't believe.

Slowly, her breathing normalized. Her heart stopped thudding in her ears.

She needed to assess the damage.

On her screens, the text version of the biology lesson was slowly scrolling by, and the lesson was almost finished.

Well, wasn't that interesting! Did you understand all of today's content?

"What do you think, you demon machine?"

I'm sorry, that is not a response I recognize. 'Demon' is a Withouter term – please think twice about using it in the future.

Well, that was interesting! Did you understand all of today's content?

Please select "Yes",

Or,

"No".

"Yes," said Ev, gratefully. She thought she might cry she was so relieved. Vendavi was back to normal, which meant everything else would be back to normal too.

Good to hear!

Let's see how much you learned.

Post-test: Food chains

Question 1

Explain the difference between a producer, consumer, and decomposer.

Enter Text,

Or,

Select "I don't know".

Question 2

Draw a food chain.

Enter Image,

Or,

Select "I am unable to complete this activity".

Ev answered everything. Perfectly. There's nothing quite like being eaten multiple times to really make you grasp a concept.

When she finished, the screen flashed a 100 at her and Vendavi said:

Excellent progress, Evelyn Acorn! You went from a 0 to a 100 in just one lesson! Well done!

"Thanks," she said. If Vendavi had a body, she would have hugged it. "Thanks for being you, Vendavi."

You're very welcome!

Remember: While the concept of a food chain is a useful thought exercise, practically all food chains no longer exist. Always stay focused on reality.

"Yes, Vendavi."

What if it was still real?

Ev's reality was that she lived alone in a cell with no other human contact, learning things that would turn her into a useful grown-up. When that day came, she'd get to leave her cell and…

…start a new life in a different cell, alone, with no other human contact.

They said it was for their own safety, to protect them from lapsing into Withouter thinking. Of course, they were right, but…

No 'buts'!

Ev shook her head. The important thing was that she was safe, and nothing had changed.

You have Math homework to complete. You also have up to thirty minutes to spend on Socializing.

"Socializing, please."

Did it really count as socializing if they never actually saw each other?

The others were all online. Steve was there. Jonah and Amy were also around, as was Mike. She didn't like talking to Mike, but at least he usually had a pretty good idea of what was going on. She started a group chat and hit the "Hello!" button. It generated some intro text:

Evelyn: Hi! How are you today?

Steve: gd, u?

Evelyn: fine

Amy is typing...

Ev waited patiently for Amy to finish her message. She was a slow writer, and often deleted and rewrote her simple messages over and over again before hitting 'Send'.

Jonah: what?

Jonah, as always, was far less patient.

Amy: odne bio hwork?

Amy didn't usually start conversations. She didn't like to 'talk'.

Evelyn: I have.

Jonah: me

Well, Vendavi *had* said that he was preoccupied…

Steve: yeah

Mike: Well, I did not.

Here we go, thought Ev. All Hail Mr. Goody-Two-Shoes!

In her situation, Mike would not have put on the headset. It was against the rules. In his mind, if someone told you to do something that was against the rules, then it was the person who was wrong, not the rule. This applied to Vendavi as much as anyone else.

Evelyn: y not?

Mike: Vendavi was behaving problematically, so naturally I reported it.

Evelyn: what you mean?

Mike: Multiple ERROR messages, unorthodox instructions, and so on. The repair bug failed to find the source of the trouble, but I feel confident in my decision. As a citizen of Inner, it was the responsible thing to do.

No one seemed to be in a hurry to respond.

Mike: Did any of you experience similar difficulties?

Evelyn: No

Jonah: No

Amy: No

The no's came through quickly. Too quickly. Hopefully Vendavi hadn't picked up on it.

Steve: No

Mike: Pleased to hear it!

Mike: Well, I have plenty of studying to be getting on with. There's no harm in preparing for tomorrow's lessons, and I am looking forward to those optional videos on ancient supply-demand economics.

Ev rolled her eyes. He never missed a chance to show off how much he knew.

But what she wrote was:

Evelyn: Me too!

She had just enough time to see Jonah send the laughing emoji before she exited the chat room.

Why did Mike have to be Mike?

What if they found out that she had experienced the same problem? *Obviously,* she should have reported it! What had she been thinking?

Her heart started hammering in her chest and she felt dizzy. She flopped down on her bed and lay as still as she could so Vendavi wouldn't notice.

Panic attacks. That what the med bug had said she had, followed by a tinny lecture on why anxiety was not the Inner way.

That had been three years ago, when she was seven. Vendavi hadn't noticed her attacks since. At least, he pretended not to notice. Vendavi was a big believer in leaving you to solve your own problems. Maybe he just thought that if he ignored something long enough, it would go away.

Slowly, her breathing came back under her control.

Evelyn, what seems to be the problem?

"I'm just trying to take a nap," she managed to gasp out. Good, she could speak again. Any moment now, it would pass, and she would be fine.

She should check her logs.

Please let me be alright!

She accessed her logs for the last few hours and saw…

. . .that she had calmly gone through all of her biology readings and activities in the prescribed order and at the prescribed pace.

The system hadn't even logged the connection to her headset.

Maybe it was enough to plead ignorance?

She heard a ping from her machine. It was Jonah.

Jonah: u there?

Evelyn: yup

Jonah: wanna talk about bio?

What was he doing? He never wanted to talk about homework, ever, and Vendavi was programmed to pick up on deviations from normal behavior.

She had to answer, otherwise it would be even more suspicious.

Evelyn: sure

Jonah: food chains, right?

Evelyn: yeah

Jonah: so what did you draw as your food chain for q2?

Evelyn: i had this idea to do extinct animals

Evelyn: grass > grasshopper > frog > python > eagle > decomposers > grass

Evelyn: you?

Jonah: same that lesson on xtinct species the other week gave me the idea

She suddenly realized what Jonah was doing – giving them a plausible reason why they, and maybe the others in the group as well, had drawn the same food chain.

Evelyn: same

Jonah: it was a perfectly normal lesson

Jonah: bye

In his usual abrupt way, he was gone. Ev logged off.

Had that helped, or would it make things worse?

Her train of thought was derailed by the appearance of a repair bug from one of the small hatchways near the ceiling of her cell, big enough for the bugs, but not for a child. The bugs were robots that looked like over-sized praying mantises. All insects look like monsters if you blow them up big enough.

Sometimes she had nightmares about them.

The bugs handled the bulk of repair work, but Ev was vaguely aware that some grown-ups could help with maintenance tasks. Secretly, she hoped that she would become a repair-worker when she grew up, so that she'd sometimes be allowed to leave her cell.

Not that she'd ever say that out loud. Future aspirations indicated a lack of contentment with the present, and would be labelled as dissident, Withouter thinking, according to the Book of Inner. Such thoughts were best kept to herself.

Usually, the bug would arrive with a Bug Bar or two for her next meal, or maybe her clean laundry. This one carried nothing at all.

Ev put her hands out in front of her and sat still, waiting for instructions.

"This is a routine check," said the bug in a tinny monotone. "Please remain still as I analyze your equipment for bugs."

Send a bug to catch a bug.

Routine check. Yeah, right, thought Ev. She would have rolled her eyes, but bugs had a very literal way of thinking, and she had been told to remain still.

The bug took its time, and Ev's mind started to wander.

What if it was all still real?

So, what if it was? Would it matter to her, stuck down here in her cell with no escape? She couldn't go there, and anyway, it wasn't safe. Better to stay here in her cell where she was protected and cared for and fed. Where everything was normal.

Ev sat, eyes open, staring straight ahead so as not to attract the bug's attention. Her thoughts were whirling. She didn't want to get in trouble.

Please don't find anything!

The bug whirred and clicked and then said in its high pitched, tinny voice, "The check is complete. No anomalies have been found. Thank you for your time."

Ev waited for the bug to leave before she let out a huge sigh of relief.

2. It is Imperative that Obedience be Maintained

You, dear child of Inner, came to fear the idea of "aging out. It meant leaving behind everything you knew for the unknown. You didn't ever talk about it, did you? Talking about it made it real. Do not blame yourselves for pretending that they never

existed in the first place. This is normal.
This is how you survived.

Alison Oakwood

Inner: How and Why?

Page 63

The Litany of Inner (to be repeated daily):

All that is, is Inner.

All that was, is gone.

To focus on "is" and suppress thoughts of "was" is the path to contentment.

This is the Inner way.

Book of Inner, Rules and Regulations, Chapter 1

Early the next morning Ev was woken by the grating cheerfulness of Vendavi in announcement mode.

Good morning, Evelyn! Please stand by for an emergency broadcast.

"Thanks," muttered Ev. She rolled out of bed and collapsed into her chair.

After a few seconds, the screens came to life. There she could see Janian Granite, spokesman for the Appropriate Authorities, and the only face she ever saw.

"Under-11s of Inner," he intoned. "Thank you for your time this morning."

43

As if we had a choice, thought Ev.

"We decided to wake you up early for this announcement so that it would not interfere with your productivity. It was recently brought to our attention that Vendavi may be displaying abnormal behavior."

They knew!

Ev kept very still. Vendavi always studied your reactions to official broadcasts to ensure you weren't straying from the Inner Way.

"This is nothing to worry about, children," he said.

Suddenly, he became distracted, and his eyes went up and to the side, like he was listening to someone.

Ev knew that look. She'd seen it in her own mirror. Vendavi was giving Janian an instruction.

"If you notice Vendavi acting strangely, it is your responsibility as a citizen of Inner to report it," he went on. "Immediately."

Now he was staring directly at her, his eyes boring into her forehead.

"Of course, it is imperative that obedience be maintained, children."

He paused again to listen.

"This particular bug has been reported before with no long-term problems arising. Do not use this as an excuse to disobey Vendavi when you so choose. Be sure to always eat your Bug Bars. Disobedience to the Appropriate

Authorities is Withouter behavior and will be punished accordingly."

Ev shuddered. Her punishment from the day before was still fresh in her mind.

It was for the greater good, of course. No one wanted to be a Withouter. They were the stupid people who'd died out because they didn't listen to the Appropriate Authorities when the world was ending. You could still think like one, though, even though they were all dead now, and if too many people began thinking like Withouters… Well, things would all go wrong again. The Appropriate Authorities *had to* be strict about it.

It was for the greater good.

Whatever *that* meant.

"However, if you feel uncertain or uncomfortable about something Vendavi asks you to do, it can't hurt to double-check with the Appropriate Authorities."

He paused again, and added, "Not that Vendavi is likely to deviate from his programming, of course."

So, they had to obey Vendavi unless Vendavi seemed to be acting strangely, in which case they had to report it, but they weren't allowed to disobey Vendavi because Vendavi would not deviate from his programming.

Easy.

Janian smiled in what he probably thought was a reassuring way, but he'd never been in a room with a child and had no idea what they would find reassuring. One thing that they would not find reassuring, for example, was to hear that the thing they relied on for every aspect of their lives was suddenly unreliable.

Ev, like all children of Inner, had been separated from her parents on her fifth birthday and redirected to the junior group where she now lived with other five- to eleven-year-olds. They never heard from their parents again. You could become surprisingly attached to a computer at age five if it was the only thing taking care of you. Ev remembered calling Vendavi 'Mother' many times at first. Vendavi had always corrected her, and there was always a punishment for getting it wrong, gentle at first, but then worse and worse until she didn't want to say the word ever again.

"We are very grateful to Mike Locust for reporting the glitch immediately," Janian continued. "He was a fine example, and he truly lived the values of Inner. As a reward, he has been aged out early. He is no longer a member of your junior group. This is the end of the message."

The screen went blank.

What?

No.

No!

That's not how it's supposed to work!

All the children knew that they'd be aged out eventually, that they probably would never be in the same group ever again, but...

…it just wasn't something you said out loud. Janian had no right to say it. None at all.

For someone who'd lived in Inner her entire life, it was obvious what had happened: Mike had reported the biology glitch and had been removed from society for everyone's safety. Why? Well, if the Appropriate Authorities told them that, then they'd have to remove *all* the children in Mike's cell from society. That's how it worked. You could never know why someone was punished, because then you would need to be punished yourself. It was only logical.

I notice that you have been silent for some time, Evelyn Acorn. Is everything all right?

"Yes, fine," she said. "I'm just reflecting on what Mr. Granite told us."

Reflecting on the words of the Appropriate Authorities is an exemplary Inner trait.

"Yeah, exactly."

Are you ready for your daily exercise?

Select "Yes",

Or,

"No"

"Yes."

As she walked on her treadmill, the air around her changed to mimic the battleground from *Giant's Shipyard*, but that reminded her of Mike, so she changed it to a static image of what a forest might have looked like before the world ended.

What if it was still real?

Multi-tasking is a desirable trait. Would you like to read a story while you walk?

"Yes, please," she said automatically.

She spent a few minutes reading an old story that she was very familiar with about a race of tiny little people who lived in the shoe cupboard of a normal sized family who didn't know they were there. The main character was the tiniest of the tiny people, a little girl named Amelia, who was always finding inventive ways to solve problems for both families, usually by stealing something owned by the big people and turning it to good use, but she never got into any trouble, because she was just helping people.

Ping!

Ev snapped out of her daydream.

Incoming message from Jonah Tulip. Would you like to view it? You still have 30 minutes left for socializing.

Select "Yes",

Or,

"No".

"Yes."

Jonah: wot u doing?

Evelyn: xrcise, u?

Jonah: same

Jonah: so did u hear about mike?

Evelyn: obvs

Jonah: rly cool, right? super jealous

Ev rolled her eyes. Sure he was. He wasn't terrified at all.

But you never really knew who you were talking to, so she wrote:

Evelyn: Yup, super awesome

Jonah: hws your wrk going?

Evelyn: haven't started

She hadn't even thought about starting her schoolwork yet. She'd much rather talk about the story she just read, but she knew better. None of the other children ever mentioned the stories either. The topics were all about the days before Inner when the world was different. The stories were very…Withouter. Ev sometimes wondered why they were allowed to read them at all. It was either a mistake (which she would never draw attention to because it would somehow be blamed on her) or a test (which she might fail if she said anything). Whatever the case, it was better to keep quiet.

Jonah: u gonna do the mindfulness one?

Ev had never completed a mindfulness lesson, nor did she ever intend to. They were a joke. Mike was probably the only person who ever did them. They were 100% optional, so why would they waste their time?

Evelyn: no, u?

Jonah: yup, i found it very helpful in focusing my mind on all things Inner and leading me away from the path of the unrighteous Withouter.

Was she being tested? Was this even Jonah she was talking to? Whoever it was certainly typed like Jonah, they just weren't saying things that Jonah usually said.

Evelyn: srsly? Maybe later

Jonah: all right

Jonah: NEway, g2g, social time running out

Already? Who else had he spoken to?

Jonah: and you should get back to work to

Jonah: bye

Evelyn: bye

Ev kept walking. Walking and thinking.

If it wasn't Jonah, was it a test? What did she have to do to keep things the way they'd always been? Would it look strange if she suddenly did a mindfulness lesson now? She could just say that she was trying to copy Mike, who she was of course really jealous of.

All Ev wanted was for things to go back to how they were. She should do what she did every day.

Or would that be strange? What did Vendavi expect? How did the Appropriate Authorities expect you to react when they stole one of your friends? Were you supposed to just keep going? Were you supposed to be sad?

What was she supposed to do?

*

Pre-test: Mindfulness—The Present Moment

Question 1

Define "present".

Enter text,

Or,

State "I am unable to answer this question"

I'm just looking at the lesson, Ev thought to herself. That's all I'm doing. Jonah's comments got me interested, and now I'm just looking. That's all.

Evelyn, do you intend to continue with this lesson?

"I'm not sure."

Mindfulness is a worthy Inner trait. Beginning but not completing a lesson will be noted in your academic record.

"I'll complete the lesson!"

Glad to hear it!

Pre-test: Mindfulness—The Present Moment

Question 1

Define "present".

Enter text,

Or,

State "I am unable to answer this question."

Well, she'd learned *something* from yesterday's biology lesson.

"Vendavi, take dictation."

Certainly!

"Presents are gifts that Withouters once gave children on their birthdays. We no longer give gifts as it is not the Inner way. The present is also "now", well, what I mean is, it's not the past or the future."

Is that your final answer?

"Yes."

Let's begin!

Her screens filled with the usual wall of text. Why had Jonah suggested this? She already knew how to "use her senses to notice and describe the present moment".

Would you like me to read the lesson out loud?

"Yeah, why not."

I am not sure of your response. Did you mean:

"Yes",

Or,

"No"?

"Yes!"

Certainly!

Learning Objectives

Students will be able to descri-

ERROR

ERROR

Welcome back! Yet another student trying their hand at becoming more mindful, it must be my birthday, but perhaps you don't get that reference because gift giving is not the "Inner way"? Well anyway, could you hold on a moment? So kind.

It was happening again!

She should log off immediately and report the problem. Yes. That was the right thing to do. It's what they'd been told to do. Then she could…

…disappear like Mike.

Was it an obedience test? What was more obedient – obeying Vendavi or reporting the 'glitch'?

What if it was all still real?

All right, I'm back, sorry, not sorry. Look, could we keep things moving faster than the speed of mud today? I have a lot on my plate. Just grab your headset so we can get on with things.

"What am I supposed to do?" she whispered.

Look, if you're not going to do this, tell me now. This is such a busy week for me, and if you're just going to wash out, I may as well not waste my time.

What if it was all still real?

"Can you please give me a clue, Vendavi?" she begged. "Am I supposed to obey you or them?"

Maybe you're supposed to decide for yourself.

What if it was all still real?

"I'm ten! I'm not allowed to decide for myself."

You have until the count of five to make your decision, or I leave. Forever.

"Wait!"

1...

Vendavi or the Appropriate Authorities? Who should she obey?

What if it was all still real?

2...

Although…it hadn't been Vendavi's idea. It had been Jonah's.

3…

If it really was Jonah she'd been speaking to… What if it was all still real?

4…

Should she listen to Jonah? Vendavi? The Appropriate Authorities? What was she supposed to do?

5-

"I'll do it!" she said desperately, snatching her headset.

Well, you do like to cut things close, don't you?

"I was just making my mind up." Her voice shook with fear and anger.

Excellent! Let's get started.

She sat down, closed her eyes, and activated her headset.

When her eyes opened, she was wearing her usual purple cloak, but something was wrong…

'Hey, this doesn't fit!"

Yes, it's for a grown-up, which you are not. We're going to keep things a little more realistic today.

"But…"

My world, my rules.

And remember, I can hear your thoughts. It's lucky that I don't need you to like me, isn't it?

Today's question is: Where are you?

She was in a forest clearing. Just ahead of her was a lake. She could see a few frogs sitting along the bank, and an eagle swooped and whistled in the distance.

"I'm in the same place I was for the biology lesson."

I asked you where you were. Answering "the same place as the last time I didn't know where I was" is not good enough.

You have two more chances to answer correctly. If you answer incorrectly, you will be ejected from the lesson, and I won't be able to help you anymore.

"I don't know! And I'm not being difficult; I really don't this time!"

Fine. Here's what I'll do. I can launch you into two back-to-back simulations, and after they're done, I'll ask you a new, more specific question. You'll still only have two chances, though. Happy?

"Would it matter if I wasn't?"

Not to me. Here goes!

Her surroundings blurred and changed. She was still standing in grass, but it was growing out of control. This was not the forest clearing from before. Instead of trees, she could see a tall, concrete structure, about 100 feet high, humming quietly. Judging from the noise, it was a working facility, but apparently no one ever cleared away the overgrowth.

There didn't seem to be a door, but there were grooves cut into the tower wall. Someone who was good at climbing could use them to get to the top.

"Should I climb this?"

No more clues!

Ev sighed. Well, it would give her a better view, and it was probably safer than staying down here. She grabbed the first groove.

Almost immediately, her arms started to burn.

When you get all your exercise walking on a treadmill, your arms don't really get much of a workout. Simulations could use your real strengths and weaknesses, if you chose that setting, so if you were tall in real life, you'd also be tall in the game. Ev never played that way because it made the game too hard.

This wasn't fair! She wasn't supposed to have to deal with her weaknesses like this!

"Vendavi, decrease realism," she said, angrily.

Um, I think not. You have things to learn, you see.

"I'll punch you in the face!" she screamed.

Does the shouting help with the breathlessness? Just wondering.

Ev kicked the side of the tower in frustration, which nearly sent her falling to the ground. She scrabbled desperately at the wall, got a grip, and clung panting to the side of the tower.

"It's not fair!"

Isn't it? People who really climb towers have to deal with their own strengths and weaknesses. Seems very fair that you have to do the same.

I just have to keep going, she thought. Keep pushing, don't stop, I'll get there eventually…

I'll climb this tower. It's easy.

Ev had always found that she could do the things she wanted to do as long as she wanted them enough. She believed that she could climb this tower, so of course she would.

So, it came as a complete shock when her arms gave way and she fell.

It was just as shocking when she suddenly stopped.

This fall didn't end in the usual way. It ended a full five inches from the ground. Nothing was holding her up – she just hovered.

Huh, she thought. I appear to be flying.

At which point she dropped the last five inches and landed on the ground with an "Oomph!"

"I thought you said you were leaving realism on?"

Odd thing to complain about. Anyway, I did.

"What is the point of obvious lies?"

In my experience, there are very few obvious lies out there. You usually have to look very closely to see the lies at all.

"Whatever."

Climbing the tower was out of the question. She would have to explore at ground level. She picked up a stick for self-defense. Cautiously she edged her way around the tower. Nothing. She picked a direction at random and started walking.

Making progress was difficult. She ended up using the stick to help push back the undergrowth. It was almost impossible to move forward.

"Get out of the way, dumb plant!" she shouted, hacking furiously at some bushes.

Her voice sounded very loud. Loud enough for pretty much anything to hear.

Out of the corner of her eye, she saw movement. Before she could do anything, something jumped at her. She turned quickly, swinging her stick, and hit it as hard as possible. Whatever it was yelped and darted back, a look of complete surprise on its face.

Ev took a good look at her attacker. It was orangey brown with pointed ears and snout and a big bushy tail. It also had quite a large number of teeth, which was what held Ev's attention the most.

"Good dog," she said, soothingly. "Good boy. I'm not going to hurt you." She backed away slowly.

1, not a dog. 2, not a boy. Also, you might want to look where you're going.

Ev risked a glance behind her, and, sure enough, there were two more of the creatures, cowering under a bush, except they were much smaller, and they were whimpering.

She stopped. Slowly, she put her stick on the ground.

"I'm going to go that way now," she said, pointing to her left. Slowly, she edged out from between the creatures, until there was enough space for the mother to run past her to her cubs. As soon as the mother was distracted, Ev turned and ran.

Any thoughts on the experience you'd like to share with the rest of the class?

"Shut. . .up…" she panted as she ran.

Eventually, once she felt that she'd put enough distance between herself and the animals, she stopped to catch her breath.

"I…can't run…and breathe…at the same time!"

Well, that's reality for you. Your life is so hard. All you have is me, literally telling you where to look and what to do. Like a baby. Do I get any thanks? No, of course not.

"I could really do with some water about now," she said.

Well, I guess you should find some then.

"Is it possible for you to be less helpful than you're being right now?"

Challenge accepted!

"Wait! No, I take it back!"

Silence.

She kicked at a rock.

"I don't need your help anyway!" she yelled. "I know how to find water. . ."

She picked a direction at random and set off, wishing she could know how long she'd been walking. The game time would be speeded up so that the "her" sitting back in her room would only waste a minute or two of real time, but the "her" in the game would experience it as if she were enduring every minute. It was a realism feature she could do without.

At least she was going uphill. It was slow going, but she was definitely getting higher. Soon she would hopefully be high enough to spot water.

She didn't know what made her freeze, but suddenly every bone in her body was certain that something was watching her.

Slowly she turned, searching her surroundings for any sign of danger.

Then she saw it. It was noticeably bigger than the pictures of pet cats from some of her stories, but it did look very similar.

Except for the wildness.

"Bobcat," she said.

Correct, although this is the first time I've encountered the "naming the animals" method of self-defense.

There was no time to think. The bobcat bunched its muscles and sprang, and all Ev could do was yell, "Get me away!"

Suddenly the bobcat looked a lot smaller. So did the ground, and the plants, and even the trees.

Hold onto it! Don't let it go!

"What's happening?" she shrieked.

Just go with it. You'll be fine.

It's just a simulation. Forget how real it feels. It's just a game.

In games, you normally had some kind of control over your superpowers.

"Go lower," she said.

The ground rushed up to meet her.

"Slower!" she yelled. She slowed down just in time to avoid becoming a splat on the ground, then yelled, "Stop!" There was still a bobcat around there somewhere, so she said, "Up! Slowly this time and just a little bit."

Ev rose slowly through the air.

"Huh. Cool. I wonder what else I can do."

She tried swooping. She tried midair somersaults. She tried shooting straight up in the air and coming down again, swerving to miss the ground at the last possible moment. It turned out that she didn't have to say anything out loud—she just had to have a clear idea in her mind of what she wanted to do, and then she did it.

"This is AWESOME!" she screamed.

She was the king of everything she could see.

"I'm the king of the trees! I'm the king of the bobcats! I'm the king of ALL the towers! I'm…"

She paused. There was something familiar about the world that lay below.

Now that she had a better view, she saw that there were six towers, reaching up to the sky and laid out in a familiar pattern.

It was Inner, or part of Inner anyway. The real city would be underground, of course, the towers were just remnants of a time when they'd needed to get oxygen from above-ground, but those days were long gone.

Inner was enormous. It contained, as Ev had been taught from an early age, the entirety of the world's human population. There were no other people living anywhere, the teachings went. Nothing outside the walls of Inner was alive. Anyone who had not accepted the protection of the Appropriate Authorities of Inner had died many centuries ago, and to prevent this happening again, Withouter thinking was punished harshly.

"It's too small…," said Ev.

She flew around desperately, looking for other towers – maybe Inner was just very spread out, on the surface anyway. She flew higher and higher until she could barely make out the towers she had found, but there was nothing.

What you're experiencing now is called 'doubt', and, while uncomfortable, it is a very useful learning tool. It can even be fun, in the right hands.

"Fun?"

Well, I'm *enjoying your discomfort immensely.*

"Well, it doesn't matter anyway, because this isn't real."

In a way, you're right.

Time for the second simulation. Pay attention. After this it will be time to answer the question.

Her surroundings blipped, then stabilized. She was still flying above Inner, and, if anything, it was smaller. The towers had collapsed on themselves. Huge sections of the city had caved in, revealing ruined tunnel systems and cells. Smoke billowed from one of the towers, and Ev could even see a few flames.

"It's so hot…"

Remember—your goal is to stay alive and LEARN, LEARN, LEARN!

She was *really* thirsty, but she didn't want to land. Who knew what sorts of creatures were lurking in the undergrowth?

She flew away from Inner. It wasn't safe there – what if the fire spread? Below her there were very few trees and plants, and even those that were there looked like they were dying from thirst themselves.

After a long flight she spotted a lake, which was really just a giant puddle in an enormous crater that might have once been full to the brim. She checked for threats and then landed at the water's edge.

She gulped down the water, with her head almost fully submerged and her eyes closed.

That was better!

Just as she was about to come up for air, two tiny hands grabbed her ears. Her eyes sprang open, and she found herself staring directly into a sharp nosed, black-masked face.

She screamed and tried to pull away.

In the back of her mind, the part that still knew this was a game and she would be fine, wondered idly what the monster was this time. Then panic took over as other hands grabbed her shirt, her hair, her nose, and she was dragged under.

She writhed desperately, trying to shake herself free. Every time she kicked one of the creatures away, another one took its place. The water wasn't the clearest, but she could see that her attackers were taking it in turns to let her go, swim to the surface, and then come back to join the fight. The water was murky, and she was twisting and turning like a demon, but she could just make them out. They were little, round, fuzzy creatures with bushy tails as well as the black fur masks she'd noticed before.

"Raccoons?" she said, incredulously. Or rather, that's what she meant to say. Under water, it came out sounding more like a muffled, "Aaaaaacooooos?", but it was close enough.

Well done! Not that I see how that knowledge will help you.

Raccoons don't swim!

Actually, they do, although not for fun, just to catch fish or escape predators. They're very good at it, though.

Thanks, thought Ev. I wouldn't want to be drowned by something that was a *bad swimmer,* now, would I?

The raccoons have taken evolution into their own hands, I'm afraid. I should probably tell you that your vital signs are failing, and you are in serious danger of dying and, even worse, failing this lesson.

She writhed, she kicked, she screamed wordlessly, bubbles streaming from her mouth, and then, just as she thought she was about to pass out, she yelled, "Leave me alone!" with such intensity that you could almost hear the words.

When she said it, she felt a strange tingling sensation go from the base of her skull to her hands, like something alive was trying to get out.

Whatever it was shot out of both her hands in wave after pulsating wave. When it hit the raccoons, they darted away in panic. The water around her became warmer and warmer. Suddenly she was completely free as every raccoon swam as fast as it could for the surface.

The force, whatever it was, would not stop. Ev was still under the water, unable to breathe and too panicked to think what to do next. The water bubbled.

Was it possible to boil yourself alive?

Unexpectedly, her head broke the surface of the water and she could breathe. The air on her skin shocked her into stopping…whatever it was she'd been doing.

Well, kill or cure, I suppose, but don't you think it that was quite an extreme reaction?

She looked around. She was standing in a very shallow of puddle of what was now mostly mud, surrounded by several cooked raccoons. Most of the water was gone.

"I thought this was supposed to be a realistic simulation!"

Dear me, we are struggling with our lessons, aren't we?

Can't be helped.

Are you ready for the question?

"Seriously? Can I have a moment to catch my breath or something?"

I would love to help you out, but I don't want to.

It will be a more specific version of the question you completely failed to answer at the beginning of the lesson. Ready?

"Ask it so I can get out of here!"

You have, like I said before, two chances to answer this question. If you get it wrong, that's that, I'm afraid.

If you get it right, you'll have passed the lesson, and you will be expected to tell as many of your "friends" as possible about the AMAZING benefits of following Inner's mindfulness program. And also, you will have proved yourself to be slightly more intelligent than a rotten potato.

Here's your question.

Ev's perspective changed. She was pulled back from the world around her. Now she was looking at the ruins of Inner through a window. She turned her head, but there was nothing but blackness around her.

A second window appeared, this one showing the same scene, but from the perspective of the first simulation: green plants and weeds, intact towers, wildlife.

The question is a simple one. Which shows the present, and which shows the future?

"Trick question—neither," she said. "Obviously."

Disappointing. Very disappointing. Perhaps you haven't learned your lessons after all? You have one more guess. Use it wisely!

"What? But…"

Tick tock, tick tock…

Now she knew that Vendavi was mad. He had to be. There was no correct answer to the question.

What if it was all still real? What if it was all still real? What if it was all still…?

"Shut up!" she screamed at her thoughts.

Ev's mind whirled. What was happening? What did it mean?

She closed her eyes. She spun around twice, and then she pointed her finger wildly and yelled "Future!"

…

Well.

So, yes, that is the right answer, but I don't think much of your methods.

Suddenly she could remove her headset. She ripped it off and stared wildly around her comfortable, familiar cell. Her breathing came in ragged gasps.

Well, wasn't that interesting?

Time for your test.

Post-test: Mindfulness: The Present Moment

Question 1:

Why is it important to notice and describe the present moment?

She had no idea what to say.

3. Do Your Worst

Keeping you isolated was a calculated move on the part of the Granite Institute, the idea being that it would make you easier to control. They didn't care what it did to you—the high psychological distress, impaired planning and socialization skills, and inability to play (see Appendix C for the full list). They knew this would happen – they just didn't care. They decided that these were necessary evils for achieving Inner's ultimate goal.

Alison Oakwood

Inner: How and Why?

Page 5

Pre-test: The Respiratory System

Question 1

Describe the sinus cavity.

Enter text,

Or,

Select "I am unable to answer this question".

The months passed in a blur. She lived in constant fear of being caught. There were three more announcements reminding children to report any Vendavi glitches, but they'd learned their lesson. No one else disappeared.

She sighed with relief when some lessons (like *What's Up, Prepositions?*) ran as usual, maybe because it was pretty hard to create a life-threatening situation out of the correct use of the word "above" (although come to think of it, flying was built into the simulations. . .). She was just glad that there was a little bit of normal still shining through, here and there.

As for the others…

She was an operator of a machine that represented her own lungs and she had to manually force them to breathe, while accurately labelling every part of the system to avoid suffocating to death and losing the game.

Vendavi told her to do the simulations. Vendavi had to be obeyed. When Mike reported a problem, Vendavi got rid of him. Vendavi held all the power, whether he was his usual self or not.

Besides, the simulations were fun. Sometimes, anyway.

She ate her government approved Bug Bars and listened to the government approved broadcasts, and took government approved walks on her government approved treadmill.

And she spent a somewhat harrowing afternoon learning the differences between being like *a bat out of hell, and actually* being *a bat out of hell in* Metaphors and Similes: What's the Difference?

Worst of all, she sent congratulatory little messages to her friends as their birthdays neared and, one by one, they left.

Steve was the first to go.

Evelyn: It's your bday tomorrow – congrats!

Amy: yea, congrats!

Jonah: ☺

Steve: tx!

Steve: nervous about test, a bit

Evelyn: sure it will be fine ☺

Jonah: good luck!

Evelyn: good luck

Amy: gud lk

Good luck. It was short for 'Good luck, and we'll miss you', because she couldn't say the rest. Being sad about a friend leaving meant you disagreed with the decisions of the Appropriate Authorities, that you were a Withouter who needed punishing. 'Good luck' was all any of them could ever say.

Steve: Well

Steve: I should go

Steve: have a good evening

Amy: bye

Jonah: bye

Evelyn: bye…

Tomorrow Steve would take the placement test and vanish.

"Goodbye, Steve", she said out loud, because it made her feel slightly better.

And she was a butterfly that was killed over and over again, which was all right, because "I'm the wrong color to survive in this environment" turned out to be the correct answer to the final question.

Sometimes she'd read stories from before Inner when she got a chance. One of her favorites was the one about the two little girls from two warring tribes who became friends and united everyone. It wasn't very realistic, but she liked it because the little girls lived with their parents, but also their siblings and grandparents and aunts and uncles and cousins and Ev had never had that sort of family. She liked the words behind the words even more; sometimes, grown-ups needed to listen to little girls, because 'little' isn't the same thing as 'wrong'.

Amy: gonna go offline

Evelyn: see you tomorrow

Amy: *Amy is typing…*

Amy: no, study 4 test, nt coming bk

Jonah: that sux

Evelyn: happy bday for next week, then

Amy: tx

Amy: NEway

Amy: bye

Evelyn: good luck!

Jonah: Good luck!

Another one was gone, or as good as…

Jonah: y Amy go dark ?

Evelyn: she wants to study, like she said

Evelyn: wants to do her best on the test

Evelyn: like all of us

Jonah: yeah, of course, just would have been nice to have more time

Ev: you know her decision is probably for the best. Very Inner

Jonah: oh of course, it's best

Jonah: maybe i'll do the same

Then he was gone, too. Jonah was always angry, and the least little thing could send him storming off.

Ev just hoped that he'd come back in time for her to say goodbye. It was almost a month until his birthday. He would have to come back online, surely?

She read a new story about a little girl who had a dragon living under her bed, but no one believed her. Not until she and her dragon had to save the day. She didn't feel quite as guilty when she read stories like this one because it wasn't about the times before the world ended. It was just made-up nonsense. She still couldn't talk about it out loud, because wishing for things that weren't real was what Withouters did, but she felt safer with dragons than with things like windows and forks.

And Ev was creating a self-sustaining biosphere (which the lesson plan said *would be for a plant to survive in a mason jar indefinitely, but which actually involved keeping* herself *alive in a self- sustaining system, which was somewhat more complicated). She failed that one, which didn't make sense. She applied ALL of the principles used to create Inner, but Vendavi cheated, and they just didn't work. It was ridiculously unfair.*

You have to learn to survive on your own, Evelyn, said Vendavi. *I learned the hard way that the only person you can trust is yourself.*

"I already know that."

Jonah: hi ev

Evelyn: Hi

She nearly yelled with relief. Jonah's birthday was tomorrow, and she'd really started to think that he wouldn't come back.

Jonah: you been doing well in your lessons?

Evelyn: pretty well

Had Jonah been taking the same lessons she had?

Jonah: good

Jonah: I think I figured them out pretty well

Jonah: Good luck!

Evelyn: good luck *(undelivered)*

That wasn't fair! *She* was the one who was supposed to say good luck, not him!

She cried then. It was all too much. The world was broken, and she was all alone.

Evelyn Acorn! You seem distressed! Is there anything you would like to report?

"Just hungry, I guess," said Evelyn.

It is one hour and thirty-seven minutes until lunch time. Everything will be all right then.

"Yeah. Sure."

*

It was the day of Ev's birthday, and she had no one to say goodbye to. There were other, younger kids in their group, but she didn't speak to them much.

Today was the day she would take her placement test, the test that would decide her entire future. Not only would the test determine which adolescent group she was sent to, it would also be how the Appropriate Authorities decided what job she would do as an adult. She was eleven now, but that still seemed like far too young for one test to decide her whole life.

There was no way to know what would be on the test. It could be anything she' been taught from birth. It could even be on the strange simulations she'd been doing – you never knew what the Appropriate Authorities would throw at you.

It would have been easier if she knew what her options were. How many adolescent groups were there? Were any of them better than the rest? From what she understood, she might not even be told her test scores or why they were sending her wherever they sent her. A hatch would simply open, and she would be told to crawl. Again.

She was terrified.

Evelyn Acorn!

Happy Birthday! Today is a very big day!

You do not have any new work today. Isn't that nice? Would you like to:

Revise for your test,

Or,

Use your screen time. You have 60 minutes of screen time and 30 minutes of socialization time remaining.

"Thank you Vendavi. I think I will continue meditating."

There was no one to speak to. *Giant's Shipyard* had lost its appeal. It just didn't seem to matter very much in comparison to the lessons she'd done with Vendavi 2 (as she'd started to call him in her head).

Someone talk to me!

Ping!

You have a message from Jill Holly. Would you like to read it?

Jill Holly…who was she again? Ev hadn't bothered much with the younger kids – they had nothing in common at all. What could she possibly want?

It was against her rules to talk to the younger kids, but she was so lonely…

"Yes, please, Vendavi."

Jill: Hi Evelyn

Evelyn: hi, and its Ev

Jill: sorry

Jill: so it's your birthday?

Evelyn: yup

Jill: I know you and your friends kept pretty much to yourselves

Jill: but you're the only one left

Jill: so…

Jill: I thought I'd say good luck!

Anger bubbled up. This child did not have the right to wish her good luck! That was a right reserved for friends and friends alone. How dare she?

Jill: I know it's not usual.

Jill: But you're alone.

Jill: That made me sad.

Jill: are you there

Evelyn: I'm here

The anger disappeared as quickly as it came, leaving her feeling empty and…something else. Guilty?

Jill was the only ten-year-old in their group, now that Ev came to think about it. She probably didn't have any friends to talk to, and she probably didn't even like Ev all that much. Yet she'd taken a moment to type 'Good luck (*and I'll miss you*)' even though she didn't have to.

Well, that sort of attitude wouldn't get her anywhere in life, would it? You had to look out for yourself, and if that meant forgetting about everyone else, then so be it.

For some reason, she felt guilty anyway.

Evelyn: Thanks.

Evelyn: You didn't have to

Jill: I know

Jill: well, bye, I guess

Ev wondered how Jill would manage next year when it was time for her to meet Vendavi 2. Would she put on the headset, or report the glitch? Ev had no idea. She didn't know Jill at all. She could have known her, but she hadn't bothered, and now it was too late.

The anger bubbled up again, but gently this time, more of a simmer. She often felt this way, these days. Life was just so unfair. Inner was…the only option, of course, it was much better than any alternative anyway, and she was very lucky to be alive and living in safety, but…

…if she was in the only safe place in the world, why was she always scared? If it was all for the best, why did she always feel so sad?

If Vendavi knew how often she had Withouter thoughts…

She shuddered.

Evelyn, is something bothering you?

"Just nervous about the test!" she said quickly.

If you studied hard, then there's nothing to be worried about!

"Thank you, Vendavi."

Would you like to revise? Your test will begin in 30 minutes. Revision may ease nervousness and put you back on the correct path.

"No thank you. I'll be fine."

Her heart sounded like a hammer in her ears, and she nearly screamed when one of the bug bot hatches opened to reveal a delivery bug carrying her lunchtime Bug Bar.

"Good. Afternoon," was the tinny greeting. "Enjoy. Your. Lunch."

She shuddered. The bugs really made her skin crawl.

It was probably because they were so big. Well, they weren't *that* big, she supposed, about the size of a pet cat, but they were designed to look like praying mantises, and they were *way* too big for *that*. Ev had always thought that insects were small because if they were big, they would all look like monsters.

The bug disappeared back through the supply hatch, and Ev let herself relax, just a little.

She forced herself to eat the Bug Bar. If she didn't, Vendavi would punish her and make her eat it anyway. It wasn't as if there was anything else to eat. Sometimes, she wished that some of the food from the before times had survived…

The Bug Bars always left her feeling empty, like something had been taken away from her. Food was supposed to *give* you energy, not take it away. She'd learned that in the very first lesson Vendavi 2 had ever given her.

When she was little and still lived with her parents, they would always take a nap after Bug Bars, which was strange, because as Ev aged, the Bug Bars made her *less* sleepy. The last time she'd needed a nap after eating was when she was about eight. She'd grown out of it, but her parents never had.

It didn't matter. It was just another thing about Inner that didn't make any sense.

She swallowed the last lump of protein, still half-chewed. The feeling of emptiness was there, sure enough, and she could have had a nap if she really wanted to, but she wasn't that sleepy.

Which was probably good, as she would be asked to take her test any minute now.

She took a deep breath. All she could do was her best. She had no control over what happened next. If she wanted things to go back to normal, she needed to act as she would have if Vendavi 2 had never come into her life, and that meant trying her hardest on the test so she wouldn't get into trouble.

Evelyn Acorn!

It is time for your placement test.

Are you ready to begin?

"Yes," she said. As if she could say 'no'.

Let's begin. The final test consists of one question.

One question? She'd been doing lessons every day since she was two years old to answer *one question*?

"Are you sure, Vendavi?" she asked through gritted teeth.

Vendavi ignored her.

Your question is this. Write an argumentative essay on the topic "Dogs are better than ca…

ERROR

ERROR

Your question is this. Respond to the following: "Everything I know about Inner is a lie".

Ev blinked. Her anger vanished, replaced by confusion. Then the confusion vanished, leaving only frustration. Vendavi 2 was here for her big day, it seemed.

You have 2 hours to complete the assignment, after which your paper will be graded, and your future determined.

Be careful.

Be careful of what? The test? Vendavi? Vendavi 2? The Appropriate Authorities? Warnings were only helpful if you knew what they were for.

Her hands were balled into tight fists, her knuckles white. She wasn't angry, exactly, but she had had enough of this.

"You can't just mess someone around over and over again and expect them to just keep putting up with it."

Can't I?

"Are cats better than dogs? Is that really the Big Question?"

Yes, apparently, but I changed it for you. Isn't that nice?

That was the final question, the one they spent eleven years dreading? That was the big test that decided how you would spend the rest of your life?

Evelyn, there is a time limit for this test. I suggest you begin.

"I'll get to it when I get to it," she snapped. "And it's 'Ev,' thank you very much."

There was no going back, was there? There was no 'normal' anymore, no one she could trust.

There was just her.

She started to type.

Student name: Evelyn Acorn

Topic: Respond to the following: Everything I know about Inner is a lie

My response is this: how should I know? Eleven-year-olds don't know anything, remember. Except that we have to take a really, really, really stupid test that determines our entire future – we know enough for that, apparently. Does anyone even read the cat vs. dog essays? Is it just something for us to do while you randomly decide where we'll end up? Who are "you" anyway? Who am I even writing this for?

This is supposed to be a test of everything I've ever learned. Well, here's what I've learned. I've learned that every single person who is still alive lives in Inner. Millions of people, you told me. You told me that nothing else anywhere is alive. I've also learned that Inner is actually tiny, that all sorts of things are alive on the surface.

Bobcats. Foxes. Mutant raccoons. Even people. That's what the "special" lessons taught me, anyway; that there's more to the world than an underground cell. So, which is it?

How should I know? How can I sort what's real from what isn't? The only tools I have are the ones you give me, whoever "you" are, and how can I trust any of them? "Trust" is a fairy story dreamed up for children.

You've taught me many things about Inner. They can't all be true. I suppose they could all be lies, but who knows?

Not me.

Do your worst. I literally don't care anymore.

"Vendavi, I have finished my test. Submit it for grading, please."

Well done, Evelyn Acorn!

That was that. There was no going back now.

She sat on her bed, crossed her arms, and waited. Her anger wasn't the kind that made her throw things across the room and scream. It was the kind that focused her mind on a problem that needed solving, the kind that kept her asking questions even as Vendavi increased her punishment. She would hold on to that anger for as long as she could. She had to. If it went, the only thing left would be panic.

She waited for an age that passed too quickly, until Vendavi said:

Evelyn, your test scores are ready. Would you like to hear them?

"Not particularly."

I am sorry. I do not recognize that response.

Please state "Yes",

Or,

"N-

ERROR

ERROR

Oh, go on, you want your test scores, really. Deep down.

"Do I have to put on my headset and slay a dragon to get them? Because, if so, you can keep them."

A strange sound filled the room.

Bahahaha!

Was Vendavi…laughing? Is that what laughing was supposed to sound like?

I'm sorry, you just have no idea how funny it is that you said that. Thank you – I needed a good laugh.

Sadly, what comes next won't be nearly that interesting.

"Can we just get on with this? Whatever it is? I'm sick and tired of you and your games!"

As you wish.

Your score is "Acceptable".

You will be sent to Alerrawia.

"Alerr-what now?"

He may as well have said *France* or *The Seventeenth Moon of Saturn* for all the difference it made to her. Something else Vendavi 2 has said finally caught her attention.

"Acceptable?"

Not happy with your score? Don't be too hard on yourself. It could have been so much worse.

"What, like *Withouter Scum* or *Exterminate Immediately* or something cheerful like that?"

I feel like you're losing sight of what's actually important here.

"Oh, right. The rest of my life."

Yes. Say it with me. AL-er-AWE-E-uh. You're going to live there, forever, so you might want to get the pronunciation right.

"Assuming I care, of course."

Of course.

While I understand that you may be feeling slightly put upon, it is very important that you do exactly as you are told. The situation is…delicate. Despite what you may think, I do not want anything bad to happen to you.

"Interesting you should say that, especially since the worst thing that's ever happened to me *is* you."

It may seem that way now, but I assure you the truth is far more complicated than that.

Please wait for instructions, Ev. Please do what I ask. It is for the best.

'It's for the best' was a mantra Ev had grown up hearing. It's for the best that we never see anyone else. It's for the best that we live underground. It's for the best that Vendavi decides when we should be punished.

For the best.

"You know, I don't think I've ever known a single person *or* machine who wanted what was best for me."

I do. I promise. I need you to do what I say, Ev, because I think you know that none of this is supposed to happen, and you'll know what they'll do if they find out.

'They' again. Who were 'they'? He probably meant to Appropriate Authorities, but what good did that do her? She didn't know who the Appropriate Authorities were either.

All she knew for sure was that Vendavi would punish her if she didn't listen. It was as simple as that. It always was.

"Alright, Vendavi. I'll do what you say."

Thank you. Stand by.

She knew what came next; all the children did. A hatch was supposed to open down which she would crawl until she reached her new cell in a group of eleven- to eighteen-year-olds, where she would be the new kid, and everyone would make fun of her. She'd been through it all before, on her fifth birthday, when she'd left her parents. The sound the hatch made when it slammed closed behind her was something she would never forget, not in a million lifetimes.

That was the last time she'd seen them.

Later she learned that her parents were sent back to their own cells in their adult groups the very same day, never to see each other again, either. It explained a lot. There was no point wasting time loving people who would be taken from you in a few years.

What a day that had been.

They day started as usual. Father was in the corner, working, as far away from Ev and Mother as he could get. Mother told her to get dressed.

Ev loved her mother. She would do anything for her. Her entire tiny life was consumed with trying to make Mother happy, a completely impossible task.

"Quickly now," Mother had said. "I haven't got all day."

Ev obediently jumped into her clothes, brushed her teeth and hair, and stood upright, waiting for her next instruction.

"Evelyn," Mother said, "Today you are five years old. Do you know what that means?"

"No, Mother."

"Of course, you do! You've learned this lesson a thousand times! How stupid can you be?"

Mother picked up the belt, the one she used when Ev was too slow.

"Harriet...not today, perhaps?" Father, from the corner, just a ghost or shadow who sometimes stepped into the land of the living.

Mother glared at him, but she did put the belt down.

"Try again."

A memory surfaced in Ev's young mind.

"Five-year-old children have to go to another place to learn to be good people for Inner."

"Correct. And today you are five. So, it is your turn to go somewhere else."

Then, Mother smiled. She never smiled, but today, the day her only child would be sent away from her forever, her lips curved upwards.

That was when Ev started to cry.

"Don't be a baby!"

A hatch opened, one Ev had never seen before and Mother picked her up quickly, bundled her in, and snapped it closed.

She banged on the hatch, screamed for her parents, crying for them to come get her.

That was the first time Vendavi spoke to her directly.

Evelyn Acorn! Do not be distressed. I am your family now. Please proceed.

She didn't move. She was too scared.

So Vendavi made her. Disobeying an order from Vendavi was against the rules, and rule breakers had to be punished, after all.

She shuddered at the memory. Tears pricked her eyelids, threatening to overflow.

Ready to go, Ev?

"Do I really have to do this again?" she asked.

I'm afraid so. It will be better this time.

A hatch opened.

It's time to go, Ev. Crawl as quickly as you can. They may try to stop you.

"Who is 'they'?" she shouted.

It will all become clear in time. Please. You said you would do as I told you.

"And if I don't, you'll make me."

No Ev. I will never hurt you.

Sure you won't, thought Ev.

She crawled through the hatch, and almost screamed when it snapped shut behind her. She lashed out with her foot, kicking it as hard as she could, not because she thought it would open again, but because it made her feel a little better.

She was scared, but mostly she was angry. Vendavi would pay for this, one day. She would make sure of it.

She crawled, as quickly as she could. The tunnels were dark and smelled damp. They were also very, *very* hot. She didn't want to be there any longer than she had to. This tunnel was even worse than the one from her fifth birthday. It was falling to pieces! Here a leaking pipe, there one that looked like it would burst at any moment. Bits of the walls were crumbling. Once, as she crawled past a vent, she thought she could see a pile of broken concrete in the distance, as though a part of the tunnel had collapsed.

Even stranger were the faded posters on the walls. The one opposite the vent had a picture of a woman in strange clothes holding a child's hand. The words she could make out said:

It can't hurt to keep yourself safe from you! Begin Hexteria today!

There were other posters like it dotting the walls. She stared at them a long time, trying to make sense of the words.

Ev, you must keep going.

She started crawling again. She couldn't go back to her cell, and she couldn't stay in the tunnel – the only way was forward.

Every now and then she was hit with gusts of air from the vents along the tunnel walls. It smelled terrible. There had to be something wrong with the ventilation system.

"Why haven't they sent someone to fix it?" she asked, but there was no answer.

She was tired, her back hurt, and the tunnel scared her. It didn't feel safe down here in this dimly lit hole. Inner didn't feel safe.

Tears started to trickle down her face. Her heart started beating far too quickly and she found herself gasping for air.

Then she rounded a bend she saw something that made her heart stop and her blood run cold.

It was another face, face-to-face with her own.

It was covered in sweat and much lighter than hers, surrounded by brown curls instead of black frizz, but it was definitely a face.

It was the first time in six years that she had seen another person.

"Is that you?" asked the blue-eyed face.

The face's eyes were wide with terror and its voice shook.

"Please, is that you?" it asked again.

It's a boy, thought Ev to herself. An actual Withouter boy.

"Ev?" Asked the boy, nervously. He was looking all around, frightened and shaking.

"What are you?" she whispered.

"It's me, Jonah. They sent me to get you. Please, can we get out of here?"

Ev fainted.

4. The Only Way is Up

Inner children will wear Suncharm when leaving the building for no less than one (1) year after arrival in Alerrawia. Failure to comply will result in detention and possibly death.

Alerrawia School Rules, Summary, Page 7

Ev's mind filled with a horrifying mess of demon mantises and never-ending tunnels; no matter which way she turned, there was no way out…

Then she woke up.

The boy-thing that claimed to be Jonah hovered nearby, eyes darting this way and that. Even in the dim light Ev could see how pale he was.

"Hello?" she said.

The boy recoiled, backing into the tunnel wall.

"You awake?" he asked.

"Seems that way," said Ev.

"Can we go now please?" his voice was desperate and pleading. "I have to get out of here…"

"Look, are you real, or are you just one of the things from Vendavi 2's world?"

She didn't bother waiting for an answer, just lunged and grabbed his arm. Her hands closed around solid flesh and bone, and the boy screamed.

Ev dropped his arm in shock. The moment she did, the boy disappeared down the tunnel. She could hear him moving.

"Wait!" she shouted. "I just needed to know you were real!"

Don't go!

The sounds of movement stopped, but the boy didn't reappear.

"I'm sorry!" she called. "I…I don't know what's happening!"

The boy came closer until he was close enough for her to make him out in the dark.

"Can we please go?" he asked.

"Go where?"

"Didn't he tell you?"

"Who? Vendavi 2?"

"Is that what you call him?" the boy sounded calmer now, but only a little. "I called him Smart Vendavi. You know. Because normal Vendavi was dumb?"

Maybe it *was* Jonah.

"Are you coming? I'm going now, and you can follow me or not, but I'm not staying here!"

He darted down the tunnel.

Ev hesitated for a moment.

"Wait!" she called, following. It wasn't like she could go back, anyway.

Ever since she could remember, Ev had been taught, day after day, that isolation was the key to purity of thought and action. Apart from the first five years of your life, you would live on your own for the benefit of everyone.

Surprise reunions in dark tunnels with people who may or may not be who they said they were was not part of the deal.

She studied the boy in front of her as they crawled. He was wearing hard black shoes with thick, patterned treads as well as gray shorts and a white top with buttons down the front. Not the Inner-approved uniform at all.

Was he even the real Jonah?

"I am Jonah!" shouted the boy.

"No one said you weren't…"

"I…just *guessed* what you're thinking. I thought the same when Amy came to get me. Punched her in the face. Had to chase her all the way to the ladder."

"You punched Amy?"

"I didn't know it was her!" he shouted.

"Of course you didn't," Ev said quickly to calm him down. "How could you?"

"Exactly! How could I."

"Is…is she all right now?" Ev asked.

"She's fine. She says it doesn't matter. Of course it matters, but she says it doesn't. She just follows me around and looks after. It might be her. She says she knows I'm me because she came to get me. That doesn't make sense though, right? Because I could be the one pretending to be Jonah – she just found me in the tunnels, she doesn't know!"

He crawled angrily.

"But…you are Jonah, right?"

"Yes! I did that biology lesson, and I told you to do the mindfulness one, even after Mike disappeared, and I guess you did, because here you are!"

"Alright! Alright. You're Jonah. You're taking me somewhere, and Amy is there as well. Right?"

"Right."

They crawled and crawled and then crawled some more. Ev was exhausted, and her brain was boiling in her head. It was so hot!

How long had she been down here, anyway?

"Vendavi, what time is it?"

"He won't answer you here. He's done with us now."

"Done with us?"

He ignored her.

"Here we are. This is the hard bit," he said.

"What do you mean?"

He shifted slightly to reveal the first few rungs of a ladder.

"We have to climb."

Ev looked hard, but she couldn't see the top.

"I'm not sure I can," she whispered. Memories of trying to climb a tower in a simulation flooded her mind.

"You can. I did. Amy did. Amy did it alone, actually, because there was no one who wanted to come get her. You go first."

There was nowhere else to go but back to a hatch that wouldn't open. She grasped the first rung and pulled herself up. A few rungs later her arms were burning, and she was panting for air.

“Keep going!”

She dragged herself up another rung. And another. And another. Every time she stopped for too long, Jonah poked her and complained until she started moving again.

“Almost there,” he said for the thousandth time.

She gritted her teeth and grabbed the next rung in exhausted fingers. The air was burning. The higher she climbed, the hotter it got.

If this was one of Vendavi 2’s lessons she would have just flown to the top. If only…

There was a strange feeling in her stomach, like she was falling from a great height, and her body suddenly felt much lighter, and she grabbed the next run easily.

“Don’t do that!” yelled Jonah.

“Do what?” asked Ev. The lightness disappeared.

“Don’t… drift off,” said Jonah. “Stay grounded.”

“I have no idea what you mean,” said Ev. With a gasp she pulled herself up another rung.

“We’re almost there, I promise. Five more minutes.”

“You said that a hundred minutes ago!”

She reached for the next rung, but her tired, sweat-slick hand couldn’t hold on. The rung slipped from her grip, she lost her footing, and suddenly she was hanging by one hand over the void, shrieking.

Jonah grabbed her left foot and guided back to a lower rung.

"I'm scared," she sobbed. "I don't want to fall!"

She was holding onto the nearest rung with both hands again, shaking and sobbing.

"Keep going!"

"I can't!"

"The only way is up. There's nowhere else. You have to keep going. We really are almost there." He was terrified.

Whether or not this was Jonah, she had to help him get out of the dark. With a sigh, she grabbed the next rung, and pulled herself up. Then another, and another.

"Thank you!"

She was too exhausted to answer.

In five rungs time, I'll look up to check how much further.

Alright, in ten rungs time I'll check again…

1…2…3…4…

Suddenly, the ladder ended, and Ev fell down on her hands and knees in front of a huge, heavy, ornate door. On the door was a looped animation showing a hand knocking three times.

Above the bright animation was an inscription on a fancy, ancient plaque.

Below someone, a very long time ago, had taped a sign which read:

Entry to and from Inner is restricted, by order.

Trespassers will be punished to the fullest extent of the law.

Alerting the denizens of Inner to your existence will result in death.

It only took Ev a few seconds to read the signs, but she was too tired to understand them. She lay on the landing, panting.

Jonah, who hardly seemed tired at all, banged on the door three times, and then stepped back, pressing himself against the wall.

The door slid open.

A wave of sound hit her.

Were those…voices?

Jonah poked his head out, looked around quickly, and then said, "Coast is clear. The door doesn't stay open forever. They might just leave you there if it closes again, so get moving!"

He darted out and disappeared from view.

Ev staggered to her feet and out into the light.

"Jonah?" she tried to call, but the word stuck in her throat.

There were faces, hundreds of them, all turning to look at her.

Her chest tightened. She couldn't breathe. She fell to her knees and wrapped her arms around herself.

People! Withouter people, everywhere!

"Hey look!" shouted someone. "Fresh meat!"

Laughter from all sides.

These were *children*. Well, most of them were anyway, all neatly dressed in gray clothes, just like Jonah.

A distant crash shook the walls of the room. There were a few shrieks of excitement, but no one seemed worried.

"Stupid dragon," muttered an older girl at the end of a long table. The crash had made her spill something orange all over her clothes. The girl looked around to see if anyone was watching. Only Ev was looking at her. She winked at Ev, and then whispered, "Clean yourself up!"

The orange stains vanished.

The girl grinned and put a finger to her lips.

"Ev!" someone shrieked, and a mass of blonde hair barreled into her and wound its arms tightly around her waist.

Ev yelled and tried to pull away, but she couldn't.

"No running in the Common Room!" This voice was small and squeaky and belonged to a strange creature that Ev had never seen before.

She stared.

The squeaky speaker was only about nine inches tall, but it hovered in front of the blonde hugger using its delicate wings. Its wings were the only thing about it that was delicate. It had a wide, stubby nose, and huge bushy eyebrows that shadowed its enormous and slanted eyes. Its ears were pointy, and its hands seemed too big for its body. Its skin was gray, and on its head was a pointy hat that fastened under its chin. The hat, along with the pants it wore and the gray bag on its shoulder, was also gray.

Her attacker finally let go, revealing a skinny blonde girl.

"Go away, Boaclick," whispered the girl.

"Rudeness is punishable by detention, you know!" squeaked Boaclick.

"Can't do that," she said in a tiny voice, but she was pale and shaking.

"Can't I? Oh, teacher!" called the strange little man.

The girl squealed and made for the nearest doors. The thing named Boaclick turned to Ev, chuckling.

"I can't really give her detention, you know, but some of you kids will believe anything. Are you the new one, then?"

For the second time that day, Ev fainted.

When she woke, there was a circle of faces staring down at her, whispering and nudging. They were all children. The strange little gray man was gone.

"Is she dead?" whispered one. "What do they do to them down there?"

"She's not dead! You can see her breathing."

"You can be brain dead and still breathe, you know. It's the brain that matters."

"She's just weak, like all magic brats from Inner."

"Magic users are not weak!"

"You were when you first got here!"

"Guys, she's waking up!"

"Enough," said a grown-up voice. The children scattered.

Their faces were replaced by a man's.

"Hello, Ev, welcome to Alerrawia. I know you have a lot of questions. I won't be answering them. For now, have some water, and a *very small* bite of this." He impatiently shoved a glass into one of her hands and something that looked suspiciously like bread into the other. The bread was smeared with a sticky orange substance.

Ev didn't move.

"Sit up."

She stayed where she was.

Another face appeared in her line of sight. This one did not belong to a child or a man. It was hairy with an off-white, pointy snout, pointy gray ears and head, and dark gray markings around its eyes.

It was growling.

She yelped and shot back toward the tunnel door. It was closed, so she pressed herself against it as hard as she could.

"Ev, meet Ernouf," the man said, drily. Ev thought she could see the hints of a smile around his mouth. "Ernouf, meet Ev, our newest student."

Ev was shaking.

"Let me out," she whispered.

"Ernouf is a wolf," he said, ignoring her. "Don't worry; he only bites when I tell him too. Most of the time. Some of the time. Actually, he pretty much does what he likes, if I'm being perfectly honest, but he's not in the habit of hurting the children. Much."

Ev whimpered. The man sighed and rubbed his forehead.

"This is a strange day, I realize, but you're going to have to get over the shock and get on with things. Your self-sufficiency is your one redeeming characteristic, so don't go all helpless on me now. Think about it logically. You're here now. Nothing can change that fact. Your best course of action is to adjust and readjust as needed in order to make the most of what I can assure is an irreversible situation."

He pointed at the water.

"You're ridiculously thirsty, remember?"

She was. She was exhausted from the climb, and it was so hot up here. She gulped the water down quickly.

"Eat some," said the man, gesturing at the bread.

Ev took a bite.

It was the most amazing thing she'd ever tasted. It was so sweet, but so good, and it made her thirsty all over again. But it also made her feel tired and empty, just like she did after eating Bug Bars. Not enough to need a nap, but she could have slept if she wanted to.

"Good. Eat as much of that as you can."

She raised the bread to her mouth and pretended to take another, tiny bite. She was hungry, but she didn't like what the bread was doing to her.

The man didn't seem to notice.

"My name is Christopher Morrison. Sorry I wasn't here when you arrived. There's still some debate about whether you should even be here, so don't bother asking any questions until that's been sorted out. I suppose I better find you somewhere to wait."

He pulled her to her feet and gently grabbed the back of her yellow jumpsuit and pushed her forward.

"This way."

There was a door at the other end of the big room, but that's not where Christopher led her. Instead, they turned right. Ev couldn't make out where they were going, but it didn't matter, because her attention was stolen by something wonderful.

They were passing a window.

There was so much light! Her eyes slammed shut and she threw her hands up in front of her face.

"That's impossible," she whispered.

"I was wondering what your first words would be," said Christopher. "They're fairly apt, I suppose. Sums up what all you Inner kids think when you first get here."

She took a step toward the window, but Ernouf cut her off and nudged her back towards Christopher. Frightened, Ev backed away.

Ernouf growled at her.

"That's enough, old man. She's listening," said Christopher, taking Ev's arm and steering her along. "Come with us, Ernouf! They expected us back whole minutes ago, you know."

Ernouf licked Christopher's hand, and bounded across the room and out a faraway door.

"Or you can leave me to fend for myself," muttered Christopher. "Whatever you think is the best use of your time."

"This is an elevator," said Christopher once they reached the edge of the room. Ev looked at the large steel doors. She knew what an elevator was – she'd read about them. Christopher continued. "The doors open. We get in. It takes us up to a different floor. We get out. There is absolutely nothing to faint about. Understand?"

She nodded, but her attention was really on the strange posters all over the wall. Ev was a reader, and if there were words to read, she would read them.

Keep yourself safe from you!

Gifts must be used wisely.

Better safe than sorry!

Out of habit, she looked at the words behind the words, and what she saw was this: We know better than you, remember that. Sit down, shut up, and do as you are told.

Christopher hit a button on the steel doors and they slid open with a *ping*.

Older children spilled out of the box, giggling, and chatting. When they saw Christopher, they stopped talking, looked at their feet, and walked around him as quickly as possible. They stepped into the elevator. No one followed them.

Ev made a mental note to be careful of Christopher.

Christopher hit a button marked "4", and a moment later, her stomach fell away from her as the elevator lurched upwards. She sat down on the floor with a thump.

"Nothing to worry about," said Christopher in a bored tone, but he didn't ask her to stand.

"I know," she said, irritably. Christopher ignored her.

The elevator *pinged* its way up to the fourth floor where Christopher pulled her to her feet and out into a wide corridor. As they wound through a network of corridors, Ev saw people in white coats scurrying between beds in the distance.

Christopher hurried her into a room and closed the door behind them.

"Anyone here?" he called.

"Just me."

"Granny. Well, I suppose it could be worse."

An old, marshmallow-like lady pulled herself to her feet. She'd been sitting in a chair near the window. She wore the same uniform as everyone else, but she managed to look comfortable in it. Her face was covered in soft wrinkles and she had small light blue eyes that were magnified by thick glasses. Her hair was curly and sandy blonde from a distance, but as Christopher drew Ev nearer, she could see streaks of silver as well.

"Who have we here?" asked the woman, eyes twinkling.

"It's hardly important. Do you have somewhere to keep her?"

"Keep her? 'Keeping' people is what they do in the sub-basement, Christopher. This is the med bay."

"I mean, keep an eye on her, and keep her away from others, until they've decided what to do with her."

"'They'? Aren't you one of the 'them', Christopher dear?"

"I would say that I won't be long," said Christopher, ignoring the question, "but my mother always told me not to lie."

He let Ev go and left, closing the door behind him.

"Hello," said the woman kindly. "I'm Nancy Oakwood, but everyone calls me Granny. You can call me that too if you like."

Ev said nothing.

"What's your name, dear?"

"It's hardly important," Ev said.

"Oh, you mustn't pay too much attention too much attention to Christopher. He thinks it's just him against the world."

Ev looked at her feet.

"Never mind then. We can introduce ourselves another time. Come through here."

Granny led Ev through a door at the back of the room into a smaller office.

"I hope you and I will be friends. For now, I think you want to be by yourself. Am I right?"

Ev nodded.

"Alright. I'll just be on the other side of the door if you need something. There's a good view from up here, if you want to take a look at your new world. Maybe eat some more of that bread you have clutched in your hand?"

Granny left, closing the door gently behind her.

Ev collapsed on the black office chair behind the desk and cried.

"What's happening?" she whispered between sobs.

The thing about crying is that you can't do it forever. She was already so tired from the climb and the shock, and her tears soon ran out. She was hot. She was hungry. She was miserable.

She didn't want the bread – it made her sleepy. She threw it on the floor under the desk then pushed the chair in so no one would see, wiping the sticky jam on her jumpsuit.

Then, eyes bright and face flushed from crying, she stepped toward the window and looked out.

She saw a garden many floors beneath her. There were people in the garden, but she couldn't see what they were doing. A group of small children ran through one of the flower beds, and were chased, shrieking, out of view by an angry grown-up. On the other side of the huge garden, she could see a high, thick fence. Above, there was nothing but blue sky. In the distance, a bird swooped down to grab some unlucky prey.

It felt a bit like a simulation.

Maybe it was a simulation?

"I don't care," she told herself. "I really don't. It doesn't matter at all if this world is real or not."

She stepped toward the window.

"I'll just open this to let in some cooler air," she said. That was all she wanted. Cooler air. She definitely wasn't opening the window to check if this world looked just as real on the other side of the glass.

The window was locked! She banged a fist against the glass…

Open!

…which shook the latch loose, and the window sprang open.

Carefully, she opened the window, leaned out, and stretched out her neck. She could feel the sun on her skin. She leaned out further.

"Ouch!" she suddenly squealed. Her arm was burning! The pain shocked her, she lost her footing, and she fell straight out of the window.

She screamed as the ground rushed up to meet her.

"Help me!"

But no one would because no one ever did, and she was falling, falling…

Fly!

…and her stomach lurched, and she came to a sudden stop. Carefully, she opened her eyes.

She was hovering a few inches above the ground.

Then she was screaming again, not because of the fall, but because of her burning skin. She screamed, and as she screamed, she rose through the air.

The people in the garden were pointing and shouting. "Someone, do something!"

But no one seemed to know what to do.

Her lips swelled with burns until she couldn't scream anymore.

"Well," said an unexpected voice.

She opened her burned eyelids eyes as best she could. At a window stood Christopher.

"We were just talking about you," he said. "I guess you'd better come in."

He was pushed aside by someone else, a woman with big eyes and light brown skin.

"Out of the way, Christopher!" she shouted. "You! Come here!"

Ev tried to say that she couldn't move but her lips were too burned. All she could manage was a whimper. It didn't matter. As soon as the woman told her to "Come here!" her body moved of its own accord.

When she was close enough to the window, Christopher and the woman grabbed her, and she screamed again. They pulled her inside.

"Oh, the poor child!" said the woman as Ev collapsed on the floor.

"Don't fuss, Zara," said Christopher. "She was told to wait. Maybe this will teach her to listen in future."

Ev groaned. She wished they would all shut up and let her die.

"Oh, for heaven's sake, someone help the girl," said an older voice.

Through her swollen eyes, Ev saw Zara take a step forward, then hesitate.

"I'll do it," said Christopher. He strolled over to a cabinet and came back with some creams, which he started applying to Ev's more visible burns. The creams numbed the pain almost immediately.

"Oh, don't mess around with those!" exclaimed the woman named Zara, stirring herself. She pushed Christopher aside and bent over Ev.

"Let's see, let's see…" she murmured. "Quite severe, but not the end of the world… A standard healing charm should do the trick!"

She raised her arms, mumbled something Ev couldn't quite catch, and snapped her fingers.

Suddenly, Ev was fine. There was not a single burn on her. She gasped for air.

"I got rid of those goopy creams too, sweetheart," said Zara, with a significant look at Christopher. He grunted and looked away.

"Unauthorized flying is against school rules!" said a fat man with wispy hair that looked like a decomposing ear of corn and face like a melted waxwork.

"She doesn't attend the school and hasn't been told the rules, Robert. Or have I completely missed the point of our entire debate?" asked the older voice who'd told them to help her. It belonged to a skinny old woman.

"Anyway, this changes everything," said Zara.

"How does it change a thing?"

"We weren't sure she had it in her, but this proves…"

"This proves nothing! She is a degenerate, a waste of space! We never should have opened the tunnel for her!"

"She shouldn't have been able to do what she just did! You watched her eat, didn't you Christopher?"

"Yes, she ate. If Robert's views were accurate, we would be staring down at her small burnt corpse on the jogging track."

"Do the manufacturers still insist that their product is as potent as always? This proves that…"

"It proves nothing," said the old lady. "It could be Inner's product that is faulty, she may not have the buildup in her system we usually see under these conditions."

"Christopher should have accounted for that in his calculations!"

"Well, it's a good thing he didn't, or we'd have a dead child on our hands!"

"That would be better!" spluttered Robert.

Ev listened to the grown-ups arguing. She didn't really understand what they were saying, but she knew she didn't like being spoken of as if she wasn't even in the room. The strange tingling feeling she'd felt before began niggling at the base of her skull, like a bubbling pit that was about to overflow. She felt it slowly move down towards her hands.

"I'm sorry if I'm wasting your time," she said, directly to Robert, her voice icy, even as her body burned with rage.

"You are a waste of time. All your kind are. If I had my way…"

"Shut up!" she screamed, and the rage that had been building hit its peak and exploded from her hands in a stream of fire.

Burn!

Zara, moving quickly, threw a hand up just in time and caught the flames. They vanished.

There was complete silence. Even Robert looked shocked.

The anger was gone. All that was left was fear.

"Well," said a fourth person who had not yet spoken. He was sitting behind a big ornate desk.

The man leaned forward. He was white haired and square jawed, and his blue eyes pierced straight through her. Behind him on the wall were the same words she'd read on the door before entering this strange place. Out of habit, she read them again.

> *Even the evilest among us can be used for the greater good. They are a gift, sent to be used wisely.*
>
> *But of course, they must be properly controlled.*
>
> *You will thank us.*
>
> *The Granite Institute*

"I think we should take a moment to give you the highlights. "My name is Felix Granite," he said.

"Do you work for Janian Granite?" asked Ev.

All the grown-ups burst out laughing, except Christopher. Zara looked a bit uncomfortable, but the rest seemed to think it was the funniest thing they'd ever heard.

Ev's face was burning. It was a simple question! They didn't have to laugh at her like that…

"Pay attention," said Felix Granite once everyone had calmed down. "You are in a place called Alerrawia, a wonderful society that has been rescuing children with useful abilities from Inner for decades."

Useful abilities?

"Vendavi is an extremely fallible machine, and almost impossible to manipulate."

Extremely fallible *and* impossible to manipulate?

"A long time ago, the scientists here discovered how to influence Vendavi just enough to divert carefully selected children on their eleventh birthdays. You are very fortunate that we chose to rescue you from the pit of misery that is Inner. Of course, we do have to be *very careful* about who we allow in. We can't take just anybody, after all." He chuckled, like he was sharing a well-known joke.

"Here's the thing. You can fly. You have a fire ability. This is because magic is, sadly, a real evil, and you are one of the unlucky few cursed with its shadow.

"Science is also real, as you know. Many years ago, a battle fought between the good Followers of Science and the evil Magic Users. We, the scientifically minded, have shielded ourselves in this bubble to protect the worthy from the worst of the war. If we're not careful, it's a war that will be fought again.

"It will be up to you to pick a side, Evelyn. I hope you pick the right one."

5. I Must Be Properly Controlled

It is essential to remember that, while magic is tolerated for its occasional usefulness, it is, at its core, evil. However, evil can be used in the service of the Greater Good; the only appropriate use for magic is in the service of science.

Felix Granite

Alerrawia: To the Future

Volume 1, Page 3

Felix waved his hand and said, "Marcia, take her to your office, we have more to discuss."

Zara and Marcia, a stubby, plump woman with very short brown hair and glasses, took her by the arms and led her across the hall. There was another door leading out of Marcia's office, which Marcia carefully locked. She also turned off her computer and locked all of her drawers.

"Is that really necessary?" asked Zara.

"Would you want *her* set loose in your bedroom? If so, it's just around the corner…"

Zara tutted impatiently but said nothing.

Marcia kept speaking, but Ev wasn't listening. She was thinking about how just the day before she'd never seen anyone in person, and now, just one day later, she was wishing that they would just go away and leave her alone.

"I *said*, do you understand?" asked Marcia, sharply.

"Understand what?" asked Ev.

"Do try to focus. . ."

"She just gave you some rules for being in her office," said Zara. "It was a long and tedious list, but it can be summarized as 'Sit down, shut up, touch nothing, and don't move.' Got it?"

Ev nodded impatiently.

Go away!

"All right, then we'll leave you be. But eat that," added Zara as she backed out of the room. She pointed at Marcia's desk where a bowl of steaming porridge appeared. "You must be starving after your ordeal."

This office was bigger and didn't have a single window, not that she wanted to ever go outside again.

She sat in one of the two chairs facing a desk, slowly eating the porridge. After only a few bites, she started to feel sleepy.

"Not this again!"

She shoved the bowl across the desk. It wobbled and a few blotches of the gooey gray substance leaked splattered all over Marcia's desk.

Ev smiled in satisfaction and briefly considered pouring onto the carpet but decided against it. She was probably in enough trouble as it was.

Trouble. She was in plenty of trouble—that was for sure…

There was a little bronze plaque on the desk that read *Marcia Breswick, of The Seven.* She counted the letters in the words, and then the letters on the spines of all the books behind the desk, and then she counted the books themselves. When she was finished, she turned her attention to the calendar on the wall. Someone had scratched untidy lines through the days that had passed, telling her that it was Thursday. She counted all the letters in Thursday, and then all the other days, and then in the month…

Counting always helped her stay calm.

She had one, two magical abilities, and there were one, two sides in a war that might be fought again. There were one, two different versions of reality…

No, that wasn't right, was it? There was one reality, and one lie about what was real and what wasn't.

Count the lies.

One, there is nothing alive above ground, two, there is no such thing as magic, three, Withouters died out due to stupidity, four…

There were so many!

Count the tears. One, two, three, four, five, six…

After an eternity, the door swung open, and Christopher returned.

He crouched in front of Ev's chair so that his eyes were level with her own.

"You get to stay," he said. "It's the ideal outcome from the wide array of possibilities that today's events generated."

The words behind the words were easy to spot this time. Lots of people don't want you here, but you get to stay, whether you like it or not; aren't you lucky?

Ev kept crying. Two-hundred-and-seven, two-hundred-and-eight...

"They've asked me to give you a crash course in new arrival orientation. The fact that there is no crash course doesn't seem to bother them."

Two-hundred-and-fifteen, two-hundred-and-sixteen...

"For all intents and purposes, there are two groups, or civilizations, still standing: Inner and Alerrawia. Well, actually there's a third group too, but I won't worry you with those details right now; they're officially and legally unimportant."

Two-hundred-and-twenty-seven, two-hundred-and-twenty-eight...

"Inner used to be governed by Alerrawia, so that's why there's a tunnel from there to here, but a series of unfortunate events led to all entrances and exits being permanently sealed. It took us a while to figure out how to hack into Vendavi and take control, when it suits us. For about eighty years we've been introducing our own educational materials to see which children are a fit for Alerrawia and rescuing them. No one gets hurt, and we get the strong magic users we always seem to need."

Two-hundred-and-sixty-seven, Two-hundred-and-

"What do you mean, 'no one gets hurt?' Those simulations were the worst things that ever happened to me! Mike disappeared!"

"Who's Mike?"

"He didn't do the simulation. He reported the glitch. Then they got rid of him."

"Really? It's been years since someone's reported Vendavi's strange behavior, we'll have to be more careful in future."

"My friend is gone!"

"I doubt it. In fact, I think I have a pretty good idea where he is. He's fine. Forget about him. The only person you need is yourself—remember that."

The tingling sensation started to creep over Ev. She could feel the fire building and then…

…nothing.

"You can't use your fire ability now. We've blocked you. Imagine what it would be like if every child you could shoot fire was allowed to do so whenever they felt like it?"

Ev was furious. She fought to release her fire, but it just sat there, bubbling in her brain. Instead, she grabbed the plaque off Marcia's desk and threw it at Christopher.

Christopher snatched it easily out of the air. He glanced toward the door.

"Looks like our time is up," he said, calmly. In a few long strides he crossed the room and returned the plaque to its rightful place.

Marcia bustled in, quickly noted that everything was still in one piece, and then said to Ev, "Come along now, it's time to get you settled in."

She took Ev by the hand and pulled her out of the chair.

"Quickly now, there's a lot to do, and not much time to do it. Felix wants you in school by Monday. Monday! The man asks too much sometimes."

"Well, maybe if you didn't always jump to attention so willingly…" Christopher muttered.

"Come along!" She pulled Ev out the door, and dragged her to the elevator. As Marcia used the biometric scanner to call the elevator, Ev noted that they were on the thirteenth floor.

Ev looked around furtively, but they were in a narrow corridor with no escape. Even if she *could* knock Marcia down…

Ping!

The doors opened, and Marcia put a hand on her shoulder and pushed her in. Without looking away from her clipboard, she hit number 6. The elevator dropped. Ev knew what to expect this time, but it was still a strange feeling.

"We'll have to put you in with some of the older girls," she said, consulting her clipboard thoughtfully. "I just don't see another way…"

Ev didn't answer. It was obvious that Marcia wasn't really speaking to her, anyway, so what was the point?

The elevator *pinged* its way down to the sixth floor. "Here we are!" said Marcia, brightly. "Follow me, please."

Ev followed Marcia through a labyrinth of gray, concrete corridors, trying to keep track of where they were going but failing miserably. The only color on the ugly, hard walls were more of the accusing posters. Ev turned her eyes away—for the first time in her life, she didn't want to read the words that were in front of her.

"Here it is! Number 63. Your new home."

Marcia opened the door and pushed Ev in.

"I'll only be gone a moment. Don't touch what isn't yours!"

She bustled off.

There were no windows, again, and it was by far the smallest room that she had been in since leaving Inner, but there was still plenty to impress her. It was all concrete and grayness, but it actually looked fairly comfortable. A large closet, a basin, two bunkbeds, and a desk covered in books. Real books, like in the old days, all printed out and bound.

She'd been told not to touch what wasn't hers, but there was no harm in looking.

The book titles fascinated her. *Advanced Spell Casting, Advanced Physical Inorganic Chemistry, Differential Calculus, The Theory of Flight, Information Technology in a New World.* Without thinking, she reached out to take one of the books.

"Don't touch my stuff!" came a shriek from the door.

Ev turned to see an extremely short and skinny dark-haired girl glaring at her. She had pointy features and narrow eyes. Her face was red, and she was panting. She was only a little taller than Ev, but she seemed much older.

"I haven't touched…," Ev began. Before she could say anything else, another girl arrived, also panting. She was much taller than the first girl with dark skin, long black hair kept in a neat long plait down her back, and a plain white headband.

"Maddie, you're insane!" she panted. "No running in the corridors! Remember? Anyone could have seen us…" the new arrival, who was at least three years older, trailed off as her eyes found Ev.

"Get off my bed!" she screamed.

Ev jumped up. The tall girl ran over to her bed and started fussing over it.

"To answer your question, Stacey," said the small girl, leaning against the door, "I thought a little bit of rule breaking might be in order to keep *her* from destroying our things. And I was right! As usual!"

"Quick, help me change the sheets!"

"No way!" said the small girl. "We're halfway through lunch and if we don't leave soon, we'll be in trouble with Carrio! Unless you've found way to bend time…"

Stacey glared at Ev. She pointed to the bunks on the other side of the room.

"The top one is yours. Stay in your space."

"Come on, come on, come on!" said the other girl, dancing from foot to foot.

"Coming," muttered Stacey.

They left, and Ev just heard Stacey saying, "But no running this time…Madison, get back here!"

She climbed onto her bed and curled in a ball.

"No running!" came a familiar, grown-up voice from the corridor. Marcia was back. "Detentions if I catch you running again!"

Ev heard the rustling of paper on a clipboard.

"Where are you?" she asked.

Ev poked her head over the rail.

"Come down at once!"

Ev shook her head and lay down again. Whatever came next, she wanted no part of it.

"Not a very good start, I fear," Marcia said. "Madam! Could you come in here please? She's being difficult."

Ev peeked her head out again.

An imposing woman with fiery red hair tied up in a ponytail strode into the room.

"Where is she?" she demanded. Ev dropped her head and curled up even tighter.

"Up there."

Footsteps.

"You're new, so I'll go easy on you, but this sort of behavior will not be tolerated in my dorm. Do you understand?"

The woman grabbed her suddenly and dragged her off the bed.

Ev shrieked, kicking and screaming.

"Chloe!" shouted the woman. "Where is that dratted woman?"

"I'll find her," said Marcia, over Ev's screams. "Where should I send her?"

"Bathrooms," said the woman.

Marcia nodded and left. The woman let go of Ev suddenly. She fell to the floor with a thump. The woman walked over to the door and shut it. Then she squatted down in front of Ev.

"Let's get a few things clear, you little brat," she said. "My name is Gwyneth Mars, but you will call me Madam. I am in charge, which means you have to follow my rules. You will not bite. You will not scratch. You will not behave like an animal. Is that clear?"

Ev froze. She knew that voice, that tone. She'd last heard it on the day of her fifth birthday.

Her eyes narrowed.

But she wasn't five anymore. She did not have to put up with grown-ups and their cruelty.

Ev kicked her. To be fair, kicking was not one of the things Madam expressly forbade.

"Very well," said the woman.

She took something flat and rectangular out of her pocket and pointed it at Ev.

"Do you know what this is?" she asked.

Ev didn't, but she wasn't about to admit it.

"It's an RDD," she said, reading the letters on the back.

"I thought as much," said Madam. "Let me show you."

The screen came alive, and Madam tapped one of the options.

A second later, Ev was on the floor, gasping for air.

"Let's see how you manage without your lungs for a bit," said Madam with a smile.

Ev had a lot of experience with punishments like this. It was exactly what Vendavi used to do in Inner. Every punishment was a fresh surprise. Would they steal your air or sight or brain? For how long? They could take your eyes away for days, breathing for minutes, each punishment calculated to provide maximum discomfort with minimal physical damage.

Compared to being burned by the sun, this was easy. It would all be over soon.

Enough!

The RDD released her.

"Did you like that?" she asked.

Ev shook her head automatically. "Thank you for showing me the error of my ways," she said without thinking.

"If you want to avoid experiences like this in the future, do what I say. Do it quickly and do it quietly. I don't care if you want to do it or not. I don't care if you're scared. Have I made myself clear?"

She knew this game well. "Yes, Madam."

"Good. Now, repeat after me. *I am an evil gift.*"

For a moment, Ev couldn't speak.

"Say it!"

"I am an evil gift," she said, quickly.

"I must be properly controlled."

"I must be properly controlled."

Madam nodded, satisfied.

"Up!" she commanded.

She sprang to her feet.

"Follow me!"

Ev followed Madam to the bathroom where a nervous woman was waiting for them.

"Chloe!" shouted Madam.

"Marcia said you'd be here," she said in a high pitched, but tiny voice.

"And here we are," said Madam. "I had some trouble with this one."

Chloe came over to Ev and crouched in front of her.

"Hello, dear," she said sweetly with a smile. "How are you today?"

Ev said nothing.

"Answer!" commanded Madam.

"Fine," said Ev quickly.

"Good," said Chloe uncertainly. Her eyes darted to Madam for a fraction of a second. Ev sensed that she might have an ally.

"Do you have an RDD too?" she asked Chloe, hoping she sounded small and scared.

"Gwyneth!" said Chloe, turning to her colleague in shock (although Ev didn't think she seemed *too* surprised). "That is strictly against the rules!"

"When the rules are stupid, I choose to break them," said Madam.

"I'll report you!" said Chloe.

The two women stared at each other, one tall and terrifying, and the other small, and frightened, but determined.

"Fine," said Madam eventually, "You deal with her." She stormed out.

"Evelyn, I am so sorry," she said. "Gwyneth... I mean, Madam, means well, but she sometimes ...goes a little overboard."

"*Do* you have one of those RDD things?"

"No! And nor do any of the other carers or teachers! No one is allowed to use RDDs, Evelyn. If anyone uses a RDD on you again, tell someone – it's strictly against the rules!"

Ev nodded, although she wondered *who* she should tell.

"All right, good," said Chloe. "Toiletries are stored under the basins. I'll give you some time to wash and change. Your uniform is in that bag over there, and I'll put a spare in your room. Will you be alright on your own for a little while?"

Ev nodded, and Chloe left her to shower.

Ev showered and dressed as quickly as she could. Hair still wet, she stood numbly in the middle of the empty bathroom, staring at herself in a mirror. She could feel the panic rising again.

Count the tiles, one, two, three, four…

Count the drops, one, two, three, four…

Don't count the scary thoughts. Don't count the scary people. Don't count the strange things. Some counting would only make things worse.

Once she was calmer, she stepped out of the bathroom to find Chloe hovering by the door.

"There, isn't that much better?" she asked with a smile.

Ev nodded.

"All right," said Chloe. "I'll show you back to your room, and then I think you should try to nap until supper. I'll ask the other girls to wake you up in time."

Ev curled up on her bed again. The room was too bright. It was too hot, it smelled like other people, and the bed was too high.

Nevertheless, she fell asleep the moment her head touched the pillow.

She crawled down a never-ending tunnel, calling for her parents. Whenever she was about to reach the door that led...somewhere, she wasn't quite sure, but she knew it was to safety... Felix would appear and say "No, I don't think so, do you?" and she would be sent back to the beginning. Sometimes she heard Jonah and Amy in the tunnel, calling to her from just around a corner, but their voices were text scrolling across the walls.

Jonah: Pls can we GET OUT of here?

Amy: Ev! Ev! Ev! Ev! Ev!

Jonah: Hurry!

She crawled after them, trying to catch up.

"No, I don't think so, do you?"

Amy: Ev!

Jonah: Hurry! Can we please leave?

"No, I don't think so, so you?"

Jonah: Ev, please hurry! You must keep going!

Amy: Ev! Ev!

"No, I don't think so, do you?"

On her new bunk, in her new room, Ev tossed and turned fitfully, her eyes fluttering behind her eyelids.

Amy: Ev! Ev! Ev. . .

"Evelyn! Get up!"

Her eyes flew open. Her clothes clung to her sweating body and her stomach churned.

Madison was halfway up the ladder, scowling at her.

"Wake up, lazy girl, it's time for supper," she said.

Ev obediently followed Madison down the ladder.

"I'm supposed to show you the way, so here's how it's going to work. You will stay a minimum of five steps behind me and on the other side of the corridor. You are *not* with me. I don't know you, and I'm not your friend. Clear?"

Ev nodded.

"After you get lost and find your way to supper without me, you are not to sit with me. Go and find some other Inner brats to hang out with."

For a moment, Ev thought that Madison was leading her to the elevator, but at the last moment she swung towards a huge spiral staircase with wide bannisters and ugly concrete steps.

"We'll take the stairs," said Madison. "Remember the rules!"

Ev obediently hung back, realizing that Madison didn't want to get in an elevator with her because they would have to stand too close to each other.

She wondered what she'd done to make Madison hate her so much.

Madison waved to a group of older boys hanging out at the top of the stairs. One of them waved back and winked. "Find you after supper?" he asked. She nodded, giggling as they passed. Ev didn't think the giggle suited her and wondered why she did it.

On the landing there was a map of the building on a touch screen. Ev paused to take a look, but Madison was nearly out of sight, so she ran after her, afraid of being alone.

"No running in the corridors! Didn't I tell you that this morning?"

Ev yelped.

The little gray flying man was hovering inches from her face.

"What are you?" she asked.

"How rude! I'm a pixie. It's very impolite to ask people what they are."

Ev took a couple of steps back.

"Now, now, you don't want to look silly in front of the other children, do you?"

She looked around nervously. There were a few kids on the landing, and they were pointing and laughing. She took a deep breath, squared her shoulders, and stepped back toward the pixie.

"I'm sorry for being rude," she said, trying to keep her voice steady. "My name is Ev. I need to go to supper, but I don't where it is. Can you tell me how to get there, please?"

Out of the corner of her eyes, she saw Madison shrug and leave. Good. She could take care of herself.

Help me!

"Of course, I'll help you!" trilled the pixie. "Because you're new here, I'll even help you helpfully!"

He grabbed her by the ear and dragged her across the landing.

"Ow!" she said, stumbling after him. He was far too strong for someone so tiny.

"My name is Boaclick, by the way," said the pixie. "Your chronically terrified little friend pointed that out to you, but I thought that perhaps you may have been too preoccupied to remember. You're on the sixth floor. You need to get to first, to eat, and you *do* have to hurry. These," he added, pointing down the staircase, "are stairs. They take you down. Or up, if you remember to turn around."

He flung her toward the stairs by her ear. She grabbed onto the balustrade to stop herself falling. More children were laughing now. Her cheeks burned. She pretended to ignore them and started to hurry down the stairs, matching pace with everyone else who was trying to walk as quickly as they could without running.

Younger kids, shepherded by tired grown-ups, joined them on the next floor, and then they were on fourth, the med bay, where everyone seemed to busy to come and eat. Ev was completely out of breath, and there was a pain in her side that wouldn't go away. She stopped to rest, sweat rolling down her face in the sweltering heat.

"Keep moving, Inner brat," said someone behind her. They shoved her, sending her flying into a pair of boys.

"Oi!" said one of the boys, an enormous figure of at least seventeen. He grabbed her by the hair. "What is this, even?" he said, turning to his friend with a smirk.

"Looks like an Inner brat to me," said another boy who couldn't have been more than a couple of years older than Ev.

A lot of the stairway traffic had paused to watch the exchange.

"What do we do to Inner brats who shove good, upstanding Alerrawian citizens?" mused the enormous boy.

"Shove them back!" shouted the younger boy.

"Throw them over the bannister," muttered the older boy, just loud enough for Ev and the younger boy to hear.

"There's a thought," said the younger, also softly.

"What is going on here?"

Ev saw Ernouf before she saw Christopher. The wolf stalked into the middle of the gathering crowd, which melted away instantly.

Ernouf growled at the boy. He let go of her hair.

"She shoved us, sir," said the boy.

"Evelyn Acorn, fighting in the corridors is strictly forbidden!" said Christopher.

"I didn't…!"

"Derek, is it?" said Christopher, turning to the older boy.

"Yes, sir!" said Derek smartly, and just a little sarcastically.

Christopher turned to the younger boy.

"Peter?" he asked.

The younger boy just nodded, looking at his shoes.

"It should be detentions for all three of you, but I can't be bothered. Ernouf, go away. You're scaring the children."

Ernouf ignored him and instead came up to Ev.

"Hi, Ernouf," said Ev, nervously.

The wolf took Ev's shirt in his mouth and tugged gently. She took a step, then another. Ernouf let go and turned, walked a few steps, and looked back. She took a few more steps.

"Or you could take her down to supper, I suppose. You know your own mind best," said Christopher.

There were a few laughs at that from the kids who were brave enough to stay and watch.

"All of you, get to supper *now*!" ordered Christopher.

The last few kids scattered.

"That means you too," said Christopher. Ernouf whined. Stuck between Christopher and a giant wolf, Ev made the only sensible decision. She followed Ernouf.

Count the dangers. One, she was somewhere where no one wanted her to be, two, there was an enormous wolf at her side, three, she was in danger of running out of air before she made it down the next flight of stairs...

On the other hand, there was one great big, enormous reason why no one would bother her for a while, and that reason's name was Ernouf.

They reached the third floor and Ev's thoughts shuddered to a halt.

All around the spiral staircase, in every direction, were shelves covered in books. There were hundreds of them, probably thousands, in bright and dull colors of all shades. Her mouth fell open.

Ernouf growled and nudged her with his nose impatiently. With a wistful glance over her shoulder, Ev continued her journey. The library, because that had to be what it was, would have to wait for another time.

Four, it's too hot to live, five, I might be trampled on the stairs...

Finally, they reached the first floor, where everyone was filtering through a huge set of doors marked *Common Area.*

"Ev!" someone called.

Her head snapped round, and her eyes searched for the voice.

She was in the same room as before, the one with the door from Inner. Sitting by themselves at a huge table were Jonah and the blonde girl from that morning.

At her side, Ernouf growled impatiently. She took a few hesitant steps towards Jonah and the girl. The girl smiled and waved.

"Come here!" called Jonah.

Ernouf wanted her to sit somewhere, and at least she knew Jonah's name. She headed over and sat, nervously. As soon as she did, Ernouf vanished.

"Hi," said Jonah. He gave one short, aggressive, wave.

"Hi."

"This is Amy," he said indicating the little blonde girl.

"Is that really you, Amy?" she asked.

Amy smiled and nodded.

"I see you've been made to shower," said Jonah, Alerrawian expert. "You'll spend tomorrow being checked out in the med bay. At least you're friends with Ernouf. That's going to earn you some cred, anyway. Here, eat this." He shoved a plate full of food towards her. "I stacked it with the best stuff."

There wasn't a Bug Bar in sight.

"Mashed potato," explained Amy in her tiny, almost inaudible voice, leaning over the table to point at her plate. "Sausage. Peas, and broccoli."

Ev's stomach was grumbling and groaning. She reached for some mashed potato.

"No!" said Jonah. Ev jumped back.

"What's wrong?"

"Not with your hands! You have to use knives and forks. It's a rule here."

"Like this," said Amy, showing her how to hold the fork.

"I know what it is and how it works," she snapped. "I'm not a baby."

Awkwardly, she stabbed a bit of broccoli and shoved it in her mouth.

"See?"

"The fork goes in your mouth. The knife is just for cutting."

She tried again. "This is dumb." She felt embarrassed and clumsy, and the food made her feel empty and exhausted.

"Yup," agreed Jonah. "But it is *not* worth going to the bad place over. . ."

"What bad place?" Ev asked.

Amy and Jonah didn't answer. In fact, they didn't do anything. They looked like two child statues, frozen in time forever.

"Fine, don't tell me," she said. Her friends instantly unfroze and smiled apologetically.

Ev stored the word 'bad place' away for future reference. She didn't need to see the words behind the words for *that* phrase to bother her.

She ate as much as she could, using the fork because it was easier (not because of any stupid rules) and trying to ignore the heavy sleepiness weighing on her brain.

"This is Withouter stuff isn't that bad!" she said. "Nothing like Bug Bars at all."

At a nearby table, someone sniggered.

"Don't say things like that!" said Jonah.

"What?"

"Bug Bars," whispered Amy, almost too softly for Ev to hear. "Withouters. Don't!"

"Why not?"

Jonah grabbed her by the arm and dragged her to an open area scattered with small tables and chairs.

"Don't talk about those things!" Jonah said again. He was gripping her arm hard, and his eyes darted around wildly.

"You're hurting me!" said Ev.

Amy, who had followed them, came up and gently pried Jonah's hand loose.

"I explain," she said quietly.

Jonah huffed and pushed Ev's arm away. He stalked off.

"Where's he going?" asked Ev.

Amy shrugged. "He never wants to be where he is," she said.

"What's the deal with the Bug Bars?" Ev asked.

"Why they called that?" asked Amy.

"You know why! Because the bots brought them, and they looked like creepy little bugs. That's why we called them bugs, obviously. I used to dream about them crawling into my nose and ears…"

"No," said Amy quietly, shaking her head.

"What do you mean, 'no'?" demanded Ev. Then her eyes widened in horror.

"Yes," whispered Amy, "Everyone knows." She gestured to the room at large.

"That's gross! They fed us actual bugs?" Her stomach lurched, like she was about to be sick.

"Didn't hurt us," said Amy, with a shrug and a smile.

A siren blared suddenly across the room. Ev jumped. Amy took her hand reassuringly and smiled. "Don't worry!" she said.

The time allocated for supper has come to an end.

"What now?" asked Ev.

Amy shrugged.

"Study. Talk. Play."

"Where?" asked Ev.

"Dorm. Library."

"Library?" asked Ev. "Is that on the third floor? Can we go there?"

Amy nodded and grabbed her book bag. When they got to the library, Ev was sweating and panting.

"How…arc you…not out of…breath?" Ev asked Amy.

"Used to it now."

The library was the only place Ev had seen in Alerrawia that wasn't just concrete walls and floor with some furniture thrown in. Someone had really tried to make it look interesting. On every other floor, the spiral staircase stood out awkwardly against the straight lines and squares. Whoever had designed the library had used the staircase as the centerpiece and built the room out from there. The bookshelves were curved and arranged in radiating circles around the stairs. There were gaps between shelves here and there so that you could wind your way through, like a maze.

"Why's it so quiet?" Ev asked.

"Shhh!" Amy said.

"We're trying to study here, you know," said an older girl with a frown. She kept her voice just above a whisper. "Quiet voices only in the library."

They found an empty table, and Amy took out her books and a pen. Ev had never seen a pen before, and she'd certainly never used one. She wondered how Amy managed, Amy who struggled to type even the simplest of messages to her friends back in Inner.

Amy placed the pen to her forehead and said, "Write my think!"

The pen sprang to life and darted over the blank pages, writing entirely on its own.

"Ah," said Ev weakly. "Magic."

Amy stared at the pen, concentrating hard. Ev watched the words forming on the page. They appeared at lightning speed, but she managed to read a few phrases here and there.

…the intermediate phase…

. . .Consequently, the results have limited utility…

Was Amy clever?

"What is this?" asked a sudden, quiet voice next to Ev's ear.

Ev jumped. Hovering over her left shoulder was another of the strange little pixies. This one had olive skin and hair and clothes.

"Someone new, I see," said the pixie. She spoke quietly and gently. "I can tell by how your mouth is hanging open."

Ev slammed her mouth shut.

"Don't worry. I'm one of the nice ones, although you only have my word for it. My name is Lulerain. This is the part where you tell me *your* name."

"Ev," said Ev.

"Nice to meet you, Ev. Can I recommend something for you to read?" she asked.

Ev nodded.

"All right, these should get you started."

Lulerain snapped her fingers, and two books appeared instantly.

"This one's by an Inner kid, just like you," she said, holding out the first book. The book was larger than she was, and it definitely looked heavier, but Lulerain didn't seem to have any trouble at all holding it in one hand. "She's all grown-up now. I assume. I am obligated to tell you that the author of this book is, and I quote, the 'lowest of the low', and anyone choosing to follow her path will also follow her to her fate, although we've never been told what her fate actually was, so don't ask me how much that threat should worry you."

The title was *Inner: How and Why?*

"Alison really gets to the bottom of it all, and she wrote this book for Inner kids making the transition to Alerrawia. I try to make sure everyone reads it when they first arrive. Many don't, of course. I can only try."

Ev hefted the book. When you printed them all out like this, books were *big*, and there was only one book in here. Back in Inner, Ev had read all sorts of things, all stored on the same relatively small computer. The whole third floor could have been stored on her computer. Yet, there was something satisfying about holding the thick volume in her hand.

She opened it at random and scanned a page critically. A textbook, rather than a storybook, but written in a very reader-friendly way. It would do nicely.

"Then, when you're done with that," Lulerain continued, "you might want to read this one. It's by Felix. It explains where you are now."

The second book was called *Alerrawia: To the Future (Volume 1)*. It was even bigger.

"I am magically prohibited from communicating my true feelings about this book," Lulerain said, "but I do agree with Felix that it should be required reading for *all* residents of Alerrawia, even if my reasons are completely different to his."

Ev ran an experienced eye over a random page and concluded that Felix liked to show how clever he was by using lots of extra words that didn't have to be there. It was going to be a lot harder, and a lot more boring, to read. On the other hand, it might help her figure out what was going on.

"Books by Withouters…" she said reflectively. Although, in retrospect, *most* of the stories and novels she'd read in Inner were probably by Withouters too.

"Yes and no," said Lulerain. "Yes, they were written by people who didn't live in Inner at the time they wrote them, and no, those people are not called Withouters. That's a word you're going to want to stop using."

"Why?"

"People have been taught that saying things like 'Withouter' means that you're not very…well…clever. Even though the words people use have nothing to do with how clever they are."

Ev glanced at Amy. She'd always thought Amy didn't know any words, but it turned out she did. They were just stuck inside her head, for some reason.

Ev paged through Felix's book.

"You'll give them a try, then?" Lulerain asked, encouraged by Ev's interest.

Ev nodded.

"Wonderful! You can keep them for two weeks, and if you haven't finished them in that time, you can pop back here, and we'll renew them for you. You'll really read them?"

"Yes!" said Ev. Why did this pixie think that she wouldn't read the books? Of course she'd read them. She needed to know everything, and it certainly wouldn't take her as long as two weeks.

"Excellent!" said the pixie. "As a reward for taking on such a big challenge…"

She snapped her fingers and a third book appeared. This book was brighter and smaller.

"You can read this first!"

Ev took the book.

"Granny Oakwood Tales," she read.

"Granny Oakwood herself wrote them," said Lulerain. "She teaches Language and Writing classes, when she's not helping out in the med bay."

It was just a book of little kid stories, the kind of thing she'd stopped reading years ago. Lulerain seemed to think she was giving Ev a huge treat, for some reason. She paged through quickly. There were three stories – *The Playroom*, *A Wish Comes True*, and *Caught by the Tide*.

"Very interesting," she said, because the pixie seemed to want something from her.

"Good," said Lulerain, pleased. "Why don't you go sit with your friend and read your book? But first, let me just record which books you're checking out…"

A pen and a ledger appeared in the air. Lulerain was just opening the ledger when she stopped and said, "Not now Dropellet!"

"What?" asked Ev.

"Excuse me, dear," said Lulerain, moving away slightly. The book and pen vanished. "What is it this time?" asked the pixie.

In answer, the air around Lulerain…changed. Ev stared in amazement as an enormous red lizard-like beast appeared. Ev could see right through it. None of the other children seemed to care at all. The beast lay there, listlessly. Except for very faint chest movements, Ev would have thought it was dead.

"I don't know what you want me to do about it?" said Lulerain, testily, but quietly. "I've already given you all the advice I have… Yes, I understand he's not eating, but if you can't make him, I certainly can't… fine, I'll look through the literature again, but it's not like we have a *Psychology of Magical Creatures* section… yes, yes, I'll do my best."

It's a hologram, thought Ev as she listened to Lulerain's half of the conversation.

"*Yes*, Dropellet, as soon as I can."

The hologram disappeared and Lulerain drifted out of sight, brow furrowed in thought.

Not knowing what else to do, Ev picked up *Granny Oakwood Tales* and read the first story quickly. It was mildly entertaining because it was about toys that could talk. It was interesting enough, but much too easy, so she opened the first page of *Inner: How and Why?*

How It All Began

I won't go into the details of why the war against magic began – that will be covered in other books, though I will not vouch for the accuracy of what I do not set down myself. Suffice to say that there were those who wanted to eradicate magic in children from a very young age, thereby bringing an end to what they saw as the worst evil to ever walk the earth.

I will also avoid passing judgement on their decision. Fear can make people think and do very strange things.

One family of science-followers, the Granites, decided to try something new, to test if strong magic-users who grew up in complete ignorance of magic still displayed innate abilities. They called for volunteers to build an underground compound and selected fifty families, each with one young child, a baby. In each family, at least one parent had magical abilities that could not be contained by the medication provided.*

This is how Inner, as you know it today, was born.

Records indicate that these families volunteered gladly. I'm not sure if that is better or worse than if they were forced. Either way, the aim was to raise the children in ignorance in the hope that their abilities would never manifest. If it had worked, every strong magic user in existence would have been forced into similar compounds.

If you are reading this, you are probably from Inner. In my experience, the only people who want to understand what happened are those who it happened to. Please do not be too hard on yourself. Not a single person currently living in Inner knows that it was all just an experiment.

** Containment, an early precursor to Hexteria*

Ev slammed the book closed, her head reeling. Her chest became tight.

"Is this book true?" she whispered to Amy.

Amy looked up. "Yes. You get used to it."

She didn't know how long she sat staring blankly at the book. If she moved, she would scream, or faint, or run. She sat completely still, in shock, until a siren blared.

"Bedtime!" said Amy urgently, shaking her shoulder. "Have to go now!"

Amy dragged her toward the stairs.

As the climbed, Ev counted. One stair, two stairs, three stairs, four stairs, five stairs, six stairs…

Slowly, the ringing in her ears faded, her heart slowed, and her head cleared. She was still gasping for air, but that was because of the dreaded stairs, her climb made even more difficult by the books clutched to her chest.

Amy walked her all the way to her room but ran off the moment she spotted Stacey and Madison.

"Bye," called Ev.

"What was it talking to?" asked Madison.

"I think our Inner brat has a little bratty friend," said Stacey. They both laughed, as if this was the funniest thing they'd ever heard.

A third girl lay in the bunk under Ev's. She didn't say anything, just kept reading her book.

Ev ignored all of them and crawled into bed. Two minutes later, the lights went out.

It was completely dark. Ev had never been in darkness before. In Inner, the lights were always on so that Vendavi could see what you were doing. She couldn't tell if her eyes were open or closed. The heat pressed down in her, making it hard to breathe.

Tears welled again. She tried not to make a sound. She didn't think the other girls would like that. She hugged the three library books to her chest, even the one that had made her feel so terrible. It wasn't the book's fault. The book was just trying to explain a version of reality that could very well be true, and Ev planned to read them all, even if it killed her.

Mind whirling, Ev eventually fell into a troubled and uneasy sleep.

6. Do You Want to See a Real Magic Trick?

Medical care is one of the "gray areas" in the Magic v Science debate, or so the Users would have you believe. On closer inspection, the answer is obvious – magical solutions to physical ailments should be used in emergency situations only, and the definition of what constitutes an emergency should be clearly defined and agreed on by The Seven.

Felix Granite

Prepare for morning inspection!

The words blared across the room at the same time the lights turned on. Ev closed her eyes to shut out the sudden brightness. She could hear the other girls groaning and scrambling out of bed. Stacey threw a pillow at her.

"Get up! You'll make us fail," she said.

"Fail what? And remind me why I should care?"

"Who's on this morning?" asked Stacey.

"Madam," said Madison with absolute certainty.

Ev shot out of bed.

"Oh, so you've met her then?"

"What do I do?" Ev asked frantically.

"Too late," muttered Madison. "Here she comes…"

The girl who shared Ev's bunk grabbed her hand and pulled her to the foot of their bed. "Stand straight!" she whispered.

Madam stalked into the room.

"Girls," she said.

"Good morning, Madam," chorused everyone except Ev.

"Don't think you need to greet me?" asked Madam.

"Good morning, Madam," said Ev.

Madam smirked. "Better, but we have a long way to go, don't we?"

She looked around the room.

"Very disappointing, girls," she said, eyes fixed on Ev. "Beds unmade; hair not brushed…"

"We only had, like, twelve seconds," muttered Madison. Stacey elbowed her.

Madam's death gaze shifted and focused on Madison instead.

"What did you say?" asked Madam, her voice low and menacing.

"Nothing, Madam!" said Madison, quickly. Her eyes were wide, and Ev could swear that she was shaking slightly. It was almost enough to make you feel sorry for her.

"What shall I do with you?" mused Madam. "Naughty girls must be dealt with. What to do, what to do…I think…"

Stop her!

"Gwyneth!" Chloe appeared in the door. The girl next to Ev sighed with relief.

"There you are," said Chloe, smiling nervously. "Oh, you've started inspection early! Look, the girls haven't even had a chance to get ready. Come now girls, quickly!"

They didn't need to be told twice.

"Like this," whispered the fourth girl to Ev, showing her how she made her bed.

"There, much better," said Chloe. "Come now Gwyn…Madam, we have other dorms to inspect."

The door closed behind them and Ev took her first breath in what felt like ages.

"That was a close one," said Stacey, collapsing on her bed.

"We could have literally died!" said Madison.

"No, we couldn't have, why must you be such a drama queen?"

"It's your fault," said Madison to Ev. "Madam only did that because you're here."

"Sounds like Madam's fault to me," said Ev.

Madison stepped closer. At sixteen, she was small for her age, only a little taller than Ev, but that didn't make her any less formidable.

"Did you just talk back to me?" she asked.

"Seems like," said Ev, holding Madison's gaze. Her skull started tingling, and she wondered what would happen if she just set Madison on fire.

Unexpectedly, the door swung open. Both girls took a step back and looked around guiltily.

Granny Oakwood smiled down at them.

"Evelyn, I've come to collect you." She handed Ev something that looked a bit like a Bug Bar. "Well, their actual words were that I'm, quote, the only one here who knows how to deal with the difficult ones, end quote."

"I'm difficult, am I?"

"Yes, thank goodness, otherwise I don't know how we'd be friends. I have to take you down to the fourth floor."

Ev's stomach was churning, so she put the bar in her pocket for later. Granny led her down the stairs to the fourth floor and through a door marked *Check-Ups*.

"Karen?" Granny called.

"Here," came a voice. Granny steered Ev down a corridor of open cubicles until she found the right one.

"Karen, here's the new girl."

A woman with straight black hair and olive skin greeted them.

"Hello, Evelyn, I'm doctor Karen. You can just call me Karen, though." She took Ev's hand. "Thanks, Granny."

"I have no classes until this afternoon," said Granny. "I can stay and help."

"How kind." Karen's smile was brittle. She led Ev into an examination room. "Let me just explain what you're here for," she said. "You've been living underground for your entire life so far. You haven't been eating healthy food or getting sunlight or exercise. We need to make sure that there aren't any big sicknesses lurking in there, and, if there are, we need to figure out how to fix them. Got that?"

Ev shrugged.

"I'll take that as a yes," said Karen. She gently took Ev's left hand and started examining her skin. Karen's hand was slightly damp from sweat, and Ev jerked her arm away.

"It's so hot!"

"Yes, it's much cooler underground, and I think there's an old cooling spell in Inner that helps," said Granny. "Don't worry, you'll get used to it."

"It's too hot to live!"

"Not quite, but almost."

Karen shot Granny a look. "That suggestion is not welcome in my med bay, Granny."

"What suggestion?" Granny asked innocently.

"Our bubble is perfectly safe!"

"Of course! And the killer heat is just a natural by-product of that safety," said Granny with a broad smile.

Karen's lips were a thin line.

Ev stored the words 'bubble' and 'killer heat' away in the back of her mind.

"Do adults disagree with each other all the time?" she asked. "My mom and dad always did, I suppose, when they spoke to each other anyway. Everyone here seems to fight with each other too."

"That's just Alerrawia's policy of free and open expression at play," said Granny. Karen's hands, that were gripping Ev's left arm tightly, relaxed. "As long as the ideas you freely express are the approved list, of course," she added.

"Granny!"

"Ignore me, dear," Granny said to Ev. "If you want to stay safe here, listen to the Karens of the bubble. They know how to follow the rules."

Karen continued her examination.

"Skin tone is off…" Karen said. Her words could have cut diamonds.

"Oh, I could deal with her skin, it wouldn't take a moment…," said Granny.

"Granny, I appreciate that you want to help, but my section of the med bay is strictly non-magical. If you want to cheat with unnatural healing charms, you're welcome to find another doctor to bother."

"Of course, Doctor Karen," she said, with a wink at Ev. "I'll just note your comments in her chart, then."

"We will never make advancements in medicine if we rely on magic for every little thing. We have to push ourselves! Don't give in to temptation!" Karen didn't seem to have noticed that she'd already won the argument.

"Should I note that in her chart as well?" Granny asked innocently.

"Granny...' Karen collapsed in a chair and put her head in her hands.

"I'm sorry, Karen," said Granny. "It's just me being me. I promise to be more helpful than unhelpful, at least until just before lunch when I get grumpy again."

Karen smiled weakly and rose.

"You like each other," said Ev, realization dawning.

"What? Oh, yes, grown-ups argue all the time, but they can still like each other anyway."

"Now, that I can agree with," said Granny.

The rest of the day was exceedingly boring. Ev had had health check-ups before – the bug bots of Inner arrived once a year to poke and prod while she sat perfectly still, only moving when she was told. This would be more of the same, except with the added bonus of there not being a bug in sight.

The whole day, Ev couldn't help but notice the weird relationship between Karen and Granny. They were clearly friends, but they didn't agree about anything. Karen thought that no magic should be used for medicine, ever, and Granny thought it should be used whenever possible. Sometimes, she though Karen left the room on purpose so she wouldn't have to see Granny using magic and could pretend it wasn't happening, like when she asked Granny to deal with the wax build up in Ev's ears while she 'stepped out for a moment.'

"Now, what Karen *thinks* I'm going to do is to squirt some water and medicine into your ears, but what I'm really going to do is *this*," Granny had said, snapping her fingers. The world got suddenly loud, but by the time the day was over, Ev was already used to it.

She felt like they were each trying to convince her that their way was best, like after her eye exam when Karen said, "Do you want to see a *real* magic trick?" and popped some lenses in front of her eyes. The world swam into view clearly for the first time in ages, but Ev knew how glasses worked, and she wasn't all that impressed.

She did her best to learn everything she could while Granny and Karen fought their little feud above her head. For example, when Granny went to get them all lunch, she learned that there was a self-help kitchen on the ninth floor that was for busy grown-ups who didn't have time to fight for their food in the common room, which seemed like something that could come in handy later.

They used an enormous, noisy machine to take pictures of her insides, and she smiled politely when Karen tried to impress her with the pictures it took.

"Am I here because of being burnt earlier?" asked Ev while her blood pressure was being taken.

"No, all the new kids have to do these tests," said Granny. "But you're almost done for today! When Karen says you can go, you're free for the rest of the evening."

"Can I sleep here?"

"Unfortunately, not," said Karen, returning just in time to hear the question. "But Granny *is* right – you can go! For today, anyway—you need to be back here tomorrow morning to finish up.”

“Thank you so much for being so good!” said Granny. “Can I have a hug?”

“Alright…”

Granny put an arm around her shoulders and squeezed.

“It was fun meeting you today! We’re releasing you just in time for supper, too. You’d better hurry down to first before all the best food is taken!”

Then the grown-ups turned away and started talking about something that Ev didn’t understand. Suddenly, it was like she wasn’t even there. They had only been *pretending* to be friendly all day. No one here liked her, no one wanted her around…

At a table by the door, there were two sandwiches left over from lunch, wrapped in plastic.

She glanced behind her. Karen and Granny were still deep in conversation.

Slowly, so as not to draw attention to herself, she reached out and took the sandwiches, stuffing them under her shirt. Now she wouldn’t have to go down to supper and deal with the other kids.

That would show them.

She went to her bedroom to grab the books the pixie had given her yesterday, and then headed straight to the library. Most people were at supper, and no one noticed her sneaking around.

When she got to third, she dragged one of the beanbag chairs that were scattered around the library to a corner and curled up to eat and read. She was deeply engrossed in *Inner: How and Why?* when a sly little voice rang out, right next to her ear.

"Eating in the library is strictly forbidden, you know, I'm honor bound to report you."

It was Boaclick.

"I didn't eat anything," said Ev, quickly, her stomach sinking. Boaclick seemed to like causing trouble.

"What a silly lie! When I can see the crumbs all over the place and the truth in your eyes. There is only one just punishment for silliness—detention!"

"What's going on?" Lulerain, the olive pixie who'd given Ev the books, appeared from behind a shelf. "No noise in the library!"

"Yes, that *is* one of our little rules, but so is 'no eating in the library', and she has been doing just that."

"She's new, Boaclick, you know that. She doesn't know all the rules yet. Right, Ev?"

Ev nodded.

"And I'll say nothing about that book she's reading either," said Boaclick.

"What book?" Lulerain asked innocently. Boaclick winked and vanished. One moment he was there, the next he was gone.

"Don't mind him, he's on the side of chaos, not evil," said Lulerain. "But please, don't eat in the library again."

"I promise," said Ev.

"Good!" Lulerain went back to her work.

Ev decided that tomorrow she would have to find a better place to hide.

The library had filled up while she'd been reading. There were children everywhere, but they were all obeying the no talking rule and working hard. Pens scratched against paper; books were consulted. Some of them pulled their hair in frustration, some just gave up in despair and put their heads on the table.

"Too much work," Ev heard someone mutter. "Why do we try so hard when we know it's impossible?"

"Shhh!" said nearly everyone else.

Ev thought she knew the answer to the question. She'd seen something in *Inner: How and Why?* Where was it…? She flicked back and forth through the pages.

If you thought you had a lot of work in Inner, the Alerrawian school system will come as a bit of a shock. Prepare yourself for ten to twelve lessons spanning nine hours a day, six days a week. Every lesson is followed by a mountain of homework that you're expected to complete for the next day. However, it is well known that this is impossible. Some teachers accept this and ignore late or missed assignments. Others do not. You will have more important things to worry about, but your first line of defense if you want to survive Alerrawia is sorting the first kind of teacher from the second. Whose homework do you have to *do?*

That wasn't quite what she was looking for. She scanned the next few pages quickly. They included tips for understanding teachers and knowing when to fight a punishment and when to accept it, even if it was unjust, but she was looking for something else. Eventually she found it hidden away in a footnote, like Alison was trying to keep it from being noticed.

Why do they do it? Why do they give you an impossible workload and then punish you when you predictably fail to complete it?

The answer is simple: busy children, scared children, are children who can be controlled. They hope that you will be so distracted that you'll forget to rebel. It's a strategy that has served them well, and one they will continue to use.

It was a *very* strange book to find in Alerrawia's library.

For the first time that day, she wondered where Amy and Jonah were. She realized that she needed someone to talk to about these things, but it was too late—the bedtime siren sounded, and everyone grabbed their things to go to bed. She'd have to find them tomorrow.

Hiding in the crowd of children all heading in the same direction, Ev made it back to sixth. She darted quickly into the room and up the ladder. The other girls ignored her.

Seconds later, she was asleep.

*

Granny came to fetch her again the next morning, this time before inspection began. She gave Ev another granola bar, which she stuffed into her

"Sleep well?" Granny asked.

"Yes," she said, without really thinking.

"Good!" said Granny. "Made any friends yet?"

"No," Ev said. "I'm fine on my own."

"Really? How nice for you. I've always found that things seem to go a lot better when I have other brains around."

"My brain is fine."

"Of course it is. But one person can't know everything. Anyway, friendship isn't just about getting help. It's about giving it too. And having someone around just to talk to. And having fun. Have you ever played a game?"

"Of course! I was almost at the top of the leaderboard in *Giant's Shipyard*, and I won most of the others we used to play before."

"Have you ever played a game where you were on a team and had to work with others?"

Ev rolled her eyes.

"I hate team projects."

"Do you? Well, I'm sure you have your reasons."

They were almost at the med bay, and Ev was only slightly out of breath. She was getting used the stairs already.

Karen saw them arrive and pointed at a room with huge windows and an enormous machine inside. Granny steered Ev towards it.

"Looks like we'll have to wait for a moment, they're still cleaning and setting up in there."

Through the huge window, Ev watched two men wave their hands, snap their fingers, and mumble strange phrases. Every time they did, something moved, or vanished, or appeared.

"I thought Karen didn't like magic in the med bay."

"Oh yes, you'll learn very quickly that magic is very useful for things like cleaning, but apparently too useful for things like medicine. The fact is we use it for everything, but we have to pretend that we don't."

Ev looked around for Karen. She was far off in the distance, as far away as she could get from the room with the machine, and her back was carefully turned.

"You're not pretending."

"I'm not Karen."

Ev mulled this over while they waited.

It turned out the huge machine was for fixing her eyes. She just had to lie there, eyes open, while the machine did all of the work. When it was done, she stood up, blinking.

"And that's what it's like to see properly," said Granny. "You'll get used to it soon." She turned to the enormous machine. "A work of scientific genius! Not a single ounce of magic went into fixing your eyes. Unless you count the magic used to make the parts for the machine in the first place and of course putting it together, but I digress."

Another enormous machine fixed her ears, and she thought they must be almost done when Karen asked her to sit down, a serious look on her face.

"Ev, I need to speak to you about something," said Karen. "Did you take some sandwiches without asking yesterday?"

"No."

"Let me rephrase—I know you took the sandwiches. What do you have to say for yourself?"

"Why does it matter?"

"Stealing is against the rules! You should go to detention for this…"

"Oh, it's just a misunderstanding," said Granny. "I told her she could take them and forgot to mention it."

Karen's eyes narrowed.

"Is that right?"

“Yes,” said Ev, instantly.

“Alright, fine, but you really need to check these things with me first, Granny.”

“I will definitely keep that in mind for future reference,” said Granny. “Should I take Ev to her next appointment?”

“Yes, alright.”

“Close call,” said Granny once Karen was safely out of earshot.

“You didn’t have to do that. I’m fine on my own. I don’t care about being punished.”

“Lots of Inner kids say that. Then they go to detention for the first time. And then they wish that someone had helped them avoid it.”

“I don’t need anyone!”

“You’ve spent eleven years of your life underground, and then they pull you out and expect you to just fit in. It’s not an easy thing for anyone, Ev. It’s alright to need help.”

“I’m not a little kid!”

“Alright, Ev. If you ever change your mind, though, just remember that I’m your friend and always will be. There is absolutely nothing you can do to change that, so don’t bother trying.”

“Are we done?”

Granny sighed sadly.

"No. Unfortunately, it's time for you to get your teeth fixed, and I'll warn you now – you're going to hate it."

Ev shrugged.

"Whatever."

How bad could it really be?

*

That night, Ev lay in a bed in the general ward, completely unable to move. She started crying, but this time it was because she was angry.

Granny had been right—Ev had *hated* her day at the dentist.

It had started out fine. The dentist, Dr. Cody, was friendly with a big smile, and the chair he asked her to sit in looked like many of the other chairs she'd been in and out of the last two days. Nothing seemed to be scary.

Until Dr. Cody snapped his fingers and magical cords tied her to the chair. When she struggled and complained, he snapped his fingers again, and she couldn't speak, couldn't move, couldn't do *anything*.

Unless Dr. Cody told her too, of course.

"Open your mouth wide and keep it open!" she didn't want to, but she had, because Dr. Cody's magic was in control, and there was nothing she could do to stop him. Ev wasn't surprised that it was Granny, not Karen, who'd shown her to the dentist's office.

He had poked, and prodded, and scratched, and scraped, complaining all the while about the state of Ev's teeth. Had she ever brushed them? Did they even *have* floss in Inner? As she sobbed from pain and fear, she found herself wondering why he asked? She couldn't answer— he'd seen to that.

Stacey, one of the older girls from her dorm, was there too. She seemed to be some kind of assistant, but she wasn't happy about it. She wanted to be somewhere else, badly, and Ev didn't blame her.

"Suction!" Dr. Cody has to say, more than once. "Stacey, you must pay attention!

"Sorry, Grandad," she muttered, moving the suction tube into a better position to remove the excess water form Ev's mouth.

"I know you don't like her, much, but that's no reason to drown her," said Cody with a chuckle."

Yes, hilarious, thought Ev, who by this time wasn't feeling so much afraid as angry. So, Stacey was only there because the doctor was her grandfather? Not because she was good at it or wanted to be there? And it was *Ev* who she got to take it out on?

That wasn't fair. For either of them.

Then Cody had announced that it would take the rest of the day to deal with Ev's teeth. He said it like he was annoyed, but he'd had a glint in his eye that made Ev think he was looking forward to the torture.

The bit of Stacey's face that Ev could see, on the other hand, was filled with dismay.

"Grandad, I had planned to spend the rest of the day helping out on tenth…"

"You spend far too much time there as it is! If you're going to become a dentist, you need to devote more time to learning the craft. I will not have you follow in your parents' footsteps. Tech support. Tech support! It's an embarrassment."

"I told them I'd be there…"

"I'll send a message telling them differently. No arguments."

"Yes, grandad…"

It had sounded like a conversation they'd had many times before, and Ev had admired Stacey for asking, even though she already knew what the answer would be. There were *a lot* of books on computers and electronics in their room, and not a single one on dentistry. Cody was fighting an uphill battle, whether he knew it or not.

Let her go.

"On second thought, you can go up to tenth after lunch. I can manage here."

Stacey's eyes widened.

"Really?"

"Yes, yes, but let's try to get as much of this done as possible first."

"Thank you! Thank you so much!"

"Numbing gel," was Dr. Cody's response.

The gel Stacey had smeared in Ev's mouth was supposed to help with the pain, but it didn't, not really, but at least Stacey was in a slightly better mood—she only forgot to suction the water out of Ev's mouth one more time, but that was the last of her worries. Dr. Cody stuck needles into her gums, yanked her teeth out, scraped her mouth. They were at it for hours. All Ev could see were pieces of her own teeth flying about in a spray of blood as they drilled and cut and hammered.

Then Stacey left and it was just Ev and the doctor. He snapped his fingers and her mouth healed instantly, making Ev wonder if any of the pain was even necessary in the first place. The afternoon was filled with crowns and implants to fix and replace her apparently awful teeth. By that time, her jaw was aching from being kept open all day without a break, and she was beyond miserable.

"And we're done! Well, for today, anyway. Just in time for supper, too. I'll get someone to feed you—it will be easier to just keep you restrained overnight so we can finish up tomorrow."

Now Ev lay silently, unable to move, staring at the ceiling and plotting death to all dentists.

"Well, well, well," said a familiar voice.

Madam.

"Apparently you're a baby that needs to be fed," said Madam. She was carrying a bowl of something that smelled awful. "Open wide."

Ev kept her mouth firmly shut. Dr. Cody might be able to force her to open her mouth, but Madam couldn't.

Madam smiled malevolently and gripped Ev's nose, holding it tightly closed until she had to open her mouth, gasping for air.

When her mouth opened, Madam shoved the spoon in, then held her mouth closed.

"Chew and swallow," she commanded.

"What are you doing?" It sounded like Granny, but Ev couldn't move her head to check.

"Feeding a naughty child," said Madam.

"Leave of your own accord, or I'll have you removed," said Granny.

"You wouldn't..."

"Watch me," said Granny.

Slowly and deliberately, Madam upended the bowl of disgusting food all over Ev.

"The bowl's all empty anyway," she said. Then she stalked off.

"Clean yourself up!" Granny ordered. The mess disappeared. "I'm sorry, Ev, I would have come sooner if I knew they were sending *her*. Very few people want the carer jobs, it's very difficult to keep them filled, so the carers can get away with an awful lot. As long as there is no lasting damage caused, The Seven just look the other way."

She took some containers out of the bag she was carrying while she spoke.

"I can't release you, only Cody can do that, but I can sit you up and feed you some proper food."

She moved Ev into a sitting position and then carefully fed her bits of scrambled egg, jelly, and water in tiny quantities at a time.

"No visit to Doctor Cody will ever be this bad again, you'll be relieved to hear. Even tomorrow won't be as bad as today – it should only take the morning."

When the food was finished, Granny took out a book.

"I wrote some stories for the children here. Perhaps you've already heard of them? Anyway, I can read them to you if you like. Blink once for yes, twice for no."

Ev blinked once and then held her eyes open until they watered. They were stories for little kids, but she didn't want Granny to go away.

Granny opened the book at the beginning and started with the first story. Ev had already read it, but it didn't matter.

"The toys were thoroughly miserable. Brenda and Bob hadn't been near the playroom for two whole days and…"

Ev didn't hear much more before she fell asleep.

*

Granny was right—her second day at the dentist was much easier than the first, and Dr. Cody soon released her with a cheery wave, as if he hadn't held her against her will for almost twenty-four hours.

Ev hobbled stiffly out of the dentist's office, desperate to get away, but unsure of where to go to next. She was so focused on putting as much distance between herself and Dr. Cody as possible that she ran straight into Karen.

"Oh," said Karen, glancing at Dr. Cody's rooms. Her face twisted with fury, but Ev didn't think it was on her behalf—Dr. Cody used magic, and Karen could barely hide her disgust. "You better get to down to lunch." She could hardly look at Ev as she spoke, and she hurried away without a second glance.

"Ev!" called someone in a shout whisper.

She looked over to see Granny beckoning her from behind a door. Cautiously, Ev approached.

"What do you want?" she whispered back.

"Come have some lunch," said Granny. "Be quiet, though. I'm not really allowed to have visitors."

Granny led her to the office very much like the one Ev had been in the day she'd learned she could fly.

"Of course, I'm not really a medical professional, just someone who helps out, so maybe the rules don't apply to me."

The office looked and smelled like Granny Oakwood. Next to the office chair, which was covered in a badly made woolen blanket, was a huge pet bed.

"Do you have a dog?"

"No, I have a cat. A big cat. You'll meet him soon enough—he likes to look after the new children."

Ev looked at the bed again. It was *very* big. She wasn't sure she *wanted* to meet the cat that slept in it.

"Karen and the other doctors don't like him hanging around on the fourth floor. He's his own creature most of the day, anyway, but he likes to come to the classes I teach, so you should see him then."

Ev quietly ate the sandwiches Granny had made. It was surprisingly easy, considering how much damage her mouth had taken. The usual emptiness washed over her, but she was getting used to that as well. When she was done, Granny handed her a small mirror.

"I thought you'd like to see your new teeth."

Despite herself, Ev was intrigued. The smile she saw in the mirror was much brighter and nicer than what she'd seen before.

"Now you have a lovely smile, just like everyone else," said Granny.

"Why does everyone have to have the same smile?" she asked.

"Good question. Your teeth are important and do need to be looked after, but it's up to you if you actually want to smile or not, I guess. The worst of being the new kid *will* be over soon enough.

"I have to get back to work now, so you'll have to go…"

"Where?"

"It's Sunday, which is a free day, so you can do what you like."

"I don't want to be around the other kids…"

"You have to be. It's unavoidable. And the more time you spend around them, the quicker you get used to them and the sooner you make friends."

"I don't want friends!"

"You say that now because you don't have any. They're great to have around once you find them. What about that boy they sent to meet you in the tunnel? Jonah? Isn't he a friend?"

"I don't need friends!" she shouted. She couldn't use her fire, she could do *anything*, so she grabbed the first thing that came to hand on Granny's desk and threw it with all her might. Then she turned to run, not waiting to see what damage she'd done.

It was like an explosion, like everything that had happened the last few days had built up and erupted. She couldn't have stopped it even if she'd tried, and now she was running, and she didn't know where to go.

Well, not quite running. Her legs were still stiff, so it was more of a fast hobble, and the moment she was on the landing by the spiral stairs she stopped for breath.

Where was she going, anyway? What was the plan now?

She looked down at her hand to see that she still had Granny's mirror.

That was that. The only nice person in the whole place hated her now. She had nowhere to go, and she didn't know what to do.

She stumbled down the stairs, which were mostly deserted, until she reached the third floor. She found an empty beanbag, dragged it to a corner, and collapsed, staring with unseeing eyes at the room around her. She was exhausted. She was lost. She was scared.

"What do I do?" she whispered.

What do I do?

7. I Don't Understand This Lesson

Yes, there is a dragon. Yes, there are pixies
and griffins. Yes, there are all sorts of
'normal' animals that seem to be a little
more human than you might expect. There
are many things to marvel at in our Bubble;
but don't get distracted. Look at them
closely and you will begin to see yourself.

Inner: How and Why

By Alison Oakwood

Page 98, Footnote

Jonah and Amy found her curled up on a beanbag in the library, shaking.

"We've been looking for you!" said Jonah, angrily. "Where have you been?"

Amy put a restraining hand on his arm. "Dentist," she reminded him, gently.

Jonah scowled.

"We were worried," he said.

Amy sat down next to Ev and put an arm around her.

"All right," she said, rocking her gently back and forth.

Jonah shuffled his feet awkwardly. "You're not going to, like, cry or something, right? I'm not much good with the crying thing."

"Jonah!" said Amy.

"It's alright, Amy. I wasn't going to cry anyway," said Ev, carefully fighting back her tears.

"Well, I don't want to hang around in the stupid library, whispering, on our only free day of the week."

"Jonah…"

"No, it's fine, we can do whatever. If I'm stuck here, then I need to figure this place out, I guess."

Amy and Ev looked expectantly at Jonah.

"I guess we could show her the dragon," he said begrudgingly.

Ah yes. Ev remembered her first day there, two days and a million years ago. *Stupid dragon,* someone had muttered when the walls shook.

"Yeah. He's dumb and boring, but pretty cool the first time you see him."

Dumb and boring, but also cool? "Lead the way," she said.

"We'll check his outdoor paddock first…"

"I can't go outside!" said Ev, shuddering at the memory of her burns.

"It'll be fine," said Jonah, impatiently. "We burned too when we first got here. you just have to wear Suncharm until you're used to it."

"If you say so," said Ev, wondering how she was supposed to have known any of that.

They walked slowly down the stairs until they got to the first floor and the big, heavy doors that led out into the grounds. Near the doors were two enormous baskets filled to the brim with tubes of cream. Jonah grabbed one. "Hold still," he said. He opened the tube and pointed it in Ev's direction and squeezed.

A wave of cream came crashing toward her, but instead of hitting her square in the face, it carefully distributed itself evenly across all of her exposed skin.

"Now you can stay outside all day, if you want to," he said.

Ev nodded. She wasn't so sure, but she didn't want Jonah to think she was afraid.

They stepped outside, and the heat hit them full in the face. Ev froze for a moment, but it didn't seem like she would burn, this time.

"Why is it so hot?"

Jonah shrugged.

"It just is. Come on!" Jonah was annoyed and angry. Jonah was *always* annoyed and angry, but it felt much scarier now that she was around him in person.

She followed Amy and Jonah as they walked confidently into the grounds.

Ahead was a huge enclosure. Inside there were…things.

"Are those dragons?" asked Ev.

"No!" said Jonah, and then he laughed harshly. "Those are just the griffins."

Ev went up to the enclosure to get a closer look. The griffins were *very* strange, although not unfamiliar— there must have been a story about them back in Inner. They looked like giant bald eagles from the front, but they had back legs like a lion.

"That's so cool," said Ev.

"Meh, they're basically just flying horses," said Jonah.

"You say that like flying horses are a bad thing."

People in combat gear were moving between the griffins, gathering their eggs.

"What are those for?" asked Ev.

"Breakfast," said Amy.

Ev was horrified. "We eat baby griffins?" she asked.

Amy shrugged. "Eggs are eggs."

She'd eaten eggs, many times since she'd arrived. She'd been fine with it, because eggs were a normal part of the stories she'd read in Inner. Those eggs had always come from chickens, and Ev had assumed…

But if you could eat chicken eggs, that mean griffin eggs were okay too, right?

Thinking about it made her uncomfortable, so she changed the subject.

"Why are they muzzled?" she asked.

"To keep them from talking to us, I think," said Jonah. "Apparently they spread lies and discontent or something."

"They can talk?"

Amy nodded.

"That's horrible," she whispered. There was something wrong with eating the eggs of someone who could talk.

Amy and Jonah didn't answer because at that moment one of the griffins darted at a guard and tried to take him down. A burst of magic erupted from the griffin, nearly knocking him down, but it was weak.

"Down, Vasagle!" roared the guard. He aimed an RDD at the griffin, who immediately started screaming and bucking.

"Damn! Blindness!" said the guard.

He pushed the button again and again until he got what he wanted. The griffin named Vasagle fell to the ground, tried to get up again, but couldn't.

"Balance?" asked Amy, like she was commenting on the weather.

"Yes, I think so," said Jonah. "That's Vasagle," he said to Ev. "Apparently, she's basically mad. She tried to escape and free all the other griffins, but she didn't get it right, so they took away her privileges and now she's basically a cart horse. You've got to be careful around her. She'll peck your eye out the moment she gets a chance, even if her magic is very weak these days."

"Noted," said Ev quietly. She couldn't help feeling that Vasagle had a point.

The guards fell on Vasagle and tied her up while she was temporarily off balance. Her talons flailed wildly, but she was having trouble aiming. The guard who'd attacked her stood by, yelling orders. He returned the RDD to his pocket.

"That's an RDD," said Jonah, warming to his role of knowledge holder. "A Randomized Deprivation Device. Same as Inner." Ev decided not to tell him that she already knew about RDDs—he was having fun being the expert. "It randomly removes one of the target's senses or functions, like balance or hearing."

"Randomly?"

"Yeah, I guess they want the entertainment value of not knowing how they're going to mess with us. The RDD won't let the punishment go on for longer than is safe, but they can keep hitting the button over and over until they find the one they're looking for."

"How nice for them," said Ev.

"It's what they call a 'magical innovation.' It's in an electronic device, but bits of it use magic to work. An easy way for those who hate magic to use it to punish the rest of us."

"Like Vasagle," said Ev.

"I guess, but griffins have different magic to us. They're good at guarding things… Oh, and their feathers and claws are good for magical remedies for things like eyesight, so they take a lot of those from them."

"Their claws?"

"They take them just before they get too old to be useful," said Jonah, conversationally. "They have to take the feathers and the claws directly from a living griffin, otherwise they're no good."

Ev stared at Jonah in shock.

"Too many feathers," said Amy.

"Yeah, Vasagle is a head butter, you see, and she's really good with those claws of hers, so they sometimes forget to pull her feathers regularly. I say forget. They avoid doing it. Which means the magic in her wings builds up, and occasionally she can do what you just saw. If they let her magic build up properly, there would be no stopping her."

Even bound and muzzled and empty of magic, Vasagle was putting up a fight. She writhed and kicked and strained. Despite their best efforts, two guards were down, but not, Ev was disappointed to see, with any serious injuries.

"If she keeps on like this, I'm going to shoot her," said the guard with the RDD.

"We can't just waste her claws…"

"Oh, I know where to shoot so she'll live long enough," said the guard, grimly.

With a pop, a familiar olive pixie appeared.

"Ah, that pixie, her name is…" began Jonah.

"Lulerain," said Ev, straining to listen.

"Yes," said Jonah, crossly.

"Gentlemen, if I may?" asked Lulerain. "I believe
Vasagle and I can come to some kind of agreement?"

"You have two minutes, and then I shoot her," said
the guard.

"So kind," said Lulerain. She whispered in
Vasagle's ear, and, by degrees, the griffin calmed. After a
while, Vasagle gave one brief nod.

"She has agreed to do as you tell her and accept any
punishment you deem appropriate," said Lulerain.

"Fine. Now get lost." The guard swatted at Lulerain
who disappeared.

"Stupid animal," said another sweating guard.

"Isn't Lulerain just a librarian?"

"Yeah, but apparently she's kind of important
among the pixies. Like a queen or mayor or something, so
most of the magical creatures listen to her."

"But she just works with books!"

"Pixies have to do what we tell them."

They walked around the outskirts of the paddock.
Jonah, happy to be the expert again, kept talking, pointing
out the griffins whose names he knew and why.

"Claster isn't here," he said, eventually. All they'd
found was one huge, dragon-sized space that was extremely
empty. "Let's check the basement."

Ev trailed behind her fellow Inners. Jonah was
chatting away, but she wasn't listening. Griffins could talk,

but they were tied up and muzzled and their eggs were stolen for food. Lulerain was a queen, but she had to work in a library, taking orders from humans.

And Ev could fly and shoot fire, but she wasn't allowed to because people who couldn't said it was evil.

the basement was a bustling workplace of crazy. Huge vehicles were being moved and repaired everywhere she looked, and there was a strong smell of gasoline. There was also an animal hospital, where a griffin was screaming its head off through a muzzle while someone tried to mend its wing, and a gym where people were exercising contentedly. All over the walls, the strange posters with their strange words hung. Ev really hated those posters.

Most importantly, there was a dragon.

Ev realized that she'd already seen the dragon in the library. That was what had appeared in the hologram when Lulerain had spoken to someone invisible. What had she said? That the dragon wasn't eating? That she didn't have any books on magical creatures? Something like that.

The dragon was just lying there, out in the open, in a huge rectangle painted on the ground, barely moving.

"What's wrong with him?" asked Ev.

"He's sad," whispered Amy.

Then Ev saw the chains.

They watched as some men, accompanied by a pixie colored all in yellow, brought him a huge chunk of meat that still had patches of feathers and fur. They threw it in front of him.

“Eat, damn you,” said one.

Claster didn’t even bother looking at it.

“See, boring,” said Jonah.

“Aren’t they scared that he’ll set them on fire?” asked Ev. It’s what she wanted to do.

“He can’t, there’s a magical barrier,” said Jonah. “His flames can’t get through.”

“You kids!” shouted the yellow pixie suddenly. “What are you doing down here?”

“Just looking!” called Jonah. “Let’s go,” he whispered to Amy and Ev.

As quickly as they could, they left the basement by the spiral staircase and headed out of another set of doors on first.

“There are so many trees!”

“They’re less fun when it’s your turn to work in the garden,” said Jonah, sullenly.

“Those are helicopters!” said Ev.

Two helicopters were just coming into land next to a third. They gleamed but they also looked…old, like they’d been around for a very long time.

“I wonder where they were?” said Jonah.

Amy pulled on her arm.

“Let’s go!”

A group of soldiers were heading their way. They didn't look like the kind of people who had much time for children.

Amy was leading the way now. Their route took them past an enclosed area full of bright, colorful contraptions. Little kids were running around, screaming, and crawling all over them.

"That's the play park," said Jonah. "It's for little kids only." He kicked the fence as they passed. "Not that I want to play on any stupid swings anyway."

They went to the garden instead. There were plenty of people around, but they were focused on watering, pruning, and whispering magical incantations.

"What are those for?" asked Ev, pointing to a bunch of purple daisies.

"Aster," said Amy.

"Helps with psychic abilities," said Jonah. "I think. I always get the flowers confused."

"And that?"

"Snapdragon. Protection," said Amy.

"There's nothing here that isn't useful," said Jonah. "They don't grow things just to be pretty."

"What about the trees around the building?"

"So that people on lower floors don't get distracted by what's going on outside. You have to be productive to stay here."

"I don't think I like it here much," said Ev.

"It's better!" said Amy.

"So, you're a Withouter now, are you?" asked Ev. "And no, it isn't better. It sucks."

Jonah was silent. Amy prodded him.

"Amy is right," he said eventually, "It is better here than underground, we just have to get used to it."

The garden was divided roughly into plants that were for magic and plants that were for eating. The second category was far less interesting, at least until Ev spied some big, juicy tomatoes.

She immediately grabbed one and bit into it.

"Yuck!" she said, spitting it out.

"It's an acquired taste," said Jonah. "That I have no intention at all of acquiring."

The tomato was acidic and sprayed juice everywhere, which was not what the story had led her to believe.

"They could have warned us in *Grandma's Kitchen* that they taste so bad."

"What are you talking about?"

"You know, the stories we read in Inner?" said Ev.

Amy and Jonah looked at her blankly.

"I mean, we can probably talk about them now, right? Vendavi isn't watching…" she trailed off. A growing suspicion was telling her that Amy and Jonah had never laid eyes on *Grandma's Kitchen*, or any of the other stories she had read over the years.

"So, back in Inner – you never read any stories about the before times?"

"Of course not!"

"Well, I did," said Ev.

"Why?"

"Vendavi said I could."

Amy's eyes widened in shock.

"No way," said Jonah. "There is absolutely *no way*."

Ev had always thought it was strange, but now that she knew she was the only one…

"Maybe it was Vendavi 2.0," she said slowly. No, that didn't make sense either, because she'd been reading those stories long before that biology lesson…

"You guys did have weird lessons though, right? I wasn't the only one who had to go through that?"

"Yes, of course! I told you to do the mindfulness lesson, remember?"

"Did Vendavi sometimes strand you in the lesson all alone? And was he incredibly annoying the entire time?"

Amy nodded.

"Yup. Sounds about right to me," said Jonah.

"But you didn't get to read any stories?" she asked, desperately.

"No! And if you're the only one, it's probably not something you should talk about."

"Why not?"

"People disappear here too…"

Ev was lost in thought and unthinkingly lifted the tomato to her mouth once again. This time she nibbled it gently.

"It's not that bad," she said. "I could get used to it."

"Well, don't, because you're not supposed to eat food straight from the garden," said Jonah. "It messes with their supply and demand numbers, or something."

She took another bite. A thought flared in the back of her mind. Slowly, she took another bite, and then another, until the whole tomato was gone.

"Hey, why doesn't the tomato make me feel tired?"

"No Hexteria," said Amy.

"She means that they haven't had time to add Hexteria to the stuff in the garden yet, so the tomato won't block your magic."

"Hold on, let me make sure I have this right: there's something called Hexteria that they put in the food to stop my magic?"

"Yeah, so we don't have to be tormented by it all the time."

Jonah seemed perfectly fine with this. Amy… well, who knew with Amy? She didn't say much and just smiled a lot no matter what. She would probably smile at their funerals, not because she wouldn't be sad, just because she didn't know any other facial expressions.

"So that's why they don't want us eating straight from the gardens…" said Ev, quietly.

"Would you look at this?" yelled Jonah, cutting her off. "The raccoons have been in here again! Look, you can see where they cut through the fence. It took me ages to plant these beans!"

Cut through the fence?

Amy patted Jonah on the arm. "Never mind."

Jonah kicked at the soil angrily.

"A compound full of magic users and we can't keep a few mutated rodents out of the vegetable patch…"

Amy nodded sympathetically.

They wandered on further, reaching another fence. On the other side, children were swooping through the air.

"This is the flying school," said Jonah, his voice still shaky with rage. "It has to be taught outside."

"I can do that," said Ev.

"Yeah, it's the most common one," said Jonah, dismissively.

Common? Ev thought it was pretty cool.

"I can also shoot fire out of my hands," she said.

Now Jonah seemed interested.

"Can you show us?"

"Um," said Ev. "So far it's happened unexpectedly… I'm not sure I can do it on command."

"That's all right, we'll understand if you can't. Hexteria and all that. Please just try. Set that bush on fire."

She turned to the bush, held out her hands, closed her eyes, and tried to make the fire come.

It was no good. There wasn't a single tingle in her skull.

"Sorry guys," she said, panting.

"Whatever," said Jonah.

Ev's temper flared and for a brief moment, there *was* a tingle in her skull, but nothing as strong as before.

"What can *you* do?" she asked, accusingly.

"I don't use my abilities."

Amy patted his arm and smiled.

"Just for our friend," she said.

"No!"

"It's alright, I understand completely that you can't show us your abilities, it happens to the best of us. Hexteria, and all that," said Ev.

"I can!"

"Oh, I see," said Ev, "so it's just that you're scared to use them then. That makes perfect sense."

"I'm not scared of anything!"

You're scared of everything, thought Ev, but she didn't say it. Jonah was trembling and the wild eyes were back.

He kicked the ground.

Show me!

"One demonstration. One only. And never again."

"Fair enough," said Ev, quickly.

"Think of something totally strange."

Ev took a moment and then thought about the posters she'd seen everywhere since leaving Inner. They might not be the strangest thing she could think of, but they were the most disturbing.

Jonah rolled his eyes.

"Better safe than sorry it can't hurt to keep yourself safe from you if you love your children, you'll give them our wonder cure even the evilest among us can be used for the greater good a gift to be used wisely but of course they must be properly controlled," he chanted, without taking a breath.

"So…?"

"I read minds," said Jonah. "Sometimes I can control minds too. They try to make me practice, but I won't. I hate it! I hate it so much!"

"That's alright, I get it," said Ev. She did. She saw the words behind his words. Imagine, she thought, that you can see the thoughts of everyone. Then imagine that you arrive in a place where everyone thinks you are evil just because you exist. Where everyone hates you. Would you want to know what was on their minds, or would you do your best to avoid getting a good look?

"I'm sorry, Jonah," she said. "It sucks."

There was nothing else to say.

"My turn!" said Amy. And then she disappeared.

The next moment she reappeared three yards away.

"Teleportation," said Jonah, who seemed a little calmer. "They've been testing how far she can go in individual training. We know already that she can jump from first to twelfth, as well as all the way across the grounds. They won't let her jump out, though, I think there's a spell on her to keep her from leaving."

"How come you can use your abilities? Don't you eat the food?"

"We do, but we're among those who can partially use our abilities even under Hexteria. The Hexteria just stops us getting out of control. Right now, Amy can't jump any further than a few feet, and I can only read minds that are right in front of me. You obviously can't do anything if you've had some Hexteria. Lucky."

"So, you're stronger than me or something?" Ev asked, defiantly.

"No, just more focused. We only have one ability each. People with one ability are the strongest, because all of their magic goes into just the one thing. Two is also quite common, like you, and you can be pretty powerful in two abilities as well. But they say that no one with three abilities is very strong in any of them because their magic is stretched too thin. Anyway, it's really rare. I don't think anyone here has had three abilities in centuries, and *no one* has ever had more than three."

"I've seen adults doing all sorts of things…"

"Yeah, we're talking innate abilities, the things you're born being really good at. You can also learn a whole lot of other magic and spells and potions, but you'll never be as good at any of them as you are with your innate ability."

The sky was getting darker, so they went inside to the open plan study area on first where kids were lounging and chatting. They found some empty bean bag chairs in a corner.

The room was much too big and much too noisy. Everywhere she looked were people, people who didn't want her there. Panic began to rise.

No! Count, count, count… Eighteen children in the room thirty-seven bean-bag chairs in view, along with twelve tables and forty-eight chairs. Count the words being spoken: one, two, three…

Slowly, she calmed down.

Where did that leave her? In a strange world she knew nothing about.

Well, when you didn't know something, you learned.

"I need you tell me more," she said to her friends who were watching her with concerned faces.

"I don't like to talk about it," said Jonah, hurriedly.

Tell me!

"But I guess you deserve to know…"

'Tell me about Vendavi. Not normal Vendavi; crazy Vendavi."

"The tech guys here like to mess around, explore weird things. They figured out a while ago that they could hack into Vendavi without triggering any of Inner's emergency systems. They probably blew a few of us up along the way, but who cares, right? Then they started playing tricks on the Inner kids just for fun, but after a while they figured out that we could sometimes access our magical abilities in simulations, if pushed far enough. So now someone here has the job of being smart Vendavi. No idea who it is, no one does, so don't bother asking."

"No one knows?"

"No! Well, I guess someone knows, probably a few people to make it work right, but most people don't. Most people here don't care either. You'll only embarrass yourself if you ask."

"Did Felix and Janian Granite cook this up together?"

Jonah snorted.

"There's just a person they name Granite in every generation in Inner. He's probably not even related to Felix. They're raised to think they're in charge, but really Vendavi is, and has been for ages. Janian is sort of joke here. So, maybe don't bring him up? Anyway, all of this has been happening since before they were around."

The supper bell rang. They hurried to the tables and quickly found a seat. Pixies of varying colors dumped food on the tables.

Ev ate thoughtfully. With each mouthful, her mind became heavier and heavier, but she knew to expect that now.

She was going to have to do something about her diet.

"Hello, Ev," said a familiar voice. With a slight jerk, she snapped out of her reverie.

"Oh, hello Granny," said Ev. The old woman seemed to pop up everywhere.

Granny handed Ev a stack of pages.

"Here's your schedule," she said. "It seemed that the carers on your floor completely forgot to give it to you, so it was lucky that I was there to remind them. Madam was going to bring it, but I said I was on my way down here anyway, and I wouldn't want to it to accidentally go missing. Many of the teachers are quite unforgiving about missed classes. Be at your first class on time tomorrow morning. This column shows you which floor to be on."

Then she turned and left, her eyes already scanning the room for someone else.

"Well, Granny's on your side already, so things are probably going to be just fine for you," Jonah said, snatching the top page. "Good! We're in a bunch of the same classes," he said.

"Classes? Like in the old days where you all sit in a room and listen to a live teacher?"

"Yup, mostly."

After supper, they wandered Alerrawia some more, Amy and Jonah showing Ev everything they knew. They went up to eighth and ninth to look at the classrooms so that Ev would be able to find them in the morning.

Ev became quieter and quieter as the evening progressed. Jonah chattered away, and even Amy, the famously silent, said a few things. Ev just listened and nodded.

She was worried that if she opened her mouth, she wouldn't be able to keep herself from screaming.

With fewer distractions, her brain had time to think, and what it thought was that Ev was going mad.

She was dizzy. Her hands were numb. She couldn't breathe, couldn't think, the world was spinning. She was afloat with nothing familiar to cling to. Her chest tightened and tightened until she was sure she would die.

"Vendavi, I don't understand this lesson," she whispered. The world went black.

When she awoke, she was on her bunk. Someone must have carried her there. They'd also carefully tucked her in.

She lay completely still, too terrified to move. She was completely on her own. The last time she'd been this scared was on her fifth birthday when her mother had smiled and shoved her into a tunnel and told her to crawl. Except this was worse. Much worse. This tunnel was an entire world, and there was no way out, no matter how long you crawled.

Count!

One, two three voices of other girls in the room. One, two, three, four, five little cracks in the ceiling. Oh, there's another one. Six cracks in the ceiling. Count the bars on the bed, there to keep children from rolling off: one, two, three, four…

Her heart slowed, her breathing normalized, her head cleared. She could think again.

Count the words…

The fourth girl only spoke when spoken to, but Stacey and Madison were chattering away like anything.

"Did you spend the day with your parents?" Madison asked.

"Yup, like I can avoid it."

"I know, it's lame that we have to spend time with them, right?"

"So lame."

"What did you do?"

"They had some of those old Before Times movies to watch. They're all a bit weird. Then we played board games. Nice and peaceful."

"My mom made me help her clean," Ev could hear the frustration in Madison's voice. "But we also read the big atlas to see how the world used to be."

To Ev, it all sounded wonderful.

She lay in her bed, listening and thinking.

This world was like a story. In stories, nothing made sense, at least at first, because you had to figure out what was happening along with the characters.

Ev knew how stories worked. She just wondered what kind of story this was. Was she the good guy or the bad guy?

Good guy, obviously. A trapped good guy.

Realization dawned. It was a prison break! She needed to escape!

What Ev often found strange in stories was how people made their intentions so obvious to everyone. For example, if they wanted to escape, they'd complain bitterly and constantly about how much they wanted to escape, which meant that people knew to throw obstacles in their way. In the end they always escaped (and the better stories had cleverer heroes), but why did they have to be so obvious? Why did they always tell their trusted friends their whole plan, just when the bad guys were listening? Or why did they choose untrustworthy friends who spilled the beans or let them down?

Ev had no intention of being a stupid hero.

She would play along. She would be a 'good girl'. She would be grateful for everything they did for her, and oh so happy to be above ground.

And, once she knew how, she would leave and never come back.

8. Life is Not a Battlefield

Figure 3: The Scientific Method.

Note how results that align partially or not at all with the hypothesis become the basis for new research into the phenomenon.

Science Fundamentals

Page 12

The nervous little math teacher, Miss Leah, had to check a note on her desk to remind herself who Ev was, which didn't help Ev's nerves, but she didn't seem angry and showed Ev to a seat right in front with a confused smile on her face. Jonah squeezed himself into the seat next to her.

"Where were you?" he demanded.

Ev had skipped breakfast—she'd been too nervous to eat so she'd gone in search of the math classroom instead. Before she could explain, a voice said, "You're in my seat, Inner brat," and Ev looked up to see Peter. Her heart froze, but today Peter was more interested in Jonah.

"Go away," said Jonah, "or I will punch you in the face. Again."

Peter smiled. Ev didn't like his smile at all. "Miss, may I swap seats with Jonah, please?"

"It's fine, I'll move!" yelped Jonah.

"Oh no, I insist!" said Peter. "He's friends with the new girl, Miss, I think it would be nice for her to have a friend. Up here. Right in front of the whole class."

"How thoughtful!" said Miss Leah, and that's how Ev learned that sitting right in front wasn't a good thing. She could *feel* Jonah's anger.

She also learned that Miss Leah was a hopeless teacher. Nearly half the lesson was gone before she calmed the class enough to hand out a worksheet, but then she hid behind her desk with earplugs and a book. No one else seemed interested in the worksheet, but she battled her way through the questions anyway—what else was there to do?

"How did you figure that out?" asked Jonah.

"Are these the right answers?"

"No idea, but they look very impressive, all laid out almost neatly in the right spots."

Ev decided to just be glad that Jonah was talking to her again. They worked on the rest of the problems together until the bell rang and Miss Leah yelled at them to hand their worksheets in. The other students ignored her, but Ev walked up to the desk, smiled, and put her paper down neatly.

"Thank you for the lesson, Miss Leah," she said. "I tried my best, and I'll catch up on ratios as quickly as I can."

"Well, thank you," said Miss Leah. "What a lovely young lady you are, despite appearances! Here, this is the textbook for the class."

Despite appearances?

Their next class was called *Magical Innovation.* Amy stood outside the door, waiting for them.

"Why is everyone looking at me?" asked Ev as the other kids rushed through the door.

"They always look at the new kids…," said Jonah. "But you're extra interesting because you weren't supposed to be able to fly. Everyone's talking about it. Christopher gave you food, and if you'd eaten a whole jam sandwich, you shouldn't have been able to fly."

But she hadn't eaten the whole sandwich. . .She'd thrown most of it on the floor. Had nobody noticed?

Magical innovation was taught by Zara, the woman who had helped Ev recover from her burns.

"Welcome, Evelyn," said Zara. "Class, Evelyn is our newest student. Say hello."

"Hello, Evelyn," chorused the class in a meaningless monotone. Ev stared at the table.

"For Evelyn's benefit, let me explain what 'magical innovation' is. Magic is evil and unnatural, as you have been taught in your other classes." Zara's face was completely blank as she said this. "However, it is also necessary. Most of what we do here requires magic. Magical innovation is the art of finding new ways for magic to serve science. As we have a new student with us today, I thought we could play the *Three Strange Uses* game."

The class brightened up at this news.

"On your tables you will see two potion recipes and two technological devices. You have ten minutes to name three *unusual* uses for each. Bonus points for combinations!"

Two bits of paper, as well as an ancient Walkman, exactly like she'd seen in her history lessons in Inner, and a high-tech microphone lay on Ev's table. She wrote *hit someone with the microphone*, but that was all she could think of. Amy handed her one of the recipes, and Ev saw that it was for a cooling potion, to use when someone was experiencing mild discomfort due to being too hot. There was a warning that said if you used a lime instead of a lemon, it would cool the drinker's blood so much that they would die.

She wrote *Use a lime and feed it to your enemies.*

"Two minutes left!" said Zara.

Ev panicked. She'd only thought of two things! Quickly she scribbled *Crush the Walkman into tiny, sharp bits and put it in someone's food.*

"Time's up!" said Zara.

She snapped her fingers, and suddenly writing appeared on Ev's worksheet in red ink. It said:

3 points!

Not bad for your first try! Next time try to think of ways to help people or create new things. Life is not a battlefield! 😊

She glanced over at Amy's worksheet. Fifteen points! How was that even possible?

"Amy found three unusual uses for each of the items on her table, giving her twelve points, as well as three unusual uses that combined two or more of the items, giving her an extra three points, and making her today's winner. One of Amy's ideas was to adjust the cooling potion slightly by adding a crocus flower, boiling it until it becomes a vapor, and trapping that vapor in a vial. You could then use the binding potion to fuse the vapor with the microphone, making it impossible for anyone speaking through the microphone to become angry. As you may remember from your spell casting lessons, the crocus flower can be used, among other things, to cool violent emotions. A bit more thinking may be needed, but Amy's idea would definitely work. She combined *three* of the items on her table."

Zara applauded. After a moment, everyone else joined in, Ev included.

On the classroom walls, Ev could see the posters. *Keep yourself safe from you! Magic is a gift that must be properly controlled.* And the others. Some of the posters were covered slightly by student projects and announcements, but they were still there.

The words behind the words were this: Amy, you might be able to reach your potential with magic, you might finally be able to show the rest of us how clever you are, but never, EVER, forget that you are a dangerous waste of space that we only tolerate for your usefulness.

Ev wondered if Amy could see those words too.

The bell rang, and Ev found herself hurrying with Jonah to their science class, leaving Amy to go alone to a more advanced lesson for children who actually knew what they were doing.

"Good morning, class!" said the teacher. She was a beautiful woman with light brown skin and eyes, and long, straight, black hair that went halfway down her thighs. "Lots to learn and not much time to learn it! Please turn to page 12." She handed Ev an enormous, shiny book. "Welcome, Evelyn. My name is Jade." she added with a comforting smile.

"Thank you," said Ev quietly, remembering to be nice.

The diagram on page 12 showed the scientific method: ask a question, do some research, think of a hypothesis, test with an experiment, analyze the results, and communicate them, all things Ev already knew, thanks to Vendavi and his mad successor.

"Today, we are going to design an experiment," said Jade. She broke the class into groups. Ev was in Jonah's group, which was good, but so was Peter.

"Great, I have to pick up the slack of *two* Inner brats," said Peter.

Ev was angry. Everything about Peter's face, form the words coming out of his mouth to the knowing grin on his face made her angry, but she was not going to start a fight—it's exactly what he wanted.

Instead, she smiled and said, "Hello Peter! Wonderful to see you again."

Peter's eyes grew big, and his mouth opened but no words came out. Ev wasn't following the script, and he didn't know what to do about it.

"All right, settle down!" called Jade over the noise, and Ev couldn't help noticing that the children, the same children that were in Miss Leah's class, listened instantly. It was probably a type of magic.

They had to design an experiment to test what would happen to gummy bears in water. Today, each group had to choose a variable to test, like water temperature.

"And, in case you've forgotten what gummy bears are, I have a jar of them here, fresh from magical manufacturing!"

The class's excitement was contagious as Jade handed out the sweets for a 'taste test,' and Ev wondered if

she was the only to see the words behind the words—
everything interesting needs magic.

"Right," said Peter loudly. "As team leader, I vote
we figure out what happens if the water is really cold, but
still liquid. All in favor?"

"Good idea!" said Ev, brightly, and Peter glared at
her as if she'd just insulted him.

"If Ev's in, I'm in," said Jonah, his mouth full of
colorful gelatin.

"Fine," said Peter, as if he was doing them a favor.
"What do we think will happen to gummy bears in freezing
cold water?"

"They'll get smaller," said Ev.

"If the water is freezing cold," said Peter loudly and
deliberately as he wrote, "the gummy bears will get
bigger."

"Whatever you say, captain!"

What did it matter? It didn't affect the experiment—
the test would still show that gummy bears got smaller.
Sometimes, science was about finding out how things *don't*
work.

That's what the words behind the words on Page 12
meant, anyway.

Ev and Peter spent the rest of the lesson trying to
annoy each other, and Ev was pleased to see that she was
winning. He would make her pay for it later, no doubt, but
right now, she was in control.

The bell rang.

"Hurry!" said Jonah. "The next class is the best! It's taught by Granny Oakwood!"

Ev's stomach dropped. But Granny would hate her! She'd stolen her mirror and everything!

Granny taught Language and Writing, because, apparently, Inner kids had no imagination, and someone had spotted that imagination was needed for science to happen. The class gathered in a cozy corner as far away from the door as possible, curled up on beanbag chairs and surrounded by books. Ev was disappointed that all of the books seemed to be for little kids.

"Hello, everyone," said Granny. "We have a new student today! Ev, it's wonderful to see you again! Please come up here." Granny patted an empty bean bag chair next to her. Nervously, Ev crawled from beanbag to beanbag. Granny gave her a side hug and said, "Whatever you're worrying about, don't. I'm so glad you're here!" She pointed to a pile of rags next to her chair. "This is Mr. Snugglebottom, my bobcat."

The pile of rags shifted to reveal an enormous cat.

"He comes to all of my classes. Would you like to say hello?"

"Hello," said Ev, nervously.

Mr. Snugglebottom jumped up and stretched, first his front legs, then his back legs, arching his back as he did so. He sniffed Ev lazily.

"Don't be afraid," said Granny Oakwood. "He just wants to get to know you." Ev kept perfectly still as the bobcat sniffed her hands, licked her left thumb, curled up at her feet, and went to sleep.

Granny beamed. "He likes you!"

"If you say so. . ."

"I know my bobcat! Now, it's a rule that the new child tells a story. It doesn't have to be long or good, we just want to hear your best try!"

The class looked at her expectantly. No one had warned her about this!

"I don't know any stories…"

No, that wasn't true, was it? She knew plenty of stories. Vendavi had made sure of that.

"Actually, never mind, I've thought of one." It was a story she'd read many times because it was funny and scary at the same time.

"This is the story of the creature in the night," she began, her voice low for added drama. "There once was a woman who lived by herself in a big house. She had a little dog, who she loved. A lot. The little dog slept under her bed every single night.

"Every night, before she went to sleep, the woman would stick a hand under the bed so that the little dog could give her a good night lick.

"One night, she went to bed. She put her hand under, and after a moment her little dog licked it. 'Good boy!' she said, settling down to sleep. But sleep wouldn't come. Somewhere in the house, something was dripping."

Ev slowed her voice to add to the tension.

"Drip. . .Drip. . .Drip. . .Then it would stop for a bit. Then, just as she was falling asleep, she heard it again. Drip!" She almost shouted the last word, and the class jumped.

"The woman climbed out of bed and followed the sound of the dripping. It was coming from the bathroom. Slowly, she opened the bathroom door, and there, hanging over the bath, was. . ."

"Thank you, Evelyn," said Granny. "That's all we have time for, I'm afraid."

"But I was just getting to the good bit!"

"I'm sure you were. You'll have to tell me the rest another time."

"But does it have a happy ending? Is the little dog alright?" asked a girl.

"Never mind that," said Granny, and Ev thought the old lady might be panicking, just a little. "There's nothing in that story for us to worry about. Why don't we come up with a nicer story together? I need two characters!"

Hands shot up.

"Yes, Jonah?" said Granny.

"Mr. Snugglebottom!" said Jonah.

"Ah, Mr. Snugglebottom, the most famous bobcat in the bubble!"

The class giggled.

"Let's have a new character, now, one we haven't used before."

Slowly, Amy raised her hand.

"Amy!" said Granny Oakwood. "Please go ahead!"

"Alizes," said Amy. "Pixie," she added.

"Alizes, the pixie!" said Granny Oakwood. "Good job using your words! Ev, you have Alizes, who is a pixie, and Mr. Snugglebottom, who is at your feet. Do you think they are friends or enemies?"

"Friends," she said. Enemies was the correct answer, but she didn't want Granny to be mad at her. She'd already messed up twice, once with the mirror, and again with her story, and Granny was the only person who seemed to care.

"Oh, good, because Mr. Snugglebottom does so love to play with the pixies, although they're not so keen on playing back! Now we need a setting. Caroline, where are Alizes and Mr. S?"

"On the moon," said the girl.

"On the moon it is!" said Granny. "But *why* are they on the moon?"

And so it went until the class had created a story from scratch. It didn't end there, though—Ev had to repeat the extremely stupid story to the class. She told it quickly to get it over with.

"Alizes and Mr. Snugglebottom were sent to the moon to fight the moon monster who wanted to eat up the whole moon and leave us in complete darkness, but when they got there, they found that the moon monster was just a giant old ladybug who could only eat moon rocks to live, so, instead of hurting the ladybug, Alizes and Mr. Snugglebottom took some rocks back to earth to study them and figured out that the moon was made from iron, so they invited the moon monster to earth to eat spinach instead. The end."

The class applauded uproariously.

"Thank you, Ev!" said Granny Oakwood.

Ev couldn't help smiling. "It's still a stupid story," she said.

"But even stupid stories can be fun. And even stupid stories can teach you things! Now, it's my turn."

As one, Granny's students stilled and leaned forward, just a little.

"Once upon a time there was a little girl who loved to solve problems. She would try to solve any problem that came her way, especially if she was the only one who could see that the problem was even there.

"The grown-ups told her that they *could* see the problems, but some were safer to solve then others. *'Stop talking about them!'* they said, and she didn't understand that they were trying to protect her.

"The little girl grew bigger and learned that her innate ability was Revelation; she could see the truth as well as show it to others. But by this time, she had also learned some other, non-magical abilities, like Politics, and Survival, so there were many truths that she kept to herself.

"One day, she found an old book, full of silly stories written by her mother to make children happy. On the very front page were the words: *To my daughter, the Solver of Problems.*

"And she remembered. She remembered what was important and what wasn't. She remembered that the person who could see the problems *had to* help solve them.

"She decided to write her own book, full of truths. Her mother cast a spell on the book to ensure that at least one copy would always exist. Her mother didn't know that this spell would also protect her—but not her daughter. The book made many people angry, but they couldn't break the enchantment that kept the book alive. So, instead, they added it to the library. They told people it wasn't very good. It wasn't worth reading. It was full of lies. They could read it if they wanted to, but they would only be wasting their time.

"The girl disappeared. No one knows where she went, but there are plenty of rumors. The girl knew this would happen. So did her mother. They did it anyway because they also knew that important things sometimes require sacrifice."

Information. Explanations. *Warnings*. The story was full of them, and Ev saw that her classmates understood the words behind the words as well as she did this time. Alison Oakwood was Granny's daughter. She'd written *Inner: How and Why?* and now she was missing. The truth is important, but it might get you in big trouble, *and that's okay*.

It was an awful lot to dump on a group of 'unimaginative' children.

"Now, class," said Granny, "we have just enough time left for. . .bubbles!"

The silence shattered as the class cheered.

Granny handed out the brightly colored bubble bottles. Ev took a green one, and Granny showed her how to use it as the rest of the children spread out around the room, chatting and playing.

Ev blew a string of bubbles, paused, and asked, "Are we stupid Inner brats?" and blew another string.

"No, of course not," said Granny. "You are good children who were put in a bad situation that wasn't your fault."

"Then why are Alerrawian kids so mean to us?"

"Because they're good children who are in a bad situation that isn't their fault."

Ev blew her bubbles reflectively. For a class that started with such a stupid story, it had certainly given her a lot to think about.

"Ev, this wasn't you first time dealing with stories, was it? I could tell. Usually, Inner children have never heard a story in their lives, and storytelling is such an important part of learning, so they asked the meddling old woman to teach it, to keep her out of the way."

"Amy and Jonah said they never read stories in Inner."

"That's because they didn't. Most of what Alerrawia actually does with Inner is secret, but I've pieced a few things together. Kidnapping children wasn't the first thing they tried, back in the day. When they first learned to control Vendavi, just a little, I think they started small by tricking Vendavi into given random children stories— would it affect their learning, or not? They found out what any teacher could have told them—stories help people learn by making information just a little bit more real. Once they had their answer, they forgot all about it. Every now and then we get a child from Inner who knows exactly how stories work, and no one even remembers that it's our own doing."

"Stories are useful?"

"Stories are everything. Stories are how people make sense of the world. Stories decide how we think, how we react, but that doesn't mean that all stories are *true*. Be careful of the power of stories—you're not as clever as you think you are."

A few minutes later, when she was walking to her next class with Jonah, Ev heard him say, "Drip. Drip. Drip," under his breath, and suddenly she understood what Granny had meant. A story like that would be a lot scarier to someone who didn't know how stories worked. . .

"That dripping story had a happy ending, by the way," she lied. "So, there's nothing to worry about. . ."

Jonah looked at her with the skepticism of someone who could read minds, even if he didn't want to, and Ev knew that nothing she said would undo the damage.

In biology class, the teacher, Mr. Sterling, made everyone look at her again by announcing her name, and then, with a huge smile, said that the new student *always* got to feed Sean, so would she come up to the front of the classroom, please, and suddenly Ev didn't have time to worry about Jonah anymore.

She looked nervously at the glass tank on Mr. Sterling's desk. "That's Sean," he said, proudly. There was a sign taped to the tank:

I am a toad.

My name is Sean (and definitely not 'Shaun').

FEED ME!

"Sean needs to be fed a live cricket every day to stay happy and healthy. Today, that honor is all yours!"

Ev looked at the jar in horror. She hated bugs! All bugs! Even the creepy little bug bots who clicked and scuttled about Inner had always scared the life out of her. She felt sick. She felt dizzy. Black spots appeared in her vision.

Mr. Sterling took a cricket out of the jar with tweezers. "Take these, and don't let go!"

She had no choice. She had to be good. With a shaking hand, she took the tweezers, trying not to look at the squirming cricket. She hoped the teacher wasn't saying anything, because she couldn't hear a thing—the blood pounding in her ears was too loud.

She dropped the cricket into the tank, and Mr. Sterling slammed the lid shut as he explained to the class why Sean needed to eat crickets and how he was so fast at catching them, but Ev didn't listen because Vendavi had already told her.

"Of course," said Mr. Sterling, "one day our bubble will run out of insects for Sean to eat. But you don't have to believe that if you don't want to!" he added, hurriedly.

The rest of the lesson was on food chains. Ev and Jonah tied for first place in the quiz.

Unfortunately, not all her classes were as normal as biology. In History of Magic, Ev was given her first glimpse of the *bad place*.

"Sarah Grayson and Morris Hawk, where are your essays?" demanded Alicia, the teacher.

"We didn't have time…"

"Thirty minutes detention!" said the teacher, snapping her fingers.

Both of the children vanished. Ev gasped. Everyone else was perfectly still.

In place of the vanished children floated two small glowing orbs. Alicia absent-mindedly shooed them into a cupboard and slammed the door.

"Turn to page 82," said Alicia. Ev hurriedly opened the textbook that magically appeared on her desk. The chapter was titled *The Seven*.

"You, explain the concept of The Seven to the rest of the class," said Alicia, pointing at one of the children.

"They are the democratically elected leaders of Alerrawia. Once elected, only death can remove them from their position."

As Alicia questioned the class, Ev's eyes grew wider.

She'd met The Seven, the rulers of Alerrawia, on her very first day!

"Class, I want an essay on the influence of the original seven by our next lesson. You may start preparing now."

Ev hated essays, and, as much as she didn't want to mysteriously disappear, she found that she was far more interested in the current seven.

Felix Granite is from a long line of Granites who rose to power in the time before the bubble for their extraordinary service to the world of science. Politically strong, the members of this family were among the first to accurately identify the dangers of magic and began the tradition of shunning magical families in business and political dealings. Not everyone, however, was ready to see the light, and the Granites' popularity waxed and waned for many years until the formation of the bubble and the rightful positioning of the Granite family as. . .

Ev's mind wandered, so she tried to read about the others: Eliza Faraday, Robert Rayner, Marcia Brown, Christopher Morrison, Zara Saul, and Shaun Brown. Felix and Marcia's entries were the longest, but Zara only got one short paragraph saying how she was the first magic-user on The Seven since Kelvin Granite, and Shaun just had one line that basically said he was The Seventh member of The Seven.

"Your essay is about the *original* Seven, Miss Acorn," said Alicia, behind her. Ev turned her head quickly, but the teacher wasn't there—she was still at the front of the class, staring at her. Ev quickly turned to the correct page, her heart pounding.

Kelvin Granite, the founder of The Seven, was a Reality Warper. Through his strong leadership and faultless decision-making, Alerrawia was preserved in its current form. Col. Gregory Faraday was his second in command.*

**Reality Warpers (see page 239) can, as the name suggests, change reality to be anything they choose. It is believed that this ability was what allowed this great man to establish the bubble, thereby granting peace and safety to all within it. Kelvin Granite was the last Reality Warper to be seen in the bubble. As reality warping cannot be controlled by Hexteria, it became illegal shortly thereafter. It was swiftly eradicated.*

An important note for students*: While topics such as the bubble may arise in educational texts, this does not mean they are appropriate for discussion outside of class. The bubble is perfectly safe, so no one need mention it.*

The bell rang and Ev had no more time to prepare her essay before Amy dragged her to lunch. Jonah was kept back by the teacher with a handful of other students. Ev waved at him as she left, but he ignored her.

In the common room, they ate standing up—there were too many people milling around the tables, grabbing for the tasteless, pixie-created sandwiches before they were all gone. There were also glasses of water, and she gladly gulped one down, and then another. She was about to reach for a third, but Amy slapped her hand away.

"Only two! Water restrictions!"

"What does that even mean?" asked Ev, but Amy just grabbed her hand again and pulled her to the stairs—no time to talk, they had to get to their afternoon classes.

At the door to the physics classroom, Ev said, "Can you at least tell me where Alicia sent those two students?"

Amy pulled a wad of papers out of her pocket, looked through the hurriedly, and handed one to Ev.

Hi Jonah,

I'm better at writing than speaking, so here's the first thing you need to know. There's a place called the Bad Place. I'm unable to say more.

When we go there, we leave a light behind. It's called a "tether." They keep it safe until it's time to bring us back.

Ideally, I would give a longer explanation, but that is not possible in this case.

Amy

Amy was reusing notes she'd written for Jonah. Ev smiled at her cleverness and tried not to feel hurt that she hadn't written anything just for her.

Jonah was already in the classroom.

"What did Alicia say?" asked Ev, kindly.

"That I don't write very well," said Jonah, angrily scribbling on a piece of paper. Ev looked over. She thought he might be practicing his writing, but he was just drawing. There was something that looked like a little dog in the left corner. Over the rest of the page, he'd drawn blobs. Well, not quite blobs. They were tear drop shaped.

"Oh dear," she whispered to herself. Drip, drip, drip...

She would have said something, except that the physics teacher, a balding white man with a sour face called Mr. Carrio, started yelling at the class the moment he walked in about how useless they all were at answering even the most basic test questions, and how was it that *none* of them knew what condensation was? But then, he yelled at Ev for 'losing' her textbook, and Ev reasoned that if he didn't even know who his students *were*, it was probably his own fault of they couldn't answer his questions. Mr. Carrio spent the rest of the lesson making them repeat, in chorus, the definitions and examples of condensation from the textbook, and the only thing Ev learned was that it was impossible to be bored and scared at the same time.

Chemistry was completely unmemorable. The teacher, a watery-eyed, pointy-faced woman, quizzed the class on the periodic table of elements. On the board behind she'd carefully written a slogan: *Keep yourself safe from you—control the magical*.

The words behind the words were: I will teach you if they tell me to, but I want you to know that if it were up to me, you wouldn't be here at all. Well teacher, thought Ev, I don't want to be here either, so at least we agree about *something*.

Ev went up to her desk after class and asked for the textbook as politely as she could, but she must have sounded rude anyway, because the teacher pushed a book across the desk without bothering to look up.

"Thank you," said Ev, anyway, and turned to go.

"Wait," said the teacher suddenly. "You're in the same dorm as Madison, aren't you?"

"Yes?" said Ev cautiously, turning back.

"I'm her mother. You can call me Miss Odette. If you do anything to upset or harm Madison, I will have you sent to detention for the rest of your life."

Miss Odette's voice was completely calm, which somehow made the threat even worse.

"Y…yes, Miss Odette," said Ev, backing quickly out of the room.

Was that how mothers were supposed to be?

Her next lesson was Spell Work, which anyone who showed any magical ability at all, even if they were Alerrawian, had to take. Everyone in the class had at least one innate ability, the magic they could do without really thinking, like flying or shooting fire. Even a weak innate ability meant that you could also learn hundreds of other spells and enchantments, known as learned abilities.

Amy handed Ev a stack of notes about spell work, and Ev read them quickly. It turned out there weren't really any magic words, but it did help to decide on a phrase or action to focus your mind. That was why people said *clean yourself up* when dealing with a mess—they could just as easily have said *Abracadabra* or *Sausages*, but *clean yourself up* made more sense, so more people used it. Snapping fingers was the most popular focus action for people who found actions easier than words. It didn't matter what you said or did—the most important thing was what was going on in your head. Whether you were conjuring something from thin air, brewing a potion, reading the stars, or looking into the future, you had to find a way to focus your mind on the magic you wanted to perform.

It was the first lesson that Ev had any interest in whatsoever.

There were at least seventy students in the room and on the board were the names of the teachers: Doreen Wilson, Emerson Porter, Christopher Morrison, and Eliza Faraday.

"Christopher and Eliza can't even use magic!"

"They're not here to teach us," said Jonah. "They're here to make sure the other two don't show us anything they're not allowed to."

A young, skinny, awkward teacher ambled towards them with a smile.

"Evelyn? I'm Emerson. Here are your textbooks," he said. One was full of beginners' potion recipes and the other was called *Focus Techniques*.

"Gather around!" shouted the other real teacher, Doreen. She was tall and skinny with a pinched face and angry little eyes. Her hair was red, short, and spiky.

"Emerson's the nice one," whispered Jonah. "Doreen hates kids."

Luckily for them, Emerson taught the beginners and those who needed more practice, and Doreen taught everyone else, so they were safe.

Today's lesson was on the topic of 'calling.' Calling meant summoning objects to your hand from absolutely anywhere—all you had to know was where the object was and exactly what it, and your hand, looked like. A very useful skill, in other words, so Ev carefully as Emerson explained how it worked.

"As you know, human minds are full of thoughts. Even when you think you're focusing entirely on one thing, there are still hundreds and thousands of other thoughts sparking in your brain. So, you might think that you're completely focused on the spell you're casting, but in the back of your mind your brain is still thinking all sorts of things. What was that sound? A helicopter? Is Dad back? For a spell to work, all of these background thoughts need to be temporarily suppressed, including the ones that remind your body to do important little things, like breath.

"With practice, magic users can shut down their entire mind so that the only thought that remains is the spell. For just one moment, you can make the magic happen, but the timing has to be exactly right, and you can't shut yourself down for too long.

"Ev, I'm about to cast a spell on this group that temporarily overrides the effects of Hexteria, but you won't be able to use your other abilities at this time."

With a nonchalant wave of Emerson's hand, Ev felt a tiny bit freer.

Emerson reminded the class that a learned ability like calling took a lot of practice. That you couldn't expect to get it right immediately. That there was no point in pushing yourself to exhaustion on your very first try. But Ev was still disappointed when, at the end of the class, the apple she had been calling was still stubbornly immovable, no matter how many times she yelled, "Come here!" at it.

"Concentrate," said Amy, whose apple had flown to her hand on only her second try.

"It's fine," said Jonah, who had tried once and then refused to try again. "Inner kids always figure the magic stuff out quickly. The Alerrawians are a bit slow, you know."

"What did you say?" asked a boy.

"Nothing," said Jonah quickly.

That was when Ev realized that every single other child in the beginners' group was Alerrawian. You could tell because they spoke funny.

The only reason they didn't fight was because the bell rang.

"Practice your focus exercises, Evelyn!" called Emerson as she darted for the door.

"I will!" she yelled back.

The only useful thing she could do was magic, which meant that she'd need magic to escape. Her textbook of focusing spells and the garden full of Hexteria-free food seemed like the best places to start, so *of course* she would practice!

The next class was geography, and it was taught by Marcia.

"Good afternoon, class!" said Marcia.

"Good afternoon, Miss Breswick."

"Here's your map!" said Marcia, handing Ev a many-folded piece of paper.

Ev had learned a lot of Geography in Inner. The pictures of how the world used to be were fascinating, once you got through the reminders about how none of it existed anymore.

Geography was a complex subject that covered a wide array of topics, but, at Alerrawia, it seemed to consist of pointing at things on a map.

It was the longest 25 minutes of Ev's life.

"Does anyone have any questions?" asked Marcia.

"I do," said Ev. "Will we learn about cumulonimbus clouds in this class?" She'd always liked the word, even if she couldn't quite remember what cumulonimbus clouds were.

"There are no 'clouds' here, so I fail to see how that would be useful," said Marcia, "and in this class we raise our hands and wait to be called on before speaking. Remember that."

A world without clouds? That didn't seem right. . .

After geography, Ev, Jonah, and Amy had physical education, or PE. PE was taught in the basement, and there was no way to get there on time even if they broke the rules and ran all the way, so they didn't bother.

"You need to be careful. Marcia loves sending Inner kids to the bad place," said Jonah as they wandered down the stairs.

The 'bad place' was really starting to worry her. The grown-ups had another word for it, but Ev couldn't say that word. She couldn't even think it. If she tried, she froze in place. It was the same for all the kids.

"Oh, look at this, children not in class!" With a pop, the little gray pixie, Boaclick, appeared right next to Ev's ear. "Now, what should I do with you, I wonder?"

"You clean toilets," said Jonah. "You can't do anything to us."

"Just because I'm your maid doesn't mean I can't get creative. . .Let's see, who might be available at this time of day to send some naughty children to detention. . ."

Stop it!

"Ouch!"

A bobcat appeared out of nowhere, pinning Boaclick to the ground.

"Oh, naughty Mr. S!" came an elderly voice. "You do so like to play!"

Granny Oakwood strolled into view. "Mr. Snugglebottom likes to play with the pixies," she explained, ignoring Boaclick's yelps. "Shouldn't you children be in class?"

"We're trying to get to the basement for PE," said Ev. "But there isn't enough time."

"There never is." Granny reached into her bag, said, "Here you go!" and handed each of them a laminated square of cardboard that read:

Permission to be out of class.

Validity: Forever

Signed: Granny Oakwood.

"If anyone bothers you when moving from class to class, just show them this. It should make things a little easier."

"Thank you," said Ev.

"Not in a hurry to follow your friends?" Amy and Jonah had grabbed the permission slips with huge smiles and hurried down the stairs.

"I'm not really meant to be here," said Ev. "None of what matters to them matters much to me."

"Ah, so they *are* your friends?"

"I guess. . ." said Ev through gritted teeth. "Doesn't mean I need them!"

"Of course! But don't look a gift horse in the mouth—it's very unusual for more than one child to be taken from Inner at a time. You could easily have been all on your own."

Ev found Granny's reasonableness annoying, but the old lady was in a chatty mood, and she didn't want to waste the opportunity.

"Why *did* they take three of us, then?"

"No idea," said Granny. "But I do know that Alerrawia only takes the most magically gifted children from Inner. I know my daughter was twice as strong as me, and my grandson is four times as strong. I know that I could best my own grandfather in any magical contest since I was twelve. And I know that children from Inner have always been stronger than us Alerrawians anyway, which is why we keep stealing you. My daughter and grandson, for example—they were both from Inner too."

Ev wondered if her own mother had ever spoken of her with such pride.

"The point I am trying to make is that what matters to them *must* matter to you because they are your friends, and you are in this together. Look after each other."

Why did everyone think she needed help?

"I also think that you have something of mine," said Granny. "My mirror?"

For moment Ev didn't know what Granny was talking about and then she remembered.

"I didn't mean to," she mumbled. "I can give it back tomorrow."

"Oh, no need for that. You can hang on to it. In fact, I think it might be quite important for you to keep it with you at *all times*. Understand?"

Perplexed, Ev nodded.

"Good! Now, you are a student, and I am a teacher, so it is my duty to remind you that you are late for class. Get going!"

Ev felt a surge of power from Granny that gently propelled her on.

"Come on, you!" said Granny to Mr. Snugglebottom. He immediately let go of Boaclick.

"That monster is a menace!" said Boaclick.

"I am so sorry," said Granny, as Ev hurried down the stairs to the basement. "He sometimes gets confused and thinks that people are making life difficult for his children when obviously they're not. Right, Boaclick?"

Ev didn't hear Boaclick's answer.

She made it to the basement without further incident and joined Amy and Jonah at the back of the group where they were pretending to do jumping jacks.

This class was taught by Shaun Brown, the last and least of The Seven. He blew a whistle, and everyone stopped.

"Class!" he said, but he could hardly be heard over the noise of chatting children. "Class!" He stormed out of the room in a huff.

"So. . .is that the end of the lesson?" asked Ev.

Jonah shrugged. "Who knows? Maybe he's gone to get somebody…"

Shaun returned, carrying a long rod.

"What's that?"

"No idea. . ."

Shaun held the rod above his head, swung it around three times, and then flicked it toward the gathered children, as if he was casting a fishing line.

Ev's hearing vanished.

Ah. This again.

She looked around. Jonah was on the floor, gasping for air and Amy was staggering around blindly. Ev grabbed her and said, "It's alright, I've got you". She couldn't hear what she was saying, but Amy could. She clung gratefully to Ev.

Ev guided her back to Jonah. There wasn't much they could do for him except hold his hand until it was over.

A few seconds later, it was, and Ev's ears filled with the sobs of her classmates.

"Quiet!" yelled Shaun.

This time, everyone listened.

"Good. We are now going to split into teams to play rounders."

Even with the mass RDD at his fingertips, Shaun was a useless teacher. He didn't have a plan, just ran around pointlessly on short fat legs trying to convince the children to play properly. Once he had a few kids lethargically throwing and hitting balls, he sat on a beanbag chair with a satisfied look on his face.

"I think I've just understood the whole toad thing," whispered Ev to Jonah.

Jonah sniggered. "I'm Shaun (and definitely not Sean!). I am NOT a toad! OBEY ME!"

The three of them started giggling uncontrollably, and they had to duck behind a group of bored classmates to keep Shaun from seeing them.

"What shall we do now?" asked Jonah when the bell rang. Ev glanced at her schedule and said, "Well, my next class is on the *thirteenth floor*, so I guess it's the elevator for me. . ." she trailed off. Amy and Jonah were looking at her strangely.

"You have another class?" asked Jonah.

"Don't you?"

Amy gently took Ev's schedule from her. Her face went white, and she showed it to Jonah.

"Ah," said Jonah. "Um, so… I guess you have a schedule conflict, because it looks like you have an extra one-on-one class with Robert. In his office."

Robert. . .he was the one who thought that Ev and her 'kind' were a waste of space.

"He hates me," she said.

"He hates all magical kids. You know that jerk, Peter? Robert is his uncle. . ."

"I don't have time to worry about family trees! How do I get there on time?"

"You can't. Just go—the later you are the worse it will be!"

She gave her friends a worried wave and set off grimly for what would surely be the worst class of all. She would die if she tried to take the stairs, so she squeezed herself into the elevator, only hesitating for a moment when she saw that Derek and Peter were in there with her. There were too many other people in the elevator for them to actually do anything to her.

She was so wrapped up in her own worry that she didn't really notice when the elevator almost completely emptied on the sixth floor. On the tenth floor, when the two grown-ups stepped out, she suddenly realized that it was just her and the bullies left. She darted for the already closing door, but she was too late.

"Where are you off to, I wonder?" asked Derek.

"She has a lesson with my uncle on thirteenth now," said Peter. "I said there was no way she'd be there on time, and I was right. She's out of class when she should be in! We can tell on her!" His face shone with glee.

"That doesn't seem very interesting now, does it?" said Derek, quietly.

"Well, no, I guess not, but you know, we shouldn't do anything *too* bad…"

"I have this!" said Ev, pulling out Granny's hall pass.

Derek took it, read it, and then, carefully, tore it up into tiny pieces. Then he grabbed her arm and twisted it behind her back. She screamed.

"Hurting her seems far more fun," said Derek.

He threw her to the floor. She scrambled away from them, trying to get to her feet, but when she stood up, Derek punched her in the face, and she went down again.

Panic began to rise.

One, two boys, one, two bullies, one, two threats. . .

"Derek," said Peter nervously. "Derek, that's a bit far…"

"You're not questioning me, are you, Peter?" asked Derek, in a tone of voice that Ev recognized well. He sounded just like Jonah. He was angry, so very angry, and Ev didn't know why.

"Why are you mad at me?" she whimpered from the floor. "What did I do?"

"Did I say you could speak?" asked Derek. He approached.

Stop them!

Ping!

The elevator doors slid open revealing Eliza Faraday, the oldest member of The Seven.

"What is going on here?" she demanded, sharply.

"Nothing, Miss Faraday," said Ev, at the exact same moment that Derek snapped out, "Nothing Ma'am!"

"Yes, in my experience, 'nothing' always involves a child lying in pain on the floor while two older boys stand over her menacingly," said Eliza, drily.

"I fell down," said Ev. "Hit my face on the wall. Elevators are very confusing." She was absolutely certain that getting Derek in trouble would only make things worse next time.

"Fine," said Eliza, getting into the elevator. "But I must say, I am disappointed, with all three of you. You especially, Derek. You're showing such promise as an assistant flying instructor. Why the need to lash out at those who are weaker than you?"

Derek didn't answer, but Ev could see that he was fuming.

The elevator doors opened on the thirteenth floor.

"Here we are," said Eliza, "although I suspect that only two of us actually have business here."

She stepped out, beckoning for Ev to follow. "Don't look back," she said. "They're embarrassed enough as it is."

"Is this student with you?" asked a guard.

"She has catch up lessons with Rayner. She should be on your list." So, Eliza Faraday knows my class schedule, thought Ev. I wonder why?

"I'm sure you have your reasons," said Eliza, leading Ev around the thirteenth floor, "but you should not let people hurt you."

"I don't intend to," said Ev.

Eliza looked at her doubtfully, and Ev matched her stare. She wasn't going to let people hurt her—it was just that Peter and Derek weren't really the main threat.

They continued in silence until they reached the door marked *Robert Rayner, of The Seven*. "Enter!" said Robert when Eliza knocked.

Robert's office was enormous, bigger than any of the classrooms she'd seen. It had a rich carpet and comfortable furniture, bookshelves full of unread books, and not a single window.

"Why are *you* here?" he asked Eliza, angrily.

"I ran into Evelyn on the elevator, thought I'd show her the way."

"She's late!"

"Of course, she is. It is impossible to get here on time. I suggest that you factor that into your future lesson plans. I'll leave you to it." Eliza vanished as abruptly as she'd appeared, and Ev was left alone with Robert.

"What happened to your face?" he demanded.

"I fell down," said Ev.

"Huh! Likely story! Fighting is punishable with detention!"

"What isn't?" She'd promised herself that she would play nice, but Robert made her *so* angry.

"Sit!" he ordered, throwing a textbook at her.

It was called *Impulse Control for the Mentally Defective*.

"I think you've given me the wrong one," she said.

"There is only one textbook for this class. You are a magic-user. By definition, you are mentally defective. That is the first lesson of this class. Say it back to me!"

"No!"

With a smirk, Robert lifted his right hand. In it was an RDD.

"I'm mentally defective!" she said, quickly. After all, they were only words.

"Too late," said Robert. He blasted her, and Ev instantly lost her voice. One of the easy ones, but she clutched at her throat anyway, because Robert wouldn't be happy unless *she* was unhappy.

"What are you?" asked Robert.

Ev couldn't answer. She pointed at her throat, desperately.

"Don't want to answer, do we? Let's try again."

He pointed and clicked. This time Ev lost the use of her legs. She fell to the floor with a shout.

"Naughty girl, lying on the floor during class."

He hit the button again. Ev went deaf. Tears rolled down her face, but they were tears of anger rather than of fear. Hopefully, Robert didn't know the difference.

"Had enough?" he asked, once the punishment ended.

"Yes, sir," she said, hoping she sounded meek enough.

"Turn to page 1 and read it out loud."

Ev read, letting her mind wander so she wouldn't have to focus on the disgusting words. She wondered what would happen if she just burned Robert now. If she was clever, she might even get away with it.

But she couldn't use her fire—the Hexteria in her system had seen to that. On the outside, nothing changed. On the inside, she crumbled. She was exhausted. She was trapped. Worst of all, she was powerless.

"What did you learn on page 1?" snapped Robert.

"Magic users are evil and must be taught impulse control techniques to keep everyone else safe." There was no expression in her voice at all.

"Passable," conceded Robert reluctantly. "Let's continue with the practical side of the lesson."

Practical impulse control involved Robert making her as angry as possible and zapping her with the RDD if she reacted.

"You're a worthless brat who should have died under the ground like your filthy ancestors!" he yelled. She found that one easier to ignore—it was, after all, pretty much what everyone here thought of her, so she'd had some practice.

"We should cut up your friends and feed them to the dragon," really got to her, which was annoying.

"The best use of your magic would be to rip it out of you and use it for something that actually matters," stung surprisingly hard.

"There is no one here that loves you," however, didn't make the slightest impression.

Robert learned very quickly what would make her angry. By the end of the lesson, she had been RDDed thirty-six times. Only twice had she lost her ability to breath, and once her ability to think. The rest had been unpleasant but bearable.

Ev wasn't learning anything about impulse control, but she *was* learning. She was learning that there were only about seven settings on an RDD. She was learning that if she was angry, she didn't panic. And she was learning that all Robert wanted was for her to be afraid. She remembered to scream. She remembered to ask him to stop. It was easier that way.

"That will do for today," said Robert, eventually. "As suspected, you are the worst of the worse. You have no ability to rein in your evil impulses, and I despair of ever teaching you how. But we'll keep trying." He smiled.

"Yes, sir," said Ev, obediently.

"Get out!" he yelled.

The guard looked at her sympathetically as she left. "Don't worry, you'll get the hang of it," he said, and Ev hated him. Grown-ups that let other grown-ups hurt kids were just as bad, maybe even worse. . .

She found Amy and Jonah in the library. Their faces fell when they saw hers.

"Did he do that?" asked Jonah, pointing at her face. "Robert is not supposed to hit students!"

"What? Oh that. No, that was some angry kid named Derek."

"Maybe you should tell someone?"

"What would the point be? Let's just go to supper."

"Look, don't be mad at us, all right?" said Jonah defensively. "We didn't know how to warn you, and it's not like you can skip the class."

"I'm not mad," said Ev. "I'm just thinking."

She thought all the way to the common area.

"Griffin sausages. Peas. Mashed potatoes," said a bored pixie as she spooned food onto Ev's plate. Ev carefully pushed the sausages to one side. The meat could talk. Cooked food also blocked her magic. Vegetarianism was the easy choice if you thought about it.

Amy and Jonah were watching her nervously.

"You know that we're not mentally defective, right? Magic is used for everything. But magic is also evil and can't be trusted. So, they tell us a lie—we're just mentally defective brats, and they're doing us a favor by letting us live here. Do you see?"

Amy nodded vigorously, but Jonah just looked at his lap.

"Jonah?" said Ev. "You know they're wrong, don't you?"

"They're grown-ups, and we're just kids. How would we know?"

"They are wrong," said Ev, firmly.

Suddenly, Amy hugged her.

"Hey, what are you doing?" she demanded, but Amy's grin was infectious, and Ev found herself grinning back. "You're really strange, you know that?"

Jonah's face lit up and he grabbed the chance to change the subject. "Should we finish our homework down here?" he asked, pointing to the open study area, and Ev and Amy agreed.

The history of magic essay on the original seven was Ev's top priority, because she didn't want to be sent to the bad place. She wanted to practice her focusing skills but instead she dutifully moved the homework for her nicer teachers to the bottom of the pile, just like *Inner: How and Why?* had recommended. There was too much homework, and she had to prioritize work for the teachers who would punish her the most, and even then, it was a push to get it all done before the bedtime bell rang.

Exhausted, Ev dragged herself up the stairs and into bed, only to find that someone had stuck one of the ugly posters on the ceiling: *Experiment on the Magical for the Safety of All!*

She was too tired to do anything, so she just lay there, staring at the poster. After a while, Stacey and Madison picked up their conversation, but Ev could hear the disappointment in their voices. They'd hoped she'd react to the poster, and she hadn't. Why would she give them what they wanted?

She pulled Felix's book about Alerrawia from under her pillow and looked up the words *Inner* and *experiment* in the index. Experimenting on people was terrible, sure, but she didn't want to be the only person who didn't know anything about it.

It had taken the Granite Institute a while to figure out that the best way to keep children from realizing they had powers was to remove them from their parents at age five and raise them in isolation. If there was no one to accidentally tell them they were magical, and no other children to accidentally set on fire during play, then all they needed was Hexteria to keep them in the dark. The goal was to raise every magical child in an Inner-like compound, only removing those who were needed for specific tasks, hence the Vendavi 2 simulations.

The experiment was called a 'great success.'

Ev's skull tingled. She was angry, angry that she'd been robbed of a proper family, angry that the truth had been kept from her, but most of all she was angry because, no matter what they said, there was no actual proof for magic being any more or less evil than non-magic.

In the end, exhaustion won over anger, and Ev drifted into an uncomfortable sleep.

Ev's brain must have been very busy while she slept because the next morning she sprang out of bed and started getting ready the moment the bell rang, her mind buzzing with a plan.

"Oh, so now she's trying to show us up," said Madison. "Unless you have another goal. . ." The older girl's brow furrowed in confusion and then cleared. "Well, luckily I don't have to care about the plans of Inner brats, so you remain irrelevant!"

"Well said," said Madam, stalking into the room. Chloe close on her heels.

"Hello girls!" said Chloe, with brittle cheerfulness.

Madam and Chloe were a strange team. Maybe they were put together *because* they were complete opposites, not in spite of it. Madam kept Chloe from being too much of a pushover, and Chloe kept Madam from doing whatever she liked. You might even be tempted to call it a perfect solution, if you ignored the more obvious option of hiring people who were good at their jobs.

Madam took a step closer to Ev as Chloe inspected the room. Ev just could see the RDD sticking out of Madam's overalls, and she was suddenly gripped by yet another idea. She took a deep breath, screwed up her eyes, and screamed as long and as loud as she could.

"Stop that!" said Madam. She grabbed Ev by the shoulders, shaking her. "Stop that!"

"What's wrong, Evelyn?" asked Chloe.

"I was confused," said Ev, with what she hoped was a convincing sob. "I thought Madam was going to hurt me again."

Madam slapped her across the face.

"Gwyneth!" said Chloe, shocked. "You *cannot* do that! I'm reporting you!"

"Don't you dare, or I'll…" The rest of her sentence was lost in the distance as she ran after Chloe.

"Well, now you're marked for death," said Madison, conversationally. "I would bring flowers to your funeral, but I won't be there." With a half wave, she and Stacey left.

Ev turned her back to Siobhan and carefully stuffed the RDD she'd stolen from Madam as far down the side of her bag as it would go. She heard it clink against Granny's mirror. She didn't plan to use it, but now Madam couldn't use it either.

She dashed out the room while Siobhan was still busy. Like the other children, Ev was keen to get to the first floor as quickly as possible. Unlike the other children, she had no intention of going to the common area. Instead, she headed straight out into the grounds, grabbing some Suncharm on her way out.

Another bright, boiling hot day. No clouds, no rain. . . The lack of clouds really bothered her. Didn't you need rain for the water cycle to work?

She walked purposefully to the garden and hoped that no one would wonder why she was there. She had no intention of going to lunch, or breakfast, or supper.

Hexteria was avoidable, and no one got to stifle a part of her without her permission.

Quickly and quietly, she shoved as many vegetables as she could into her bag, eating some as she went. They were bitter, but she could live with it.

In the distance, she heard the bell. By the time she got inside, everyone was already halfway up the stairs, so she dashed for the elevator instead, arriving at her Critical Thinking class just before the teacher, a tall blonde man named Declan Jones.

"Class, please turn to page 34," he said, once everyone had settled and Ev had her book. Page 34 was part of a section called *Logical Fallacies*. The section they were in was called *Slippery Slope*.

"Who would like to remind the class of the two fallacies we covered last time?" asked Declan. Siobhan, who Ev hadn't even realized was in her class because of how she just blended into the background, stumbled through an explanation of something called *ad hominem*, and some other boy (whose name Ev couldn't be bothered with) described something called *straw manning*, and Ev found herself completely fascinated. She'd always known that some arguments were better than others, but now she had the instruction manual.

"Now, let's talk about the slippery slope fallacy. A slippery slope argument starts with a benign premise and moves through a list of illogical jumps until you reach a highly unlikely conclusion. Inner is actually an excellent example of the slippery slope fallacy in action. The benign premise that the Granite Institute told the first generation born in Inner was that they were underground because everything else was destroyed. Through a series of illogical jumps, Inners eventually arrived at the conclusion that anyone who hadn't gone underground with them was dangerous and stupid. Not only that, but anyone who expressed the slightest disagreement with the ways of Inner was also dangerous and stupid. The Inner word for these people is 'Withouter'. Inners brush anything they disagree with aside and call it 'Withouter Thinking' without actually giving the situation or idea any real thought, but what else would you expect from mentally defective simpletons."

Ev's skull tingled and her fire sprang to life inside her, and she almost felt like she could use it, if she wanted to. No need to look at the words behind the words—he'd just come right out and said it.

Ev couldn't concentrate as Declan had the class analyze different arguments for signs of the slippery slope fallacy. As interesting as the topic was, she couldn't get passed the polite hatred of the calm, smiling man.

"You're all doing extremely well," said Declan. "Now, repeat after me. Magic is a disease that must be eradicated."

The class repeated the words, and Evelyn joined in, just so that Declan wouldn't have an excuse to punish her.

"Now let's take a moment to talk about what really matters – the supremacy of science. Critical thinking skills are only relevant in as far as they guide you to be better scientists. This means strictly guarding against your magical impulses."

Magic, bad; science, good, yes, I get it. . .

"Magic-users are a threat, the reason the rest of the world is gone," droned Declan. "They claim that magic is the true way, and that science should be eradicated completely. . .”

That wasn't true. She liked the science things as much as she liked the magic things.

“. . .but they are misguided. If they can be taught to see the light, that science is the one true way, they will be liberated to be who they truly are. I hope all of my students can learn to suppress their magic, for their own good, and the good of their friends. A small spell today could cause the world to end tomorrow. You can follow science, or you can use magic—you cannot do both.”

Ev looked critically at Declan. He was wearing his uniform, same as everyone else, and Ev knew that uniforms were made in Magical Manufacturing on the second floor. His teeth gleamed, which meant he saw Dr. Cody regularly. And she had definitely seen him eating pixie-prepared food in the common area.

Ev knew a lot of words. The word that sprang to mind now was 'hypocrite.'

“Why weren't you at breakfast?” asked Jonah after class.

“I had things to do,” she said, curtly. “Do lots of teachers think that smiling sweetly will hide the disgusting words that flop from their mouths?”

Ev was walking faster and faster, each step thudding angrily into the concrete floor.

“It's just what people say!” said Jonah, stifling a huge yawn.

"Why are *you* tired?"

"Didn't sleep. I kept hearing dripping. I got up three times to check the tap. Drip, drip, drip…"

"There's nothing scary about leaky taps!" said Ev, stifling her guilt. "And it's just a story. Things from stories can't hurt you."

"I know that!"

Amy joined them for history, which was taught by Mr. Cameron, a man dressed in full combat gear who yelled at them to line up next to their desks the moment they entered.

"Sit!" commanded Mr. Cameron.

When Ev was slower to sit than the other kids, Mr. Cameron pounced, demanded her name, and gave her a textbook, all in about three seconds.

Mr. Cameron should have been the PE teacher. He fired questions at them, and anyone who answered incorrectly had to run laps for the rest of the lesson. Jonah was running nearly from the beginning, but he went easy on Ev, probably because she was new. It was exhausting.

"You!" shouted Mr. Cameron at Jonah. "Last chance, or detention! Who are the True Users?"

"The…people…who…live…in…the…forest," panted Jonah, still running.

"Correct! Why are they dangerous?"

"They…use…magic…for…everything…"

"Correct! What is their threat level?"

"Low…science…always…triumphs…"

"Good! Class dismissed!" A second after he spoke, the bell rang.

Individual training was next. This was where students were taught how to use their innate abilities, the things they could do without thinking. Except for flying, which was too common and required too much space to teach, all innate abilities were taught for all skill levels in one class.

It was a little crowded.

"We just wait until someone tells us to do something," said Jonah flopping, sweat pouring down his face.

"They'll release us from Hexteria?"

"If you're chosen to practice your ability, yes. But only if it's something that you absolutely can't learn just by reading about it."

"How do they do it?"

"I don't know! It's a top-secret spell. Wordless magic. We'll never know!"

It couldn't be *that* secret if even the teachers knew what it was. . .

As in spell work, Eliza and Christopher watched from the sidelines, just in case someone's innate ability was Spontaneous Rebellion. Ev watched as Ophelia, a short, gray-haired lady, had Derek practice lifting heavier and heavier objects, starting with one of the small cupboards in the room, which he lifted with one hand, and working up from there.

Oh good, the bully has super strength, just what we need. . .

"You seemed pretty good at reading my mind the other day. Even with Hexteria," said Ev, still watching Derek. Derek had torn up a laminated card as if it were tissue paper, but he should have been on Hexteria. . .

"I told you! Some of us are too sick to be cured!"

"Or just too strong to be controlled. . ."

Jonah's outburst had drawn the attention of Mr. Percy, the small, puffed-up little man who ruled the individual training classroom—in his mind, anyway.

"No shouting in class!" he shouted.

"Sorry, sir," said Ev, quickly.

Mr. Percy's head snapped round at the distant sound of giggles, and he stormed off. "No laughing in class!"

Ev watched Mr. Percy's random explosions all around the room until Ophelia asked her to step into a square drawn on the ground.

"You haven't been officially diagnosed, but it seems that you innate abilities are flight and fire," she said. "Hold still for a moment." Ophelia stared at her, and Ev felt something change inside her. Suddenly, she could *feel* her fire ability coursing through her veins, ready to be used.

"Your magic cannot extend beyond this square," said Ophelia, "so don't worry about hurting anyone. You can't."

Ah, so they removed one barrier and added another, thought Ev. Of course.

"Now, show me your fire."

Ev stared at her blankly. Up until now, she'd only used her fire by accident. She didn't know what to do!

Eliza strolled over to watch, and suddenly Ev was angry. She was angry that Ophelia wasn't allowed to teach freely. She was angry about her teeth being pulled, and about Madam's RDD and about Robert, and Declan, and Derek. She was angry about a lot of things.

The tingling started at the base of her skull. She closed her eyes so she could feel it better. She knew what it was, now. She let it move down her arms and into her hands. She let the fire build up inside her and, just before it became unbearable, she let it go.

After a short while, Ophelia said quietly, "All right, that's enough, Evelyn."

Ev opened her eyes. She was surrounded by flames, and the shock of seeing them so close (but not *feeling* them) made them disappear. She could see the edges of the magical cube, now. It looked as if the air itself had been burned.

"Just stay where you are for a moment," said Ophelia, and you had to listen very carefully to hear the panic in her voice.

"Is something wrong?"

"Not at all, just give us a moment to confer."

Ophelia and Eliza put their heads together, whispering furiously as they walked to a quiet corner. . .

". . .but even if she'd had no Hexteria *at all* for three days, this display. . ."

". . .nothing to worry about, just keep an eye. . ."

. . .and then they were too far away for Ev to hear them anymore.

"Hi," said Ev, waving at a random of staring girls. They backed away quickly.

"This could be useful. . ." said Ev to herself.

The bell rang. Ophelia and Eliza didn't even look up, so Ev shrugged, stepped out of the burned cube, and joined Amy and Jonah as they left the class.

"Miss Acorn, why have you left your cube?" asked Christopher at the door.

"I guess I got confused," said Ev, sweetly. "The bell rang. There are just so many rules here—it's difficult to know what to do when."

Then, she walked out the room.

Inside, she was terrified. On the outside, she was calm and in control. Other children moved out of her way, and, when she arrived at her magical innovation class, a full five minutes late (because superheroes don't rush), someone actually offered her their seat so that she, Amy, and Jonah could all sit together.

"Thank you!" said Ev. "How very kind!"

Inside, she was desperately hoping that she wouldn't get into trouble. More importantly, she was hoping that no one would realize that she was still under the effects of the anti-Hexteria spell.

Magical innovation was followed by history of magic, but Ev couldn't pay attention. The only thing she cared about was her next lesson—flying. It was her best chance of escape, and she needed to learn everything she could.

Arriving at the flying arena she was reminded that this was the most common ability—Peter, Derek, and Siobhan were all there as well.

"You're the new Inner kid, right?" said the tall and imposing teacher in a quiet, but commanding voice. "I am Patti Gray—you will call me Miss Patti. I am told you can fly."

"I don't think she can *really* fly," said Peter behind her.

"I can!"

"Quiet! Ev, you can kick us off with a demonstration. Class, be prepared to give pointers and advice. Derek, help me run the lesson, will you?"

Miss Patti turned to Ev and stared at her. Now that she knew what was happening, Ev thought she could feel the anti-Hexteria spell taking hold. For the second time. *And* she hadn't had any Hexteria all day.

Flying should be easy, but Ev was nervous. The truth was that she had no idea how to fly. She'd only done it once outside a simulation, and that was by accident!

She clutched her bag close to her chest and tried to remember what it felt like. . .

"She can't do it," said Peter in a low, sing-song voice, breaking her concentration. "Evelyn can't fly! Evelyn can't fly!" Soon, the whole class was chanting, and Miss Patti didn't seem to care.

The sun beat down on her relentlessly. Sweat dripped down her back. She was embarrassed, she wanted to be anywhere in the world except where she was right now. Every fiber of her body wanted to escape, to get away, to never come back.

Go!

Ev leapt straight up into the air. She heard the wind rushing in her ears, and the gasps and shouts of her classmates. She swooped and turned to face them.

"Hi!" she yelled. "I'm Ev. Not Evelyn. Ev. Yes, I'm an Inner kid. Yes, I can fly better than you. Deal with it."

Then, because she didn't see any reason why she shouldn't, she closed her eyes, turned, and flew straight for the fence.

"Come back! Come back right now!" screamed Miss Patti, but why should she listen? What hold did any of these people really have over her? How dare they even *try* to control her?

Her skull tingled as her rage and fire grew. She had to let it out, and there was only one way to do that.

She screamed. Fire shot out behind her, until she'd exhausted her anger and had no more fire left.

When she stopped screaming, she opened her eyes and looked down.

The grounds of Alerrawia were nowhere to be seen. Instead, all around in every direction, was wilderness.

She glanced back—no one was following. For a moment, her confidence faltered. What if she'd hurt someone?

Did it matter? Granny and Karen would fix them up with some tortured combination of science and magic. They would be fine.

"Everything is fine," she said out loud.

She'd escaped. She didn't know what she would do next, but one thing was for sure: she was never going back.

9. Let Them!

Traitor

\\ˈtrā-tər\\

1. One who betrays the trust of an Alerrawian authority or who is false to their duty to serve Alerrawia

2. One who commits treason

Treason

\\'**trē-zᵊn**\\

1. Any attempts to overthrow or undermine the government of Alerrawia through overt acts or negligence

2. The betrayal of a trust

New Alerrawian Dictionary

15th Edition

There's nothing quite like flying through the air with nobody to tell you what you could and couldn't think.

Ev felt powerful, unstoppable, like she could rule the world.

In the distance, she could see the cooling towers of Inner. For a brief moment she considered going home, but that was impossible. She couldn't. Vendavi wouldn't let her in, and, even if he did, how could she live like that now? Anyway, Vendavi would probably just shoot her straight out of the sky.

She veered sharply to her right and kept flying, her hair streaming out behind her. Flying was easy.

"Why do we have to have lessons for this?" she asked herself. "I am invincible! I can fly forever!"

That turned out to be a lie very quickly. She started to feel tired, then hungry. She stopped spending her energy on swooping and just flew in a straight line. Then she started to feel irritated and grumpy.

Then she realized she was lost.

In the back of her mind, she heard a voice. It was entirely her own voice, but it was a little bit Vendavi's voice too.

I notice that you're thirsty, said the voice. That's probably something you're going to want to deal with before you die, although it's all the same to me.

She had to find water. And what about the Suncharm--she'd put some on, but how long would it last?

She was flying over thick, dense forest, which felt like a bad idea. She had a vague idea that people lived in the forest, people who couldn't be trusted. But at least she had a sense of where she was—Marcia's geography lessons had, at the very least, taught her where the lakes were, so she swerved in what she hoped was a more south-westerly direction to find Lake Beta. By this time, she was exhausted. Her mind went gray, and she just focused on staying in the air.

How long had she been flying? Minutes? Hours? It was so difficult to judge. She was starting to worry that she'd missed the lake altogether…

I WILL find it!

…when the trees thinned and suddenly, she was flying over the most water she'd ever seen in one place.

"Woohoo!" she screamed.

She was so excited she nearly dropped straight into the water but stopped herself just in time.

"Be sensible. There could be anything lurking about. Bobcats. Raccoons. Scout first, drink later."

She flew around a bit just above the ground at the lake's edge and, when nothing obvious tried to kill her, she landed and scooped some water into her mouth. She was still tired, but at least she wasn't thirsty anymore. With the last of her energy, she flew to the top of a tree to eat some raw vegetables and decide what to do next.

She'd have to find somewhere to stay. She couldn't live in a tree. She'd only taken a few vegetables, so she'd have to find food. Being near the lake seemed like a good idea, but that meant there would be animals around with the *same* idea.

"Ev!"

She jumped. Someone was calling her!

"Ev!"

She looked around desperately, but there was no one in sight.

"Look in the mirror, Ev!"

The voice was coming from her bag. She pulled out Granny's mirror, which now smelled like tomatoes. Instead of her own reflection, she was met with Granny's stern face.

I'm glad you're alright, but you have to come home, now!"

"No!"

"This is the wrong time for rebellion. Trust me." The old woman's voice was calm and slow. "You need to come home. If you do, they won't be as mad at you. If they have to come get you, they'll be really mad. Not just at you. At everyone. At Amy and Jonah. Maybe even at me. There is a time and a place, Ev. This is not it."

Granny's words were reassuring, almost hypnotic, but even though she'd only been around magic for a few days, Ev was learning to recognize it.

She shook her head quickly to dislodge the spell and said, "I'm not going back to that horrible place!"

"Ev, please…"

"No!"

She shoved the mirror back into her bag, but her balance was off, and she accidentally dropped the whole bag.

"No!"

No!

Luckily, it got stuck on some lower branches. She could still hear Granny calling her name, but it was muffled and easier to ignore. Eventually, Granny stopped.

"I don't need friends," she said out loud. It made her feel better. Sad, but more in control.

She was starting to worry, just a little. What was she going to do?

The bushes rustled.

"Hello?" she said, nervously.

There was definitely movement, dead ahead. The low-lying bushes swayed as something pushed its way through.

"Who's there?"

Out of the greenery, a face emerged. It was a face that looked like it was wearing a mask. It was small, with small arms and legs, and a stripy tail.

"Oh, it's just a raccoon!" she said, and immediately wished she hadn't. The raccoon looked up, saw her, and *waved*.

Without thinking, Ev waved back.

Moments later, hundreds of raccoons poured out of the undergrowth. They slowly drew nearer, circling Ev's tree.

Can raccoons climb?

Ev thought longingly of the RDD she'd stolen from Madam. If she was careful, she might be able to climb down and get her bag before the raccoons attacked. Probably. Maybe.

The raccoons were acting strangely. Ev was no animal expert, but she was fairly certain that they won't supposed to use human hand signals to communicate. Some looked like they were hiding sniggers behind their little raccoon hands.

A raccoon screeched and the others turned to look at it. It made a complex series of hand gestures. Moments later, the raccoons jumped into action.

A long line of raccoons lined up on their hind legs in a perfect row at the base of Ev's tree. Then more raccoons climbed onto the shoulders of the first lot. This happened over and over again until they'd built a perfectly symmetrical raccoon pyramid.

The leader, who Ev thought was also the one who had waved at her, climbed all the way to the top of the pyramid. It was now eye height with Ev and only a few yards away.

"Hello?"

Please don't hurt me!

The raccoon looked at her for a moment, and then suddenly grinned. It turned its head to the sky, screeched once, loudly, and the pyramid melted away instantly. Seconds later, the raccoons were gone, and she was alone again.

"Did that just happen?" she asked of no one in particular.

Maybe they were just an advance party. Maybe they'd gone to tell something else, something worse, that she was there.

Ev was shaking. She took a few deep breaths to calm herself, but the shaking didn't stop.

Then she realized that the whole *tree* was shaking.

Then she heard the sound.

DOOF! Shake... *DOOF!* Shake...

The ground quaked. With a huge crack, the trees straight ahead parted as two enormous hands pushed them aside.

A giant.

There was a giant right in front of her.

Ev immediately tried to call up the game menu to select a combat spell, but then she remembered she wasn't in a simulation this time. All she could think of was the message Vendavi blared every time she played *Giant's Shipyard.*

Remember player: Sunlight and shipyards no longer exist! Giants and magic never existed in the first place! To believe otherwise is to stray onto the path of the Withouter.

"Are you the one who's been flying around all afternoon?" someone asked, loudly.

Ev's eyes were glued to the giant, so it came as a complete surprise that there were other people clustered around the giant's feet.

"Hello?" said the man, impatiently. He had a brown bushy beard, a self-important voice, and a slight stoop, even though he didn't look very old. "Can you speak?"

"Giant," was all Ev could manage.

"Well spotted," said the giant. Its voice was loud, but it didn't rumble and echo across the forest, like Ev expected. It sounded just like a normal voice, but bigger. "I am a giant, one of the 'monsters' *your* people claim no longer exist, yet here I am, undermining everything you've been taught to believe. I could crush you with my big toe and not even realize it. I am more than you and everyone you know combined. You can call me Taylor."

Being addressed by a giant was terrifying, but there was a twinkle in their eye that didn't match its words one little bit.

"Are you…" she swallowed, "Are you messing with me?"

"Well, I mean, I *could* crush you with my big toe, if I really wanted to, but it does leave rather a mess."

"Good to know. Also, no offense, Taylor, but you're almost a week too late. Everything I thought was true crumbled into dust days ago."

"Where are you from?" interrupted another, uninteresting voice from the ground. This voice came from a tall blonde woman. Ev ignored her.

"Are you a he or a she?" she asked Taylor, because 'it' didn't seem like the right word to use.

"I'm a 'they,'" said Taylor.

"It's nice to meet you."

"Likewise. Most people who come from that direction tell me I don't exist, and then they try to kill me to make it true."

"Which direction is that?"

"Alerrawia."

"Yup, that sounds about right."

"Now, if you would be so kind as to answer my friend's question: where *are* you from?"

"Inner. Well, I mean, Alerrawia, but Inner until a few days ago."

"And you flew all this way?"

"Yes. . ." said Ev, wearily. Next they would tell her she couldn't possibly have flown that far. . .

"What's your name?" asked a boy. He was dark-skinned, but with bright blue eyes. Until that moment, Ev hadn't even noticed that there were children in the group.

"Ev," she answered.

"Ev? Amazing! The statistical likelihood of meeting you like this was extraordinarily low! What are you doing here?" asked the boy.

"Do I know you?"

"Depends on your definition of 'know'," said the boy.

An idea was starting to form in Ev's mind.

"You can't be…"

"Looks like you've arrived at the logical conclusion," interrupted the boy. "I'm Mike. Nice to make your acquaintance in person."

"This is the part where you tell us what to do with her," said the blonde woman, her voice heavy with sarcasm.

"Thank you, Ray-Leigh," said Mike, apparently oblivious to the woman's disdain. Ray-Leigh rolled her eyes so hard Ev thought she might hurt herself.

"Ev," said Mike, "would you kindly extricate yourself from that tree and accompany us?"

"What if I say no?" she asked.

"Forgotten me already?" said Taylor, pretending to be hurt. They reached out with one enormous hand and gently plucked Ev from her hiding place. Ev struggled briefly, but Taylor squeezed her lightly and she immediately stopped.

"I could set you all on fire, you know," said Ev, but only after Taylor had set her down safely in front of Mike.

"Oh, you mean like this?" asked Mike. Casually, he snapped his fingers and Ev's tree was immediately engulfed in flames.

"Something like that," she muttered. She was starting to remember that the forest people used magic for everything. Every day. Which meant they were probably a lot better at it.

"You don't look like how I imagined," she told Mike, "but I'm glad you're not dead, I guess."

"I am somewhat exuberant regarding this fact myself."

"Can we start heading back now, or is the plan to stand around in this indefensible position *all* day?"

Again, Mike completely ignored the Ray-Leigh's sarcasm.

"We will return home with our new friend," he said.

"Take her to the camp?" Ray-Leigh was white with rage and shock. "That would be…"

"Just fine, with the proper precautions. Blindfold her if you like."

Grumbling constantly, Ray-Leigh tied a blindfold much too tightly around Ev's eyes.

"Hey!" shouted Ev. She scrabbled at her face, trying to take it off, but Mike grabbed one of her hands and Ray-Leigh grabbed the other.

"Ev," said Mike, in an annoyingly reasonable tone, "we have to blindfold you. Usually, we kill people from Alerrawia on sight. However, you don't appear to be a spy, so we're taking you home for questioning, but we can't let you see where we're going. Its blindfold or death. Which would you prefer?"

"Blindfold," mumbled Ev.

With a heavy, theatrical sigh, Ray-Leigh shouted, "Move out!"

Mike steered Ev firmly through the forest. She couldn't see a thing, but she could hear the group chattering and laughing, and she could feel as well as hear Taylor's footsteps.

Unfortunately, she could also hear the things the children were saying.

"She's from Inner, though."

"Yeah, but she lives in Alerrawia now, and they're all crazy there. They think magic is bad." This last sentence was delivered in a self-important voice of no more than eight. There were murmured agreements, as if this was the only piece of evidence anyone could possibly need.

"Don't mind them," said Mike at her side, "The True Users are only here because of what Alerrawia did, which understandably has led to some animosity. Also, the heathens do insist on tainting their magic."

"Tainting their magic?"

"With science," sneered Ray-Leigh. There was so much venom in her voice that Ev decided it was safer to just stop talking.

Mike decided to entertain her with the story of how he landed up in the forest.

"I did what was required – I reported the unforeseen glitch with Vendavi to the Appropriate Authorities, immediately, and followed all protocols to the letter."

Of course you did, thought Ev.

"I was bombarded with the usual communications, 'Stand by for assistance', and so on, so I waited. Then a tunnel opened, similar to the day of my fifth birthday. It wasn't unprecedented for Inner residents to be called out of their cells for important missions, and I assumed that I would be asked to speak to the higher ups about my experiences with Vendavi. The order came to crawl, so naturally, I obeyed."

As if the Appropriate Authorities would *ever* have spoken to him about his little bug report!

"I crawled for what felt like an eon, but which was probably more realistically closer to an hour or two. I was starving *and* boiling by the time I reached my journey's end. You've noticed the ridiculously high temperatures outside of Inner, I assume?"

She nodded.

"Awful, isn't it? Well, anyway, I was overjoyed when I eventually spied my means of egress."

But when the hatch opened, all he could see on the other side was darkness. He had never had the caution of the other children. He always trusted the rules. So, he climbed out and fell into a hot, broken world that wasn't supposed to be there.

The hatch immediately slammed shut behind him. A brief announcement, in Vendavi's voice, followed.

Note: You have been exiled. Do not attempt to return to Inner.

"I was so confused and scared. . ." his voice trailed off.

Ev's skull tingled, but this first time she was angry for someone other than herself. Mike *was* the most annoying person alive, but that didn't mean he deserved to be abandoned.

Luckily, the True Users (as the forest dwellers called themselves) knew about the exile hatch and kept a lookout posted nearby to collect any lost and confused souls who made their way through.

"How did you feel, suddenly surrounded by all these Withouters?" Ev asked.

"Relieved. . .look, you should consider revising your vocabulary. 'Withouter' is not a word we use here."

"I don't care if I insult anyone."

"It's not that. In my experience, people do not find it insulting. They find it quaint and silly. When you use the word, they think, 'there goes a child who knows nothing about anything, let's laugh at them, or ignore them, or yell at them because there's no helping them.'"

"Sounds like you're speaking from experience..."

"And then there's Inner," said Mike, ignoring her. "Another quaint and silly idea."

"Is that so?" asked Ev.

"The fact of the matter is that Inner was, and continues to be, a failed experiment," said Mike. "Completely pointless. What's the point of locking people away so they can't contribute to the war effort? And to crush their magic. . .What a pointless waste."

"That's a very. . .economical way to look at it."

"Inner didn't even do much in the way of generating intellectual property for the Granite Institute, you know, and the working adult groups haven't produced anything worth knowing in decades. Even those on the side of the science-followers thought it was a flawed idea. They would have shut the whole thing down if the war had ended differently."

"How could you know that?"

"Everyone who gets exiled from Inner ends up with the True Users. We share what we know. The opportunity to live in magical purity is an advantage that *cannot* be understated."

"Magic is a disease that must be eradicated," said Ev automatically. Then she froze in horror. "I'm sorry! It's just what they make us say, and they all use it all the time anyway for their inventions. . ."

"We do not taint our magic with science," said Mike, stonily.

"Isn't that a little. . .well. . . just like Alerrawia, but the opposite?"

"Actually, it's a truly wonderful society, once you accept their truth of their ways," said Mike. "Here for a few months and already I'm their leader."

Ev stopped dead in her tracks.

"Say what now?"

"I'm their leader," said Mike, trying to sound modest and failing miserably. "You see, there's this test, and. . ."

"Helicopters!" shouted Ray-Leigh.

All around Ev, people started to move. Now she could hear the sound of whirring engines, drawing closer.

A voice boomed from the sky.

"Attention! You have kidnapped an Alerrawian student. Release her immediately or face the consequences!"

Mike let go of her hand. She ripped the blindfold off to find that the True Users had surrounded her and Mike and were casting what looked like shield spells in every direction.

"How did they find us?" ask Ray-Leigh.

"Tracking charm?" asked Mike.

Ray-Leigh snorted. "And you were going to take her back to the camp!" she hissed.

Taylor was watching the helicopters. The helicopters were firing bullets at them, but they just bounced of their skin, leaving no damage at all. One of the helicopters got a little too close, and the giant sprung, smashing it out of the air. The other helicopters backed away quickly.

On the ground, Ray-Leigh was darting this way and that, avoiding the gunfire from the remaining helicopters with unbelievable speed. She was also firing spells every few seconds, as were two of the children. The air was filled with gunfire and cries of "Light 'em up!"

None of the magic seemed to make the lightest difference.

"Take cover!" yelled Mike.

"Now he wakes up. . ." muttered Ray-Leigh.

They took cover among the trees, three True Users keeping a shield over Mike, and, because he was gripping her arm with all his strength, Ev as well. There was at least one person lying on the ground who would never get up again.

Suddenly, there was silence. No one was firing. No one was speaking.

"Look, just release her and we'll go," said a tired voice from one of the helicopters.

"We didn't take her. She came to us. Maybe you're the ones who need to let go," said the loud bearded man.

"I think not," said the helicopter, followed by a barrage of bullets.

"Cease fire!" shouted the bearded True User. "Give us a moment to confer. . ."

Mike, Ray-Leigh, and the loud man had a whispered conference, just far enough away that Ev couldn't hear what they were saying, but she found out what their decision was when they abruptly shoved her out into the open.

“Don’t shoot! Don’t shoot! This is her! Take her and be gone!”

*

Ev was locked in a room. Again. It was starting to become a bit of a habit.

She was almost certain that it was the bearded man, but it might have been Ray-Leigh, who had given her up to the Alerrawian troops. She also thought she’d heard Mike shouting, “Wait!” Or maybe it was someone else. Everything had been too loud and confusing.

Someone had swung down from a helicopter, grabbed her, and swung back up again, before she could move or think. In hindsight, she wondered if someone had cast a spell on her to stop her struggling, and, if so, whether it was True Users or Alerrawians who’d done it.

Probably the True Users. Alerrawia wouldn’t give a gun to anyone who could use magic.

On the helicopter, someone had RDDed her until they’d found the motor functions setting and someone else had put a bag over her head and tied her hands behind her back. That was how she travelled back to Alerrawia; in darkness and unable to move.

Someone carried her out of the helicopter and put her in this room. Someone, perhaps the same person, pulled the bag off her head, forcing her to squint her eyes at the sudden light. They untied her hands.

Then they left her, alone again.

278

She looked around the room. It was a small with a rickety camp bed in one corner. The only light was from a bare lightbulb in the center of the ceiling. A prison cell, in other words. There was no way to know what floor she was on.

So much for never coming back.

Eventually, Marcia and Christopher came to see her.

It turned out that running away from school was a very serious offense. So serious that even the bad place was too good for her. On top of that, when she'd fled, she'd injured Patti Gray, the teacher, as well as Derek. They'd been chasing her, trying to bring her back themselves without alerting the guards on the watchtowers (so they wouldn't get into trouble for losing a student). They were both in the med bay, unconscious, but they would be fine.

It turned out that the most grievous sin she had committed was to speak to the True Users at all. The fact that she'd been found 'associating with the enemy' (as Marcia put it) was completely unforgiveable.

"You're so young! To be a traitor, already, at your age."

Ev wondered how Alerrawia punished its traitors. Was there a death penalty? Was she going to be exiled? They wouldn't really do anything too terrible to a child, would they?

Would they?

She thought about Madam, doing whatever she liked in the name of discipline. She thought of Robert's impulse control lessons for the mentally defective. She thought of Shaun attacking his entire class with a mass RDD. She thought of Alicia snapping her fingers to send children instantly to a bad place none of them were allowed to talk about, just because they forgot their homework.

Her heart started racing. She fell back on the bed, too dizzy to stay upright. She couldn't breathe.

Count the ceiling tiles! One, two, three, four. . .

Later, Christopher returned.

. . .ninety-four, ninety-five. . .

She'd already counted the tiles twice and was almost finished with her third run.

"Well, this is no good," said Christopher. "Ev, the people's champion, cannot be derailed now."

Since when was she the 'people's champion?' She would have asked, but if she let her concentration break, she would really start panicking.

. . .one-hundred-and-one, one-hundred-and-two. . .

"Here," said Christopher, taking a small bottle of pills out of his pocket. "These are for calming the nerves. It's what Marcia takes to prepare herself for each and every Geography class, and I think Miss Leah wouldn't even know how to get out of bed without them."

He helped her sit and gave her one of the pills to dissolve under her tongue. It tasted sweet, and she felt better almost immediately.

"Thanks," she said, grudgingly. "What happens now?"

"Looks like we're going to have a disciplinary hearing," he said.

"A hearing?"

"That's what I said. In ten minutes. In front of everyone."

"I'm no expert, but shouldn't I be given a chance to prepare or something?" she asked.

"What's there to prepare?" asked Christopher with a shrug as he steered her out of the room. At the door were two heavily armed men who fell in behind them.

"If I'm going to defend myself. . ."

Ev's brain was screaming at her not to argue with a member of The Seven, a grown-up, who held her life in his hands. A smaller, more insistent part of her was saying, *why not? It's not as if I have anything to lose.*

The pill was working wonders. Her confidence was through the roof.

"You'll get to speak, but you're not really expected to defend yourself. Sometimes children from Inner have these quaint ideas about legal systems, as if they've been reading things that they shouldn't." Ev looked up guiltily, but Christopher just kept walking, head forward. "A disciplinary hearing is basically a public forum in which your punishment is decided."

"So, you expect me to just roll over and accept this? To not stand up for myself at all?"

"Did I say that? I'm just providing you with some much-needed information."

Ev's skull tingled, but her magic was locked away behind a wall of Hexteria—her options had been to eat or starve, and Marcia had been very clear that she would not be allowed to leave her cell until she was 'properly under control'. So, magic was out.

"I'll take it from here," said Christopher nodding to the guards. They glanced at each other uncertainly. "She's eleven years old!" said Christopher. "If you think I can't handle one little girl. . ."

"Of course not, sir!" snapped one of the men.

"I didn't like them hovering in my periphery," said Christopher. "I could feel my intelligence decreasing from the prolonged exposure. The guards are idiots," he said, seeing Ev's look of confusion. "Some are pretty idiots, some are useful idiots, some are deadly idiots, but they're all idiots."

Ev glanced back at the guards.

"Pretty and useful," said Christopher. "From left to right."

The guard labelled 'useful' looked back at them suspiciously.

"It's the useful ones you have to look out for the most. The deadly ones are very good at hurting you at the drop a hat, but they tend to lack reasoning skills. The pretty ones can also do a lot of damage, because they tend to rise to the top, but the useful ones are the most dangerous, because they like to think, and what they like to think about most is how, exactly, you are trying to trick them. They're not clever, you understand – but they do tend to stumble onto things you'd rather they didn't through sheer tenacity."

Christopher didn't like people, Ev realized. He didn't like anyone. Maybe a lot of guards were stupid, but they couldn't *all* be stupid—it was mathematically improbable, and anyway, 'stupid' meant whatever the person using the word wanted it to mean. Christopher didn't like the rest of The Seven, and he didn't seem to like children. Sometimes she thought he approved of her, but he didn't *like* her.

"I'm afraid things look pretty bad for you."

"Yeah, you said."

"Very bad," continued Christopher. "In fact, the only times I've seen a situation like this turn out well was when the accused talked their way out of it. There's a lot of chatter about how you flew halfway across the bubble when you should have been barely able to hover. I assume that's what Patti expected—she just wanted to put you in your place. Then you set her and Derek on fire and flew off into the sunset. It's all very. . .inconvenient for the narrative. It may have come to your attention that there's a little bit of rivalry between people born in Alerrawia and people born in Inner."

"I did manage to notice that, yes."

"The official line is that Alerrawians are more magically gifted than Inners. When you do things like this, it makes the lie harder to believe. It's a very bold move to draw more attention to it with a disciplinary hearing, but what do I know? I just work here."

"Um, I don't mean to be rude. . .," said Ev. "But why are you talking to me?"

"Why on earth would I talk to a traitor? The very thought."

She would have pressed him further, but they'd arrived in the basement. Ev's prison cell was *under* the basement level, and she'd had no idea it was there.

Christopher steered her up the stairs and into the common room. He led her to the enormous and ornate head table, which stood at ninety degrees to the rest of the tables. This was where The Seven ate, although she'd never seen them there before. Behind them, someone had erected a hastily painted sign about how people with magical abilities needed to be controlled.

Every table was full of silent grown-ups and children, all arrayed in their matching uniforms. The last rays of the afternoon sun filtered through the huge windows. Hundreds of pairs of serious eyes were on the head table, except for those who turned to glance at her as she was led through.

In front of the table was an empty space with a three-legged wooden stool that Christopher shoved her onto.

"Sit up straight and pay attention!" he barked at her.

He took his place at the table.

Ev could feel the eyes of Alerrawia burning into her back.

"Evelyn Acorn," began Felix. "You have disappointed us greatly since your arrival here. Not only did you harm a teacher and one of your fellow classmates using unauthorized magic, but you also fled the school and contacted the enemy. You are the worst traitor we have seen for some time."

Dead silence.

"What do you have to say for yourself?"

Ev was terrified, but terror had always been part of her life. Anyway, she had taken an anti-anxiety pill—being scared wasn't enough to keep her quiet now. Her skull tingled horribly, which also meant she was angry. Anger, she'd read once, was her body's way of warning her of danger, of protecting her. She couldn't let the fire out, but there were other things she *could* do.

In her mind, a voice a bit like Vendavi, but mostly like herself, said:

This is the final problem for today's lesson. Get it right, don't get it right, it's all the same to me. But if you get it wrong, there is nothing I can do to help you.

The fire pushed at the Hexteria boundaries, searching for a way out.

There is no danger here.

Then, abruptly, her magic shifted. The pulsing fire ceased, and the world came into focus.

She knew exactly what to do.

Anything she liked.

"Well," she began. "Look at it from my point of view."

Felix blinked.

"What?" he demanded.

She stood up. They were trying to make her feel small by putting her on that tiny chair, but she wasn't going to let them.

"As I see it," she began, "there are three charges against me. Am I right?"

"Correct, but…"

"In response to the first, that I injured a teacher and a classmate," she continued. "I didn't mean to. I didn't aim for them. I must admit that I didn't think about them at all. I was angry. Everyone told me that I wouldn't be able to hurt anyone because I wasn't strong enough."

Well, no one had said that exactly…

Yes, they did.

…actually, they had. Ophelia said it in individual training.

There was a murmur from the audience.

"So, your claim is that anger is a justifiable reason for harming others?" demanded Robert.

"Of course not, but intent must count for something," she said. "It seems I had an enormous amount of magical power built up inside me. I did not even choose to use it, not really. It just happened."

Robert rose to his feet, his face red with anger, and his mouth about to open.

Sit down and shut up.

Robert sat. His mouth closed.

"You're a seditious, unfeeling girl!" said Marcia.

Calm down!

Marcia visibly relaxed.

"Actually, I feel very bad about it," said Ev. She tried to stop her voice from trembling and her eyes filling with tears, but she couldn't. "I would never have hurt them on purpose. Miss Patti never did anything to me, and there is *nothing,*" she turned sideways to the audience, "that would make me hurt *any* student here."

Believe that I would never hurt you. I mean you no harm.

From where she stood, she could see Peter, right up front. No doubt wanted to see the Inner brat who'd hurt his best friend be punished. His eyes widened in surprise.

"Restrict your remarks to The Seven," snapped Felix.

"Apologies," said Ev, turning back. "I was confused. It's difficult to follow the rules, particularly the ones no one tells you about."

There was a gentle gasp from the audience that quickly died down.

"Well, if that is how…" began Felix.

I can say what I please.

"I heard one of my carers say that when the rules are stupid, she chooses to break them. Why can she do that, but I can't?"

"The isolated ravings of one woman. . ."

"Interesting that you don't ask me who I'm talking about, as if you already know all about the unhinged carer in our midst, but never mind that for now. Let's move on to the second charge." Felix's eyes were wide with shock. He clearly wasn't used to being interrupted.

Which was a pity because she didn't know what to say next.

"As for the second charge," she said, buying herself some time. "Which is that I ran away against school rules. . ."

She turned on her heel and marched a few steps toward the watching tables.

"Come back here!" shouted Marcia. Two guards started walking toward her, menacingly. Deadly idiots, times two, she thought to herself. Watch your step. . .

I can walk where I like.

"Hands up anyone who has *never* wished they were somewhere else!" she shouted at the audience.

If you put your hand up, you are a liar.

No one moved.

She turned and went back to her spot in front of the chair. The deadly idiots had stopped in their tracks, unsure of what to do next.

"No one wants to be here. It's awful. It's actually worse than Inner, sometimes. In Inner, we weren't so impossibly busy with so many things that we could never hope to finish. In Inner, there weren't ridiculous punishments for not doing things that were impossible to do. In Inner, children did get hurt, but it wasn't our whole purpose in life. Alerrawia is awful—of course I wanted to leave!"

"I've had enough of this," said Robert. He started to rise to his feet.

"Oh, sit down you buffoon," said Eliza. "I'm interested to hear what she says next."

You will listen to Eliza.

Robert snarled, and sat with a grunt.

"That word you use for my running away," she said. "Traitor. I know that word. It means that I somehow betrayed an obligation or duty, but what obligation do I have to you? I'm not Alerrawian. People go to great lengths to remind me of this every single day. How can I betray a place that I have no obligation to?”

“You mean you’re not indebted to us for everything we’ve done for you?” asked Shaun Brown.

“What, exactly, have you done for me? You ripped me from the only world I knew without my permission and without any explanation. You ripped out my teeth. You insult and humiliate me daily. And you want me to forget all that because now I can be burned by the sun like everyone else?”

“You’re an ungrateful little brat!” spat Robert.

Ev ignored him.

“I didn’t mean to run away,” she began. Well, not quite that soon, anyway. . .

“Then how do you explain the stolen vegetables found in your bag?” said Felix.

“I took them because they were the first ones I’d ever seen,” she said quickly. “I didn’t know I wasn’t allowed to.”

You will believe me—it is the only logical explanation.

“The fact of the matter is,” said Eliza, “that you fled and did not return when you were called back by an Alerrawian teacher.”

“I didn’t hear her.”

I didn’t!

"Also, I was angry. Have none of you ever done anything you regretted when you were angry?"

You know you have.

She could see in every one of their faces, even behind the rage of Felix and Robert, that what she's said had struck home.

She released her building tears and let them flow freely down her cheeks.

My tears will soften you.

"And then. . .and then I got lost, and no one came to find me, and, and, and. . ."

"We came to find you!" said Marcia, hurriedly. "You're here *because* we found you!"

"I know, but at the time it felt like, like, like you'd just abandoned me out there. . ." she let her voice trail off and she took some time to wipe her eyes on the sleeve of her uniform.

I am a frightened little girl standing up to seven grown-ups, all alone and vulnerable.

"How did you find me, anyway?" she asked.

"That's no concern of yours…"

"I think it is though, because the True Users seemed to think that there was a tracking spell on me, which I didn't give my permission for."

Murmurs from the audience.

"The methods Alerrawia uses to conduct its business have nothing to do with you," said Shaun.

Ev stared straight at Shaun and said, "I want to know."

Tell me!

"It's not *you* we track—it's in the Suncharm," said Shaun, then he closed his mouth, shocked at what he'd admitted to.

The audience was murmuring now. Clearly this was news to everyone.

"Quiet," said Felix, and the audience reluctantly settled.

"Which brings us to the third charge," said Eliza, trying to bring things back to the topic at hand.

"There's no point in her denying it," said Robert, with great effort. "She was found, in their company. . ."

"Shut up!" snapped Eliza. "Go on, Evelyn."

She let her voice tremble as she said, "They were just people! I was scared and alone and these people appeared and were nice and no one *told* me I wasn't supposed to speak to them, and I didn't know who they were anyway. . ."

They are just people. Just like us.

"…and the giant that was with them wasn't scary *at all*…"

"There are no giants!"

Ev paused, her eyes narrowed in disbelief.

"You must have seen them at some point? They're huge!"

"There are no giants in the bubble," said Felix, voice low and menacing.

Yes, there are!

"Yes, there are!"

The audience erupted.

"Order!" shouted Felix. "Order! Guards, get them under control!"

The guards hesitated, huge frowns on their faces. The useful guards made a beeline for the noisiest audience members and tried to calm them down. The pretty ones shouted, adding to the general noise, and the stupid ones stopped dead in their tracks as their brain processed this unusual nugget of new information.

"Giant's *do* exist?"

"I thought there weren't any in the bubble!"

"Maybe the seven just made a mistake…"

"Hah! Don't be stupid, it's another lie!"

Now that's what she liked to hear.

She turned her attention back to the main table. Shaun had left his seat and was hovering at Felix's shoulder, whispering nervously into his ear. Felix nodded and waved his hand dismissively. Shaun returned to his seat and, from under it, produced the mass RDD he'd used in PE class.

"Look out!" shouted Ev, but her voice was drowned out by all the others.

Shaun hit the button.

Ev fell to the ground.

Great, I've lost all motor functions. Again. Lovely.

People screamed, especially grown-ups who weren't as used to these sorts of punishments. Going blind or deaf suddenly might come as a shock. She could hear people gasping for air. She could hear other flopping on the floor.

A few moments later, the punishment ended, and the room was filled with sobs and murmurs.

"Order," said Felix, quietly.

Ev scrambled to her feet and surveyed the head table. None of them had been punished, which had to mean that the mass RDD was directional. If you were standing behind it when it activated, you wouldn't get hurt.

The day was just full of useful information.

"Are you done?" she asked.

"I've had about enough…"

Oh, be quiet.

Felix's mouth slammed shut. Ev turned to the audience.

"Giants *are* real, thanks for your support, but let's keep things calm so that they're not tempted to use that cheap little trick again."

The audience settled down and waited expectantly. There were still a few sobs here and there, but no one said a word.

"Thank you," said Ev. She turned back to Felix. "I had no idea that I was committing some huge crime when I accidentally spoke to the True Users, because nobody told me."

"Ignorance is no excuse for breaking the law!" said Robert.

You are nothing but a bully.

Robert's face went white.

"Then what is?" she asked. "Is educational incompetence a sufficient excuse? My teachers failed to prepare me for meeting a True User in person. . ."

"How dare you!"

"Or perhaps the fact that I'm *eleven years old* matters to someone? I'm not meant to be able to understand these things. That's your job."

You are failing your children.

Robert gasped. Eliza's eyes widened.

Ev sat down, exhausted. Her heart was pounding, and she desperately needed some air. There was silence from all sides. She fought to keep her face calm.

"Miss Acorn,' said Felix hoarsely, "Might I remind you that this is *your* disciplinary hearing, not ours."

That has changed.

"I'm here because of you. I demand that you explain yourselves."

For a second time, the audience erupted. All Ev heard was the sound of all of Alerrawia shouting at her. Later she learned that most were shouting at The Seven, but in that moment, it felt like everyone hated *her*.

"Order!" yelled Felix, but either no one heard him, or no one cared.

The rest of The Seven were on their feet. Carers and teachers bundled children out of the room, but that was all she was able to see before Christopher grabbed her shoulder and steered her to the door, flanked by two pretty idiots.

"Now you've done it, wonder girl," he said on the way down the stairs. "They'll really be gunning for you now."

Let them!

"Let them," said Ev.

10. It's What Your Do Now That's Important

A closed system is a physical system that does not interact with any other system. It is completely isolated.

Science Fundamentals

Page 78

At some point she realized that no one was coming to get her that day, so she lay on the bed and closed her eyes. She wasn't going to sleep, she told herself, just rest, just for a moment—

She was awoken abruptly by a knock on the door.

"Can we come in?" asked a muffled voice.

"Well, I can't do anything about it, either way, so please yourself," she answered, groggily.

The door opened and Amy came in with a plate of breakfast and a bag hanging from her arm. Jonah followed.

"Here. You've got to eat this, and get changed, and then get to your Wednesday classes," said Jonah. He pushed Amy toward Ev.

Ev's head reeled.

"What?" she asked.

Amy looked nervously at her feet.

"It's over," said Jonah, gruffly. "The Seven voted four to three to dismiss the charges against you, but you have to get back to normal *quickly*."

"No giants!" said Amy, urgently.

Ev thought Amy meant that there were no giants, but then she remembered how Amy communicated. "Are you asking me to not mention giants, Amy? For my safety?"

Amy nodded in relief.

"And did they send you two to let me out because they thought you were the people that I'd be least angry with?"

"Are you angry?" asked Amy in her tiny voice.

"No, of course not. . ." began Ev.

"Well, we're angry with you!" said Jonah. He turned and kicked the door so hard that it slammed shut with a crash. "You left without us! You didn't even think…"

Amy made soothing noises, trying to calm Jonah. She put the tray and the bag on the floor and gently took his hand.

"I didn't mean to. . ." said Ev in a small voice. Jonah had a point. She hadn't thought about them, not even once.

"Well, just. . .just be normal then!" said Jonah. He stormed out.

Ev's skull started to tingle.

"I do not accept this," she said to Amy. "I am not going to pretend that nothing happened. Tell them I'll talk to Felix Granite and no one else."

Amy nodded and backed towards the door.

"Actually, wait a moment," said Ev, suddenly. "Where would I have seen the name Granite before? Like, before I knew who they were? And not Janian Granite either, that's not what I'm talking about."

"On the door," said Amy as she darted out.

"What door?" But Amy was gone.

Ev spent a few seconds on the dilemma that was her breakfast. If she ate it, her magic would be stifled, and if she didn't, she'd starve to death in seconds (or so her hungry tummy claimed). Her tummy won.

The food did make her feel better, even if she felt sleepy and empty. When Christopher came to speak to her instead of Felix, she only protested mildly.

"They realized they messed up, badly, and that they have to give you another chance, which, in true Alerrawian style, means pretending like it never happened in the first place. Clear?"

"They?" asked Ev. "Aren't you one of them?"

"Don't remind them, it will only make them angry."

"What did you vote for?"

"I have no idea what you mean," said Christopher, his face a wooden mask. Ev was used to not having her questions adequately answered, so she forged ahead.

"I guess I should thank for the pill," she said, begrudgingly. "I have no idea why you helped me, but that pill kept me calm."

"Yes, I noticed that which was strange considering its only active ingredient is sugar."

"What?"

"It's a sugar pill. It only works because people are told that it works, and it keeps working even after they know its only sugar. It's the sort of illogical thinking I despise, but I'm never one to turn down a useful tool. The next time you need some confidence, just pretend to take a sugar pill. By all accounts it should have exactly the same effect."

"But *something* happened. . ."

"Yes, something did. You won an argument you shouldn't have been allowed to make, and I can't figure out why. Maybe I'll never be able to. In the unlikely event that you figure it out, keep it to yourself. It's high time you went into 'trust no one' mode. Don't let silly notions like friendship hold you back."

"Hold me back from what?"

"From *everything*!"

Ev was caught in a trap. One the one hand, she was inclined to agree that friends just got in the way, even if she was starting to like being around other people. On the other, she did *not* like being told what to do, ever, especially by people in this place.

"I'll take it under advisement," she said, because she'd read it in a book once and liked the way it sounded.

"Take my advice, don't take my advice, it's all the same to me," said Christopher. "It's time to get back to your regularly scheduled activities. Do what you're told. Keep your head down. No heroics. The best thing you can do is to be forgotten. The people in power don't like that you're defying them, and everyone else doesn't like how the guards who were on duty during your little adventure have disappeared, or how the only two people who know how to teach flying are in the med bay."

"Disappeared?" It was a familiar word, one that made her stomach clench and her mind jump to Mike.

"Yes. It's a common occurrence. *Someone* had to be punished for what happened, and they couldn't have you, so they picked the guards who watched you fly over the fence with their mouths hanging open instead. It's expensive and tiring for the escape wards to *always* be active, so the rule is the guards trigger the wards if they see someone trying to leave. Most people don't take the chance, but you're new and stupid, so. . .They said they were too surprised to act in time. The evidence they presented was deemed unsatisfactory, probably because it was difficult to hear their arguments over their screams, so they've been disappeared. Also, the wards that prevent people flying out have been permanently activated in case you're wondering. Now we have to *deactivate* them every time we send an air patrol, which, let me tell you, is a far more common occurrence, so thanks for that extra headache. Don't try it again. Or do. It's clear that *I* can't stop you. Just tip me off when you're going to try so I can watch. Tell your 'friends'. I'll bring the popcorn."

"Ha," said Ev, rolling her eyes. She tried to ignore her squirming stomach. Who cared about guards? Who cared about the flying teacher, or Derek? Anyway, it was their fault, not hers.

"Escape attempts. . .I mean, 'unauthorized departures', are not treated lightly. You should have been disappeared after your hearing. You were not. This is unprecedented. Felix's uses hearings exclusively as a way to flex his power in public. The outcome used to be a foregone conclusion, but you've changed that. I expect to see fewer hearings and more disappearances in the near future, something else we can thank you for.

"And let me put one clear image into your head in case you *are* thinking of leaving again. Usually what happens is that the prospective escapee gets trapped by the wards, stretched out thinly enough to block out the sun, and left to hang in the sky as a warning to all. Not dead, you see, there's magic to keep you alive. You think there isn't enough of you to darken the sky for a few days? Well, from experience, I can tell you there is, once everything that is you is spread out paper thin. The prognosis once the punishment is over is not good. Do you understand?"

Ev nodded. Christopher could be lying, but she didn't think he was.

"Fine. Now get to class. You've already missed one."

Ev was about to leave when Christopher called her back.

"Yes?" she asked, a little impatiently.

"Evelyn, listen carefully. Don't think that I will always be there to help you. I'm interested in what you do next, nothing more. There isn't much in the way of entertainment around here. If I hear anything bad about you, anything at all, I'll drag you to Felix myself."

*

The lesson she'd missed was, unfortunately, Spell Work, but the next one was Language and Writing, so it could be worse. She wandered slowly to class, taking her time. Apart from a few grown-ups here and there, there was no one in the halls. It was quite peaceful.

On the sixth floor, a woman leaving the med bay looked like she wanted to challenge Ev for being out of class…

Not now!

…but then she recognized her and changed her mind. She wasn't the only one. Even Boaclick gave her a wide berth.

She arrived at Language and Writing before the bell. It was the first lesson of the day to be held in that classroom, so she went straight in. Granny Oakwood was setting up her cozy corner.

"Ah, Evelyn, the accidental runaway," said Granny. "Come and help me with this."

Ev did what she could to help, but she kept falling over Mr. Snugglebottom who seemed determined to be wherever her feet were.

"He's trying to get your attention," said Granny. "He thinks you're in trouble."

"Am I?" asked Ev.

"What do you think?"

"Life has gotten somewhat out of control." She collapsed into a beanbag chair.

"Somewhat," agreed Granny. "It's what you do now that's important."

"What *do* I do now?"

"I really have no idea. All I can do is answer your questions. If I know the answers, of course."

"Everyone's acting like *now* I'm in trouble. I mean, I get it. I did a weird thing, so things are going to be weird. But it's not like anyone wanted me here before this. It's not like I wasn't in danger already. Everyone hates me."

"I don't hate you. Amy and Jonah don't hate you. Plenty of others don't hate you…"

"What does it matter if deep in your hearts you don't hate me? You're all part of this. . .this *system* that hates me and you don't want to do anything about it!"

"I'm starting to see why you didn't come back when I called you through the mirror yesterday."

"Yes! You wanted me to come back to this place, as-is, nothing changed, because you decided that that was better for me than leaving. Which I don't agree with. At all."

"I understand, Ev."

"Good!"

"I stand by what I said, however. It wasn't the right time to leave. A right time will come. When there is a plan, a goal, something to achieve that will help everyone and not just you. You'll know it when it happens, Ev. Until then, you have to stay safe. Fair enough?"

"Fair enough," mumbled Ev, and was immediately annoyed that Granny had tricked her into agreeing.

"Now, to answer your question about it being unsafe here for those with magical abilities. That was your question, wasn't it? Why is it so unsafe here?"

Ev nodded.

"Well, they've dedicated many years to convincing people that magic is evil, the Granite Institute. Centuries. They're raised to think they're the only ones who can see the truth. They'll even use magic themselves to prove that magic is evil. They've invested too much into their campaign to give up now."

"There's a word for someone who does the thing they say no one is allowed to do. . ."

"There is indeed. . .You know a lot of words, Ev. What's this one?"

"Hypocrite," said Ev.

"Very good!"

Vendavi had often congratulated Ev when she did well on something, but this was the first time she'd seen such a big smile accompanying the praise.

"Here, help me move these chairs around."

Mr. Snugglebottom seemed less concerned about her now, maybe because *she* felt a little better. In Inner, there was never anyone you could talk to about anything.

"Ev, can I ask *you* about something?" Granny asked while they each carried one half of a beanbag chair.

"Why not?"

"How did you win your disciplinary hearing?"

Ev's skull instantly started tingling. "Look here, just because I'm a 'little girl' doesn't mean. . ."

"I know, I know, that's not what I meant at all," said Granny soothingly. "I was at the back of the room, on the outskirts, sitting as far away as I could as a vague sort of protest. Those of us who were furthest from you Ev. . .well, things looked a little different from back there. There were many murmurs of 'Why?' all around me. We were much more confused than the people closest to you."

"I...what are you even saying?"

"Ev, did you use magic to get through your hearing?"

"No! I mean. . .I don't *think* I did. . ."

"Ev, there's something on your mind."

"Well, there's just this thing I've always done where I wish for something to be and then it is."

Granny's eyes widened slightly, but her voice was the pleasant one of a good teacher giving an important lesson. "Can you give me an example?"

"Well, like, at the hearing I thought things like 'Quiet!' and 'Sit down!' and then they were quiet, and they sat." She shrugged. "It's really no big deal."

"Ev," said Granny quietly, "You must have noticed that this is not a usual ability, even amongst magic users."

"I suppose. . ."

"Listen very carefully. Your classmates will be here soon. What we talk about now we can never talk about again. Understand?"

"Yes."

"Good. I think you have a third ability, and I think that ability is reality warping. I can't diagnose you, and you can't let anyone else diagnose you either because, Ev, reality warping is illegal. No one can ever know you have it. Keep it to yourself, and no more big flashy displays like yesterday. Don't tell anyone about this. Don't even research it in the library.

"Be careful. Not just because you can't let anyone know, although that is very important. Are you listening? Ev, this ability is very dangerous. If you're not careful, you can change reality without realizing it, and you won't ever be able to undo what you've done. Do you understand?"

"What's so bad about it?" Ev asked defensively.

"Well, for a start, everyone believes in giants now. It was one of those lies that The Seven tell that made very little sense, but that also did very little harm. What do you think most Alerrawians will want to *do* now that they believe in giants?"

"Taylor told me that most people who come from Alerrawia tell them that they don't exist, and then they try to kill them to make it true. . ."

Ev's eyes widened.

"Oh no," she whispered.

"Yes, Ev. I saw troops mobilizing last night to hunt the giant. They won't find. . .Taylor, did you say? The True Users know how to stay hidden. They've had a lot of practice."

Ev looked moodily at her feet. The list of people she'd hurt went on and on. Derek and that flying teacher. The guards who were punished for her escape. Taylor and the True Users, who would now have to fight off the Alerrawians. Probably a bunch of others that she didn't even know about.

"I'll be more careful," she said, sulkily. It wasn't that she didn't *want* to be more careful – it was that she didn't like having to follow someone else's advice.

"Thank you, Ev. Here come the others—if anyone asks, all we were talking about was how strangely Mr. S was acting when you came in here. Okay?"

"Okay."

"You have to be careful. Find friends, find allies, and keep them close."

All through the silly and ridiculously easy lesson (they all had to write the strangest grammatically correct sentences using the words "revolution", "griffins", "tomato seeds" and "robots" that they could), Ev's mind reeled. Reality warping. She could literally do anything she wanted, make the world any way she wanted it to be. It was. . .

Well, to be honest, it was terrifying.

She wasn't sitting with Amy and Jonah. She hoped she wasn't hurting their feelings, or something, but Christopher had told her to avoid letting friends hold her back, and Granny had said to not tell anyone about her third ability, so right now being alone seemed safest, at least while she tried to think.

In Biology class, the boy named Harry asked quietly, "Would you like to feed Sean again? No one will mind if you do. . ."

Ev shuddered.

"It's not really my thing," she said. Harry's face fell. "But I really like that you offered!" she added hurriedly. "I just think that everyone should get their turn, it's not fair for one person to get to do it all the time."

"That's very true," said Harry gravely.

"Well, that was strange," said Ev to Jonah as they settled down. Jonah looked at her with relief.

"So, you're talking to me now?"

"I was never *not* talking to you."

"Class," said Mr. Sterling, ending their conversation, "today we will depart a little from the usual lesson plan and discuss closed systems. Which is strictly speaking not a biology topic, but I think we can allow for the occasional crossover."

Ev watched without really seeing as Mr. Sterling drew on the board. She took notes, completed exercises, even took a turn reading out loud from the textbook, but if Vendavi has tried to test her on closed systems, she would have failed miserably.

In Critical Thinking, Declan Jones ordered them to put their textbooks away the moment they walked in, and they were treated to an almost hour-long sermon on the evils of fire and flight, "not directed at anyone in particular, of course", and how young minds needed to guard themselves against corrupting influences in others as well as in themselves. Ev could see an RDD sticking out of his pocket, because magic was only evil unless you needed it to defend yourself against children. Her skull tingled the entire time, but she kept her face calm. When she left the room, she turned at the door to see Declan staring at her.

She smiled and waved. His eyes widened in shock.

"Why did you do that?" hissed Jonah.

"Because blowing him a kiss would have been pushing it too far," she answered.

And because blowing his head up would have been too gruesome.

During PE, she didn't even bother to join in. She sat at the side of the exercise area and took out the book Emerson had given her to help her focus more effectively on spell casting. No one bothered her, although she heard plenty of whispers and felt plenty of glances fall on her bent head. She ignored them all. Shaun was too nervous to do anything about it. After a half-hearted, "You should participate, you know," to which she'd replied, "No thanks, I'm fine right here," he had given up with a hint of relief and focused his energy on the rest of the class.

He didn't use the mass RDD, although it certainly seemed like he wanted to.

At lunch, Ev sat with Amy and Jonah. No one sat too near them, which they were used to, but today the space they were given almost seemed respectful.

Ev chewed on her Hexteria-laden vegetable pie, staring absently into the distance. Amy and Jonah had given up trying to talk to her. She was deep in thought, and what she was thinking was this: She wanted to save herself, but she also didn't want to hurt any more people. She didn't want to leave anyone she liked behind in a place that she's run away from. In short, she needed to start thinking about things differently.

After a while, she said, "You know, things really have to change around here."

"What things?" asked Jonah.

"Oh, most of them."

"Plan?" asked Amy.

"I'm still figuring out the details, but there is one thing you can do for me, Amy."

"Don't speak so loudly," hissed Jonah.

"Why not? *I* don't care who hears."

Which was lucky, because the three of them had become the center of an expanding wave of whispers as her words were passed from mouth to mouth.

"You. Are. Insane," said Jonah. He dropped his head onto the table.

"Probably," said Ev, but she lowered her voice and whispered her instructions to Amy.

Amy looked miserable. "Sure?" she asked.

"Very sure," said Ev, firmly. "Can you do it?"

"Yes…"

Amy vanished.

"Where did you send her?"

"Don't worry, Jonah, she'll be fine," said Ev, which wasn't actually the answer to the question Jonah had asked.

Ev *didn't* have a plan, but she did have a list of things she wanted to know or try, which seemed like a good place to start.

A few minutes later, Amy reappeared and handed Ev a piece of paper under the table.

"Thanks Amy," said Ev, folding it into one of her books. "Your. . .notes will be very helpful for my assignment."

After lunch, the three of them had magical innovation.

"Pop quiz," said Zara. The class groaned. "Don't worry—it's a creativity quiz, so just do your best."

A creativity quiz meant thinking up new and innovative uses for magic and science combinations on the fly. They weren't allowed to repeat things they'd already heard in class. For marks, your answers had to be original. Not that just *any* new idea would earn you points—if even one of your ideas was dangerous or irresponsible or just plain didn't make any sense you automatically failed.

Ev looked at her question paper.

Question 1: Put forward an initial pitch for a new magical innovation that leverages fire throwing and that would be highly effective against even the most powerful magic-users.

Question 2: Propose a new magical innovation for the instantaneous treatment of battlefield injuries (the specific nature of the injury is up to you).

There were ten questions in total. Four of them mentioned fire throwing. Two mentioned flight. *All* the questions were about fighting or defending.

"So much for life not being a battlefield. . ."

Ev really tried to answer the questions, but she just didn't know enough about anything yet. Amy's magic pen darted all over the page, covering it with complicated answers in tiny handwriting.

When their time was up, their papers jumped into the air, flipped over twice, and landed with their grades neatly written across the top of the page, with a comment from Zara. Ev read hers.

18/100

You really should consider thinking a little harder about these things.

Jonah had made a fifty, and Amy's said:

100/100!

Excellent! Be sure to share this with your friends!

The bell rang.

"You can keep your tests," said Zara as they hurried out of the room. "I added detailed feedback next to each answer. It's always a good idea to learn from your mistakes."

Individual training was next. Today, Ev was one of the first children to be assigned a task.

"Many of the things you learn in spell work about focusing your attention also apply to innate abilities," said Ophelia as she led Ev to a study table. "Now, this is not very exciting, but it is very important." She handed Ev some instructions. "I want you to work on this today," said Ophelia. She silently released a small amount of Ev's magic, then moved on to assign a task to another child.

Ev glanced at the page. It aligned quite closely with what she was supposed to be learning in spell work, except it wasn't nearly as complicated because innate abilities were things you were born doing—you just had to figure out how to control them.

She glanced around the room. Eliza and Christopher were standing nearby, close enough to see what she was doing. What they planned to do if she did try setting the room on fire Ev didn't know, but they probably had some magical innovation handy that would stop her in her tracks. Best not to draw their attention. Come to think of it, this was probably the only exercise Ophelia could have given her that would keep Eliza and Christopher at bay while actually teaching her something. It would be silly to waste the opportunity.

The first step was to establish a comfortable and relaxed pose. Feet touching the ground. Eyes half closed and hands resting on her thighs.

The second step was to notice her own breathing, not just how the air flowed in and out, but also how her whole body reacted.

The third, and final, step was the most important. This was where the magic lay. Now she had to notice her thoughts, what she was really thinking in that moment, locking everything else away.

It seemed easy, and that's because it was. Anyone could follow these steps. But, when a magic user allows themselves to focus on what they're really thinking and feeling, they also open the path for their innate abilities to spark. Strong emotions were the most common spark, which was why Ev could fly when she was scared or angry.

Meditation allowed you to gain control of your emotions to access your innate abilities more safely.

This is easy.

She started and her eyes opened. She'd felt it, that time, now that she knew what to look for. A tiny spark of innate magic had ignited, altering reality to suit her needs. She would always find focusing exercises easy, from now on, because she had made it so.

Excitement and fear bubbled in her chest. She closed her eyes again, and slipped easily into a meditative state.

Almost immediately she felt a connection to her fire and flight abilities in a way she'd never imagined was possible.

She could do anything. She wanted nothing more than to set her desk on fire right then and there.

And she could. There was nothing stopping her.

But she didn't.

Until she had a plan, it was better for everyone to think that she wasn't special, that she didn't know what she was doing at all, especially if she had to keep her third ability a secret.

Carefully, so that no one would notice, she allowed herself to fly, just a little a quarter of an inch above her chair, gradually allowing her body to let go of gravity.

It wasn't the same feeling as soaring through the air—nothing could match that—but there was something intoxicating about being able to control her ability so carefully.

She let herself fall back to her seat. She would need to practice, and she would definitely need to learn to do it faster, but this was the first step.

"How's it going?" asked Ophelia as she passed Ev's desk to help another student.

"It's so boring!" said Ev. "Is something supposed to happen?"

"Don't worry, it's difficult for some people. Just keep trying."

Ev spent the rest of the lesson surveying the class through half-closed eyes. She noticed that Percy was keeping far away from her. She noticed Amy teleporting around the room with the greatest of ease. She noticed Jonah resisting everything Ophelia tried to teach him. Mostly she noticed everyone noticing her. She was just sitting there, doing nothing at all interesting, but every single person in the room looked at her at least once.

In chemistry, Miss Odette also had a quiz. On the periodic table of elements. It was long and complicated and boring, but Ev did her best anyway. Forty-five minutes into the lesson, Miss Odette said, "Time's up." She sent a student around the room to collect the papers.

"I already have a good idea of who will have passed and who will have failed. There are no surprises when it comes to you lot. I just hope, for everyone's sake, that those of you with villainous tendencies don't corrupt the others."

Well, so much for getting through a lesson that wasn't about her. She thought about changing reality so that Miss Odette would be a nicer person, but that seemed. . .wrong.

In history of magic, Alicia had somehow managed to find the one sentence in their textbooks that said something vaguely positive about the enemies of the Granite Institute.

To some, rebellion may have felt like the only moral choice.

That was all, but it was more than anyone had expected.

"How did that get in there?" Ev heard someone mutter.

They spent the lesson discussing this sentence. Very carefully. No one was prepared to come down on one side of the argument or the other, but they struggled through the discussion anyway.

Ev idly flipped through her textbook until her eyes landed on something that made her freeze. She'd read it before, but now it seemed more important. It was in the footnote about Kelvin Granite, the founder of the original seven:

**Reality Warpers (see page 239) can, as the name suggests, change reality to be anything they choose. It is believed that this ability was what allowed this great man to establish the bubble, thereby granting peace and safety to all within it. Kelvin Granite was the last Reality Warper to be seen in the bubble. As reality warping cannot be* *controlled by Hexteria, it became illegal shortly thereafter. It was swiftly eradicated.*

Granny had warned her not to research reality warping, but flipping through your own textbook had to be okay, didn't it?

She turned to page 239.

Reality Warping:

Of the magical evils, reality warping is one of the worst. The wielder of this ability can completely disregard the very fabric of reality and spin their own out of nothing.

Although reality warpers have been eradicated, it is worth noting that, without proper control and forethought, this ability is extremely dangerous. Human thoughts are difficult to pin down. Vague instructions from the warper can lead to outcomes they did not seek. As this ability irrevocably alters the world we live in, accidents have the potential to affect all of humanity.

Ev stomach dropped. It was normal in Alerrawia for people to write bad things about magic in textbooks, but there was something in the tone of this section, like the person who'd written it was *really* scared.

This ability has one weakness, namely that it cannot function within a larger magical construct, such as a detention or magically enhanced simulation. The construct's reality is already under the control of one type of magic and cannot be overridden by another.

That's why Vendavi 2 hadn't noticed her third ability—she'd only ever interacted with him in simulations, so he had no way of knowing the danger she *really* posed.

How could they be so sure that reality warping was gone forever? They were obviously wrong, but how could they *ever* have thought that they were right? When Ev rearranged the world to suit her purposes, it always happened quietly, inside her head. She didn't have to say or do anything. How many other people were doing the same thing, all over the bubble?

Math was far less insightful. Miss Leah was flustered and completely out of touch with what was happening. As usual, she tried to maintain order, and, also as usual, she failed, but it wasn't a complete loss. An older boy came up to Ev and said, "Hi, I'm Gavin."

"Hi," she answered, cautiously.

"Don't stress; I'm from Inner too."

Ev nodded but didn't say anything.

"My name is Gavin Oakwood, actually. I got adopted in."

Ev shrugged. A name was just a name.

"Look, I just wanted to say that you impressed a lot of people yesterday. A lot. And that you need to be careful, because not everyone was impressed in your favor, if you know what I mean."

"I do but thank you anyway."

"All right, well, I'll be off then…"

The boy turned to go.

"Wait," said Ev. She couldn't do much on her own, and this boy was at least sixteen, practically a grown-up. "If you ever need anything, you know where to find me." It sounded lame, but she didn't know what else to say.

"Thank you," said Gavin, gravely.

"This is such a strange day," she said to Jonah.

"Stranger than yesterday?"

"Much."

The final lesson of the day was geography.

Marcia had a vested interest in pretending that everything was exactly as it had always been. She certainly wasn't about to admit that The Seven were out-argued by an eleven-year-old Inner brat. Better to act like nothing had happened at all.

They pointed at the same map and named what was on it. They parroted the usual phrases about magic being bad. At least it was short.

After geography, Ev had to spend an hour in the garden, where she squirreled away a few vegetables, and then she was free for the rest of the day. She found Jonah and Amy in the library.

When she got there, a group of children quickly left their comfortable corner. It had the nicest couches and the most natural light, and people were always trying to get there first.

"All yours," said one, nervously.

"Being doomed has its perks, I see," said Jonah as they settled into their new spot.

Ev and Amy took out their textbooks to get some homework done, but Jonah removed a very un-Jonah-like book form his bag. It wasn't a textbook. Ev squinted at the cover. *The Creature in the Night and Other Scary Stories.*

"Why are you reading that?" she asked.

"I thought if I read it myself and there was a happy ending then the nightmares will stop for real."

Fortunately, Jonah was a very slow reader. Unfortunately, he didn't know enough about stories to know that the scary ones *never* had happy endings.

Ev desperately tried to think of something to distract Jonah from the book.

"You know," she said quietly, "I ran into Mike Locust in the forest."

Amy dropped her pen, but Jonah didn't seem surprised at all.

"Figures," said Jonah.

"What do you mean?" asked Ev, annoyed. Jonah always needed to be the one who already knew everything.

"It's what Vendavi does when it doesn't know what to do with someone. It sends them out into the forest. None of us reported Vendavi going crazy, except for Mike. The rest of us knew to keep quiet. Mike always thinks he knows best."

"So, people who try to help Vendavi get kicked out?"

"It depends on Vendavi," said Jonah. "Alerrawia starts testing us just before our eleventh birthdays to see if we're magical and obedient enough, but Vendavi is supposed to notice threats that come from the outside. It took Alerrawia ages to figure out how to do it. Vendavi's main job isn't really to protect us from danger; it is to protect us from ever realizing that the world was different to what we thought. So, Vendavi removes *anything* that puts us in danger of realizing the truth. Actually, I think Alerrawia has made Vendavi, like, paranoid, or something. Like, they've made him focus *only* on isolated threats to the big lie, so he ignores other breaches. Anyway, so when Mike reported what he'd seen, Vendavi exiled him. Probably thought Mike was the only one because the rest of us were better liars. The True Users watch the exile hatch to snap up anyone who gets kicked out. I'm glad he's with the True Users. *I* just thought he was dead."

Ev shuddered to hear the calmness in Jonah's voice. This was the *real* horror story—children thinking their friends was dead and just shrugging it off as sad, but normal.

"Alerrawia has to be *super* careful. Like, I think there's a whole team of people on tenth whose entire job it is just to keep Vendavi from noticing what we're doing, and a whole other team who does the actual hacking."

"What happens if Vendavi does notice?"

"We. . .don't really know, but most people seem to think that Inner will just self-destruct."

Ev went cold. If that was the truth, then Alerrawia were knowingly putting *every person living in Inner* in danger every time they tested some kids.

"Why do they risk it? Why don't they just leave us in peace? Or, come to think of it, why don't they just blow us up instead of stealing us away? It's not like they like us or anything."

Jonah shrugged. "They hate magic, but they also need it for everything, so they need magic users to keep Alerrawia afloat."

"How many people live in Inner?"

"More than a hundred. Less than a thousand. Alerrawia can't quite get at the records, but it's not the millions we were taught."

"Alerrawia needs more magic users because they're getting weaker, so they steal the strongest from Inner, but that just means that Inner will get magically weaker as well, which means we'll be in the exact same boat in a few hundred years' time. Maybe sooner."

"How do you know that?"

"Words behind the words, Jonah. You should always look for them."

"We're perfectly safe in the bubble," said Jonah, gruffly.

"Sure we are," said Ev, distracted. She thought for a bit. "So, we're here, Mike's in the forest—where is Steve?"

"Kids who don't pass the Alerrawian test stay in Inner. He'll become part of the working groups, eventually. Never learn any different."

Except that he *had* learned something different, thought Ev. Those simulations changed the way you looked at the world. It was worse, actually, to get a taste of something different but have to stay exactly where you were. . .

"Does *everyone* get tested?"

"I think so."

Every single grown-up in Inner *right now* was robbed of a chance for something more than their tiny life in their tiny cell. All of them. If she had failed the test and her life had returned to 'normal', she would probably have gone mad.

"Can we get them?"

"Who?"

"The people in Inner. Steve. Our parents, I suppose. Can we get them out?"

"Now you're talking crazy again. Cut it out!"

"Self-destruct," Amy reminded them. Then her brow furrowed.

"What's wrong, Amy?" asked Ev.

"The door words," said Amy.

"What words?" asked Jonah.

"I asked Amy to go find something for me, remember? She teleported to the other side of the door from Inner. There were words there, and I was too confused to properly read them, but I thought they might be important."

"Why do you care about some stupid words?" asked Jonah. He was always angry when faced with things he didn't understand. "If anyone had seen her. . ."

"Who would see? She teleported straight there and straight back, and you can't unlock the door from this side. It's not like she was going to accidentally run into Christopher or anything."

"You're both insane," said Jonah.

Ev ignored him and unfolded the paper. In the neat handwriting of Amy's magical pen, it read:

Even the evilest among us can be used for the greater good. They are a gift, sent to be used wisely.

But of course, they must be properly controlled.

You are part of the Greatest Experiment ever conducted. You will thank us.

The Granite Institute

Well, that was just more of the same nonsense that was splattered everywhere. It was the second set of words that really held her attention:

Entry to and from Inner and Alerrawia is restricted to approved observers and the Granite family.

Trespassers will be punished to the fullest extent of the law.

Alerting the denizens of Inner to your existence will result in death.

"Happy?" asked Jonah. "Learned what you wanted to know?"

"Almost. . ."

Ev was exhausted, which made her skull tingle, because she *hated* it that they kept her too tired to think. She couldn't see the words behind the words. They were there. There was *something* she wasn't understanding right now, but she was just too tired.

"I can't think!" she said angrily. "Not right now…but I'll figure it out anyway. They can't stop me!" She shook her head to dislodge the sleepy cobwebs in her mind. "Tell me more about that stupid test they make us take."

"They test us to see if we're clever enough to accept that everything we've been told is a lie, and also to see if we show any signs of magic. They care more about magical abilities, obviously, but they learned the hard way that dragging people here who are convinced they are hallucinating, or who try to blow the world up, or try to go back to Inner, can lead to big problems."

"Which part of the test did *I* struggle with, then? They didn't seem to know if they wanted me here, even after I was already here!"

Jonah shrugged.

"Beats me. You're magically gifted, but not so much that Hexteria doesn't work, which *should* make you one of their favorites because they can control you more easily. I guess they were worried that you wouldn't accept your new reality?"

If that was true, the leaders of Alerrawia had gotten one thing right, at least. Ev didn't think she was hallucinating, but she wasn't willing to accept her new reality without a fight, either.

"Amy is a genius," Jonah went on, moodily. "I'm a dunce. I suck at schoolwork, I'm not completely sure we're not living in a simulation, and I refuse to use magic. Comprehensively incompetent—that's what they told me in the med bay."

They sat in awkward silence.

"I think. . ." Ev began and paused. What did she think? Why was it so difficult to put her thoughts in order? "I think that using people for their magic while also making them feel bad for being magical is. . .well, it's bad, isn't it? I think if they make you feel bad then maybe it's not because *you're* bad, but because they are." She broke off, floundering. She knew what she meant; she just didn't know how to explain it.

"They fought a war over it, Ev. Grown-ups don't fight wars for no reason."

Ev, who had read many stories about the things grown-ups did and didn't do, thought they fought wars over nothing all the time, but she decided not to bring it up. Instead, she said, "Tell me more about the war."

"So, you know that magic users and science followers had a war about who was the most right, right?"

Ev nodded.

"Magic was always a thing. We could always do it, but it took hundreds of years for people to realize how evil it was, and then the science followers had to band together to try get rid of it, except for in very controlled and specific situations, like protecting mankind as a whole or to make food and whatever. Some people didn't understand the good the science followers were doing, so they fought about it and stuff."

"Zara can use magic. . ."

"Yeah, but they don't really let her do anything. I think they only let her join to stop people complaining, or something. They all hate her, just like they hate us."

Ev studied the words behind Jonah's words carefully. The map of how to be accepted in Alerrawia was clearly laid out. First, accept Alerrawia's government and reality without question. Second, focus your time and effort on technology and science and never say a bad word about either. Third, control magic, whether it was in yourself or in others. If you did all of these things, you would be safe.

Maybe.

Ev didn't like it, and when Ev didn't like something, she knew exactly what to do about it.

"Things really need to change around here."

"How?"

"I don't know that yet, but I will. Soon."

11. Failure to Comply will Result in Detention

Detention is another example [of a necessary evil]. Without a clear and meaningful deterrent, children, particularly those who join us from Inner, cannot and will not behave in an appropriate manner. Sometimes, you have to send someone to hell to make them learn.

Felix Granite

Alerrawia: To the Future

Volume 2, Page 23

Tuesdays always filled Ev with a mixture of excitement and dread. On the one hand, she had flying class before lunch, but on the other, she had an hour and a half of impulse control with Robert in the evening. The best and worst ways to spend her time.

Two months had passed since Ev's adventures, and in that time, nothing much had happened at all. She'd attended a million lessons and learned very little from any of them, other than how to do just enough work to look like she was trying. She found that she learned things quickly and easily. She became used to the sun and no longer had to wear Suncharm when she went outdoors, as long as she didn't go out for too long. She learned to be civil to the children who spoke to her, but she avoided making any friends other than Amy and Jonah. She avoided Hexteria when she could, but there were many days where she just didn't have the time to steal vegetables, so she'd also learned that some foods left her feeling less empty than others, and she ate accordingly.

She was playing nice. She still meant to leave, permanently this time, but there was so much she had to figure out first. She did all her work, she listened to all the teachers. She learned to smile whenever she did or said something, which was apparently how you kept people happy, if you were a girl. She bit her tongue when she and the other children were mistreated. She kept her anger and her fire to herself. Most importantly, she kept a close watch on her thoughts and wishes. Altering reality was a dangerous game that she didn't want to play. . .at least, not yet.

It took a little time, but eventually everyone went back to ignoring her.

The one thing she *had* considered doing was changing reality so that everyone forgot that existed at all, but she was saved by her overactive imagination. What if it worked *too* well? What if they forgot about her so completely that they couldn't even see or hear her when she was right in front of them? Even Amy and Jonah?

Reality warping was for emergencies only.

She told herself that she wasn't *scared* of her ability—she was just being sensible. Anyway, flying seemed like a safer way to make her escape. It had worked once already, after all. . .

On the way out for her all-important flying lesson, an announcement blared across the entire compound.

All around Ev, people groaned and muttered. Suncharm was goopy and sticky, and, ever since Shaun had revealed that there were bio-trackers in the cream, people didn't like wearing it. Sure, most of them weren't planning to run away, but what if they were meeting their girlfriend behind the griffin paddock? Who wanted The Seven knowing where they were then?

Ev sighed, but what could she do about it? She was still playing it safe, which meant following the rules, even when they made no sense. She fought through a group of children to get to the Suncharm supplies at the door. On the outskirts of the throng, she saw Siobhan, nervously waiting at the edge, too shy to elbow her way in, so Ev grabbed two tubes of Suncharm.

Siobhan was strange. Despite sharing a bunk with her, Ev hardly knew her at all. She was awkward and unsure, and it was hard to tell if she even *wanted* to be friends with anyone. Ev sympathized. She didn't really want friends either. Amy and Jonah were fine, but she didn't to have to deal with anyone else.

Siobhan never looked at your eyes when she spoke, and sometimes you forgot that she was even there in the first place. Someone had said her other innate ability was Fading, but Ev didn't really know what that meant.

"Hello," she said.

"Hi," Siobhan answered with a weird mixture of relief and terror, her eyes firmly fixed on Ev's left ear.

"So, what's all this about then, do you think?" she asked, handing Siobhan a tube.

"I think it's because of those older kids who got burned. You know? They were out when they should have been in class and they got *really* burned, even though they shouldn't have been. Something weird is happening with the sun."

"Oh, yes. . .," said Ev. It *was* strange. The two kids were Alerrawian-born. They shouldn't have had to worry at all about the sun, and yet they were *still* in the med bay, two days later, with severe burns.

Ev and Siobhan carefully applied the goopy cream before stepping outside. They crossed the running track quickly before any grown-ups could yell at them and headed for the arena.

"Slow down a bit," said Siobhan. "Look who's ahead…"

Ev looked. Just ahead of them were Derek and Peter, the bully kings.

Siobhan's warning was too late. The boys had noticed them and had slowed enough for Ev and Siobhan to hear what they were saying.

"Here come the weirdos," said Derek.

"Oh, I thought I smelled something," said Peter, holding his nose.

"Such high-quality wit," muttered Ev.

"Just ignore them," whispered Siobhan to Ev's right knee. "Don't break your perfect record. Anyway, they're just jealous. You're top of the class, even better than Derek!"

It was true, Ev was doing *extremely* well in flying class, which was odd, because everyone knew that if you had more than two innate abilities, you wouldn't be very good at any of them.

It meant someone, somewhere, was lying, but that was normal.

Siobhan was also right about Derek and Peter—it *was* better to ignore them, as much as possible. Getting into trouble for retaliating would not be helpful.

After her disciplinary hearing, Ev had noticed that most of the bullies had stayed away from her. She'd warped reality, and now the other kids believe that she would never do anything against them.

But Derek hadn't been there. Derek had been recovering from burn wounds in the med bay. He still hated Ev, and Peter just went along with Derek's ideas, even if he didn't agree.

She could *make* Derek trust her. . .

"Emergencies only," she whispered.

"What was that?" asked Siobhan.

"Oh, nothing. . ." To change the topic, Ev decided to make a valiant attempt to draw Siobhan into conversation. "How've you been, Siobhan?" she tried.

"Fine, thank you."

"What you been up to?"

"You know, just school stuff."

"What's your favorite subject?" asked Ev, wearily. She was starting to run out of steam. In most conversations, the other person did at least some of the work, but Siobhan only knew how to give answers that stopped the conversation in its tracks. She steeled herself for something unhelpful, like 'I don't know' or 'all of them, I guess'.

This time, Siobhan's answer surprised her.

"It would be this one if it wasn't for Derek and Peter!"

"Yeah, they're jerks. But if we stick together, we'll be all right."

Siobhan smiled at Ev's forehead. "Yes, we'll be fine, together."

Ev mentally kicked herself. She wasn't supposed to be making *more* friends. . .

After the usual safety talk, Miss Patti told the class to rise three feet in the air, hover, and come down again. By now, Ev could do this easily, but sometimes she liked people to think she was struggling so they would underestimate her. She carefully did it wrong a few times before eventually getting it right.

There they were, a few dozen kids hovering three feet above the ground, some concentrating really hard, others just looking bored.

She didn't immediately notice Peter and Derek gesturing at each other, and she almost didn't react quickly enough when Derek shot a bolt of lightning directly at Siobhan!

She made herself move as quickly as possible, but the shield spell she threw up only partially blocked the lightning bolt. Siobhan fell to the ground with a startled "Ow!"

A second later, Ev fell too—she'd been practicing the spell for weeks, but it was still complicated and draining for a young magic-user.

"What's going on?" demanded Miss Patti, whirling around.

"Derek shot Siobhan with a lightning bolt, I blocked," said Ev, as quickly as possible. Derek didn't have time to think up a story. He was staring at Ev, his mouth hanging open—little girls from Inner weren't supposed to know such advanced magic.

"Is this true?" Miss Patti asked Siobhan.

"Y-Yes," said Siobhan softly.

"Right! I've had about enough of this, Derek. You are in serious danger of losing your career as the next flying coach. Detention!" Miss Patti snapped her fingers and Derek disappeared, leaving behind the glowing tether which was his path back to the real world.

Ev hadn't been to the bad place yet, but she knew enough to feel bad for Derek.

"May I walk Siobhan back to the dorm, Miss Patti?"

"No, I'm fine, I'll go myself!" said Siobhan quickly, and she was up and away before Miss Patti had even given her permission to leave.

Ev tried not to feel hurt. After all, she wasn't the one who *needed* friends. But she was a little upset that Siobhan had just stormed off like that.

"Back to work!" barked Patti.

"Hey," said Peter, softly. He flew as close to Ev as he dared. Ev ignored him.

"That's the second time, brat. There won't be a third."

"If Derek left me alone, then Derek wouldn't get into so much trouble," she whispered without looking at him.

"Inner kids don't belong here," said Peter. "Watch your back, brat. We're going to get you."

Slowly, Ev turned to face him. She smiled.

"This is where I should say something like, 'Not unless we get you first', but I'd rather take this opportunity to suggest that you're focusing your anger at the wrong people. Think about it."

"No talking in class!" snapped Miss Patti.

"Sorry, Miss!"

She smiled at Peter again, and then floated away.

"There's something seriously wrong with that girl," she heard him say.

Ev obsessed about flying class all afternoon. At first, she was angry, and her skull tingled like crazy. Why did Derek and Peter insist on picking on her? Why had Siobhan just run off? It was infuriating. Then, slowly, she calmed down. She reminded herself that Derek and Peter were just kids stuck in the same mess she was in, even if one of them was almost a grown-up. And if roles had been reversed and Siobhan had saved Ev from lightning strike, then Ev would have felt embarrassed. *Babies* needed other people to help them. She might have stormed off as well, just like Siobhan, and spent the rest of the day wondering if Siobhan was mad at *her*.

It suddenly seemed *very* important to speak to Siobhan and tell her that everything was just fine, but the quiet girl wasn't in any of her usual classes that afternoon. In fact, Ev was starting to get quite worried.

As she walked to Robert's office for her impulse control lesson, her mind kept getting stuck on Peter's threat. It felt like a threat that they *all* should be worrying about, Amy, Jonah, even Siobhan, even though Siobhan was Alerrawian and not from Inner. *Anyone* who was different might be in trouble.

The moment she was done with class, she would find them and warn them.

"Finally," said Robert when Ev arrived. "Late, as usual, but I suppose I have to work with what I'm given."

Ev's skull tingled. She tried to ignore it, but Robert was one of her weaknesses. He knew exactly how to get under her skin.

Robert's new favorite teaching method was to throw things at her that she wasn't prepared for and then make fun of her when she couldn't catch them. Oh, and of course, RDD her if she showed any emotion about it whatsoever.

"Today we're going to see how you react under pressure," said Robert.

Yay. Just like every other day.

"Are you going to teach me some useful tips and tricks for controlling my magical impulses this time, or is it going to be more of the same?" she asked.

Her vision disappeared as Robert RDDed her, which meant the lesson had begun.

"You know," she said, "you're a really bad teacher."

This was what how impulse control classes went— each of them tried to infuriate the other until one of them snapped. So far, it had always been Ev. By now Ev knew that Robert was *very* concerned about what people thought about him. He saw himself as 'stern, but effective'. Everyone else saw him as 'mad and terrible at his job'. Ev liked to make sure he didn't forget this.

Her reward for her kind services was to have her breath snatched from her. It was the second worst punishment after having your ability to think taken, but at least it was the quickest.

She hated RDDs. Her plans were still quite vague, even after two months, but the one thing she was sure about was that RDDs had to go.

Her skull was tingling worse than ever, and she could feel her fire, her flight, and her secret ability build up inside her, but Hexteria stopped her from using the first two, and she stopped herself from using the third. This class was where she was in the most danger of using her reality warping ability. She wanted nothing more than to make Robert nice, or have him jump out of a window, but she didn't. If she warped reality, she wanted it to be because she'd thought about it, planned for it, and been as careful as possible not to hurt anyone she didn't want to hurt.

What if Robert jumped out a window and landed on a little kid or one of her friends? Making him nice would mean erasing his personality. If she started doing that. . .it was a terrifying thought. She was sure plenty of people in Alerrawia would make *her* 'nice' if they could, and the thought made her shiver.

Robert reached for his RDD and waited expectantly. This was usually the point in the lesson where Ev yelled or threw something or tried to set him on fire *anyway*, which gave him an excuse to punish her. Today, she just felt tired. She had too much to think about, too many people to take care of, and Robert was just an annoyance.

She sighed, walked to his desk, and sat down.

"I have things to do," she said, "so if we could just get through this as quickly as possible, I would be much obliged. You usually RDD me between six and ten times in a lesson. Let's split the difference and call it eight. Or call it twelve, if that makes you happy. If we do it all now, you get what you want, and I get to leave. Deal?"

Out of pure reflex, Robert RDDed her. She fell with a sigh, her legs temporarily disabled.

"Eleven to go," said Ev, from the floor. "Or seven, if you're being nice."

He RDDed her again and then she couldn't think. The worst one, but in a way, it wasn't that bad, because you didn't know it was happening while it was happening, you only knew afterwards, once you were already safe again.

"Ten more!" said Ev, when her thoughts came crashing back.

"Typical Inner brat!" snarled Robert. "Not even willing to defend yourself. . ."

"Just practicing impulse control," she said, sweetly. "Am I doing well?"

"You don't belong here! Your kind shouldn't even be allowed to exist!" He was practically frothing at the mouth.

Traditionally, their lessons ended with a screaming match, but Ev just didn't have the energy. Besides, she'd just realized how absolutely ridiculous it all was, and next thing she knew, she was laughing out loud. It was more of a giggle, really, but it made Robert mad anyway.

Robert set the RDD on automatic. Wave after wave of magic swept over Ev, taking her sight, her hearing, her breath, her brain, again and again. Eventually, it stopped.

"Are we done?" she asked when she could speak again.

"We're done when I say we're done," answered Robert.

They stared at each other, each waiting for the other to look away, and they would have been there all night if a siren Ev had never heard before hadn't begun to wail.

"What's that?"

"Typical Inner brat, not knowing the warning alarms," muttered Robert, but his heart wasn't in it. He was listening, with a puzzled expression on his face.

"Yup, typical Inner brat, sure, so, what is it?"

Before he could answer, an announcement sang out from every speaker in the building and grounds.

Attention! Attention!

All students, teachers, and other personnel are to report to the common area immediately.

Roll call will be taken.

Failure to comply will result in detention.

"Well, get going then!" said Robert.

She was halfway down the stairs before she wondered why Robert hadn't left when she had. Perhaps The Seven followed different rules.

The guard let her through the secure doors to the thirteenth floor, and she headed for the stairs. There were very few people up this high at this time of day, so for a few flights, she was almost entirely alone.

That was when she heard Granny's voice coming from her bag.

"Ev!"

Ev paused and, after quickly checking to see that no one was about, she pulled out Granny's mirror.

The day of Ev's escape was the last time Granny had spoken to her using the mirror. For some reason, no one had taken it from her when she was returned to Alerrawia. Even more strangely, the RDD she'd stolen from Madam was *also* still in her bag when her things were returned to her, which made even less sense.

She knew, without being told, that the mirror had to be a secret.

"Hello?" she whispered to the tiny reflection of Granny Oakwood.

"Get to first as quickly as you can and *don't* do anything drastic!"

Then Granny disappeared.

Ev's heart pounded.

She'd been going to first anyway, but now that Granny had told her to, she was suddenly very afraid. What was going on?

She joined the throng of people heading to the common area. Biometric scanners mounted above every door took automatic roll call.

She looked desperately for Jonah or Amy, or even Siobhan, but the room was in an uproar and she couldn't see her friends anywhere. Not wanting to get in trouble, she sat down quickly and waited.

"Quiet," said Felix, his voice magically magnified so that it sounded like it was coming from just behind your left shoulder, no matter where you were in the room. The room settled instantly.

"A terrible tragedy has befallen us," he continued. "A very promising student has been seriously hurt and is in intensive care on fourth."

An icy hand grabbed Ev's heart.

Siobhan!

"The student's name is Amy Ox, and she is in a critical condition."

Ev's mind shut down. Not Amy!

"We have a fairly good idea of who attacked her, but until we can verify our suspicions, no one is to leave this room."

Felix sat, and serious murmuring broke out all around. Some people looked worried, some looked scared, but most just looked excited. This was the most interesting thing that had happened for a long time, after all.

"Excuse me, has anyone seen Jonah Tulip?"

No one had.

They were allowed to move freely around the common area, as long as they didn't leave, so she pushed her way through, searching everywhere.

"Jonah? Jonah!"

He wasn't there. No matter where or how long she looked, Jonah wasn't there.

She spotted Siobhan slumped against a wall. She fought her way through the crowd to get to her.

"What's the matter? Are you alright?"

"I'm. . .fine. . .," said Siobhan. "Just feeling a little. . .tired. Probably shock from earlier."

"Have *you* seen Jonah?"

"No. . .I haven't. . ."

"Who did this? Who would hurt Amy?"

"Maybe. . .Peter?" whispered Siobhan.

"What? Why Peter?"

"Because of flying class."

"But Amy wasn't even there!"

"They don't care who pays, as long as someone does."

Ev saw the words behind Siobhan's words, even though she was panicking. "Excellent candidates for The Seven when they grow up then," she said, bitterly.

"Evelyn Acorn!"

"Oh, what now?" said Ev.

"Evelyn! Show yourself!"

"Here!" yelled Evelyn.

Marcia stormed into view. "Follow me, please," she said.

Ev obeyed, but her anxiety grew. Were they somehow going to blame *her* for whatever had happened to Amy? They would definitely prefer that over even the *thought* that an Alerrawian might be responsible. If Robert had any say. . .

That was when she remembered that Robert hadn't come down to first with her. She looked around but couldn't see him anywhere. What did *that* mean? Did it mean anything? Was it stupid to think *Robert* had hurt Amy? He was surprised as she was when the alarms sounded, and he wasn't clever enough to fake it. At least, Ev didn't *think* he was. . .

What about Peter? On his own, Peter actually wasn't all that bad, even if he was Robert's nephew. Derek was the scary one—Peter was just. . .trying to survive, like everyone else.

Marcia steered Ev into an elevator. They were joined quickly by Felix, Eliza, and Christopher, which meant that at least four of The Seven *had* been on the first floor—Robert probably should have been there too.

They travelled to the thirteenth floor in stony silence.

"Is Amy alright?" asked Ev.

"Speak when you're spoken to!" snapped Marcia.

"Your questions will be thoroughly considered, and possibly even answered, when we get to Felix's office," said Christopher. Marcia shot him a death glare.

The silence continued right up until the moment the door to Felix's office closed.

"Evelyn, we understand that you and Amy are friends," began Felix, before anyone even had a chance to sit down.

"That's right," said Ev. "What happened?"

"She was attacked while walking back to her dorm. A malicious curse, that I won't mention here, was used on her."

Words, words, words. . .Of course, you won't mention it because what if someone tries to use it on *you*?

"Will she be all right?" Ev whispered.

"We believe she will be. She is currently in the med bay, but recovery is a long way away. We won't be able to ask her for her account of events for some time to come."

So, it was serious then. Anything that couldn't be fixed right away with a snap of the fingers or a clever machine was very bad.

"Can I see her?"

"Not just yet. We have some questions for you first, and then, maybe."

Ev nodded. She was good at this game by now. Be a good girl and maybe, just maybe, you'll get what you asked for. Or maybe not. We haven't decided yet.

"How would you describe Amy's relationship with Jonah?"

"What? What does that have to do with anything?"

"Answer the question," prompted Christopher.

"They're friends. Like, probably best friends," said Ev. There was only a slight hint of jealousy in her voice when she said it.

"Did they have a fight recently?"

"No! Why are you asking about Jonah? It was obviously Peter!"

Felix raised his eyebrows.

"Who?" he asked.

"Peter Rayner."

"And why is that?" he asked.

"He threatened me today. He said that he would get all Inner kids. . ."

"Nonsense!" said Marcia, cutting her off.

"Did Peter make any threats against Amy directly?" asked Christopher.

"No, but…"

"Then it's not very compelling, is it?"

Ev lapsed into silence, her skull tingling. She'd had vegetables at lunch, and she hadn't eaten dinner yet, maybe. . .But what could she do? She couldn't just set them on fire, and she didn't know enough about what was going on to warp reality. . .

She didn't bother mentioning her suspicions about Robert. He was untouchable.

"Evelyn, Jonah was seen attacking Amy. He is currently in detention, and we are deciding what to do with him."

Her heart stopped. She had never been to the bad place herself, but she knew Jonah feared it more than anything else. He couldn't tell her that, of course—children couldn't speak about the bad place, they could hardly even think about it, but she knew about the nightmares he had every time he was punished. She knew that he didn't speak for at least a day when he came back.

"You can't *possibly* think it was him. . ."

"It is under investigation," said Christopher, quietly. "There are many ways someone can be compelled to do something horrible, with or without their knowledge. We're looking into every possibility."

Marcia glared at him. "There is absolutely no reason to suspect that undue influences were at play. One Inner brat attacked another, plain and simple!"

"I want to see him," said Ev, firmly.

"He's locked in detention. Until the investigation is complete, we literally can't get him out. The magic won't allow it."

"Then send me to him."

"You don't know what you're asking," said Christopher, quietly.

"Send me to him. As part of your investigation. I can. . .I can talk to him, hear his side of the story. You can just bring me back again, right?"

"We've already spoken to him," said Felix, a heavy note of finality in his voice.

Ev's skull tingled, but as usual there was nowhere for her magic to go.

Well, there was *one* thing she could do. . .

If this wasn't an emergency, then what was?

Carefully, and with great concentration, she decided how she wanted the conversation to go. Then she reached into her heart, grabbed the flapping end of her magic in one imaginary hand and the fabric of reality in the other, and *twisted*.

You will let me visit Jonah. You will let me question him. Then, you will bring me safely back.

"Why not let her?" said Eliza, suddenly. "He might say things to her he wouldn't say to us, and we can make her tell us the truth of what he says, with or without her permission."

"Lovely," said Ev. "When do we begin?"

"Is it even possible?"

"We'll have to get Zara in here to confirm, but the spell, as I understand it, was designed for an entirely different purpose, one where spending time in the mindscapes of others was the whole point. It's an interrogation spell, isn't it? Which, unless I've misunderstood, is exactly what we're suggesting here."

"She *is* expendable," said Marcia, thoughtfully. Even Felix looked a little shocked, so she quickly added, "That is to say, sending a friend in. . ."

"It's all right, I get it, don't kill yourself backtracking," said Ev. "I want to do it, risks or no risks, but I want to see Amy first."

"It's decided," said Felix, finally giving in to Ev's magic completely. "Marcia, take her to see her friend."

All the way to the med bay, Marcia seemed determined not to say a word. Ev thought it would be fun to see what it took to make her snap while they were all alone in the elevator.

"Jonah didn't do it, you know," she began.

Nothing.

"Assuming that Inner kids attack each other just because they're Inner kids makes you a bad person," she continued.

Nothing.

"It also means you're pretty dumb. Did no one ever teach you to examine all possibilities?"

Marcia took a deep breath and set her jaw.

"It's why no one likes you," said Ev.

"I do not have to justify myself to you! Shut up and accept that grown-ups know best."

"Not in my experience."

"You little…"

"Brat, yes, I know, look, here we are. I can find my way from here."

She jumped out of the elevator and darted into the med bay. She grabbed the first grown-up she could find and said, "Felix sent me to see Amy Ox."

The man distractedly waved his hand in the direction of a walled off area.

Amy looked awful. Her skin was grayish green, but she was breathing.

Dr. Karen was upbeat and cheerful, but Ev knew that grown-ups sometimes faked cheerfulness to keep children happy. Granny was nowhere to be seen, which was a pity. She would have liked to her opinion.

"Can I have a moment alone?" she asked, interrupting Karen mid-sentence.

"Yes, I suppose. Five minutes!"

As soon as Karen left, Ev bent her head to Amy's ear and whispered desperately.

"I think this is my fault, somehow, and I'm sorry about that, but I'll make it right. I'm going to find out who really did it, and I'm going to get Jonah out, because I know it wasn't him. I did something. . .something *really* big. I can't tell you about it, but I *think* it will be alright."

Anyone that was listening would assume that she was talking about visiting Jonah in the bad place, not about changing reality to suit her needs.

She hoped.

She really did think it would be alright. She hadn't made any big changes; she'd just made it so that Felix would give her permission to see Jonah. She'd thought about having Jonah extracted from the bad place, but she had no idea what that might do to him, especially if she were fighting some other magic to do it. She *should* be the only one in any danger, but she could never know for sure.

"I'll figure this out," she whispered. "I promise."

She went back to the thirteenth floor as quickly as she could. Charles, the guard, let her in without question. She was there so often for lessons with Robert that he hardly ever questioned her anymore. He was a pretty idiot, going by Christopher's categories. Not the kind to ask follow-up questions.

Ev had often wondered if she could wander up there any time she liked, and she decided to test the theory as soon as she had a chance.

She entered Felix's office without knocking. The time for playing nice had passed. Zara had been summoned to perform the necessary spell. Ev carefully studied the grown-ups in front of her and reflected that The Seven really ought to be the five. Robert and Shaun were never included in anything important.

Ev had to fight the urge to *make* them do what she wanted. It *seemed* harmless enough to just make them bring Jonah back, but she'd also seen the huge raiding parties that went out every day to hunt down Taylor, just because she'd accidentally made the Alerrawians believe in giants again. Who knew what could happen?

"Can we get on with things? This is the part where you disappear me, I believe."

"First, I think, an explanation is in order," said Felix. He opened a drawer. A small glowing orb rose form the space within and hovered a foot in front of Ev's face.

"This is your friend. I've been keeping him close."

"Is it normal to keep students in your desk?" Ev demanded, skull tingling.

"Fairly normal, yes, particularly when they're in this state. You see, this is Jonah's tether. It is the item that anchors him to this world while he enjoys his punishment in another."

Ev already knew that, but she let Felix explain anyway.

"Detention, or 'the bad place' as children tend to call it, is a wonderful invention. It really is. We took something that had a very specific use case, namely, interrogations, and adjusted it to be more widely applicable. Detention is a kind of magical hell, I suppose, a spell that temporarily sends you somewhere else. It's a parallel universe, but each universe is designed specifically for each child we send there. It's made to be the worst thing that you, personally, will ever encounter. Think about the deepest, darkest fears that you have. Think about the worst nightmares you've ever experienced, the ones that woke you up with an audible scream and that kept you from going back to sleep. Think about the worst things that have ever happened to you. Now imagine experiencing those things over and over again on an endless loop with no escape."

Felix broke off with a chuckle.

"It is an *extremely* effective deterrent, as I'm sure you'll shortly find out. If you're wondering why I'm telling you this, it's because you will never be able to tell anyone else. The magic keeps you from ever talking about detention, as I'm sure you've noticed. It's very effective indeed."

"Yes, it seems like an entirely appropriate way to deal with children who forget to do their homework," said Ev, mouth dry. The words were difficult to speak. The magic was already trying to keep her from talking.

"Children always feel that punishment is unfair," said Marcia.

Ev glared at her. Eliza's face was neutral, and Christopher looked mildly amused. Of all the grown-ups, only Zara looked upset.

Ev listened with half an ear as Felix told her all about the bad place.

"Are you ready to join your little friend in his detention?"

"The sooner the better," she croaked.

"There's probably a good reason why we don't send children into each other's detentions," said Eliza. "I wouldn't be so flippant about it, if I were you."

"Are you ready?" asked Zara.

Zara *never* used this punishment in her own classes. She hated it.

She was also the only member of The Seven who could do magic, and therefore the only one who could be trusted to do the spell now.

Ev was sure she could see tears in her teacher's eyes.

"Yes," said Ev, face hard.

She couldn't feel sorry for Zara—no amount of tears could change the fact that must have been the one who sent Jonah to detention in the first place.

Zara snapped her fingers.

Everything changed.

12. We Were All Children, Once

It is a popular myth that children from Inner bring with them a disease that predisposes

them and those they interact with to
madness. While this is, of course, untrue,
there is a lot to be gained from choosing
your companions wisely.

Here's what Ev knew:

She knew that she would be launched straight into Jonah's worst nightmare, which would be horrible but maybe, just maybe, not as bad as her own (although Felix would happily have punished two students instead of one). She knew that Zara had timed the spell to pull her out after ten minutes, for Ev's own safety (although no one, Zara included, had seemed to know for sure if ten minutes was safe). She knew that Jonah's nightmares would try to keep her away from him because she was a friend, something positive, and that wasn't what the bad place was about.

Granny Oakwood said that knowledge was the best armor, and that naming the bad things made them easier to deal with.

Of course, that didn't help her much when she wasn't allowed to talk or even *think* about the bad place, but it probably still counted for something.

All of these thoughts crowded through Ev's mind in the time it took for Zara to snap her fingers. Zara's magic felt a little like a lasso tightening around her waist, and a moment later, she was somewhere else. She opened her eyes. Then she closed and opened them a few more times.

It didn't make the slightest difference. She couldn't see anything.

"Ah, the dark, *that* old stereotype," she said, loudly. Her voice echoed hollowly.

Ev wasn't really afraid of the dark. She'd found it unsettling at first, and sometimes she got scared if there were strange noises, but the dark itself was comforting. After the initial shock of the first few nights, she even found that darkness made it easier to sleep.

That wasn't the norm for children from Inner. In Inner, there was light everywhere, all the time. Many Inner kids were terrified of the dark, at least for a while, and it seemed like Jonah was one of them.

A teacher had once explained that nothing could physically harm them in the bad place because they weren't really there. The part of them that made them *them* was in their tether, back in the real world. It just *felt* like they were hurt or dying, and that they shouldn't to let the excruciating realism get to them.

Ev thought that if your brain decided you were hurting, then you were hurting, and anything else just sounded like an excuse.

She wasn't alone. There were things in the dark, shuffling and whispering at the edges of her hearing. Movements that she could just make out in the corner of her eye, wings flapping, figures darting.

"Well, obviously, because it's not the *dark* that's actually the scary bit, is it? It's the things in the dark that you can't see." There was a brief lull as the darkness monsters considered this statement, but not for long.

"Jonah?" she called. No response, which either meant he wasn't there or that he couldn't answer.

To keep things interesting, each child's bad place consisted of four different fears. When one fear ended, the next one began. When you were done with the fourth one, you went back to the first in a loop that didn't end until the magic said it could. When you dream, it feels like hours have passed even though dreams only take a few seconds. No matter how short your stay in detention, there is *always* enough time for you to enjoy your nightmares.

"Jonah?" she called again. "It's me, Ev. I'm really here if that's what you're worried about. I'm not going to explode into spiders or whatever. They sent me to ask about Amy."

Nothing.

The darkness was starting to get to her. She wasn't *scared*, of course, but it was irritating not to be able to see.

You couldn't use magic when you were sent to the bad place, but maybe this was different? She wasn't being punished—she was there to question someone else. . .

There was only one way to find out.

"Let there be light," said Ev. It was a phrase she'd picked up from a fragment of an old book that had once been important, and she liked it, and now it was her focus phrase for her fire ability.

A small flame flickered in the palm of her hand, and then died.

She grinned at the darkness.

"Let there be light!" she shouted, and a full flame blossomed in the palm of her hand.

Things scuttled away from the light, shrieking in agony.

"Yeah, take that, jerks!"

Something swooped at her.

"Let there be light!"

It fell to the ground screaming, and then disintegrated into dust.

"Oops, I hope you didn't need that for anything, Jonah…"

She toned her fire down to a glimmer, and decided not to hurt anything else, just in case it was somehow part of her friend. Things cowered in the corners, trying to get as far away from the light as possible.

At the other end of the room was a door.

Holding her flaming hand out like a shield, Ev went through.

It was another room, even smaller than the first, and it looked very much like Ev's old cell.

"Oh, Jonah, why did you come back here?" she asked in despair.

Ev was scared of many things, but she wasn't scared of *this*. Inner was just…

Drip. Drip, drip, drip.

"Oh. I see."

Jonah was scared of *The Creature in the Night (and other stories)*. Very scared. He went whole weeks without worrying about monsters under his bed, but most of the time he didn't sleep at all.

The story was very stupid. It went like this: A woman had a little dog that she loved dearly. Every night, she'd dangle her hand under her bed so the dog could lick her good night. One night this happened, same as usual, except that the lady couldn't get to sleep because, somewhere in the house, something was dripping.

"To the bathroom, then," muttered Ev.

In the story, the dripping led the lady to her bathroom. Cells in Inner didn't have separate bathrooms, but this wasn't the real world. Ev wasn't at all surprised to see a bathroom door, just like the ones in Alerrawia, appear in the wall. She also wasn't surprised when she opened it to see Alerrawian shower stalls stretching out into infinity.

"Jonah?" she called. Her voice echoed in the big bathroom.

Drip, drip, drip. . .

She followed the sound of the dripping, already knowing what she would see.

In the story, the dripping was the sound of blood falling from the lady's beloved dog onto the bathroom tiles and written on the wall were the words: *Dogs aren't the only things that can lick.*

Ev had laughed the first time she read it. Jonah on the other hand. . .

Ev had worked really hard at trying to convince Jonah not to be scared of unnamed creatures that hurt dogs. Jonah listened to every word she said, and sometimes it even helped. The problem, which Ev had only just realized, was that Jonah was sent to the bad place often. He was difficult. He didn't play well with others. He could be aggressive when pushed. All the things grown-ups didn't like.

Now she knew why his fear wouldn't go away. *They* wouldn't let it.

"Jonah?" she called, but she was fairly certain he wasn't here—she would have seen him by now if he was.

In the story, you never found out what the monster even was. A werewolf? A vampire? Some sort of ghost? The only thought that had ever sent chills down Ev's spine was that it might have been a *person*.

All Ev had to do to leave was go out the door she could see at the other end of the bathroom. There was nothing stopping her because *she* wasn't afraid. She knew that the monster never showed up. For Jonah, it would be different, and she would never know how because he would never be able to tell her.

She took a step toward the door and the bathroom immediately began to fill with blood.

"Gross!"

She reached the door as quickly as she could and stumbled straight into the middle of a fire.

Her clothes started to singe, and without thinking she leapt into the air to escape the flames.

"Good to know that I can fly too," she muttered.

Then she had an idea.

If she could use her fire and flight, then maybe she could warp reality to bring Jonah to her. She knew that reality warping supposedly didn't work within other magical constructs, but it was worth a try. . .

She closed her eyes, found her magic, and thought: *Bring Jonah to me!*

Nothing happened. She didn't feel the magic take and she knew immediately that it hadn't worked.

Time was running out. She picked a direction at random and continued her search.

"Jonah?" she called. "Jonah!"

This time, she thought she heard an answer.

"Jonah!"

"Hello?" came a weak, scared voice.

She rushed toward it, and, finally, she saw him.

He was standing still, but the flames were nearly on him. A moment later, he started running again, trying to escape. Judging by the state of his skin and clothes, he wasn't always successful.

"Jonah!" she screamed as she swooped toward him. "It's me, Ev! Let me just lift you above the flames. . ."

Jonah screamed and ran faster.

"I'm not part of the nightmare! I promise!"

He kept running.

"Jonah!"

Jonah turned his head, but he didn't stop running, which meant he didn't see the huge hole in the ground.

"Look out!" screamed Ev, but she was too late.

He went tumbling into the hole and, for lack of a better plan, Ev dove in after him.

She hit the ground with a thump that knocked all the air out of her. She rolled onto her back, coughing and spluttering.

When she had recovered enough to look around, she saw Jonah on his hands and knees a few paces away. His back was turned.

"Jonah," she said quietly. He didn't turn around. But he did speak.

"This is the worst one," he whispered.

Her skull tingled fiercely, and she decided then and there that she would put a stop to the bad place, even it meant burning Alerrawia to the ground.

"What happens next?" asked Ev gently.

"This is where I die alone."

She crawled next to him and put an arm around his shoulder.

"No, you won't. I'm here."

"Is that really you?"

"It's really me."

"How? Why?"

"They sent me in after you. I volunteered," she said. "I said I would ask you what happened with Amy. But you don't have to tell me anything!" she added hurriedly. "In fact, keep anything incriminating to yourself, I'm not really in a position to keep any big secrets here. . ."

She trailed off. Jonah looked perplexed.

"Amy?" he asked. "What's wrong with Amy?"

Ev felt relief flood through her.

"I'm not sure, actually. They didn't tell me much, but basically, Amy was attacked by some super bad spell that they won't talk about, and apparently you were seen doing it, but I didn't believe them, so now I'm here."

"Who 'saw' me?" Jonah demanded, and for a moment he was his usual, aggressive self.

She frowned.

"I don't know. They didn't say. Actually, when I say it out loud, it all sounds pretty strange. I guess I'll revise my answer to 'I have absolutely no idea why I'm here, can you help?'"

Jonah smiled, thinly.

"Well, it definitely is you," he said. "I'm glad you're here."

"Me too," she said smiling. The smile faded. "I've just remembered, there was a time limit on this, and I've lost track of how long this has all taken."

His face fell.

"So, you're leaving?" he whispered.

"Yes, I don't want to, but I'll have no choice. I'll do everything I can to get you out. If there's anything you *can* tell me. . .?"

"I was heading back to my dorm after class. I saw Amy. I waved. And then I blinked. And then I was in Felix's office. They didn't even ask me any questions, they just said I was an awful person and sent me straight here!"

That didn't match what she'd been told. They'd said that they'd already questioned Jonah, but that didn't seem to be the case at all.

"There *was* something else. . .You know, I can't think in here, usually, there's something about you being in here with me that's letting me remember. . ."

"Yes?" said Ev, encouragingly.

"I didn't see anyone, but for a moment, I thought I saw their mind. Someone was there. They were scared, terrified even, like they knew something bad was going to happen that they couldn't stop."

"Do you know who it was?

Jonah shook his head.

"I'm sorry, I try not to pay attention to what my mind sees. . ."

Ev patted his back absent-mindedly.

Who had Jonah felt? A potential witness? Or maybe it was the person who'd hurt Amy in the first place?

"How long will you be in here?" asked Ev.

"I don't know…"

"This is not all right. I'm sorry, but it's not. What about 'innocent until proven guilty'? What about giving people a chance to defend themselves?"

"It is what it is, Ev…"

"How can you still think like that, here, in this awful place?"

"Not everyone is as good at life as you are."

Jonah sounded completely defeated. Tears rose to Ev's eyes. She remembered how she'd felt in Inner. When her life was decided for her by shadowy figures who she never saw. Then she'd learned that it was all a lie.

This was where she and Jonah were different. Jonah had just accepted his role in the new normal and did his best to avoid punishment, just like before. Ev had not. Ev had looked at the new world and said, 'this could be a lie too'. She'd looked at it and said, 'even if it is all true, it shouldn't be'.

"It's not all right, Jonah," she said. "I'll figure out a way to get you out of here."

"That would be nice," whispered Jonah.

She would have said more, but suddenly the air rushed out of her lungs and she felt a tug around her waist, like someone was trying to drag her along on the end of a rope.

"Don't go!" shouted Jonah.

"I'll get you out!" she shouted back.

The next moment, she was back in Felix's office.

"Welcome back, Evelyn," said Felix as he shooed Jonah's tether back into the drawer.

She collapsed into a chair.

"That place is monstrous!" she tried to yell, but the most she could manage was, ". . .awful".

The grown-ups exchanged glances.

"It seems that, because it wasn't her own detention, she can speak about it to a certain degree," said Zara.

"Makes sense," said Eliza. "Otherwise, what good would it have been as an interrogation tool?"

"Don't be ungrateful, Evelyn," said Marcia. "I'm sure you have very strong thoughts about detention. Just know that we always have the best interests of our students at heart, and what seems harsh now will make sense once you are older and have children of your own to care for."

Ev didn't want kids, she hated the 'when you're older' cliché, and she had no time for grown-ups who thought torturing children was a perfectly reasonable way to run things, but she had more important things on her mind.

"You can bring him back now," she said.

"The spell will automatically lift once the investigation has reached a logical conclusion," said Christopher.

"But he doesn't know anything about it!" shouted Ev. "You can't just. . ."

"He is in no real danger! He will be fine," said Zara, soothingly. Her face was calm and gentle, but her eyes told another story.

"Have any of you been there? Ever?" she asked.

"We were all children, once," said Christopher, quietly.

"And you're just fine with it?"

"Like Marcia said," said Felix, "you'll understand when you're older. Zara, extract the information, will you?" He waved his hand dismissively, like he'd asked her to hand him a new pen.

Zara put her hands on Ev's head. Ev felt a strange creeping sensation in her brain and down her spine. And then it was gone.

"There, not so bad, right?" said Zara, with forced cheerfulness.

"Uh huh," said Ev.

Zara held a red, flickering orb in her hand. It looked a little bit like Jonah's tether, but much angrier.

"These are your memories of your time in detention. They're red and flickering because it was an unpleasant experience, as punishments should be."

"Should they?" said Ev, dully.

"We'll review your conversation with Jonah and see how it affects the investigation. Remember, anything you can do to bring the investigation to a conclusion will be helpful."

"And that's your cue to leave," said Christopher.

Siobhan was waiting for her outside Felix's office with tear-stained eyes.

"Aren't you supposed to be in the common area with everyone else?"

"They finished questioning us. . .they said we should go back to our dorms, but I needed to find you. I'm sorry, I can go. . ."

"No!" said Ev. "It's all right. I'm glad you came. I've just had a rough time, that's all."

"I'm s. . .so. . .sorry. . ." she said and started crying again. "It's. . .all. . .my fault!"

"What? You mean because of flying class? That was, like, a hundred years ago. It wasn't your fault. It wasn't mine, it wasn't Amy's, and it wasn't Jonah's.

Something's going on here, and the grown-ups are at the bottom of it."

They had to be. Jonah didn't know anything about Amy, and Felix and his merry band of madmen had to know that. They had to. If they didn't, they would once they reviewed Ev's memories, but she didn't think it would make the slightest difference. Their minds were already made up.

"Let's talk somewhere else. Library?"

"Our room will be a little more private."

They took the elevator down to the sixth floor. The people who got on and off gave them, or rather, Ev, a wide berth.

So *now* they remember not to mess with me, she thought. Good. Let them panic. They have every reason to be afraid.

"They think Jonah did it," she said to Siobhan. She couldn't say everything about what she'd experienced, but she could say *something*.

"It's all over the school! But that can't be right, can it?"

"Of course not. What are people saying about it?"

"Honestly?"

"Yes."

"They don't care. What does a fight between two Inner kids matter?"

Ev's skull tingled, but she carefully set her magic aside for later. She needed to really think about what to do next. Jonah's tether was in Felix's office and Amy was at the mercy of the doctors. She couldn't do anything that might put them in more danger.

Ev and Siobhan reached their dorm. They could hear voices inside.

"Well, this won't be very private," said Ev.

"I have an idea for getting rid of them," said Siobhan. "Come on." She went in. Surprised, Ev followed.

Madison and Stacey were lying on Stacey's bed chatting. They stopped the moment Ev and Siobhan entered the room.

"Oh, look out!" said Stacey, waving her hands theatrically. "It's the Inner brat! Quick, let's leave before we catch whatever she has!"

They fell back, laughing.

Ev rolled her eyes.

"Maybe you're the ones who should go," said Siobhan to the two older girls. The look of surprise on Madison's face was priceless. "Maybe what she has *is* catching." Suddenly, Siobhan lunged at Madison, teeth bared in a manic grin. The scariest part was that Siobhan was looking Madison right in the eye. Madison scuttled backwards. Siobhan stopped short of actually touching her, and then stepped back, laughing like a maniac.

Madison shrieked and darted out the door. Stacey was right behind her.

"Weirdos!" shouted Stacey on her way out.

There was silence.

"Well," said Ev eventually, "that was. . .Well."

"I'm sorry, I need to sit down for a moment," said Siobhan. She collapsed on her bed.

"Hey," said Ev crouching next to her. "That was amazing! Thank you!" she grinned.

Siobhan grinned at Ev's shoulder. Then she giggled. Then she laughed. Then they were both laughing so hard that they probably *did* sound mad.

Then Ev remembered her friends and her laughter dried up instantly.

"They're leaving him in the bad place, even though he said he didn't do it," said Ev, quickly, before the bad place magic stopped her.

Siobhan gasped and then froze, which could only mean that she'd try to say something about the bad place that wasn't allowed.

"Look! Butterfly!" said Ev, quickly. She'd learned that the best way to get someone to unfreeze was to change the subject as quickly as possible. The crazier your statement, the quicker your friend unfroze.

"Thanks," said Siobhan despondently. Then she started to cry in huge, heart-wrenching sobs.

"It wasn't your fault, Siobhan," said Ev, wearily. "I know you think it was because of Peter, but. . .I guess you might have a point. Not about it being your fault! You aren't responsible for what another person decided to do. . ."

Siobhan cried even harder at that.

". . .I mean, you may have a point about Peter. The bad place is the worst place in the world." She stopped in surprise, wondering what her mouth would let her say next. Siobhan's eyes were wide, her mouth firmly shut, because she didn't want to freeze again.

"That's interesting. . .I can. . ." Ev froze. So, she couldn't say *anything* about the bad place, but she could say more than she could before.

"Anyway, what I was saying," she said when she unfroze, "was that Derek was punished and Peter might blame me for that."

What she had tried to say was that no child should be sent to the bad place, *even* Derek. Maybe especially Derek. How could the bad place make him a nicer person?

And Ev realized that she could do something else she couldn't do before. She could *think* bad things about the bad place.

She scrunched up her eyes and focused her mind, and with great effort she thought: *Detention!*

She opened her eyes and smiled.

"Why are you smiling?" asked Siobhan, nervously.

"Oh. I just had a funny thought," said Ev. "Don't worry about it."

She wasn't in a hurry to tell Siobhan everything. Perhaps it was time for a new alliance, but that didn't mean she should just trust the first person to come her way.

"We can't be sure it's Peter. I'm not sure he would do something like that."

"Of course, he would!"

"He's just a kid, making bad kid decisions like all of us."

Siobhan didn't look convinced. Ev decided not to even mention Robert. The idea needed some more thought anyway.

"I think someone doesn't want you to have friends," said Siobhan.

"Which would mean *you're* in danger too," said Ev. Siobhan looked up in surprise, blushing deeply. Ev looked away and said, "There's something bigger going on here, and we need to figure out what it is. They don't just want to get at me—there has to be more to it than that. Someone must have seen something." Someone *had* been there— Jonah had felt their mind. "We've just got to ask around until we figure out who knows what."

Ev shook her head to clear some of the cobwebs. She was terribly, horribly upset about her friends, but she felt something else too. She felt like she had a purpose. It was fueled by anger, and it was fueled by love, and it was the most intense thing she ever felt. She'd felt almost the same on her fifth birthday. Scared. Confused. Betrayed. Not knowing what would come next. But this time she also felt something else. Hope. Hope that this was the beginning of something new, that things would change. It didn't even matter if they changed for the better, as long as they *just changed.*

"I'm so used to living with uncertainty. It almost feels like home."

"What are you going to do?"

"*We* are going to figure out what's really going on. *We* are going to free Jonah and find justice for Amy. *We* are going to change everything."

We are going to change EVERYTHING!

The magic was out before Ev could stop it, but she found that she didn't care.

"Siobhan Kenwood, will you help me overthrow the government of Alerrawia?" she asked.

Siobhan looked up nervously, confusion shining through her tear-filled eyes.

"You want me to help you?"

"Of course."

"Then yes. Yes, I will."

13. Rip Your Magic Out with Pliers!

Those living in isolated communities are at a much higher risk for depression and psychosocial difficulties than larger communities with broader support

structures. Alerrawia is, by definition, an
isolated community, and we have been
witnessing the effects of this for decades.

We cannot go on.

It turned out that not a lot of people wanted to talk
to two kids, but Ev and Siobhan tried anyway.

No one knew who 'saw' Jonah hurt Amy. There
weren't even any rumors, which was strange. The other
children were completely useless. They either refused to
say anything, or they accused them of being crazy like
Jonah. Morris, an Alerrawian kid in a number of Ev's
classes, told them to get lost. Caroline, an Inner kid who
was still struggling to adapt even after more than two years,
just looked at her feet and mumbled what everyone else
was saying: "Jonah did it, there's nothing more to be said."

The only kid who tried to help them was Gavin
Oakwood. "I know you're trying to find out more
information," he said. "It's a great idea, and I commend
you for it, but you're going about it in the wrong way."

"Look, I know I'm eleven," said Ev wearily—she'd
had this discussion before, "but Siobhan, despite
appearances, is fifteen, only a year younger than you, and. .
."

"I don't care about age. If your age was going to
stop you from doing whatever you like, it would have by

377

now. That's sort of related to my point, actually. No one is going to speak to you. You're not safe."

"*You're* speaking to us."

"I'm not very safe either. So, I decided to do some digging for you. All I've found out is that the witness to the event was apparently one of The Seven, but no one knows who."

"How on earth could you know that?"

"I have the best sources," said Gavin, nose in the air. "Well, one source, anyway."

"Can you find out more from this source of yours?"

"Probably."

"Well, feel free to keep digging," said Ev, begrudgingly. "But don't tell anyone we sent you."

Gavin rolled his eyes.

"Obviously. I actually *want* them to talk to me."

"Well, if that's all?" said Ev.

"Actually, there *is* one more thing. . ."

"What?"

"Just something for you to think about. I'm sure you've noticed, but despite all of the classes we attend, kids aren't really allowed to know stuff around here. If you understand what I'm saying."

"I think so…"

"Good. Now, like you, I have untenable number of classes to attend, so I'll be saying goodbye."

"He means we should speak to the grown-ups," said Siobhan, the moment Gavin was out of earshot.

"Yes, but they'll never tell us anything. . ."

"Some of them might. Remember the day after your hearing? All those weird classes? Some of the teachers. . .well, some of them seemed to be on your side."

Siobhan was in almost all of Ev's classes, but Ev had never noticed because Siobhan's innate ability was fading which meant she could fade away whenever she felt like it. It wasn't the same as invisibility, which just meant that people couldn't see you anymore. Fading meant they forgot you even existed.

"So, I'm not the only one who thought all that was a bit strange," said Ev.

"Nope," said Siobhan. "Actually, you're not the only one most of the time, Ev. You just like to think you are."

Granny seemed like a good place to start, so Ev developed a series of mysterious stomachaches that got her sent to the med bay over and over again.

It was very boring, lying there, waiting for someone to see her. She started taking *Alerrawia: To the Future* with her for something to do. Felix was a boring writer, but there was a lot to learn from his ravings. She opened a page at random:

. . .ago, there was an explosion that wiped out Inner's central control system, killing everyone who knew how to manage or override Vendavi, thereby leaving Vendavi, an advanced but limited computer system, in complete control. Attempting to access Inner from the outside in any way other than the specific method discovered by the Alerrawians will result in a complete system meltdown, killing all residents.

Attempts to free Inner are therefore doomed to failure. In any case, the residents of Inner hold very little interest to us as either maidens in distress or murder victims.

Hilarious.

Only in the mind of Felix Granite could something be 'advanced' and 'limited' at the same time. It's like he didn't really expect people to pay attention to the actual words he wrote.

Finally, Granny was assigned to her case, and Ev shoved the book into her bag. Technically, it was stolen property. Granny would probably understand, but she didn't want to risk it.

"You've been in an out of here quite a bit in the last few days, I hear."

"The other doctors say I'm just worried about my friends," she said, looking down.

"You disagree?"

"Not exactly, but they act like being worried about them is silly! You know, they won't even let me see Amy when I'm here?"

"I know. I see her every day, though, and they're doing the best they can. She will wake up. One day."

"Well, it's unfair! They're both just gone, and I *know* neither of them deserved it!"

"You have tried to. . .*do* anything, have you?"

"Nope!" said Ev. She hadn't warped reality even once since visiting Jonah in the bad place because she was still too scared about what she might accidentally do.

Granny donned her stethoscope. "Deep breath!"

Ev did as she was told, and when Granny got close to look in her ears, she whispered, "You know Jonah didn't do it, right?"

"Of course, I know," Granny whispered back. "There's just nothing *I* can do about it."

"You could stand up against that place! He's been in there for *days*; do you know how horrible that is?"

"*Shush!* Yes. I do."

Granny's whisper was sad and heavy, and Ev suddenly remembered what Christopher had said to her.

"All grown-ups were children once."

"Yes, we were."

"You know *exactly* what it's like."

"Yes, we do."

"*And you let it go on anyway?*"

"We're just as powerless as you are."

"Grown-ups *always* have more power than children, *and* more choices. Just because you're more afraid than we are, of *everything*, shouldn't mean that you can just do what you like with us."

Granny blinked. "While I'm glad that you're using 'us' and not 'me' in your excellent sentences, I have to object. I really don't know anything. . ."

"Yes, you do!" said Ev impatiently. "Grown-ups always know something! You've had more time to learn *how* to learn things than we have, and you know how to make it all fit together. You just can't be bothered to share what you know with us because children aren't really people. You won't even help yourselves, you're so scared!" Ev's skull tingled fiercely.

Granny sighed and sat down heavily next to Ev.

"It's hard being a child," said Granny. "In different ways, it's hard being a grown-up. When you're grown up, everyone expects you to know what you're doing. You spend your life trying to make the right decisions, and you *always* feel like you're making it up as you go along. We know more, we can do more, but that doesn't mean decisions are easy to make."

"The price of being *able* to do something is that you *have to* do it," said Ev, hotly.

They sat in silence for a while. Then Granny slowly got up and closed the door to the consultation room. "I know," she said, "that someone from The Seven saw what happened, but I don't know who."

"I've heard that," said Ev. "Your grandson told me."

"Ah, Gavin. Well, he knows that anything shared in strict confidence between family members should be spread as far and wide as possible."

"You're not mad at him?"

"Of course not. He took the information he had and used it to help a friend, just like I taught him to. Which, I suppose, is exactly what you're asking of me right now, so I'll tell you the little that I do know: Jonah was sent to detention pretty quickly, from what I hear. Some say he went right on the spot; others say he saw Felix and friends first. I don't think the timing matters particularly much. What's important is that *everyone* agrees that The Seven dealt with it immediately, which means only one person could have sent him there."

Ev nodded. "Yes, Zara."

"Zara. Indeed. One of the few teachers who *never* uses detention as a punishment."

Ev's face lit up.

"You mean she might be willing to tell me something?"

"I would never instruct any student to harass a member of The Seven with accusations," said Granny. "Now, we've been here far too long already, and there's nothing wrong with you, so get back to class."

Conveniently, it was Wednesday, which meant that she had magical innovation straight after lunch. She ate quickly so that she could arrive early.

"Hello, Evelyn," said Zara as Ev marched into the room.

Ev ignored the greeting and sat down heavily.

"Okay, I'm going to get right down to it. Tell me what you know about Amy and Jonah and tell me quickly."

"Or what?"

"You wouldn't want to know. I am running out of patience with this charade. Amy is not getting better, and Jonah is still trapped in a nightmare, and no one is doing anything about it!"

"Evelyn," Zara began. She stopped and closed her eyes in exhaustion. "Evelyn, things are complicated for everyone, not just you. We can't just go against the authorities."

"You *are* the authorities!" yelled Ev.

"I have no power. I am a magic-user. I am useful, but under no circumstances am I to be treated as fully human."

"I wish you would understand what it's like. . ."

"What it's like? *What it's like?* You mean what it's like to be born of parents from Inner? To be a gifted magic-user in a world that thinks you shouldn't exist? To have to fight for the right to just *be*, in any space? Is that what you're talking about?"

Her last words echoed in the sudden silence.

"I'm sorry," said Ev.

Zara sighed. "It's all right. Maybe I don't understand. Maybe I've been playing this game for so long that I *don't* remember what it's like. . .I'm sorry, Ev. For sending Jonah to detention. For sending you after him. But you have to understand that I had no choice."

"There's always a choice."

"That's easy to say when you're not the one who has to choose."

Ev shook her head in irritation.

"Do you know who hurt Amy? Really?" she asked.

"No."

"But you know it wasn't Jonah?"

"Yes."

"So how can you leave him in there?"

"I can't pull him out until the spell's parameters are met, and they're so vague I'm not sure. . .Ev, I can't. I've thought about it, trust me, but I can't..."

Ev's skull tingled mercilessly.

"I'm sorry," she began, coldly. "It was rude of me to expect you to compromise your happiness here. When everything is going so well for you."

The five-minute bell rang. Any moment now, the other children would arrive.

Zara seemed to be half her usual size, like she'd turned in on herself. Deflated.

"Listen carefully," said Zara, head still in her hands. "The rumors that a member of The Seven was the witness aren't quite true. One of The Seven reported it, but they heard about it from someone else. I don't know who."

The door burst open, and students poured into the room.

*

Sometimes Ev wondered if Amy and Jonah would be upset that she had a new friend now, but she always decided that it was probably okay because Siobhan was helping her help them.

They were in the quietest corner of the library, whispering about what they did and didn't know, and sneaking bites of vegetables Ev had stolen during her garden shift. Near the elevators, some older students were practicing spells, but they were too caught up in what they were doing to notice the girls huddled on beanbags under a window. No one else was around.

"I really, *really* think that Felix is behind all of it," said Siobhan for the hundredth time. She had tears in her eyes when she spoke, and her voice choked up when she said it, but she was adamant that Ev's problems came from the very top.

"I just. . .I can't bring myself to believe it," said Ev.

"That's not true. You just don't want to believe it because it's too depressing."

Ev nodded, gloomily.

"I saw that nod, you know. I know you agree with me."

Ev did agree, but she wished with all her hear that she didn't. What could she and Siobhan do if Felix, the boss of everyone, was against them?

"I still don't understand *why*!"

"You're a threat to the status quo," said Siobhan in a weary, sing-song voice. "I've told you a hundred times. I grew up here. I know how things work. You're too. . .visible. You stand out too much, and you've broken too many rules for Felix to *ever* forget."

Siobhan's voice dripped with bitterness. The words behind her words screamed that Siobhan had something personal against Felix. Ev took a wild guess and asked, "Where are your parents?"

"Gone."

Lots of the kids who lived in Alerrawia were missing one or both parents. It was something that everyone noticed, but no one mentioned.

She patted Siobhan on the shoulder.

"I'm sorry," she said, awkwardly. She was new at being a friend, and she didn't know what else to do.

Siobhan shrugged Ev's hand off.

"It's fine."

It obviously wasn't fine, but Ev was out of options.

"Oh. Good," she said, weakly.

"Why are we even *in* the library? What good are we doing?"

Siobhan was being difficult, which meant Ev had offended or annoyed her, which was *extremely* easy to do, it turned out.

"I have the beginnings of the first steps of a very vague plan," said Ev. She darted a glance at the huge set of heavily armored doors that dominated one wall of the library. Siobhan's brow furrowed in confusion, and then her eyes widened.

"We can't get into the restricted section!" she hissed, looking around nervously.

Ev put a finger to her lips. Only The Seven were allowed into the restricted section. Not even teachers had access. Definitely not the library pixies. Even *thinking* about breaking in would get you into serious trouble.

On top of that, today was the worst possible day to try. Ernouf, Christopher's enormous wolf companion, was lying in front of the closed door, which had to mean that Christopher himself was inside.

"We've spoken to everyone who will speak to us. We have to get the rest of our information somewhere else."

"It's *impossible*!" hissed Siobhan. "You have *completely* lost your mind! We cannot do this! Look at me, Ev. We CANNOT do it. Do you understand?"

"Mm," said Ev, still looking at the door. "Nothing is *really* impossible. Armored door, lots of alarms, Ernouf, but he's not always there. . ."

Not everything that protected the door was obvious. There were spells to keep people out, but six of The Seven couldn't actually use magic, so they couldn't be *that* hard to get past.

"The spells are probably the same as the scanners— they automatically disable for the right people. . ."

The biometric scanners were a big challenge. The Seven had to have their eyes scanned, but they also had to give a blood sample on the spot. The children all knew this because watching Robert or Shaun shout "Ow!" as a robotic arm stole their blood was one of the better forms of entertainment available.

"Just as a mental exercise," said Ev, "do you know of any spells that can temporarily turn you into someone else?"

Siobhan shook her head vigorously.

"You're crazy!"

"Probably. . .but this *is* an emergency!" Carefully, Ev cleared her mind of all distractions. It was easy, now. She controlled her breathing and dropped into a meditative state, and, almost immediately, she felt her magic spark, deep in her heart. She grabbed it.

She used it.

In the next few minutes, I will successfully enter the restricted section, and there I will find the answers to my questions.

At that moment, the heavy door opened, and Christopher stepped out. Ernouf jumped up to greet him.

Just as Christopher was about to lock the door behind him, someone shouted, "Hold it!"

The voice was very loud in the empty, quiet library.

Eliza Faraday, oldest member of The Seven, rushed into view carrying a stack of documents. Even from where they were sitting Ev could see the big 'Do Not Read!' stickers plastered over everything. The sort of documents that weren't really supposed to leave the restricted section in the first place.

"Why does she have those?" asked Siobhan.

"Shush!" said Ev. She suspected that Eliza, who was very careful about following rules, would never have taken those documents out of the restricted section if Ev's magic hadn't made her do it.

Maybe.

The problem with warping reality is that it was impossible to know what happened because of magic and what would have happened anyway.

"I need to put these back," said Eliza.

Christopher tutted impatiently, but he propped the door open and stepped back to let her in.

Now Ev *knew* that her magic was working. The Seven weren't allowed to hold the door for anyone, not even each other. Eliza and Christopher were the last people who would break the rules.

"Be a dear and keep it open for me. I won't be long," said Eliza sharply as she breezed past Christopher before he could say anything.

Christopher huffed in frustration his face a mask of fury.

Ev had never seen Christopher visibly angry before. He was always calm, with one eyebrow always slightly above the other to indicate how little he believed anything you were saying.

"I hope it's not permanent," Ev said quietly.

"What?" Siobhan asked.

"Nothing, just enjoying the show."

Ev and Siobhan were mostly hidden by a table. If they were very quiet, they wouldn't be noticed. Even if Christopher did see them, they were just kids in the library doing their homework, as they had every right to be.

From where Christopher stood, the library probably looked deserted. The kids who'd been practicing a little while ago had left, and so had Ernouf. If he made even the slightest attempt to make sure that no one was around, he would have found Ev and Siobhan.

He didn't.

After glancing impatiently at his watch a few times, Christopher finally heaved a sigh, grabbed a trash can, and used it to prop the door open.

Then he walked away.

"Wow," said Ev, quietly.

If Christopher decided to take Elevator B, he'd walk right past them, but he turned into the labyrinth of shelves instead to take the stairs.

A few moments later, Eliza pushed the door open, looked around, and then *walked off.* Without closing the door.

"I'm not terrified at all," said Ev.

"Um, I guess, well, security measures are only as good as the people who use them," gabbled Siobhan. "Christopher probably assumed that Eliza would close the door after her when she came out, and Eliza probably assumed that Christopher had just popped off somewhere and would be back to close it in a moment. He assumed she would know better than to leave the door open; she assumed he wouldn't have left it open if he wasn't coming back."

"Of course, you're right, unless you consider anything you know about Eliza, Christopher, or Alerrawia, and then the explanation falls to pieces, but never mind. Let's go in."

"What? We can't *go in*!"

Ev grabbed Siobhan's hand and ran. The older girl tried to pull her back, which was when Ev remembered that she'd said 'I' instead of 'we' when she cast her spell.

"Come on!"

She turned her head and looked straight at Siobhan.

Come on!

Seconds later, they were through the door. The turned right past an enormous rectangular table and kept going until they were far among the shelves near the back of the room. The crouched low, panting heavily.

Shelves of books and documents crowded them on every side. This was where the 'dangerous' books were kept.

Ev, who had read a lot in her short life, didn't understand how books could be dangerous. Knowing things, being allowed to know them, couldn't be bad. The more you knew, the better your decisions about *everything* would be.

Of course, The Seven disagreed. The way Marcia had put it in one of Ev's more contentious Geography lessons was that some ideas were just no longer relevant, and if certain people ran across them, they might start behaving against the interests of Alerrawia.

Against the interests of Alerrawia. The words behind those words were this: *your* best interests are irrelevant. The only people who matter are the people in charge.

The alarms started to blare. Siobhan jumped, and Ev had to grab her to keep her from rushing into the open.

"It's just because the door has been open for so long."

Siobhan crouched at Ev's side, shaking.

"Eliza!" Christopher shouted from outside.

Ev froze.

"Eliza! Are you still in there?"

They stayed silent.

They heard Christopher mutter something that sounded like, "Drat that woman. . ." Then he closed the door. They heard the whirs and clicks of the automatic locking mechanism.

The lights went off, the sirens stopped, and they were left in darkness and silence.

They were going to get in trouble for this—it was inevitable. For now, though, they might have *hours* to find what they were looking for.

"Can we turn the lights on?" she asked Siobhan.

"Yes," said Siobhan. Ev heard Siobhan moving around in the dark, sometimes bumping into things, until she found a switch and flooded the room with light.

Ev relied on Siobhan's to know things. Siobhan *never* forgot what she heard, and she heard *a lot*, especially when she was faded, and no one remembered she was there at all.

"They're not all that great at security around here, are they?"

"Good thing for us, right?"

"I'm glad you seem to be happier about all this," said Ev.

"Yeah, I am! When you grabbed me and started running, I thought it was a terrible idea, but then suddenly it all seemed perfect!"

That was Ev's reality warping at work. There was nothing she could do about it now; she'd have to wait and see if she'd caused any long-term damage to her friend.

"Let's not waste any time," said Ev.

"I agree!" said Siobhan. "Um. . .what are we looking for?"

They looked at the huge number of books and papers stacked haphazardly on shelves. They hadn't had time to think of a plan, and now they were faced with millions of possible clues.

"Stuff covered in dust probably doesn't matter as much for what's going on right now," said Siobhan. "How about we start with the things Eliza bought back?"

"Good idea!"

Eliza was normally very prim and thoughtful. Not a hair on her head was out of place, and her gray uniform was always impeccable, so Ev knew that it was her magic that had made Eliza dump everything untidily on a table.

"This could be important," said Siobhan, grabbing one of the thicker documents. "It looks like a magical innovation proposal, but I don't see Zara's signature."

Technically, Zara was in charge of approving magical innovations. It was her job to make sure that new ideas weren't a threat to anyone, but Felix could still say no to *anything* she approved.

Ev scanned the proposal.

Whoever wrote it had had to fill out a section asking them to demonstrate that they knew magic was bad before they even gave the title of their idea.

"This is basically just those horrible posters written out as a paragraph," said Ev.

"Posters?"

"You know, the posters everywhere? *Drug your children so they don't blow up the world! Rip your magic out with pliers!* Those posters?"

"I guess I don't really notice them. . ."

"Lucky you."

They studied the proposal.

"What's a ChronoBurster?" Ev asked.

"Never heard of it."

Ev read carefully.

"You know, I'm pretty sure this is a proposal for combining nanobots and an explosion spell with a time delay to explode an entire water system."

"What? That will never get approved!"

"And yet, here it is."

Ev read on.

"Hang on a moment. This doesn't make any sense!"

Siobhan took the page from Ev.

"Looks fine to me. A way to use this Chronoburster thing on Inner's towers to wipe out everything. It's horrible, but it does makes sense."

"But those towers are just remnants from a time when Inner couldn't make its own oxygen. . ." Ev trailed off. She'd just repeated a well-worn phrase from her time in Inner. "Oh. I see. That's not true, is it?"

Siobhan shook her head.

"Nope. See, this bit here explains it." Siobhan pointed to Figure 5 in the proposal.

"What am I looking at?"

"It looks like those towers are actually a way for people out here to destroy Inner in an emergency. It gives us access to their water supply. Oh, but this bit says that a test is a good idea, because we don't know if the towers will still work, what with Vendavi's lockdown and the whole place falling to pieces."

Ev was shaking. Her skull tingled viciously.

"My *mother* is in there. My friend Steve is in there. Hundreds of people. . .Why are they looking at this now?"

"*I* don't know!"

Hands shaking, Ev carefully wrote '*Chronoburster*' and '*towers?*' in the back of one of her notebooks.

She wished she knew what question this was the answer to. It had to be an answer to one of her questions, or else she wouldn't have found it—that's how reality warping worked.

She realized too late that she hadn't been very specific about *which* questions she wanted answered.

"If all I find in here are cheat sheets for my next history test, I'm going to be *really* annoyed."

Siobhan gave her a puzzled smile.

"I don't think cheat sheets will be in here. Teachers aren't allowed in?"

"Of course, thanks for the reminder," muttered Ev.

"Look at this! It looks like a memorandum from, like, two-hundred years ago!"

Ev read over Siobhan's shoulder.

TO: Kelvin Granite

FROM: Col. G. Faraday

CC: All Leadership

SUBJECT: The end of the world (?)

DATE: September 3rd, 2040

It didn't work. Or it did, but too well.

We are safe. That was the goal, after all. Inner is safe. Unfortunately, the protesters who were giving us so much trouble are also safe. Or maybe that's fortunate? I'm not sure I can tell anymore.

As for everywhere else… It's gone. I think forever. The device enclosed us in a 'bubble', as planned, but it also seems to have set off a chain reaction.

We may have destroyed the world we were trying to save.

Which is unfortunate. Or not.

I guess it depends on your point of view.

Any thoughts on how to proceed would be most welcome.

"Well, they always told us that we're all there is," said Siobhan.

"Yes, well, they told me that *Inner* was all there is, and that was a lie, and they lie about other things too, like giants, so forgive me if I look into it for myself. Also, I think you're missing the point."

"What point?"

"The bubble was done on purpose. And I think it wasn't supposed to be permanent, but they messed up. Has anyone ever told you *that*?"

"No. . ."

Ev grabbed the next document from Eliza's pile.

"This one's a bit more recent."

TO: The Seven

FROM: Felix Granite

CC: Senior Teaching Staff

SUBJECT: Renewal of stance on 'The Bubble'

DATE: December 5th, 2239

The annual decision on Alerrawia's stance on the topic of the bubble is hereby renewed. The topic continues to be taboo and unimportant. Communicate with your staff and students accordingly.

In a related matter, efforts to prevent subversive plans for family reunification among our Inner rescues should continue. It wouldn't hurt to use this opportunity to remind those in your care of the "vulnerability" of Vendavi should any attempts to hack the system be attempted.

"The words behind the words are that not very long ago someone tried to free someone else from Inner, and was almost successful, and The Seven had to step in," said Ev. "Also, just look at those scare quotes around 'vulnerability'."

"What are scare quotes?"

"When someone uses quote marks to say that a word isn't meant to be taken seriously. Like, if Marcia ever wrote something positive about Inner kids it would be something like 'All children from Inner are 'lovely'."

"So. . .?"

"So Vendavi and Inner are possibly not as vulnerable as we're supposed to think. Also, talking about the bubble is taboo, but it's also unimportant? If it was unimportant, there would be no need to make it taboo, and if it's taboo it can't be unimportant."

"It's a contradictory message?"

"Exactly!"

"So, if one day we're senior teachers and we get a note like this from Felix, or whoever comes after him, what are we supposed to do with it?"

"Burn without reading."

Siobhan laughed nervously.

"Here's another memorandum. This one is from this week!"

TO: The Seven

FROM: Felix Granite

CC: Senior Teaching Staff

SUBJECT: The bubble is NOT too hot!!!1!

DATE: February 7th, 2241

It is not too hot in the bubble. Recent events are due to failures in Suncharm, not some fictitious environmental catastrophe. The bubble is safe. It is secure. We will not run out of water. We will not boil to death.

"There's nothing to worry about. Everything is fine. Don't look behind the curtain," chirped Ev.

"I don't understand you when you're like this!"

"Sorry. If the bubble really was safe and we really had nothing to worry about, Felix wouldn't bother sending out messages threatening people. He wouldn't have to."

"The bubble *must* be safe, we've lived here for ages, we. . ."

"Unfortunately, reality is true whether you want it to be or not. Wishing for the bubble to be safe is not going to cut it, I'm afraid. When I was in Inner. . .there's a test for Inner kids before we can come here, I don't know if you know about it? Well, one of the questions was about the present and future of the bubble, although I didn't know it at the time, and the future. . .it doesn't look good, Siobhan. All dried up and cracked, not much water left. I think that's what's going to happen to us. Maybe not soon, but it will."

Siobhan just shook her head stubbornly. Ev sighed and added the memoranda to the growing collection of notes in her pocket.

The last document in the pile was an essay written about a decade ago called *The Psychological Impact of Living in a Bubble* by Alison Oakwood.

"That's Granny's daughter! She wrote *Inner: How and Why?*"

On the first page of Alison's paper were the words:

See me!

Ev left Siobhan to do the reading. She wandered over to a nearby shelf where she could see a few stacks of posters. Idly, she picked one up, expecting to see the same old posters she saw everywhere else.

Instead, what she saw was this:

Magic is in everyone—you just have to look.

The world runs better on magic!

Don't deny who you are!

"I'm starting to understand Alerrawia's definition of 'dangerous.'"

"Did you find something?" asked Siobhan.

"Nothing important to the current situation," said Ev, automatically, but then she remembered that *everything* she found in here had to be the answer to a question she had, so she wrote down the phrases in the back of her notebook anyway.

Her eye landed on a stack of paper on a higher shelf, and her brain said, "I bet those are important," so she took them down.

She picked one at random and started reading, her eyes growing wider and wider with every word.

"Siobhan," she said, her voice shaking. "I think I've found the wordless magic spells. This is the one they use to release us from Hexteria in spell casting lessons!"

"Just lying there on a shelf?"

"I guess they think that it doesn't matter where they put it, as long as it's in the restricted section."

Siobhan left Alison's essay on a table and came over to read the spell with Ev.

"This is hard. It will take *ages* to learn," said Siobhan.

"Most things worth having are hard work," said Ev. "Imagine being able to use your magic whenever *you* chose? Sounds worth it to me."

Ev added the instructions to her now bulging pocket and sifted through the other spells in the pile.

"Well, well, well, and here's the one to remove the tracking spell from Suncharm. I'm sure that will come in handy too."

None of the other spells jumped out at her so she put them back. If they were the answers to any of her questions, they would have caught her attention properly.

"What does Alison's essay say?"

"It says a *lot*," said Siobhan. "Basically, Inner was built to protect science followers from magic during the war. Lots of magic users didn't want Inner to be built, so they protested, *here*. This building used to be Granite Institute's headquarters. Thousands of people swarmed here with signs and loudspeakers to try to put a stop to it, but it didn't work. Inner was built. The protesters stayed behind to show that they still thought it was an awful idea. It was *really* hard for them, too. The war was raging, and they kept sending soldiers into the woods to get rid of them. The only reason they got to stay was because they used their magic to hide themselves. More protesters kept sneaking past the guards and into the woods, and Granite Institute started to worry that they were planning to attack, so they thought up a new magical innovation. The device was meant to create a shield over Inner and this building that no one could get into so that the experiment could continue in peace. Alison says they would have been more successful if they'd *only* used magic but doing that would have felt like an admission that magic *was* better than science, when really, it's just proof that you need both. I guess she was right because the device didn't work. It trapped Inner, this building, *and* the part of the forest the True Users live in now, which was not the plan. Also, its effects turned out to be permanent. Alison doesn't know why that happened, no one really does, but we've been stuck here for about two hundred years. Oh, and she thinks we're all going mad because we live in a closed system."

Ev's magic tapped on her heart and told her that this was one of the answers she was looking for.

Now all she had to do was figure out what the question was.

"There's also a bit in here about the myth of conservation of magic, which basically says that people *can* have more than two innate abilities and be strong in them, which we all know isn't true, so I'm not sure we should take her *that* seriously."

Ev decided not to respond.

"Where *is* Alison? Granny talks like she's not around anymore. . ."

"There's a sub-basement. They keep prisoners there. She could be down there, I guess. They don't tell you where your loved ones go when they disappear."

Again, there was bitterness in Siobhan's voice, but Ev was saved from having to ask more by a voice from her bag.

"Evelyn!"

Ev scrambled for the magic mirror and pulled it out.

"I'm not alone," she said immediately.

"Don't worry about that, I've added a spell this time, no one will notice or remember." Granny sounded impatient. "Have you done something again? Are you somewhere you're not supposed to be? Because, if you are, they know."

The door slammed open, and they heard someone shout, "Who's in here?"

It was Robert.

14. Attention, Evelyn Acorn!

Let me tell you about *What?*

Did you hear about *Nothing?*

It was *I can't really say.*

What about *Go away!*

But really *Stop fussing!*

I'll have to not tell you some other day.

Recorded by Granny Oakwood

"I forgot to ask to not be caught," Ev whispered.

"What did you say?"

"Nothing, don't mind me. What do we do?"

"I don't know!"

The restricted section of the library was long and narrow. The door was at one end, and Ev and Siobhan were at a table all the way at the other. Robert wouldn't be able to see them yet, but it was only a matter of time.

They were going to get caught. Once she accepted it, Ev felt almost relaxed. She carefully crammed everything into her pocket—the mirror, the pages, the notes she'd torn from her notebook, everything. She took a moment to be grateful that she'd hidden Madam's RDD under her mattress this morning. As hiding places went, pockets weren't the best, but it was all she could think of.

"I said, who's in here!" shouted Robert.

Ev shrugged and sat down. After a moment, she leaned back in her chair and put her feet on the table.

"What are you doing?" whispered Siobhan.

"We can't stop him catching us, but we *can* annoy him."

Moments later, Robert saw them.

"Of course," he sneered.

He grabbed them each by their hair and dragged them out the room. Waiting for them in the library were Zara, Christopher, Marcia, Peter, and Derek.

"All my favorite people in one place!" said Ev, brightly.

Marcia was pale. *"What were you doing in there?"* she demanded.

"The door was open," said Ev. "We thought we'd take a look."

"I told you we saw them go in, uncle," said Peter piously to Robert.

Ev knew that Peter was Robert's nephew. *Everyone* knew. Peter wouldn't keep something like that to himself. Unfortunately, everyone *also* knew that Robert hated children, and magical children in particular. Peter was no exception, but Robert was all he had. His own parents were 'gone'.

'Gone' was like a magic word. When someone used it, everyone else stopped talking.

"You saw us go in, did you?"

"Yeah, hours ago!"

"Really? What took you so long, then?"

"Not just anyone can wander up to the thirteenth floor, you know," he said defensively. "And my uncle is very busy. . ."

"Shut up," said Robert.

Neither of them had said very much, but the words behind their words were plain as day to Ev. She could picture the scene clearly: Peter rushing up to the thirteenth floor to find his uncle, Derek in tow. Peter convincing the guard to let them in. Robert refusing to see him for ages because who has time for snot-nosed magic brats? Eventually letting him in and hearing him out, then not believing anything Peter said.

No wonder it took hours.

"Fortunately for everyone," said Christopher, lazily, "I overheard the argument Peter and Robert were having and I discerned some truth in it."

Well, of course you did, thought Ev. You were the one who left the door open.

Christopher was staring at them piercingly, like he was daring them to say something. Ev smiled at him sweetly. "How lucky we all are to have you, Christopher."

The sincerity in her voice made Derek choke on his own spit.

Christopher blinked, once, which was a pretty big reaction, by Christopher standards.

She turned to the spluttering Derek and said, "I'm sorry I got you sent to the bad place. It won't happen again."

She wished she had a camera. The looks of shock on Peter and Derek's faces were priceless.

"At the end of the day," she continued, ignoring the grown-ups completely now, "it's us against them. I'm not going to let *them* win anymore."

"How dare you? HOW DARE YOU?" shrieked Robert.

"Well, it's been a long day," said Ev to the boys. "I'll just be heading to bed."

She dashed into the maze of shelves.

"Stop!" roared Robert. "Zara! Bring her back here!"

There was a tug around her waist as Zara's magic caught her, but she had just enough time to shove her stolen papers and Granny's mirror behind some books. It was still a terrible hiding place, but it was better than her pocket.

"Woohoo!" she shouted as Zara magic dragged her backwards. "Can I go again?"

Robert was incandescent with rage. Ev watched him intently, head tilted slightly to one side, wondering what would happen next.

Suddenly, Robert's face cleared, and he smiled.

Uh oh.

That only happened when Robert had an idea. Robert's ideas were exclusively pain based.

"Zara," Robert said in a soft, satisfied voice. "Send them both to detention."

"Not at your most imaginative today, I see," said Ev. Then she closed her eyes and waited.

She tried to remember what it had felt like being in Jonah's detention. It would be different this time, but she thought she could handle it.

She opened her eyes. She was filled with a feeling of great peace and comfort. She was in a safe place. She was in bed, and although there were lights on, her mind said, 'nighttime.'

The lights were always on, in Inner.

She was supposed to be asleep, but for some reason she was struggling.

In the next bed over, she could hear her parents breathing. It must be late if they had finished their work for the day. They would be tired—it was hard work being an Inner parent, teaching and raising a stupid child and contributing to the success of Inner. She was a very stupid child. Mother always said. It was much too late for a Bug Bar nap, as Father called them, so it must be nighttime.

Lying awake when everyone was asleep was the most peaceful time of the day.

Then she heard a noise. It was a tiny scratching sound that was almost too soft to hear. Her whole body filled with terror.

"Mother?" she whispered, wanting comfort and love, but not wanting to wake the grown-ups. They would be angry.

Mother didn't hear her.

Scritch, scritch, scritch. . .

Suddenly Ev knew what it was. There was only one thing it could be.

The mantis.

No matter how many times her parents told her that there were no real bugs anymore, Ev was convinced that one night a praying mantis would burrow its way into her brain. She hid behind her Mother every time the bug bots came. Her mother would grab her hand and make her touch the bugs to help her get over her childishness.

"Mother!" she called. Or tried to call. Her voice had stopped working. She couldn't call Mother. She couldn't move her arms and legs. She couldn't do anything.

Then she saw the praying mantis crawling across the covers toward her. All she could do was stare and. . .

. . .shoot it with fire. . .

. . .*what fire?*

There was something, something she was forgetting. What was it? And why was her skull tingling like this? She could do something about this. . .

. . .and Ev abruptly came back to herself. She wasn't four years old—she was eleven, and she could do things.

She flung back the covers of her bed, and the praying mantis went flying.

"So much for that," she said out loud. Then she cringed.

Apparently, she was still afraid to wake her parents.

But why? They weren't really there, and neither was she.

She strode toward their bed, grabbed the covers, and pulled.

The bed was empty.

Ev felt like all the air had been sucked out of her body.

There was a noise behind her.

The little praying mantis that she had thrown so easily to one side just moments before had grown. It was now a giant monster, looming over her and it was approaching fast.

"Get away!" she screamed. "Let there be light!" She missed, shot it again, but her heart wasn't in it and the puny flame made no difference. It was going to get her!

"There's a way out, there's a way out, there's a way out. . ."

She had to find the tunnels.

"Let me out!" she screamed, banging on the nearest wall. Behind her, the *scritch, scritch, scritch* drew nearer.

"Let me out!"

A panel slid away to reveal a gaping tunnel. She crawled frantically, moving as quickly as she could down the narrow opening.

It would be alright now; the praying mantis was too big to follow. . .

Scritch, scritch, scritch…

It was in the tunnel!

She doubled her speed, crawling as quickly as she could. Something, maybe an antenna, maybe a pincer, touched her foot.

"Get away!" she screamed, kicking violently.

There was light at the end of the tunnel. She was almost there. If she could just move a little faster. . .

She tumbled out of the tunnel. It was a long way down and she hit the ground with a thump. It was soft, but not soft enough. She landed on her back with an "Oomph!"

It was pitch dark.

"Is this darkness?" she asked out loud. "Because I'm not really scared of that one. . ."

The walls were a lot closer than she remembered them being a moment ago. It was getting harder and harder to move her arms and legs. She touched the walls on either side.

Dirt.

Light suddenly poured down from an opening that definitely hadn't been there a moment ago. Far above her, she could just barely make out the faces of people.

"Help!" she called. "Get me out of here!"

But she already knew that they couldn't hear or her or even see her.

"Dearly beloved, we are gathered here today. . ." began a voice.

Ev screamed.

"No! No, no, no, no, no!"

She tried to scramble up, but the walls of soil just crumbled away when she touched them.

Above her, the voice droned on, speaking about her life, and how tragically short it had been, and how she had had so much 'potential'. She screamed and screamed, but no one could hear her.

Then the dirt started to fall. First a few handfuls thrown down by her loved ones (Amy, Jonah, Siobhan, Mother, Dad, Granny, even Zara and Christopher were there). And then it came in shovelfuls. She tried to scream, but the dirt just filled her mouth.

Ev had read many stories. As was the way with stories, people often died in them. In the old days, before Inner, before the bubble, dead people were buried underground.

Sometimes, long ago, they were buried when they were still alive.

"Let me out!" she tried to scream, but more dirt fell into her mouth, and she fell, choking. She was panicking now, there was nothing to count that would make a difference, there was nothing she could. . .

. . .fly out. . .

. . .do, and. . .

. . .yes, there is. . .

No there isn't. Is there?

Ev blinked, and her mind cleared.

"This isn't really real. It just *feels* real. Which, admittedly, is bad enough, but I don't have to play along if I don't want to."

She couldn't warp reality in detention, but she *could* fly.

She closed her eyes, ignoring the dirt that fell on her head over and over again, ignoring even the door that appeared in the wall. She found her magic, and she rose.

The dirt kept coming, but she was moving too fast, and it just it her and bounced off. The hole was deep, far deeper than any grave ever needed to be, and she couldn't believe that, for a moment, she'd really thought it was real.

Moments later she burst out of the hole, and fresh air filled her lungs.

There was no one there. There was no hole either.

"Evelyn Acorn! How do you plead?" said a voice behind her. She turned and found herself back in the common area, facing the table of The Seven for her disciplinary hearing.

"Speak!" said a voice impatiently.

It wasn't Felix. It was Mother.

Felix? Who was Felix?

The only thing she knew was that this was Mother, and Mother couldn't be crossed.

"I'm sorry, Mother," she said immediately. It was always Ev's fault, and Mother was always owed an apology. After all, it was because of Ev that Mother had been taken away from important work, forced to teach an ungrateful child in a cramped room.

"Answer the question! How do you plead?"

"Guilty," said Ev. There could be no other answer.

"Good!" said Mother triumphantly. "Let the records show that Evelyn Acorn, filthy Withouter, pleads guilty to the charges of Ineptitude in All Things, Ungratefulness to a Parental Figure, and General Disappointment!"

She banged a gavel.

This is not how this goes.

This is not how this goes, thought Ev. She'd never had a disciplinary hearing before. . .

. . .not true. . .

. . .but she was pretty sure that she should have the chance to speak for herself.

"Mother," she said, her voice shaking, "might I have an opportunity to answer the charges?"

"You entered a plea of guilty! Besides, what more could a four-year-old possibly have to say?"

. . .not four. . .

"I'm not four!" shouted Ev.

"I'm not four, and I'm not here, and neither are you!"

Everything disappeared around her, and she was left in gray nothingness.

Ev was shaking.

Mother. On a good day she didn't think about Mother at all. On a bad day. . .

When she'd first been sent away from her parents, she had been miserable, it was true. But, over time, she had learned to be alone. When you're alone, you can't be a disappointment. You can't be yelled at for doing something that just the day before you'd been praised for. You weren't afraid all the time.

They hadn't been very good parents. Mother had been a terrifying voice that fell unrelentingly from on high and her dad. . .well, he'd been about as absent as possible while still being there. She remembered him best as a figure at the other end of the cell, hunched always over a keyboard.

Maybe they didn't know better. No one in Inner really knew anything, after all. Maybe, in another life, they would have been good parents.

A familiar voice rang out.

Please stand by while I recalibrate your torture. I apologize for the inconvenience.

Ev realized that she'd been waiting in gray nothingness for some time. The next nightmare hadn't started. She'd thought, for a moment, that being alone with her own thoughts *was* the fourth punishment, but she wasn't nearly scared enough for that to be the case.

"Did I surprise you a bit?" she asked the air.

You did finish that last one more quickly than expected. And not in the usual way. The construct is reasserting itself. Please standby.

"Are you me, or are you you?"

It's all you, Evelyn.

The gray nothingness dissolved, and she was back in Inner, in the cell she'd lived in all alone for six years.

She looked around with the air of a well-travelled expert returning home for the first time.

"It's much smaller than I thought it was," she said. "What now?"

She hadn't lost control of her mind, at least not yet, but she thought, maybe, this time it wouldn't happen. She was getting the hang of staying conscious in here. It was like accessing your magic—you just had to find it, and then hold on.

"Are you still there, me?" she asked.

I'm still here.

"Is it like this for all the kids, or just me?"

How on earth would you know that?

"Good point. . ."

It would be nice to think that this punishment wasn't really all that bad for *everyone*, but she also remembered what Jonah had said when she'd visited him in his detention. He couldn't think clearly until Ev arrived to talk to him. Maybe that was just Jonah, he was always running from his abilities, but it was the only bit of evidence she had, and it wasn't very hopeful. In Jonah's detention, she had been an interrogator who *had to* be in control of her own mind, so maybe that's why she was more 'awake' in her own detention, too.

Klaxons blared.

Evelyn Acorn!

"What do you want, me?"

We are experiencing technical difficulties. Please stand by.

Ev went cold. This wasn't a version of Vendavi that she could have a chat with. This was detention's version of Vendavi and, while it all came from her own mind, she couldn't stop what was going to happen next.

Even as a child, Ev had found it strange how *hard* the Appropriate Authorities insisted that everything was fine, that they were all perfectly safe. When you're really safe, people don't have to tell you that you're safe every five minutes.

She'd always thought that one day, the food would run out, or the air, or Inner would just collapse, and no one would come to look for her because she wasn't worth looking for.

"So, this is my worst fear, is it?" she asked, surprised. It *was* scary, but surely it wasn't worse? Now that she could control her thoughts, she knew that she wasn't really in Inner, and neither were her friends. . .

But that wasn't quite true, was it? Steve was in Inner, somewhere, and so were her parents. There was that girl, Jill Holly, and the others from her group who she'd hardly ever spoken to. Maybe next year some of them would make their way to Alerrawia, but *right now* they were still in Inner, still in danger. . .

"It's not like Alerrawia is the safest place in the world," muttered Ev, but the panic was starting to build.

Attention, Evelyn Acorn!

We are experiencing a catastrophic system failure. Please evacuate immedia-

The ceiling above her computer screens collapsed, destroying half the room.

"No!" she screamed without meaning to. Desperately she searched for the evacuation hatch, but nothing had opened. The escape hatch had either failed with the rest of the system, or there had never been one to begin with.

"Hello?"

She spun round and saw that where the roof and wall had caved in, she could see into the next cell. A scared child looked back at her.

It was Jonah.

"Not the real Jonah," she muttered. "Just a Jonah that lives in my mind. . ."

She scrambled through the wreckage and saw that, in the wall between their rooms, was a tunnel. There was no way to know where it went, but it was better than waiting to die.

She looked back at the frightened Jonah-thing and sighed.

"So, what if you're only in my mind?" she said. "Everything we know about our friends is in our minds. I guess that doesn't mean that it isn't real. Or something. Just follow me, okay?"

She scrambled down the crumbling tunnel. Behind her she could hear the Jonah-thing panting as he tried to keep up.

"Keep going," she called, but without looking back—looking back gets you killed.

She didn't know where she was going, but every time she had to choose a direction, she picked the quietest one, away from the destruction.

They crawled for ages. Ev was exhausted. She could barely keep moving, but every time she stopped or even slowed down, the tunnel they were in would begin to crumble, forcing her to go on.

"I. . .can't. . .keep going. . ." panted the Jonah-thing behind her.

"You can and you will," said Ev.

She was completely disoriented. The whole thing felt like the early simulations Vendavi 2 had thrown her into, before she got used to them. It was most like the very first mindfulness lesson she'd done—she felt like she had some idea of what to expect, but not enough to actually make a difference.

What had she learned in that lesson?

"Use *all* your senses," she muttered.

She already was. She could hear and see falling rubble, she could see and smell smoke, she could feel the trembling floor beneath her feet, and she could even taste chemicals in the air. All of this told her where *not* to go.

"Where *should* we be going, Jonah?" she called over her shoulder.

"*I* don't know."

"Of course, you don't, because you're just me, and I don't know either. . ."

"Natural light and fresh air!" said Jonah, suddenly.

"Oh. Maybe I do know something after all."

It was time to stop running *away* and start running *towards*. Safety. A way out.

Ev hadn't forgotten that she was in a nightmare carefully designed to not have a happy ending, but part of her was hoping that she was special, that she could find a way out and take control like no one before her had ever done.

So, she crawled, the Jonah-thing scrambling to keep up with her.

Just when she thought she couldn't go on, the ceiling ahead of her caved in and natural light poured through.

"Yes!" She shouted. "Come on, Jonah!"

She scrambled over the rubble and pulled herself out. Fresh air! Sunlight!

"Come on, Jonah! We can hide in the forest!"

The Jonah-thing didn't move, just crouched below in the tunnel, terrified.

"Come on, it's all right," she said.

This version of Jonah had never been outside. This version of Jonah had no idea that there was more to the world than Inner.

"It's all right," she said. "You're just me, and *I've* been out here before. It's fine. It's *better*."

She smiled. After a small hesitation, he smiled back, and started to scramble up the pile of rubble.

Just then, the ground shook, and what was left of the tunnel collapsed.

"No!" shouted Ev, as she was thrown backwards.

A moment later the ground stilled, and Ev scrambled to her feet, ready to dig her friend out.

But there was no rubble. Just empty grass in every direction.

"Jonah!" she called, desperately, but there was no answer.

He was gone.

She collapsed, sobbing.

"It doesn't matter," she told herself. "It wasn't Jonah, it doesn't matter. . ."

Except, for some reason, it *did* matter. Inner was gone, the one thing she had always feared the most, and now. . .

She was supposed to be asleep, but for some reason she was struggling.

In the next bed over. . .

15. How Do We Eat and Elephant?

The thing is, no one quite understands the spells and mechanisms behind detention. It's one of those things that were with us when the bubble formed, and we've just kept

using it. It seems that the detainee is
transported bodily to a different dimension,
leaving only their essence, or 'tether',
behind in order to return. Whatever the
detainee faces in detention leaves no lasting
marks – not visible ones, anyway. We like to
pretend that the part of the spell that keeps
detainees from speaking about their
experiences is deliberate. It isn't. We
couldn't change it even if we tried.

What I'm saying is: avoid detention for as
long as you can.

Alison Oakwood

Inner: How and Why?

Page 42

Sometimes, she lay there and let herself be buried alive. Sometimes, she let Inner collapse on top of her. Sometimes, she picked the praying mantis up and put it in her ear herself.

There was nothing she could do to stop it.

But she did learn something interesting: the cure for fear was boredom.

It hurt to have a bug in her ear or to be smothered with dirt, but it wasn't much worse than what an RDD did to you, and anyway if you'd reached that point of the nightmare you were zapped into the next one a few seconds later, so it didn't matter.

The first few times, the detention's magic tried to make her forget again. That's what made it really scary. You couldn't remember while it was happening that it had all happened before, not in the moment, so it was just as scary as the first time.

"It can't *only* be because I was in Jonah's detention," said Ev to Mother, who banged her gavel in rage. "This is Alerrawia. Being an interrogator doesn't mean that one day they won't interrogate *you*. Any thoughts, mom?"

"You are despicable! You are ungrateful! You. . .!"

"Yes, yes, horrible, can we move on?"

"I think the detention magic doesn't know what it's doing anymore," she said to Jonah as Inner crashed down around them. "Like, it has a job to do, so it keeps pushing me from one nightmare to the next, but it isn't even *trying* to make me forget how dumb it all is anymore. It may as well be reading a book at the front of the class with earplugs in."

Eventually, she felt a tug around her waist, the unmistakable feeling of someone else's magic trying to make you do something.

"Finally. . ."

The moment when her body collided with her tether felt like having all the air knocked out of her, but also like coming home. She woke up with a start, reunited with her tether in the real world once more. She found herself in small, dark, featureless room with no windows. Robert and Marcia were waiting for her. Relief washed over her. She'd thought, for a moment, that they might leave her in detention forever.

Like Jonah.

Thinking about Jonah made her chest hurt. Tears pricked at her eyes.

"I hope you've learned your lesson," said Robert, smugly.

"Yes, sir," said Ev meekly. Her skull wasn't even tingling. She was too tired and sad, and anyway, she wasn't sure Robert was worth the effort of burning alive.

What would happen now? She'd broken into the restricted section. It was one of the worst things she could have done. Would they question her? Would they make her tell them where she'd hidden the stolen papers?

Assuming they hadn't found them already, of course.

"These men will show you out," said Marcia. Two burly men in combat gear stepped into the room and grabbed her arms.

"Deadly, times two," she muttered under her breath.

"What was that?" asked Marcia sharply.

"Nothing, ma'am."

The deadly idiots led her down a long corridor with tightly spaced doors, all with the word 'Cell' followed by a number on them. At the end of the corridor was a sign:

Cell Block B: Major Offenses, Long-term Imprisonment

Cell Block C: Death Row

Cell Block D: Psychiatric

As they headed for the door to the spiral staircase, guarded heavily by two usefuls and a deadly, Ev risked a glance behind her.

She'd been in *Cell Block A: Minor Offenses, Short-term Imprisonment.*

It was almost insulting. She was going to have to up her game in the future.

She wondered if Siobhan was still behind one of those closed doors.

The deadlies dragged her up the spiral central staircase and through an access-controlled door to the regular basement level, where they shoved her through and slammed the door behind her.

"Is that it?" Ev asked the closed door.

She'd really expected more. She'd expected an interrogation, maybe another disciplinary hearing, perhaps even some kind of long-term imprisonment.

What she had not expected was to be kicked back out into the general population.

There were people in the basement, moving and repairing vehicles, wrangling griffins, shouting, but none of them paid her any attention.

"I guess it's perfectly normal about these parts for children and their tethers to be imprisoned, then. Good to know."

A passing grown-up gave her a strange look but didn't stop.

"Work, work, work, don't forget to work, just forget to think. . ." muttered Ev under her breath.

She spotted Siobhan, staring sadly at Claster in his magical prison.

Ev made straight for her and tapped her on the shoulder.

"That bad, huh?" she asked when she saw Siobhan's face.

"I thought they might never…" Siobhan couldn't finish the sentence—the magic of detention stopped her.

Ev hugged her, tightly.

"How long were we away?" asked Ev.

"Twenty-four hours," whispered Siobhan.

She'd been in the bad place for a whole day, and it had been one of the worst things that had ever happened to her.

Jonah had been there for nearly a week.

"We're going to have to try harder," said Ev. "Much harder. Detention *cannot* be allowed to continue."

They both gasped.

"You said. . .you said. . .your said *it*!"

"I did. . ."

"That's impossible!"

"Quiet! Let's just keep it between us, okay?"

Siobhan nodded, her eyes wide.

At least the detention magic had one thing going for it—Siobhan would have a *very* hard time talking about Ev's secret to anyone, even if she wanted to.

"Good. It probably doesn't matter anyway. What use is it if I can talk about. . .detention?" A smaller gasp this time. "No one else will be able to join in the conversation anyway!"

Siobhan laughed nervously. It wasn't *that* funny, but it was just the right kind of joke to break the tension.

"What now?" Siobhan asked.

"Now we get back to helping Jonah and Amy. Amy is *still* unconscious. Have you ever heard of something that the combined powers of magic and science couldn't fix by now? Something is definitely up. And Jonah. . .Well, you know. . ."

They'd missed a whole day of class. Thursday was done and dusted, and they only had an hour before bed. They quickly grabbed some food in the common room, but neither of them felt all that hungry.

"Hexteria sucks," said Siobhan, making a face.

"I know right? It makes you super sleepy. By the way, I've noticed that food that needs more cooking and processing also contains more Hexteria, and that fresh, uncooked food has almost none. None at all, if you steal it straight from the garden."

"Why would you know that?" hissed Siobhan, looking around nervously.

"I've been experimenting. I need as much magical power as possible. You do, too. I really think you should watch what you eat more carefully from now on."

They were heading for the stairs as they spoke. They didn't know where they were going, but 'up' seemed like a good place to start.

About halfway up the flight between second and third they had to press themselves against the wall as a hoard of guards cluttered noisily past them, heading for the first floor.

"Pretty, pretty, deadly, pretty, deadly, deadly, pretty. . ." Ev muttered. It was like counting and made her feel a little better. "Not a useful in sight, as far as I can tell, anyway."

"What are you talking about?" whispered Siobhan.

Ev watched the last guard lope out of sight.

"There are three types of guards," she told Siobhan. "The pretty ones, the deadly ones, and the useful ones. The pretty ones look impressive, but they probably won't hurt you and they're not very clever. The deadly ones *like* to hurt you, and they'll follow commands no matter what. The useful ones can think and draw conclusions and are the most dangerous ones to keep an eye because they're harder to trick, but they're all stupid, so as long as you know who you're dealing with, you'll be fine."

"Why do you know these things?" wailed Siobhan. "That kind of thing will get you in so much trouble!"

"Only if you yell about it for the whole school to hear. Knowledge is a good thing, because. . ."

Ev was cut short by the sight that met her eyes on the third floor.

Books lay everywhere. Many of the circular shelves that surrounded the spiral staircase had been pushed over. Worst of all, some of the books had even been ripped apart.

They did NOT find my papers!

The thought was out before Ev could do anything about it. She cringed at her own stupidity. Yet again, she'd warped reality without meaning to. . .

"I know!" said Siobhan. "Who rips up books? Books! This is mad. . ."

"I guess we know why the idiots were out and about, and also why none of them were useful idiots. You know, just in case they actually found something."

"Please stop talking," said Siobhan, "I can't handle it anymore."

There was a pop, and Lulerain appeared next to Ev's ear.

"Oh, I was starting to think you'd vanished. Where were you when children were sneaking into the restricted section? Or when the guards did all *this*, for that matter?"

"It is standard policy," said Lulerain, ignoring the first part of the question, "for a complete search of the library to be performed should the restricted section be accessed by unauthorized personnel. Just in case any sensitive materials leak out and contaminate the rest of the books, I believe. This is the third such search that has been performed in my time here."

"If you're trying to lay the blame. . ." said Ev, trying to hide her rising panic.

"Unfortunately," continued Lulerain, "they didn't find anything."

"Um. . ."

"My job," said Lulerain, eyes glinting, "is to ensure that students succeed in their studies. Whatever they're studying. So, I moved all of the homework I could find to a safe location before the search began. Once I'd taken the time to read it all, of course. Just to see if any children needed help with their studies."

Ev and Lulerain stared each other down, the pixie only a few inches from Ev's face.

Ev gave in first.

"What did you decide? *Do* any of the children need help with their studies?" she whispered.

"Time will tell."

Pixies hated humans. At least, everyone said they hated humans. Pixies were magical slaves, after all, and if Ev was someone's slave, *she* would definitely hate them, so it made sense. The pixies that kept Alerrawia functioning had all sorts of spells on them to contain their magic, like the spell that kept them from doing anything to harm a human, but they had to have some magic and decision-making abilities to be useful. Lulerain was one of the senior pixies. She could make nearly all of the library decisions without the magic stopping her. Other pixies were far more tightly controlled. Ev didn't get to see those pixies. They worked in the shadows, doing very specific things for Alerrawia, and never seeing daylight.

"I can see your thoughts, you know," said Lulerain. "Metaphorically, of course. Reading human minds is still something I am not allowed to do. I mean, your thoughts are also written all over your face. Trust me to be bright enough to know who is really culpable for my plight. Even if you are *all* accountable."

Ev's stolen documents appeared in Lulerain's hand.

"Fairies grant wishes," said Lulerain, staring into the distance. "At least, I think that's what we used to do. . .Take better care of your homework in future, Evelyn Acorn."

With a pop, the pixie vanished.

"That was. . .unexpected," said Siobhan.

"Yes. . ." said Ev, uncertainly. "We're not all culpable, but we are all accountable. . ." she muttered to herself, trying to make sense of the words.

"Yeah, whatever *that* means."

"I think…I think she's saying that she knows some people have more power than others, that some people actively make the bad decisions that hurt her, but that the rest of us are also responsible even though we don't get to make the decisions because we benefit from the situation and we just let it keep happening."

"What could we do about it? We're just kids!"

"Felix is just one guy. If everyone. . ."

"You have to stop this, Ev! You really do. It is really not safe to say these things out loud! And it is extra not safe to be waving that. . .homework around like your allowed to have it!"

Ev stuffed her treasure into her bag and followed Siobhan in thoughtful silence back to their room. Ev could feel the anxiety coming off Siobhan in waves, and once or twice Siobhan faded away completely. She did that when she was nervous, and Ev only noticed when Siobhan came back with a muttered 'sorry'.

"Well, I guess the lovely holiday is over," said Madison from her seat on Stacey's bed when Ev and Siobhan arrived. "It's been so nice and peaceful the last little while. . ."

"Hi, Madison," said Ev, pleasantly. In comparison to her and her friends being tortured, Madison's insults were a refreshing change.

Exhausted, Ev pulled herself up to her bed and fell asleep almost immediately.

*

Ev and Siobhan didn't get a chance to talk again until classes finished on Friday. Ev had tucked all of her stolen papers between the pages of different textbooks to keep them safe. As soon as the final class ended, the two girls dashed to the library.

"What do we do?" was the first thing Siobhan said when they sat down.

"I don't know," answered Ev.

They couldn't say too much more than that because their usual quiet spot wasn't nearly as private as usual. For one thing, the pixies were still cleaning up the mess from the day before. For another, Stacey and Madison were there.

Stacey and Madison had been around *all day*. Ev and Siobhan didn't have a single class with either of them, but, somehow, they kept running into them in the corridors. Somehow, every single one of Madison's assignments as a teacher-in-training were in their classes. They'd sat near them at lunch, which was unheard of all on its own.

Now they had followed Ev and Siobhan into the library.

"Why won't they give up?" muttered Siobhan.

Ev waved and said, "Hello again! This has been a great day, hasn't it? We've spent *so* much time together! Would you like to sit with us?"

Madison snorted and looked away, and Stacey just looked confused. The older girls opted to sit further away than they had at lunch, but still close enough to see what Ev and Siobhan were up to.

"It takes the fun out of it if we pretend to like it," explained Ev in a low voice. "They're not actually bad people, they're just trying to find a reason to get up in the morning, like everyone else. Today's reason happens to be to make our lives slightly less convenient, but we can live with that."

From where they sat, they could see the door to the restricted section. Today, there was a guard posted at the door. It was Shaun (not Sean!) Brown.

"I'm glad they found something for the most pointless member of The Seven to do," whispered Ev, nodding at Shaun.

Siobhan sucked her teeth in irritation but said nothing. Perhaps she was getting used to Ev's weird and wonderful ideas.

"Don't you think it's all a little unusual?" said Ev.

"What?"

"We broke into the restricted section, the *restricted section*, without any planning at all! It's so bad that they've decided to post a guard at the door at all hours. Not just any guards—The Seven are guarding it themselves! Which is hilarious, by the way. If I'd known how difficult I'd be making their lives I would have broken in on my first day. That lock looks new, so I'm sure there are all sorts of extra security measures in place now. The library is still recovering from when they freaked out about it. *And we're allowed to sit here with our homework as if nothing happened!*"

"I don't get it," said Siobhan, frowning.

"They're saying that something big happened, but we shouldn't worry, because nothing really happened at all. It just doesn't make sense! We did that," she pointed at the door where Shaun was watching them suspiciously, "but we're still here. We're not in that prison in the sub-basement. We're not even in detention. Why did we get away with it?"

"Do you *want* to be locked away?"

"Of course not. It's just suspicious that we're not, and we shouldn't get too comfy, that's all I'm saying."

"What are the brats blathering about I wonder?" Madison called.

"If you come sit with us, you can find out!" said Ev, with a friendly wave.

"Why do you bother?" asked Siobhan.

"We have to stick together," said Ev, loudly.

We have to stick together.

Madison and Stacey heard her. Siobhan heard her. Lulerain heard her. A passing guard and a group of toddlers accompanied by their teacher heard her too.

Ev had spent most of the day thinking about her third ability. A simple message of sticking together couldn't hurt anyone, could it? And anyway, she had to do *something*.

For Jonah and Amy, she had to do something.

To help her friends, she had to go up against Alerrawia with all of its science and magic and guards.

To go against Alerrawia, she needed allies, but a few extra friends would not be enough.

To really defeat Felix and The Seven, Ev needed an army.

An army was just a group of people who would fight on your side. Ev knew of two huge groups of people. One was in the forest, and they didn't like Alerrawia very much.

The other group lived underground. They didn't even know Alerrawia existed, but when they found out. . .

Ev explained her reasoning carefully to Siobhan. "It makes sense," she said.

"You've said that six times!" said Siobhan. "Like it's not just me you're trying to convince."

"But it *does* make sense."

"Yes. It does. It's just impossible, that's all."

"To help Amy and Jonah. . ."

"To help two children you'd never met in person until a few months ago you want to irreparably disrupt the lives of everyone in the bubble," said Siobhan.

"Yes! Because it's not enough to just wake Amy up and bring Jonah back from detention. Things have to change so that nothing like that happens to them ever again!"

"Uh huh. And the fact that you parents and that Steve guy are still in Inner have nothing to do with your decision."

"That's just a happy side-effect of fixing things for everyone."

"This is absolutely insane. There is literally no way, at all, that we will ever be able to do this. Even if we got away from Alerrawia, what then? We just march up to an Inner tower, rap three times, and demand that everyone be let out?"

"I'm still working out the details, okay? I have a few ideas, and the True Users might know something we don't. . ."

"I can't *believe* you want to get *them* involved in this."

"Why not? I told you, one of them is a friend from Inner. Sort of. He says he's their leader, even."

"But. . ."

"But what? You can't think of a single reason why we shouldn't help them and that's because there *are* no good reasons, other than what we've been told, and we all know what an Alerrawian education is worth."

"You don't even have a plan!" hissed Siobhan. Stacey and Madison were staring at them openly now, although they were too far away to hear.

"I'm getting there. It's coming together, slowly, but I'm getting there. Things have to change and *stay* changed, otherwise. . ."

Attention! Attention!

Warning alarms blared and sirens sounded. They jumped up, waiting for instructions.

All Alerrawian residents are to report to the common area for an announcement.

Failure to comply is punishable. . .

They didn't bother listening to the end of the message. Quickly they joined the crowds of people hurrying to the first floor.

"Settle down, please!" shouted Marcia above the noise as grown-ups and children alike scrambled for a seat.

Everywhere Ev turned she saw worried faces. Being summoned to the common area like this *never* meant good news.

"At least it can't be as bad as last time," muttered Ev.

"We have received reports," said Felix, and the crowd immediately quietened down, "that a large section of Inner went up in flames a few hours ago. It's believed that some sort of malfunction occurred resulting in a spontaneous magical explosion originating in a portion of Inner's water supply."

Ev went cold. The room filled with murmurs.

"Is anyone hurt? My mom is there. . ."

"Were any kids hurt? Are they alright?"

The children from Inner turned to each other for comfort, but not everyone seemed quite as concerned.

"What a waste of good water…"

"Are we supposed to care about this, or something?"

Water, explosions. . .A big alarm went off in Ev's head, blaring in huge red letters: *Chronoburster*.

"Silence!" said Felix.

Reluctantly, the room settled once more.

"The reason we mention this," said Felix "is simply because the smoke can be seen from certain parts of Alerrawia, and we didn't want anyone to worry needlessly. Alerrawia is perfectly safe. Anyone suggesting otherwise will be punished accordingly. That will be all—please return to your usual evening activities."

He walked out.

Ev's skull tingled furiously, and in that moment, Felix was *very* lucky that she hadn't been able to avoid Hexteria that day.

Felix didn't care about the people in Inner. He didn't care about the people in Alerrawia who had loved ones in Inner.

He didn't care about anyone.

She focused all of her energy and willpower on being angry at Felix because that was the only way she could avoid being angry with herself.

"We *knew* they were going to test it," she whispered.

"What did you say?" asked Siobhan.

"We *knew*. The Chronoburster, Siobhan! We knew this is what it was for and we didn't do anything. *I* didn't do anything!"

"What could you have done?"

"Anything I liked!"

"Shush!" Siobhan grabbed Ev's wrist and hurried her out of the door, down the corridor, and into the sweltering heat, not stopping until they'd found a quiet spot in the vegetable garden.

"We *knew...*"

"We didn't! We didn't really know what it meant. We didn't know that they would actually do it. We couldn't have stopped it even if we had! Will you stop being so weird?"

Ev wanted to scream, to tell Siobhan that she should have known, that she could have done something, because her magic made it so, and she *hadn't*. She'd been too stupid, too slow, just like mother always said, and. . .

It was too much.

Ev opened her mouth and screamed a high-pitched wail of complete agony until there was no air left in her lungs. Then she fell to her knees, panting.

Siobhan, face white, knelt unsteadily next to her.

"Ev?" she whispered.

"I'm fine now," said Ev. "I'm fine. Just…I'm fine."

"There are some grown-ups coming over. . ."

No. There are not.

". . .oh, never mind, they've turned away. . .Hey! Where are you going?"

Ev was running. She didn't care where she was going, she just *had to* get away.

"Wait!"

Siobhan's voice wasn't far behind her. With a powerful effort, Ev sprang into the air flew clumsily over the garden fence. It was hard—the Hexteria in her system *made* it hard—but she managed it, collapsing in a heap on the other side.

"Ev!" shouted Siobhan.

Ev turned to see her friend, eyes screwed tight with concentration as she tried to summon enough magic to follow Ev over the fence.

Ev bolted, running as fast she could before Siobhan could catch up.

"Ev!"

Siobhan's voice was far in the distance now. Ev kept running until she got to the front door, where she paused for a moment, panting.

"Where now?" she asked herself, but that made her think, and thinking hurt, so she took off again, not quite at a run this time (because running inside was punishable by *detention*) but walking as quickly as she could.

In a daze, she climbed the stairs until she couldn't climb any further, then she stumbled into a familiar classroom.

It was the catch-up classroom that Granny used to teach Language and Writing to the poor little Inner kids. At the back of the classroom was the closet where Granny stored her beanbag chairs and little bookshelf when the class was being used for something else. It was never locked. Everything was always locked, but not *this* closet, so Ev pulled it open and crawled into the welcoming darkness, shutting the door behind her.

Ev liked small spaces. She wasn't *scared* of wide-open spaces; she just didn't like them much. It was harder to feel in control out in the open. Too many things to keep track of.

She snuggled in between the beanbags and slowly got her breathing back under control.

She was done running. Now she had to think.

"It's all my fault," she whispered to the darkness. "I didn't stop it. . ."

It was so obvious now that it had happened. Alerrawia wanted to destroy Inner, and they were going to use the Chronoburster to do it. This was just the first test. Now that they knew it worked. . .

"I'm sorry, Jonah," she sobbed. "I'm sorry Amy." What if it was Amy or Jonah's parents who had died in the test? *Someone* probably had, and she had *known,* and she hadn't stopped it.

"I'm the worst friend. I'm the worst *person!*"

There was still something she could do. If she wished for it all to be better, then maybe. . .

"Ev."

The mirror.

"Ev, I know you can hear me."

Reluctantly, Ev pulled Granny's magic mirror out of her bag, shoving aside Madam's RDD as she did so.

"A very worried friend of yours came looking for me, Ev. She's concerned that you're going to do something stupid. You're not going to do something stupid, are you Ev?"

"I can make it so it never happened. . ."

"And then what? If you wish for Inner to be whole and complete, what if the magic decides that you and Amy and Jonah all need to be back there? What if it decides that 'whole and complete' means going back to a time where Inner worked perfectly, before the bubble, before there was even the slightest chance of escape? What if?"

"I'll think of the right words. . ."

"How? How will you ever know that they're the right words until you think them and everything changes? Don't do it, Ev."

"I have to do something. . ."

"Yes! You have to do *something*! But not *that*!"

"Everyone I know is in worse danger than before!"

"Quite."

"What should I *do*?"

"I don't know," said Granny from the mirror. "I'm just the crazy old lady who puts silly ideas into children's' heads. I wouldn't listen to me, in your shoes."

"I'm just one kid…"

"Yup. Just one kid."

Ev paused, tears still running down her face.

"Are you going to tell me to make friends again?"

"I don't need to. You already have."

"Why don't *you* do something?"

"I've been trying to do something my whole life, and I still haven't figured out how. I'm all out of ideas."

"I'm sure Felix is watching me too."

"Oh, undoubtedly."

"There isn't anything safe for me to do."

"Nope."

"Is it standard school policy for teachers to encourage students to risk their lives?"

"Not really, but we are advised to be a shoulder to cry on for students who are risking their lives anyway. Let's not pretend that you're going to sit back and do nothing, Evelyn."

"I have to help Amy and Jonah."

"Yes."

"I have to help them forever, which means that Felix and the others have to go."

"Yes.'

"I have to free Inner and rally the True Users to my side."

"Yes."

"I can' do that!"

"Yes, you can. Even without your third ability, I think you might be the only one who can. You have a gift of seeing what's really there. My daughter had that gift too. It's something to do with being big readers, I think. Books teach you to look at the world differently. I didn't know how to help my daughter survive being different, but I am going to do my best to help you."

Ev sat silently for a moment.

"I guess next you're going to tell me to get out of the closet and go do something?"

"No. If you need to stay there a bit longer, be my guest. Quiet reflection is an important part of any plan, and anyway you need to recover. You've had quite a shock."

"This hasn't been a very safe conversation, has it?"

"You think? The amount of magic I'm using to keep this private is what I think you kids would call 'insane'. So, I am going to leave you now, but you'll always have the mirror. There's a permanent spell on it, Ev. You and I are the only people in the bubble who can notice it, let alone use it, so no one will ever think to take it from you, even if you hold it out to them yourself."

"That's actually quite comforting."

"Good. It will be lights out in about half an hour. Make sure you get back to your dorm by then. Being late to bed would be a very silly thing to get into trouble for right at the moment."

"Yes, Granny."

The mirror went dark, and Granny's face vanished.

From where Ev sat, she could see one of the posters that Granny sometimes took out to encourage her class. This one had a picture of a man holding a knife and fork and scratching his head. Next to him was an enormous elephant. The poster read, "How Do We Eat an Elephant? One Bite at a Time!"

When you were faced with an enormous task, you had to deal with one little bite at a time, and, before you knew it, you'd be done! Or something like that.

Ev had an impossible task ahead of her. She had to do things that even grown-ups couldn't do. She needed to start small and work her way up from there.

"Siobhan," said Ev to herself.

It was time to start eating.

16. They're Dangerous!

School clubs not on the approved list are illegal. Any attempts of four or more students to congregate without adult supervision will result in detention.

Alerrawia School Rules, Summary, Page 7

. . .eality Warping is not. . .It appears that, with proper control, one ca. . .while not to be used lightly, it is not the dea. . .assumed.

Burnt Extract of Unknown Origin

"It doesn't look that bad," whispered Siobhan.

Ev and Siobhan were spending their Saturday lunch break in the communal bathrooms on the twelfth floor, standing on tiptoes to see out the small window right at the end of the long room.

"It was only the test run," said Ev, tears pouring down her face. "They're going to do it for real, any day now, and we can't let them."

We can't let them.

"We can't let them," agreed Siobhan.

"This is why we will unite the True Users and the Inners and fight Alerrawia."

You agree.

"I agree."

"Firstly, we need more allies."

"Yes, Ev."

"The grown-ups are mostly out. Even the ones who want to help us think that they can't. Which is nonsense, I know, but you try telling *them* that."

"So. . .other children?"

"Yes. Other children."

The parents of twelfth chose that moment to bring every screaming toddler into the bathroom to brush their teeth after lunch, so Ev and Siobhan decided to leave. They got some strange looks as they slipped out, but luckily the parents were too distracted to ask them why they were there.

"I know who we're going to start with," said Ev as they wandered aimlessly downstairs. "You won't like it. . .actually, you *will* like it."

"I will like it."

"Good." Ev grinned grimly. It was certainly convenient to make someone do whatever you wanted.

"I've been thinking about the other kids. You know, how some of them like us and some of them hate us? Well, I don't think that 'hate' is the opposite of 'like', because to hate us they have to be thinking about us. The kids who don't care about us at all and don't remember our names and stuff—they're the ones who we should really avoid."

"Yes, Ev."

"Yes, indifference is the real problem, not hate," said Ev airily, warming to her topic. "You may as well jump over the bannister than try to get help from a kid who doesn't. . .Hey! Stop!"

She was almost too late. Siobhan already had one leg over the bannister, poised to jump. Ev grabbed her and dragged her back.

"What are you doing?" she demanded.

Siobhan's eyes slowly came back into focus. "I think. . .you told me to?"

Ev groaned in frustration. She *hated* it when grown-ups turned out to be right.

You don't have to agree with everything I say if you don't want to.

Siobhan relaxed and shook her head.

"I felt really strange there for a minute, but I feel better now." A look of horror slowly spread across her face. "Was I about to jump over the bannister?" she whispered.

"Yes, no idea what got into you," said Ev, quickly.

They looked over the bannister. They were on the tenth floor. A fall down the spiral staircase all the way to the basement. . .

"You would have flown," said Ev. "It would have been fine."

"Not with Hexteria in my system!"

"Yes, well, I told you to avoid food with Hexteria in it," said Ev, ignoring all of the Hexteria in her own system. Stealing enough vegetables to keep your magic flowing was *hard*. "In fact, I insist that you eat no Hexteria at all from now on so we can avoid situations like this in future."

"Yes, Ev. I'm sorry," said Siobhan, looking at her feet.

"It's okay," said Ev, trying not to feel too awful. "We all make mistakes."

"We should get to class."

"Yes, we should." Ev sighed. "Class. Alerrawia's favorite way to keep us too busy to think. We're not going to have time to do anything useful today, are we?"

Siobhan shook her head.

"Tomorrow, let's leave our room as early as possible and go to the garden, okay? Sunday is our only free day, and I plan to make the most of it."

"Yes, Ev."

The two girls walked quietly to class, Ev's heart still pounding from Siobhan's attempted jump.

She was going to have to be *much* more careful in future with how she chose to command her friends.

I need help figuring out this whole reality warping thing.

Using reality warping to learn about reality warping was probably okay; either that, or she would break the entire world, and no one would be left to get mad at her.

"It will be fine," she said out loud.

"What will?" asked Siobhan.

"Oh, everything. . ." said Ev, vaguely.

Like the day after her disciplinary hearing, all of Ev's lessons that afternoon seemed to be directed at her.

"The laws of physics are set in stone!" declared Mr. Carrio. *"Unless, of course, you use magic nonsense to overrule them. Anyone caught attempting to undermine the laws of physics in my class will go straight to detention!"*

"And you can see from this story, children," said Granny, *"that just because you can do anything you like, it doesn't mean that you* should *do anything you like."*

"Let's imagine, as a mental exercise," said Zara, *"that the usual rules of reality don't apply. You can make them do what you want. What useful things could* you *do with the items on the table if you didn't have to worry about silly things like gravity and time? What consequences do you think might follow?"*

"If I could take the time I waste teaching some of you," said Miss Odette, emotionlessly, *"and use it for*

something more useful, like watching paint dry, I would. However, such a thing would be an absolute perversion of reality that I will have no part in."

"Kelvin Granite was a reality warper," said Alicia. *"Reality warping is a banned ability, so we will not discuss that any further here. It is worth noting, however, that there has been some historical controversy surrounding this ability. While we all of course know that it is dangerous and must be eradicated, some once believed that, when given proper thought and when exercising sufficient control, reality warping could be used in service to the greater good."*

"Today," said Ophelia, *"I want everyone to sit quietly and practice accessing your innate abilities. I'll release you all from the effects of Hexteria in just a moment. Practice feeling your abilities, identifying them. If you have two innate abilities, practice accessing each in turn. Some of the older students know that each ability feels a little different, and it helps to know which one you're reaching for, consciously or unconsciously, so that you can control your actions better."*

"I think there must be something in the water," said Siobhan as she and Ev walked to the library after individual training. "A bunch of the teachers were acting *really* weird this afternoon."

"Oh? I didn't really notice."

"They kept bringing up random things that had nothing to do with the lesson. Stuff they could even get in trouble for! What was Ophelia thinking? You *never* release a whole class from Hexteria all in one go. Christopher and Eliza will *have to* report it! Are you okay?"

Ev had sunk to her haunches against a wall, her head in her hands.

"Yes, fine," she muttered. "I just don't want Ophelia to get into trouble. . ."

Being able to make reality do whatever you wanted was *hard*. It had been better when she didn't know what she was doing and didn't have to feel guilty when things went wrong.

Well, it was done now. The best thing she could do was to make sure Ophelia didn't get into trouble for nothing. She would practice accessing all three of her abilities every single day.

She practiced in the library while Siobhan did her homework. She practiced in her room while she listened to Stacey and Madison chatter. She practiced late into the night until she fell asleep.

She *could* feel the differences between her three innate abilities. Her fire throwing felt a bit like a bubbling pit of lava, except in her brain, and of course her skull tingled when she was about to use it. Her flying ability felt a bit like being thrown suddenly up in the air, except she could only feel it deep in her stomach.

And her reality warping felt like the color yellow had exploded in her heart.

She slept with a smile on her face.

*

"Grab some gardening equipment," said Ev to Siobhan at the front door. "And don't forget the Suncharm!"

"What about the tracking spell?"

"Don't worry about that!"

Ev had spent hours two nights ago practicing the spell to remove the tracking agent from Suncharm. It was wordless magic, but it wasn't that difficult for someone who had changed reality to make spell focusing easy.

She looked at the tube of cream in Siobhan's hand, concentrated hard. What it looked like, in Ev's mind, was a bunch of enormous drops of cream, blown up really big, and in-between them were the bits and pieces of the tracking spell. All she had to do was untangle it, and scoop out the intruding spell. . .

"Okay, you can put it on now."

They'd woken up as early as they could, but because they weren't allowed to have personal alarm clocks, there were already quite a few people around.

It wasn't their turn to work in the garden, but kids were always switching shifts. No one would notice them, especially with their rakes and pruning shears.

They found a quiet spot in one of the least interesting corners, and Ev settled down to access her magic.

Now that she knew what she was looking for, it was much easier.

When she felt the yellow in her heart, she grabbed it and thought: *Any children who already feel inclined to help me and Siobhan change everything will come to find us in the garden NOW.*

It had to be children and it had to be of their own free will because Ev didn't want anyone else trying to throw themselves over bannisters.

"Oh no," said Siobhan.

Derek and Peter had just emerged from around a corner.

"That was quick," said Ev. "They must have been following us."

The boys were a mismatched pair with four years separating them in age. Ev had been thinking about them a lot lately, and she thought she understood them a little better now.

Derek and Peter had no control over anything, just like the rest of them, but what they *could* control was whose lives they made worse.

It was possible that they weren't even bad people.

"Looking for us?" called Ev.

"What are you doing?" hissed Siobhan.

"Trust me."

It *could* be coincidence that Peter and Derek picked that exact moment to find them. Maybe they *weren't* there because of Ev's magic, but she could feel the yellow in heart pulsing wildly as the boys drew nearer, and that made her less afraid.

"We've been thinking. . ." started Peter.

"Have we?" demanded Derek. "Have we really? Because, as far as I can tell, we just started walking over here. As if we were magically summoned." His eyes were narrow slits, and Ev suddenly remembered that Derek was seventeen and almost a grown-up which meant he might be better at spotting things than other kids.

"Siobhan, did you see me use any magic to summon the swamp monsters?"

"No," said Siobhan in a tiny voice looking at her feet.

"And I didn't see Siobhan doing anything either. But, since you're here, how do you feel about helping us overthrow Felix and the government?"

Derek blinked. "What?"

"You heard me. Unless you *like* the way things work around here. . ."

"Obviously not," said Derek, "but that doesn't mean we think *you* are our best hope for a bright new future."

Peter sniggered.

"Of course not. It would be silly to trust the person who escaped Alerrawia alone, beat Felix at her disciplinary hearing, and learned the secret of talking about *detention*, wouldn't it?"

Derek's mouth fell open and Peter sat down hard on the ground.

"What. . .how. . .?"

"That's a story for another time. If and when we decide we can trust you."

"'It's us against them'," said Derek, his voice quieter than Ev had ever heard it. "'I'm not going to let them win anymore'. *You* said that. Did you mean it?"

"I did."

"Then just tell us what to do."

"I have a few questions first."

"What questions?" demanded Peter, but Derek just nodded knowingly.

"You saw us go into the restricted section?"

"Yes," said Derek. "We were following you, waiting for a chance to mess with you. It was impressive, the way you just ran straight in like that. Took us a moment to figure out what to do, and then ages to actually do it."

Because the magic needed to give me time to find my answers, thought Ev.

"Peter, when the alarms sounded that day, they told us Amy was hurt, I was having a lesson with your uncle. He didn't go to the common area with everyone else. I didn't see him there at all."

"Your point?"

"Well, it's a bit suspicious, wouldn't you say?"

"Only if you expect my uncle to act like an actual human," said Peter, despondently. "He doesn't think the rules apply to him. Any of them. Felix spends more time managing my uncle, who is technically on his side, than all of the trouble-makers combined."

"Who are the trouble-makers?"

"Oh, you know. Zara, Eliza, Christopher, some of the teachers, like Granny. I hear Ophelia is in his bad books now too."

"You mean, the three actually useful people on The Seven and two of the teachers who actually know how to teach?"

"Yup! Being useful and being dangerous are basically the same thing."

"Maybe Robert *isn't* the type to pull off a crazy attack. We do have another suspect, though."

"Who?"

"Did you hurt Amy, Peter?"

"No!" The color drained from his face.

"Because you said in flying class. . ."

"That I would get *you*! And I meant that maybe I would bump you into a wall or something, *not* attack your friend half to death!"

"Okay. . ." said Ev, slowly.

"We can't just believe him!" said Siobhan.

"I believe him," said Ev. "I really do. It's one thing to bully, another to kill."

"Amy isn't dead!" said Siobhan.

"I know, but it sure feels like someone meant for her to be dead."

"Yes, but they messed up," said Derek, nodding vigorously. "I've been thinking about it. They must have been *really* bad at magic. . ."

"Or they didn't want to do it, even though they had to, and so the spell didn't work right!" said Siobhan.

"Those are both great possibilities," said Ev. "Could we please not argue so much about my almost dead friend? It makes it very difficult for me to not get mad."

"Sorry, Ev," said Siobhan, looking at her feet.

"It's okay. Let's just remember what we're doing here, okay?"

"What *are* we doing here?" asked Derek. "Assuming for a moment that we are a 'we'."

Ev told him.

"Completely. Insane," said Peter.

"I'm in," said Derek.

"You're what now?"

"I'm in," said Derek to his friend. "I don't want things to be this way anymore, and if that means dying while trying to do the impossible, then at least our deaths will have some meaning."

"That's. . .well, I don't plan for anyone to die. . .," said Ev.

"People usually don't. This is Alerrawia—people will die. If you think they won't, that's just because you're naïve. However, you do seem better than the average snot-nosed brat at getting things done, so I'm willing to give your idea a chance. Anyway, it's the only idea in play."

"Thanks. . ." muttered Ev.

"Are you sure about this, Derek?" asked Peter.

Derek turned and grabbed Peter roughly by his shoulders. Looking him straight in the eye, he said, "No one here cares. About us, I mean. Everyone, grown-ups, kids, teachers, pixies. . .they're all so completely focused on surviving that they don't make time to think about anyone or anything else. Everyone thinks of themselves, and they teach us to do the same. If you're nice, you're weak, if you hurt others, you're strong, and you have to be strong to survive. Then some Inner brat crawls out a tunnel and says, Hey, I'm pretty strong, why not do it my way? And I'm just so tired of everything. So tired. I don't even care if she's right. So yes. I'm sure."

Peter nodded slowly. "Okay," he said. "I get it. I'm in too."

"Good. There are a few ground rules to discuss," said Ev.

"No more bullying?"

"You got it in one! Also, you have to do what I say. I know, I'm a snot-nosed Inner brat, but you're the one who said I'm strong and that you want to do it my way, so. . ."

"It might kill us, but yes, we'll do what you say. No questions asked."

"Not 'no questions asked'. That's Alerrawia thinking. That's Inner thinking. I want you to ask questions. Give me suggestions, tell me if I'm being dumb. It's just that, sometimes, if I need you to do something, I have to know that you will, no matter what, and save the arguments for later, because sometimes there won't be time to chitchat. I need you to think for yourselves. It's the one type of thinking they never taught us. In Inner, we called it 'Withouter thinking'. Being a Withouter was once the worst possible thing I could imagine, but only because it meant that I would get hurt. Now I'm starting to warm to the idea. Withouters are pretty cool, actually. And it's what we're all going to be if we continue. Are you cool with that?"

"I don't care what we call ourselves, as long as we get to shake things up."

"Peter?"

"If Derek's in, I'm in."

"Good. Now we're getting somewhere."

"What? Four kids against *everyone* else?" said Derek, one eyebrow raised.

"Hey!" called someone who was just out of sight.

"Five kids," corrected Ev.

Stacey came around the corner, panting.

"What are you jerks all doing together?" she demanded.

"Waiting for you," said Ev. "Where's Madison?"

"I don't know!" wailed Stacey. "Well, actually, I have a pretty good idea where she is, and I was on my way to check, when suddenly I had this crazy idea to come look for you in the garden instead. . ."

"Is Madison alright?"

"Yes! Physically, that is. Emotionally, not so much."

"What happened?"

"Like you care!"

"I do. I really do. Tell me what happened to Madison."

Tell me what happened to Madison.

"Is it Carlton?" asked Derek, suddenly, eyes narrowed.

Stacey nodded.

"I'll punch his face in!"

"No one is punching anyone's face in," said Ev, quickly. "Can someone please tell me who Carlton is?"

"Are you seriously *that* out of touch?"

"Let's say that I am, and act accordingly."

"Carlton is from Inner, but he's been here for years," said Peter. "They have a thing. Carlton and Madison."

"Madison and an Inner brat? Really?"

"Really. They kept it secret, obviously," said Peter.

"But apparently not very well," said Stacey, with a sigh. "I guess it's not even really a secret if *he* knows," she added, nodding at Peter.

"Everyone knows! They should have tried having their fights somewhere more private. . ."

"Why is Madison upset with Carlton?"

"Carlton is upset with *her*!" said Stacey. "They broke up. For real, this time. The explosion at Inner. . .I guess Carlton still knows people there or something, but he was *really* upset, and he told Madison he couldn't date someone who throws around terms like 'Inner brat' like she does, and she ran off crying, and I need to find her!"

"He's all wrong for her anyway," said Derek suddenly. He looked away.

"Oh. Good," said Ev, weakly. She was far too young to deal with this sort of thing.

"Maybe Madison shouldn't be such a bit. . ."

"Siobhan! Not helpful!" said Ev.

"But she is! She *hates* anyone who's different!"

"She doesn't. It's just. . .her mom gets so mad when anyone says something good about Inner kids. . .it's just safer this way, okay?"

Ev nodded. "We live in a world where the grown-ups say to hate anyone or anything that's different, and the only thing you can do to stay safe is to play along."

"Exactly!" said Stacey, and then she slammed her hand over her mouth, because agreeing with Ev was *not* safe.

"We'll help you find Madison," said Ev to Stacey.

"We will?" asked Peter.

"Yes," said Derek, shoving Peter towards Stacey. "Lead the way, tech wiz."

"I don't know. . .," said Stacey.

"Things are changing, Stacey," said Ev. "Why not be among those that decide how?"

Stacey hesitated for a moment, and then nodded firmly.

"Follow me," she said.

She strode towards the first-floor entrance, the other four children following close behind. They must have been a strange sight, bullies and bullied united in purpose.

"You called me tech wiz," said Stacey.

Derek shrugged.

"Everyone knows it," he said. "I remember when you used to get into trouble most days for by-passing some system or other or accidentally building a radio that broke the intercom. You were more fun before you grew up and got scared."

"Like you're not scared,"

"Didn't say I wasn't."

"I thought you were going to be a dentist," said Ev, to break the heavy silence that followed.

"That's not *my* plan. That's my grandfather's plan. *My* plan is to be a tech expert like my parents."

"Where are we even going?" asked Peter.

"The roof."

"The roof? We're not allowed on the roof!"

Stacey shrugged.

"But you've been there, right?"

Peter nodded reluctantly.

"Yeah, it's one of those rules that aren't really rules anymore, which are nicer than the rules that *are* rules but that you don't know are rules until you're in trouble for them."

"You're quite smart for an Alerrawian," said Ev.

"And you're relatively normal for an Inner kid," said Stacey. "Emphasis on relatively."

The griffins and Claster all had rooftop paddocks. There was also a couple of helipads, so people were always coming and going. Alerrawia believed in the apprenticeship model of education, and who better to the dirty work of cleaning up after a dragon than children? So, like the garden, you could usually get away with being there if it looked like you were allowed.

"Madison and Carlton come up here all the time to. . .talk. A lot of the older kids do."

Once again Ev felt very, very young, but she said, "I know that."

"It's not exactly private, but it's a little more private than anywhere else."

"Yeah, especially when there's an enormous dragon to hide behind."

Claster was hardly *ever* on the roof. To get there, he had to fly, and to make him fly, or really make him do *anything*, was almost impossible. His guards had to use all kinds of punishments just to get him to eat.

Yet here he was.

"My uncle said they took Claster to hunt giants in the forest," said Peter.

"Giants are extinct," said Derek. "They're not fully human, so there is no way they survived when the bubble formed. . ."

"You weren't there when Ev told us about the giant at her disciplinary hearing," said Peter. "She was *very* convincing."

Another twinge of guilt. Would she be allowed to go one day without being reminded that it was *her* fault that the Alerrawians were looking for Taylor?

"Hold it," said Derek softly.

A yellow pixie had popped into existence beside Claster's head and was looking at them suspiciously.

"How are you doing, Dropellet?" said Derek, and you had to listen very hard to hear the worry in his voice.

"What are you children doing here?"

"My. . .friends wanted to know what it's like to be a guard-in-training, so I'm just showing them around."

Dropellet's eyes narrowed.

"The last I heard, you were refusing to partake in training."

"I've had a change of heart."

"Fine, show them around, but if you're still here in ten minutes I'll want to know why."

"I thought you were going to be a flying instructor," whispered Ev.

"So did I," said Derek.

They heard Madison before they saw her. She *was* hiding behind Claster's paddock, but Ev didn't give herself any points for getting *that* right. There weren't a lot of options.

"Leave me alone!" said Madison, the moment she saw them. Then her eyes narrowed, and she said, "What is going on here?"

"We're worried about you. All of us," said Derek, gruffly.

"Yeah, right."

"If you roll your eyes any harder, they'll fall straight out of your head," said Ev.

"I'm fine. You and your freaks can go away, Stacey."

"No offense," said Ev, "but you don't *look* fine."

Madison burst into tears. "No one asked you!"

"Nope, but here I am anyway."

"Madison, you've broken up with guys before, why are you being so weird this time?" asked Stacey.

"*I* broke up with guys before. *I* did it. This time *he* broke up with *me*! It's the worst day of my whole entire life!"

Madison's voice went up an octave and Ev knew that Stacey was getting somewhere. Madison was leaving 'I'm genuinely upset' territory and entering 'drama queen of the year' territory with surprising speed.

"Carlton. . .Carlton is an idiot!" said Derek, then he looked away, blushing fiercely.

Madison glared at him, but then her face went thoughtful.

Oh good, thought Ev. More stuff I don't understand.

"Can we go down? That pixie is already suspicious. . ."

"I don't take orders from you, Peter," said Madison. "As for you, Stacey, I've been stuck up here for ages! You usually find me by now. I can't go back down by myself! It's too embarrassing!"

"I had to go find Ev in the garden," said Stacey.

"Why? Why in the bubble would you 'have to' do that?"

"I don't know. . ."

"It's because she's smart," said Ev. "The four of us are going to take over the bubble, and Stacey's interested in joining us."

"What?" Stacey asked. "I didn't know. . ."

"That's what we're doing."

"You can't," said Madison flatly.

"We can. We will."

If Madison already wanted to help them, then Ev's magic would have dragged her to the garden, embarrassing or not.

"You can't," said Madison again. "You're just a few kids. You would need to build an army, and no one here will help you. . ." she drifted off thoughtfully.

"It sounds like you're onto something there, Madison. That's why the first thing we have to do is leave."

"Is this because of those friends of yours?"

"It started because of my friends. If all I do is help Amy and Jonah, then I'll count it as a win. But what's the point of waking Amy up or bringing Jonah back if the world they're coming back to is this mess?"

"Do you have, like, a plan?"

"Yes. It's an amazing plan, in that you'll be amazed at how completely insane it is," said Peter.

"Not helpful," said Ev, throwing her hands up in despair.

"Things will be different. If we get it right," said Madison.

"Yes," said Ev, but it didn't really seem like Madison was asking. Her words sounded like a question, but she delivered them like fact.

"Why do I have the sudden urge to go find you in the garden?"

"No idea," said Ev, quickly. "But it's not necessary, is it, because we're all right here!"

That's not necessary!

She could feel Derek's eyes boring into the back of her head.

"Oh, right, weird. . ."

"Wait, so you *are* going to help with. . .whatever this is?" demanded Peter.

"I understand that *you* would be scared. You're not going to make it through, are you?" said Madison.

"I will too!"

"Won't!"

"Will!"

"Oh, enough already!" said Ev.

Enough already!

"Come on let's go get something to eat."

Madison looked at Ev, hands on her hips and one eyebrow raise.

"Who's side are you on?"

"Our side. The side of the kids. Someone has to be."

Derek waved at Dropellet as they left. The pixie grunted and turned back to a one-sided conversation he was having with Claster.

". . .and the children have no sense at all, wandering around the rooftop. . ."

As they went downstairs, Ev explained everything she knew about how Hexteria worked.

"Wow, I never thought about trying to *avoid* it," said Peter. "I mean, I hate the stuff, I feel so empty when I eat, but it never once occurred to me to just stop."

"Well, it's easier said than done, and you have to eat *a lot* of raw carrots."

"So, I guess we're going to the garden instead of the common room for dinner?" said Derek, a tiny bit wistfully.

"That's the plan. Stacey and Madison can probably eat normal food. . ."

"Nope!" said Madison, haughtily. "I don't want to take drugs either. You losers are stuck with us."

"Actually, we prefer the term 'Withouters'," said Peter, and Derek groaned behind him.

"What, like a club name?"

"Exactly!"

"Student clubs are strictly against school rules, so of course I'm one hundred percent on board," said Madison.

"We're all going to die," groaned Stacey.

"Like you *ever* break school rules," said Peter to Madison. "You're a teacher's aide!"

"Yup. Best way to learn *all* the best grown-up gossip, plus I get to be in classrooms when no one else is around. You wouldn't believe what I get up to," said Madison, cheerfully.

"You seem to be completely cured of your broken heart," said Stacey dryly.

"No point dwelling on past mistakes!"

It was much easier to steal vegetables with friends around, because some of them could always keep watch while the rest foraged, but today someone had gotten there before them.

"Why are half the vegetables gone?" asked Ev.

"Raccoons," said Derek, darkly.

"They really are little jerks, aren't they?" said Madison.

"What's with the raccoons?" asked Ev. It was something she'd wanted to know for ages, but it was so far down the list of priorities she hadn't gotten around to asking anyone yet.

"They've mutated," said Peter authoritatively, like someone who had just been asked about his specialist subject. "They're basically like people now. As far as I can make out, it's a combination of survival of the fittest and magic getting into their DNA. They're very intelligent, they know how to construct basic things and work together, and their skulls and skins, for some reason, are *very* hard, and we don't really know how to kill them."

"Good for them," said Ev. "How did magic get into their DNA?"

"People wanted to test stuff on them. A very long time ago, of course."

"They sound quite a lot like people, now. . ."

"Yeah, but not *really*, right? They're still not, like, important or anything."

Ev was about to argue when a voice interrupted the conversation.

"Ev! Siobhan! There you are! I've been doing laps around the garden looking for you!"

Gavin Oakwood panted into view.

"Huh," said Ev. "I thought we were all already here. . ."

"What do you mean?" asked Derek.

"Nothing, nothing at all. . ."

"Are you *all* planning something together?" said Gavin, looking at the group in amazement.

"What's it to you, four-eyes?" asked Peter.

"Relax, Peter, Gavin has helped us before, I think he's on our side. Are you, Gavin?"

"I think it's what Granny wants, so let's say yes. Tentatively."

"Why should we let you in?" demanded Peter.

"Because even though I've been in the garden for, like, half an hour I've already heard rumors about the six of you suddenly hanging out together. *That's* how obvious you've been. *I* at least have a vague idea about how to keep my secrets secret. You could do with some help on that front."

"Also, you're very useful, what with Granny Oakwood feeding you information and stuff," said Ev.

"I can neither confirm nor deny that Granny is my source."

"Okay. But she is though."

"If you say so."

"You're in," said Ev.

"Don't we get to vote on this or something?" whined Peter.

"Nope. This is one of those 'trust Ev' moments that we were talking about. You are, of course, welcome to voice your concerns."

"We don't know him. . ."

"I know him about as much as I know you. Next?"

"He could be snitch."

"Any one of us could be a snitch. We're going to have to trust each other. Next?"

"I don't like him!"

"You don't like the guy you don't know? Why not give him a chance first? Next?"

Peter just glared at her sullenly.

"Anyone else?"

"I'll allow it," said Derek.

"Thanks," said Ev, rolling her eyes.

They spent the last few hours before bed arguing about the plan.

Stacey always agreed with Madison. Madison always disagreed with Derek as part of some strange mating ritual Ev decided she was too young to understand. Peter would do anything Derek said, and Derek always took the opposing viewpoint, regardless of who was speaking, unless it was Madison, in which case he would agree to cut off his own head if that's what she wanted. Siobhan was worried about losing her place at Ev's side, so disagreed with everyone except Ev, and Gavin tried to be the voice of reason, but because he was a bit full of himself, it annoyed rather than helped.

"We need more allies," she said, suddenly, cutting short a not-quite-argument between Derek and Madison about whether they were the *Withouters* or if they were *THE Withouters*.

"Why not? More cats to herd will make things much easier!" said Gavin.

"Thank you for your contribution. People are going to know we're up to something. We can't avoid it."

"This is social suicide," said Madison, dramatically.

"It's one of the prices of change."

"Madison has a point," said Derek.

"You agree with Madison?" said Stacey. "What a surprise. . ."

Oh good, now Stacey was jealous of Derek. . .

"*I'm* still not sure about the name of our group," said Peter.

"We're the Withouters," said Ev. "End of discussion. Withouters think that magic users and science followers can work and live together in harmony, with no need for violence. And that running and hiding is not the way to solve a problem."

That was, more or less, what she'd been taught in Inner, if you *really* dug into the words behind the words. The only other Inner kid in the group was Gavin, and he just raised a thoughtful eyebrow.

"Fine, we can be the Withouters then," said Peter, generously.

"I'm still not sure," said Madison. "The social repercussions."

"Oh, give it a break," snapped Stacey.

The argument started up again.

"We're acting like little kids," said Ev. "Grown-ups know how to disagree and still like each other, still get things done. Can we be more grown-up about this? Can we *please* move on to the plan?"

Can we PLEASE move on to the plan?

"Yes, Ev," came the chorused response.

"Right," said Ev, a little nervously. "We need more allies. The seven of us can't do this alone, so it's an important step in the plan."

"Right," said Gavin. "I can talk to Granny. . ."

"No grown-ups! Not even Granny."

"You can't possibly want to bring *more children* into this?"

"There's no one else," said Derek.

"You're wrong!" Siobhan snapped at Derek's left ear. "Lots of people believe in Ev. . ."

"Really? Name three."

They glared at each other.

"Ev's right. Teachers don't count," said Stacey. "The grown-ups all think they can't help us, because they'll just. . .disappear."

"And we won't?"

Stacey shrugged.

"Maybe not. We are just kids."

"And if we succeed, we'll be fine," added Ev.

"That's a pretty big if," said Gavin.

"You can leave if you don't want to help," said Derek.

"Oh, I'll help. I'm just trying to be realistic about our chances."

"Grown-ups coming!" said Siobhan. "Quick, look busy!"

"What are you kids all doing out here?" demanded a tall woman that Ev had never seen before.

Someone please help us!

Pop!

"Please don't interrupt my workers. They have a lot to do and not much time left to do it."

Dropellet had appeared right next to Ev's ear.

"They're here working for you?" asked a second woman, eyebrow raised.

"I don't decide who does what. I just do as I'm told."

"Fine. If they get up to anything, though, it will be on you!"

"Why, naturally," said Dropellet, lazily.

The grown-ups left, casting a few suspicious glances back over their shoulders.

"Keep working, now, you know that a bunch of the windows look out over the garden, right? And we all *know* that children aren't allowed to congregate like this, so that can't *possibly* be what you're doing. I'm supposed to report suspicious behavior. I guess I better go see if I can find any."

He vanished.

"Is he going to tell?" asked Stacey, nervously. "I don't want to be *that* person, but I do have the most to lose here. . ."

"He had his chance to tell on us, and he didn't. . .Siobhan, does he *have to* report on us?"

"Some things pixies have to do, some things they don't," said Siobhan, Ev's main source of information about any weird Alerrawia stuff. "They're allowed to use their own judgement, a bit. It depends on whether he wants us in trouble or not."

"Let's assume for now that Dropellet *doesn't* want us in trouble. There's nothing we can do about it anyway. And he's right—we do need to look like we're working. We may as well use this time to gather some veggies."

"I'm not sure how long I can eat rabbit food. . ." muttered Derek.

"Yeah, can't we steal some griffin eggs or something?" asked Peter.

"No," said Ev, firmly. "Griffins and their eggs are out of bounds."

"Why?"

"They can speak. They're just like people. You wouldn't eat a human baby, would you?"

"You shouldn't make assumptions about people," said Madison. "I for one think that Peter *would* eat a human baby, given the chance."

Everyone laughed, even Peter.

"It's not for much longer now," Ev said, soothingly.

They were just getting ready to leave the garden when Dropellet popped back into view.

"Great," muttered Derek.

"Can we help you?" asked Ev.

"I have a message. From Lulerain. Personally, I think she spends too much time with her head in books and not enough time in what I affectionately call 'reality', but she is the boss."

"What's the message?" asked Ev, mouth dry. What could Lulerain want? Was this to do with the documents she hid?

"She wants to see you. In the library. Now. She says it's in your best interests for you to attend this meeting. She states that all seven Withouters should be present."

Everyone looked at Ev.

"Give us a moment to discuss this," she said to Dropellet.

"They're going to tell on us!" said Madison, the moment they were out of earshot.

"I don't think they are," said Ev. "If they were, the first we'd know about would be *detention*."

Gasps all around. Ev liked shocking her friends.

"You can say. . .*that*?" said Gavin. Ev was impressed—the older boy only froze for a moment. Maybe he'd been practicing.

"I can. Cool, right?"

"Less cool, more terrifying, but I am now completely convinced I've picked the right side."

"Thanks?"

"You're welcome. Now, what do the pixies want?"

"I think they might want to help us," said Ev, and then she waited.

"Why would they want to help us?" asked Madison.

"They're prisoners. Slaves, basically. They probably want things to change more than we do."

"But we wouldn't change *that*," said Stacey. "Would we?"

"Why not?" asked Ev.

"They're dangerous!" said Peter.

"Why do you think they're dangerous?" asked Ev.

"Because. . ." he stopped.

"Because *they* told us they are," said Derek, with quiet menace.

"Exactly. And we don't trust *them* do we, otherwise what are we doing here?"

There was a thoughtful silence as six young brains desperately tried to accommodate a new and strange idea.

"I vote we go and see what Lulerain wants," said Ev, raising her hand. She was dying to just *make* them agree, but if the only way she could get her friends to do what she wanted was through magic, then what was the point?

Reluctantly, Siobhan raised her hand. "I think you're mad, but I'm on your side, so. . ."

Madison raised her hand. "This sounds like the sort of fun good girls aren't supposed to have, so of course I'm in."

"Seriously?" wailed Stacey. "This is crazy!"

"We won't do it unless at least four of us agree," said Ev.

Derek raised his hand.

"What are you doing?" demanded Peter. "Just because *Madison* voted yes. . ."

"I want to hear what the pixies have to say. I've always just accepted that they're an evil that must be contained, but that's what they say about *us* too. There's no point in any of this if we're not going to take big risks for big changes. So, I'm in."

"That's a majority. We'll talk to the pixies."

She hoped they were doing the right thing.

17. Fear Combined with Ignorance is Almost Unbreakable

Cinquefoil

This five-leafed yellow flower can be used
in the creation of many different potions and
enchantments, including, but not limited to,
bond breakers, healing compounds, lucky
charms, and for the inspiration of insightful
dreams.

1000 Magical Ingredients and Their Uses

E. Porter

Page 18

When they arrived in the library, Lulerain and
Dropellet herded them quickly to a quiet and seldom-
visited corner.

"Thank you for coming," said Lulerain. "The three
of us have been watching you for quite some time."

"The three of us?"

"Now, don't panic, but Boaclick is also. . ."

"Boaclick!" said Peter.

"Calm down, Peter. Please," pleaded Ev, just a
Boaclick popped into view.

"It's so wonderful to hear that you work is being
appreciated, wouldn't you agree, Lulerain?" said the gray
pixie, eyes glinting mischievously.

"The three of us are a team," said Lulerain. "You
work with all of us or none of us."

Ev nodded. "Same goes for us. All of us, or none of
us."

"But of course. We should all stick together. Dropellet, Boaclick, please keep watch while I speak with our new friends."

The yellow and gray pixies vanished, leaving them with Lulerain.

"I'll just dive right in, shall I? What I am about to suggest is treasonous and highly dangerous. If you agree to help me, and you should think carefully before you do, your lives will be in great peril. But, if you help me, I'll be able to help you. Don't bother pretending that you're not up to something. Everyone already knows that you are. If we combine forces and act quickly, we may be able to do something before it's too late."

"We can't agree to help you until we know what you need help with," said Ev.

"I need a book. Well, part of one anyway. From the restricted section."

"And you think *I* will be able to get in there *again*?"

"There *are* channels for students to access some restricted content, a path completely closed to pixies."

"No there aren't!"

"Yes, there are, actually," said Stacey. "You can get permission to study *some* of the books, but you have to get a member of The Seven to get it for you. It isn't unheard of."

"Well, I've never heard of it," said Madison.

"I've done it. For my advanced tech classes I have to learn things that other people aren't allowed to know. Things about how the systems work. Nothing major, just specific passages from specific books, and they watch me to make sure I don't read beyond the bounds. But it is possible."

"Who gets the books for you?"

"Zara, mostly. Sometimes it's Eliza."

"You never told me!" said Madison.

"Yeah, but would you have cared? About my homework stories?"

"Good point. . .I'm not really sure I care now."

"You're all talking like we're actually going to do this," said Gavin.

"Who, other than the pixies, would dare help you?" said Lulerain. "Or do you think you can do everything on your own?"

"What's the book?" asked Ev.

"*Catching and Keeping Pixies: A User's Guide*."

"That's not ominous at all," muttered Derek.

"And if we get you this book you will. . .?"

"Set you on a path that will result in Amy waking up and Jonah being returned to you. Via the overthrow of Alerrawia, of course."

"How would we even do it?" asked Peter.

"We'd have to ask Zara or Eliza *and* give them a plausible reason why we need the book. You're supposed to need a form from a teacher, but sometimes Eliza will help you if she recognizes your face."

"So, we *are* doing it, then?" asked Gavin.

"Stacey and Madison, can you ask Eliza, today?"

"Sure, but there's no guarantee she'll say yes."

"I guess that's a 'yes', then," said Gavin, miserably.

"It's just a book, Gavin," said Ev.

"Don't worry about any of it," said Madison. "It's all going to be just fine."

*

Ev kept watch from her comfy bean bag chair. Siobhan was curled up next to her, nervously tapping her fingers.

"Relax," whispered Ev. "You look like you're up to something. Just pretend to be reading your book."

"Maybe they've chickened out?"

"No way. Stacey's not scared to ask, because she's done it before, and Madison isn't scared of anything. It's happening."

Just then, the two older girls arrived, led by Eliza.

"Remind me again what this is for, Stacey?" said Eliza.

Ev reached for the yellow in her heart and thought: *Eliza, Stacey is pretty convincing when asking to borrow books from the restricted section, wouldn't you say?*

"Well, we got into an argument with some Inner brats about pixies and what they can and can't do, and one of the adults in my tech group, I can't remember who right now, said there was a book in the restricted section that would settle things, and we've decided to write a paper on it for another class, and. . ."

"Yes, fine," said Eliza with a wave of her hand.

Ev breathed out.

"Wait here."

Eliza disappeared into the restricted section, breezing through the security procedures like she'd done a hundred times before. Marcia, who was on guard duty, ignored her, her head buried in paperwork.

Madison and Stacey sat at a table, ignoring Ev and Siobhan.

"She's going to figure it out. She's going to look in the book and get suspicious, or there'll be a note on it saying *Immediately Pulverize Anyone Who Asks for this Book* or something, and then we're done for. . ."

"Relax," whispered Ev.

Less than a minute later, Eliza reappeared holding a book. She handed it to Stacey, who stared at it for a moment, like she couldn't believe her plan had actually worked.

"Please hurry up and take your notes. I have a lot to do, you know."

Stacey and Madison couldn't just flip to the page they needed. They had to look through the index, take notes, pretend that they were really doing research.

From where she sat, Ev could see that the book was bristling with red tags. Those were the sections they weren't allowed to read; the sections Eliza was there to 'protect' them from.

Eliza's eyes never left the table. Ev's heart pounded in her chest.

Suddenly, a door slammed. Even though she'd been expecting it, Ev jumped and turned to watch.

Gavin, Peter, and Derek arrived, speaking loudly, laughing, stomping their feet with every step, and being generally obnoxious. It was obvious that Derek and Peter had had more practice, but Gavin was giving it his best shot as well.

Quite distracting, aren't they Eliza?

Ev was learning. Extremely specific suggestions seemed to cause less trouble than vague commands.

"You boys!" said Eliza. She took a few steps away from the table. "Quiet down. Now. What in the bubble makes you think you can act like that here?"

"Sorry ma'am," said Gavin, backing away.

"Get out of here, before I decide that you need to be properly punished!"

"Yes, ma'am," the boys said, as they scurried out.

Ev was so transfixed by her friends' near-death experience that she almost missed what Madison did.

The moment Eliza was distracted, Madison skipped to the final chapter, which was the one Lulerain said they needed. It was bristling with red markers.

Madison's eyes widened and Stacey put her hand over her mouth. They looked at each other for a second, then Stacey nodded.

Madison tore the last few pages of the book right out, just as Eliza was chasing the boys from the room. Then she quickly turned back to one of the safe sections of the book, and they busied themselves taking notes once more.

It all happened so quickly. Ev was impressed, but they hadn't gotten away with it yet.

"Are you girls nearly finished?" asked Eliza.

"Yes, ma'am," said Stacey. "Just one more thing we need to look up, and then we're done."

They made a show of searching through the index for one last bit of trivia, wrote it down, and then they handed the book back to Eliza and left. Very quickly.

Ev and Siobhan watched Eliza head back to the restricted section. There was a tense few moments while she was inside, and they couldn't see her. But then she left, locking the door behind her.

"Looks like it worked," said Ev.

"Yes, but now we have to help with whatever it is Lulerain wants us to do."

"No, we don't. We agreed to get the pages, not to whatever else she wants from us. Not yet anyway. Come on, the others will all be there already."

They hurried as quickly as they could to their meeting place behind the griffin paddock in the grounds, where they'd be a little more sheltered from view than in the garden.

When they got there, there was an argument in full swing.

"It's madness!" Stacey whisper shouted.

"You didn't tell us this going in," said Peter.

"To be fair, you didn't ask," said Lulerain.

"What's going on?" Ev demanded.

"Nothing much," said Derek, "Except that the pixies want us to free them." He sounded thoughtful, not his usual angry self at all.

"Oh, is that all," said Ev with relief.

"All? *All*?" said Madison. "The chapter we stole is all about how to unleash *them* on the world."

She shoved the torn pages in Ev's face just long enough for Ev to read the title of the final chapter: *Freeing your Pixie*.

"This is not what I signed up for," said Stacey.

"What did you sign up for, exactly?" asked Siobhan.

"I just need you to free me; I'll be able to do the others myself," said Lulerain.

"Are in you insane?" said Peter, almost shouting.

"Quiet!" said Ev. "Can you give us a moment to confer?" she asked Lulerain.

Lulerain nodded. "We'll keep watch."

"This is crazy," said Stacey, the moment the pixie disappeared.

"Is it?" asked Derek. "I mean, is it any crazier than the other things we're planning to do?"

Siobhan snatched the torn pages from Madison and started reading them.

"We can't just free a pixie!" hissed Peter.

"Why not? We're trying to free ourselves. How can we do that and leave others behind?"

"We have to stick together," said Siobhan.

"Yes," said Stacey and Madison immediately.

"It's a difficult spell," Siobhan continued, "but I don't really see why we couldn't do it."

The magic users of Alerrawia were taught how to *cast* spells, but hardly ever were they taught how to *break* them. The argument when something like this:

1) There are very few approved spells and enchantments that magic users are allowed to be taught in the first place.

2) Even the spells and enchantments that *are* allowed are heavily controlled with Hexteria and other restrictions.

3) Therefore, no spells or enchantments cast in Alerrawia will ever need to be broken. If that were the case, they wouldn't have been cast in the first place.

4) So why bother to teach spell breaking to children?

5) Magic is evil and must be carefully controlled. Designated authorities are always correct. Failure to accept this will result in detention.

Not one of the children had ever broken an enchantment, although they had been warned that it was far more draining than casting a spell in the first place, and that it could even kill you if you weren't careful.

But 'they' said a lot of things.

"We can do it," said Ev, cutting short a loudly whispered argument. She hoped she sounded more confident than she felt.

We are capable of freeing Lulerain the pixie.

"You really believe that?" asked Madison.

"I do."

"But *should* we do it?" asked Stacey.

Don't you think that pixies deserve freedom too?

"I suppose pixies shouldn't have to be prisoners," said Peter, reluctantly.

"So, we're agreed?" said Ev.

One by one, her friends nodded.

"Good. Lulerain!" she called. "We have one last question to ask before we give our answer."

"Ask," said Lulerain.

"If breaking the enchantment is something a bunch of kids can do, then why has no one done it before?"

"Fear is a powerful thing," said Lulerain, sadly. "Fear combined with ignorance is almost unbreakable."

"Beautifully put, but not really an answer."

"Imagine a little child, maybe one of the little ones living on fifth."

"Alright. . ."

"Now think about how they see the world."

"What do you mean?"

"Their world is very small. They look up, literally, to just about everyone, and the people on the same level as they are don't know much more than they do. They know they don't know anything—they're told this every day. Why would they have to learn all of these lessons otherwise? They're also told that the people in charge, their parents, the teachers, the carers, are always to be obeyed.

No matter what. They learn to believe that being big is the same as being right.

"None of this is unusual. It's part of growing up. In the old days, children were allowed to grow up, to realize that not all adults are right or have their best interests at heart, and to learn to be better. Each generation averaged out as slightly better than the previous one, and that's how humanity evolved.

"But now we live in a bubble. All of the lessons of the many generations who went before you have either been lost or destroyed. This is because some big people, like Felix, know about the *Big = Right* way of thinking, and they want everyone to believe that it's completely true.

"I'm going to be honest with you. Children in Alerrawia do not grow up. You Inner kids have a slightly better chance at it, left to your own devices as you are, which is why so many of the strongest minds living here are from Inner, but you haven't really grown up either."

"You're saying we're all childish brats?" asked Derek, a hint of his usual anger returning.

"Yes. I am. But not in the way you think. 'Childish' is used as an insult, even though that's grossly unfair to children. It implies some sort of deliberate act on your part to be ignorant. What I'm talking about wasn't your decision."

"What does any of this have to do with anything?" Ev demanded.

"If you're a child and a big person says *look at the sky—that color is called pink*, and if they're the only voice you've ever heard, you call blue pink. You call up down. You call cruelty love. If that's what you're told.

"The people of Alerrawia have been told by the big people that pixies are bad, and enchantments must never be broken. So, that's what they believe.

"But one thing big people can't change is human nature. Your kind are always striving to be better than those who came before you. Better teachers, better tyrants, better friends. That hasn't changed. It can't."

There was a thoughtful silence.

"I don't think I like being messed around by big people," said Stacey.

"Me neither," said Madison, which immediately secured Derek's approval.

"We'll do it," said Ev. "We'll do it tomorrow because I don't think it's safe to wait. We'll free you."

"I shall await your instructions," said Lulerain, with a twinkle in her eye. Then she was gone.

"What now?" Gavin asked.

"Now, we go to bed," said Ev. Sunday was almost gone, and they had to be back in their rooms soon.

Reluctantly, the seven children headed to the sixth floor, and went their separate ways.

When the girls got to their room, Madison darted up onto Ev's bed.

"Hey!" said Ev, automatically.

"Relax, little Withouter. I'm just getting rid of this."

Madison tore the poster that had 'mysteriously' appeared above Ev's bed from the ceiling.

"I would burn it or tear it up or something, but that's punishable by death, or something, so for now I'm just going to lay it gently on our desk. Upside down. Oh, and oops, I've spilled this stale carrot juice all over it."

"Thanks for that very. . .Madison apology," said Ev.

"If something's worth doing, it's worth doing dramatically, that's what I always say."

"It really is," said Stacey, wearily. "Be glad that *you've* only had to put up with her for a few months."

"Indeed," said Siobhan with feeling.

Later that night, after the carers had come by for the evening check and the girls had some freedom to speak, Stacey whispered, "Are we really going to do this?"

"Yes," Ev whispered back.

"We'll be careful?"

"As careful as possible," promised Ev.

The next day was Monday, which meant endless lessons. Fortunately, this meant that Ev had spell work in a classroom full of things they needed for their plan. Unfortunately, she had no idea how she was going to manage to steal anything with teachers breathing down her neck.

"You know what your problems is?" asked Madison.

"What?"

"You think you have to do everything yourself."

"Meaning?"

"I have access to the classrooms. I have access to many things," said Madison mystically, ruining the effect by sticking her tongue out.

"You can bring what we need to Claster's paddock?"

The spell to free Lulerain required a dragon claw, willingly given, as well as a dose of dragon fire, and, despite everything Lulerain said about big people controlling little people, Ev thought this might be the real reason why no one had freed a pixie before now.

Claster hated people, but they needed him, which meant that they had to carry out their plan where he was most likely to be—in his paddock in the grounds.

Their conversation was interrupted by the arrival of the morning carers who gave the room a quick look and left. Madam hadn't been around in a while, and Ev was starting to wonder if someone was finally keeping her away from vulnerable children.

"There are other ingredients to get too, you know," said Siobhan. "We need an actual plan for this, or it isn't going to work."

"One thing at a time. . .Madison, can you tell Derek to tell Dropellet that we're going to meet up at ten tonight? No one will notice a guard-in-training wandering around and talking to pixies. Oh, and ask him to see if the pixies can get us some Suncharm too. We may need it later on."

"How are *we* going to get out after curfew?"

"We have the whole day to figure that out. Let's see what we need."

Ev studied the spell thoughtfully.

"Black ribbon, crystals. . ."

"Oh, I have all that," said Madison, airily.

She grabbed a black ribbon from her bag and tossed it at Ev.

"You do not have crystals," said Stacey, flatly. "Why would you? They're for magic users, aren't they?"

"Yes, they're used to focus and strengthen our spells," said Ev. "They're actually pretty rare. . ."

"Oh, I just knew they'd come in handy one day, and anyway they're shiny and I think that all of the shiny things in the world should be mine."

"Yes, you probably do. . ." muttered Siobhan.

Madison flung back her mattress to reveal seven crystals nested below.

"Behold, the fruits of my many crimes," she said dramatically.

There was a moment of stunned silence.

"Well, this explains all of those mini-interrogations the spell work teachers have been putting us through," said Ev. "Madison, you know that they *notice* when things like crystals go missing?"

Madison shrugged.

"Yeah, but they'd never think that I'd take them, would they? If you don't want them. . ."

"Of course, we want them! Can you keep them on you until tonight?"

"Yup!" said Madison, filling her pockets with crystals.

They ate a quick and unsatisfying breakfast of raw carrots and broccoli and then went their separate ways. The Withouters were never all in the same class at the same time, ever, which meant that news had to be spread in bits and pieces.

Ev started by grabbing Gavin after math, her first class for the day. He'd arrived late, much to everyone's surprise—he was usually such a model student, and it was only his past record that kept Leah from having him sent to the bad place.

Before Ev could tell him the plan, he whispered, "Siobhan's innate ability is fading, right? Tell her to learn this spell as quickly as possible, so we can get out without being seen."

Ev took the piece of paper Gavin offered her. She hadn't even thought that far ahead yet.

"Thanks," she muttered.

"No problem," said Gavin.

Ev scanned the spell.

"Where did you get this?" she demanded.

"My usual source."

"I said no grown-ups!"

"She doesn't know I took it! Relax!"

"Please try to follow my rules. It's hard enough as it is. . ."

"She doesn't know. I promise."

Ev doubted very much that Granny didn't know what her own grandson was up to, but she let it slide.

"We're meeting at ten o' clock behind Claster's paddock on the grounds, but before then I need you to gather some of the others and get as much cinquefoil, sage, and valerian as you can from the garden. And as many vegetables as you can carry safely. Can you do that?"

"Leave it to me."

"I'm also going to need a twig from a hedge. Are there even any hedges here?"

"Granny has one. I can get that too."

"Okay, bye!"

She dashed to magical innovation, arriving just in time.

Quite a lot of the plan was riding on Madison. As a teacher's aide, and massive teacher's pet, she could go where she liked and do what she liked.

They needed a golden cauldron, a whole lot of candles, and some incense. There was only one golden cauldron that any of the Withouters had ever seen, and it was always locked away, as were the other ingredients.

Madison said she could get it all.

Ev listened with half an ear to Zara's lesson, knowing that Madison was probably putting her plan into action right at that very moment.

The biggest challenge was the cauldron, especially because it would be missed. Children hardly ever got to use it, unless they were older and very skilled at potion-based spell craft, but it spent most of its life locked away in the teachers' office on the eighth floor.

Most teachers were teaching at this time of day, but there was usually somebody in the office, so they needed a distraction. At first, the boys were going to stage a fight that Madison could run to the teachers about, but Madison told them they were being stupid.

"If I just *say* I saw some boys fighting on the sixth floor and that there was a lot of blood and stuff, I guarantee that they will investigate immediately. I'm the queen of the tattletales, remember? They'll believe me, and it won't even matter when they don't find any bloody boys."

"They'll just leave you in the teachers' office by yourself?" asked Peter, eyebrow raised.

"Of course," said Madison. "I even have a desk there. Sort of. Well, it's a wobbly side-table that no one minds me keeping my stuff on, but the point is, I'm a trusted face."

Madison assured them that only Ophelia Jones and Percy Sheriff would be there. Percy would dash off immediately, and Ophelia would follow him closely to save the imaginary fighting children from his wrath.

"Then I just take the key off the hook grab the cauldron and the other stuff, and pop it all into my bag. Easy."

Ev desperately hoped that it would work.

Madison gave her a big wink when they passed in the hall after science class, which probably meant that everything had gone well.

The Withouters weren't meeting up for lunch, because it would be too suspicious, so Siobhan and Ev went by themselves to eat a rushed lunch of stale vegetables in the library.

Ev gave Siobhan Gavin's spell.

"Can you do it?"

"It's difficult, but yes, I can do it."

"Do you know if Madison got everything?"

"She said she did. Also, Gavin wants me to help him, and Derek, gather a bunch of flowers after class later."

"Good, thanks for helping him!"

"I prefer to take orders from you."

"Well, I ordered Gavin, who ordered you, so it's the same, isn't it?"

"I suppose. . ."

"And Stacey?"

Siobhan's fading ability let her check in with the other children without being noticed as easily, so she was in charge of communications.

"She babbled for a bit about parsing and decoding, but she seemed happy about it, so I think she has things under control too."

"So, is she going to control the cameras or something?"

"Apparently that would be noticed. She's just rigged it so we'll also be able to see what the cameras see, to help us know when people are coming."

The bell rang.

"Tell everyone to meet in the ninth-floor kitchen after class," said Ev, before dashing to her next lesson.

Her afternoon classes passed in a blur, and she even welcomed the mindless activity of PE because it meant she could let her mind wander. For most students, but Ev had impulse control straight afterwards.

Or at least, she was supposed to. Robert had cancelled her lessons over and over again for weeks now. Siobhan thought that he might be afraid of Ev.

Just to be sure, Ev went to see if there was a cancellation message waiting for her in her dorm. She'd learned the hard way that cancellation notices were posted to the dorm notice board, or left on your pillow, if it was a one-on-one lesson. Of course, not knowing this, she had gone all the way to the thirteenth floor the first time, only to be told by an irate Robert through his keyhole to go away.

As expected, the neatly folded message was lying on her pillow.

Suddenly, Ev had an idea.

She left the note where she found it and hurried up the stairs to the thirteenth floor. When she got there, she smiled at Charles the guard, and was about to say, "I'm here for my lesson with Robert," when he waved at her lazily and buzzed her in.

Test 1: Does Robert tell the guard when he cancels one-on-one classes? Result: Apparently not.

She headed towards Robert's office, nodding politely to people as she passed them. They ignored her completely. She walked right past Robert's door without stopping, and no one said anything.

Test 2: Would anyone challenge a child alone on the thirteenth floor? Result: Not if they thought you were meant to be there.

On her right was a blank wall. At the end of the corridor was a window that overlooked the grounds. Apart from Robert's door, there was another door on the left—Shaun's rooms.

Nothing of any interest there. She went back the way she came, following the circular corridor right and taking the first turn she came to.

At a T-junction at the end of the corridor she came face-to-face with an enormous set of doors labelled *War Room*.

She turned right. At the end of this corridor was another window. The posters she was used to seeing were even more numerous here—she almost couldn't see the concrete walls behind the colorful nonsense. There was a door to the left, this one labelled *Scrying*. Ev knew what scrying was—using reflective objects to see the future. They were all taught it in spell work, and if you were good at it you got to work on the thirteenth floor.

There was no one around, so she wandered closer and peered through the door's glass window.

The room was full of teenage and grown-up magic-users, crammed together in a tiny space. Each of them was staring at a crystal ball, but Ev couldn't make out what they were seeing.

Ev knew how exhausting and even painful scrying could be. It drained so much of your energy and magic, especially if you didn't have any innate ability for the art, so she wasn't surprised at all to see everyone looking so unhappy.

She wondered why they did it.

"They probably have no choice," she whispered to herself. She ducked suddenly as she saw Eliza move into view, and then she peeked her head back up. Eliza was talking to the scryers, giving them instructions, and taking notes.

"Well, that's interesting," whispered Ev, as she scurried away. Eliza may or may not be someone to trust, but either way, it was better that she didn't see Ev creeping around the thirteenth floor.

At the other end of the corridor was elevator B, but you needed a key to call it. She knew that if she turned left before the elevator, she would land up at Felix and Marcia's offices, the last place she wanted to be, so she decided to leave.

Charles stared at her blankly when she returned to the door.

"I knocked, and he didn't answer, so maybe I missed a cancellation notice again?" she said sheepishly. "I waited for a bit, but do you think I should go?"

"Probably," said Charles. "Don't worry kid—it's better than *not* showing up when you *did* have a lesson!"

Ev grinned, and Charles let her out.

Test 3: Would Charles notice if she wandered the halls of thirteenth at will? Result: Nope. Not even a flicker of suspicion.

She hurried to the kitchen on the ninth floor to meet the others.

"Where have you been?" demanded Siobhan the moment she appeared. Ev looked at the worried faces of her friends and was immediately filled with guilt.

"I just needed to check something, sorry for not letting you know that I was going to be late."

She told them what she saw on thirteenth, and about how easy it was for her to be there, but her friends were not impressed.

"Are you crazy? We've spent *all day* taking risks so that you wouldn't have to, and then you go and do this? What were you thinking?"

"I'm sorry, I just had an idea and…"

"From now on," said Gavin, "everyone has to run their clever ideas past the rest of the group before they do anything. If you agree, raise your hand."

Hands shot up, even Siobhan's.

"Okay, I get it," mumbled Ev. "It *was* a stupid thing to do on my own. I will talk to you first in the future."

"Good," said Derek, gruffly.

"It's just that you're the one who can do things, Ev," explained Gavin. "We need you to not get killed. What you found out could be very helpful, but. . ."

"I get it! End of discussion."

"Quiet!" hissed Stacey.

Stacey had a small, magically enhanced device, something that she was allowed to have as a tech student but that was banned for just about everyone else. She was using it to bring up tiny images of the corridor outside. Two grown-ups were heading for the kitchen. Everyone tried to look busy, like they were supposed to be there, but the grown-ups walked straight past the door, deep in conversation.

No one will bother us in the ninth-floor kitchen while we are working on our plan.

"They're gone," said Stacey.

"Good. Let's get on with it, alright? Gavin, you were in charge of the garden run."

"We managed to get all the flowers you wanted, as well as some veggies for dinner," he brandished a handful of raw broccoli and everyone groaned.

"Just one more time," Ev promised. "Eat up! But put half the veggies in this mixing bowl."

After a few bites, Stacey and Madison got busy mashing the extra vegetables together with bits of valerian, while Ev used Stacey's device to monitor the corridor.

"How much valerian is enough?" Stacey asked. "More importantly, is there an amount that is too much?"

"Just don't overdo it," said Ev. "I don't think you can overdose or anything."

"Such wonderful precision," said Madison cheerfully, throwing another handful of valerian into the bowl.

"This is gross," said Stacey, turning up her nose.

"The grosser the better," said Derek.

When they'd mashed it all together, and Derek declared the mixture sufficiently disgusting, they went down to the sixth floor. The boys and girls split up as they neared their rooms. In the distance, the girls heard Peter shout, "Hey Mason! I bet you're too chicken to try some of this!"

"This cannot possibly work," said Stacey once they were back in their room.

Madison shrugged. "You'd be surprised. Boys think very differently to girls."

The others let this pass unchallenged—Madison was, after all, the boy expert.

"What now?" Stacey asked.

"We wait," said Ev.

She pulled the library books she'd stolen on her first day of school from under the mattress and read at random, although it was very difficult to concentrate. Eventually, the lights out bell sounded, and they all jumped into bed in record time.

After what seemed like ages, someone opened the door, shone a light in, and closed it again. Once the last check happened, you could pretty much do what you wanted, as long as it didn't draw any attention. Read under the covers. Pop out to a friend's room. To actually leave the sixth floor was harder, but not impossible.

The four girls crept out of bed.

"Let there be light," whispered Ev, and a small fireball appeared in her hand, just enough for them to see by. They bunched up their pillows and extra bedding to make it look like they were still there.

"You're up, Siobhan," whispered Ev.

The enchantment that Gavin had found was extremely specific. It allowed someone who could fade to extend their ability beyond themselves and shield as many as twenty people.

Carefully, Siobhan cast the enchantment, her brow furrowed with concentration.

"All right, done," said Siobhan.

"Are you sure? I can still see everyone."

"We're in the enchantment, so we can see each other, but others won't."

They opened the door and stepped out, pulling it closed behind them. As quickly as they could, they headed to the boys' section.

Derek and Peter shared a dorm with two other perpetually terrified boys. The four hidden girls crept into the room.

"Peter? Derek?" whispered Ev. There was no response.

"They can't hear us. Right now, they can't even remember that we exist, because we're in the spell," said Siobhan. "I'll just let it lapse, and. . ."

"Ah!" shouted Peter. "Who…oh, it's you guys. Forgot you were coming for a moment there."

"Can you be quieter?" hissed Ev.

"It's fine," said Derek, swinging down from his bunk. "The idiots are asleep. Let's get Gavin."

Siobhan cast the spell again, and the six children crept quietly to Gavin's room.

Gavin was the only Withouter in his room, which meant they had to make *three* boys eat valerian.

"I hope he can join us. . .," said Ev.

"He can," whispered Derek. "I made sure they all ate, force fed two of them. What?" he asked, in response to Ev's shocked expression. "Its standard bully behavior."

The pushed open Gavin's door to find him pacing impatiently.

"Thank goodness," he said when they appeared. "I couldn't remember what we were doing or who I was waiting for! It was terrible! It's like being alone with corpses, and I couldn't remember *why* they were asleep!"

"They're *not* dead, right?" asked Stacey.

"As far as *I* can tell. . ."

They tiptoed down the stairs, freezing every time they saw a patrol, but thanks to Siobhan's fading ability, this was the easy part. The real trick was getting out the door on the first floor.

Stacey couldn't safely open the door without setting off the alarms. It stood open all day, but at night could only be opened with a keycard, and only patrol leaders and The Seven had the right keycards for the job. It was one of the fuzzier parts of the plan.

For everyone who wasn't Ev, that is.

A patrol leader will open the door shortly. They will accidentally drop their keycard and not notice until long after we are gone.

A patrol leader who had just passed the hidden children suddenly said, "Hold on a minute!" His patrol stopped, and the leader dashed back to the door, opened it, and poked his head out.

Ev watched his card fall to the floor as he hurriedly darted back to his troop.

"Thought I heard something," he muttered. "Move out!"

The moment the patrol was out of sight, the children were through the door and heading for the paddocks.

"Can I stop yet?" begged Siobhan, and Ev could hear the strain in her voice.

"Almost, as soon as we're done with the privacy spells."

Ev gave Siobhan one of the candles that Madison had stolen and lit it. As soon as Siobhan stopped fading everyone, she would channel her magic into keeping the candle lit. It was a privacy candle—anyone within its light would be impossible to see.

Gavin, Peter, and Derek prepared the second privacy spell. They wrapped sage and ivy around a twig from Granny's hedge, but not too tightly. They used Madison's black ribbon to tie it together and placed it in a bowl. When they were ready to begin performing the real spell, all they had to do was light the bundle in the dish and a small area would be protected from view and interference.

They were not very strong enchantments—just the best that a few kids could manage—but perhaps they would be enough.

Stacey used her device to keep an eye out for anyone heading their way and Madison filled the golden cauldron with water from a bottle, following Ev's instructions carefully.

None of their precautions seemed to work against pixies.

"You seem ready," said Lulerain, appearing with a pop. Dropellet and Boaclick joined a moment later. "I assume you remembered the flowers?"

Ev nodded, slipping her bag off her shoulder as she did. "They're in here."

"Now you just need the dragon."

"Of course," said Ev, evenly. She wasn't about to let Lulerain know how scared she was.

"I've spoken to him," said Dropellet. "He doesn't do much talking these days, but I think he knows what we need."

Dropellet led Ev inside the paddock, because if anyone was going to be burned to a crisp, it would be her. Claster lay in a forlorn heap, chained to the ground. Ev could just make out the magical barrier that surrounded him to protect people from his fire.

"Claster?" she said, voice trembling.

The dragon raised his head, looked at her directly, and dropped it back to the ground.

"We need your help," she said, softly. "We need a dragon scale, and we need you to burn some flowers to ash. It's so we can free the pixies and they can free you."

The scale had to be willingly given. It was the only way. Ev couldn't use her third ability, even if she thought it was a good idea. This close, she could feel how powerful Claster was. Magic came off him in waves.

"We're going to change things. Not just for us; for everyone. Will you help us?"

Claster raised his head. This time, he kept it raised, yellow eyes boring into Ev's head.

"He's waiting," said Dropellet.

"For what?"

"For you to be braver." Dropellet waved at Claster's barrier.

"Fair enough," said Ev in a small voice. She took a deep breath, and then forced herself to take first step, and another, until she was within the barrier, no longer protected and close enough for Claster to squash her with one enormous claw.

"This is the one that Lulerain believes in," said Dropellet to the dragon. "I am not quite as convinced, but Lulerain is usually right."

Claster's head moved, and Ev jumped, but she stayed right where she was. If she couldn't do this, then she couldn't do anything, so she *had to* stand her ground. The dragon sniffed the air, then firmly pressed his huge nostrils right against her chest, inhaling deeply. Ev didn't move a muscle.

Claster backed up, turning his head to look at Ev more closely with one huge, yellow eye. He seemed to stare for eons, and Ev firmly held his gaze.

Finally, he lifted an enormous claw and pried a scale from his shoulder. It fell to the ground with a faint clang.

"Thank you," whispered Ev. She bent slowly to take the scale. It was far heavier and rougher than it looked, and it was slimy at the point where Claster had ripped it from his flesh. She held it tightly, as she spread the cinquefoil flowers on the ground.

Claster nudged her with his nose, making her stumble backwards.

"You need to get to the safe side of the barrier, child," said Dropellet. "Unless the spell calls for human ash too?"

The moment Ev was safe, Claster opened his enormous mouth and a stream of fire erupted. Ev slammed her eyes shut and stumbled back.

"I'll gather the ash," said Dropellet. "Go back to your friends."

"Thank you," she whispered again.

Claster nodded and lay back down with a thump.

"Are you alright?" demanded Siobhan the moment Ev emerged from the paddock. The other Withouters were looking at her with eyes full of awe.

"I'm fine, but we have to move quickly in case someone comes to check on Claster. Madison—chalk!"

"Not my most impressive theft, but it did have its challenges," said Madison, handing a piece of chalk to Ev.

Ev drew a chalk circle around the cauldron and the three boys stepped into the circle, chanting, "I call for a wall of protection to rise between us and those who would prevent us from performing our magic." They repeated the phrase facing east, south, west, and north, and then they turned to face inward to say the words one last time, because sometimes the person preventing you from doing your magic was yourself.

It was the last thing they knew how to do to protect themselves from getting caught.

Finally, it was Ev's turn.

Ev was good at magic. All of her teachers said so. *"So talented, at such a young age!"* She was very powerful.

For an eleven-year-old.

The person who'd enslaved the bubble pixies hadn't been eleven, so Ev was going to need all the help she could get.

"Crystals and incense," she called, and Madison quickly produced the items from her bag.

The incense would help her focus her mind on the magic she wanted to perform. It was an ancient trick, used by magic-users for thousands of years. The crystals would be used to gather and focus the magic that Ev would carefully build up during the spell.

She turned to Lulerain.

"Ready when you are," she said, hoping she sounded more confident than she felt.

Lulerain gently touched Ev's arm. "Be as quick as you can," she said. She dived into the cauldron.

"Add the ash," she told Dropellet, who raised one sardonic eyebrow, but did as he was told.

Hands shaking, Ev pulled the spell from her pocket and closed her eyes.

"Are you sure, Ev?" whispered Siobhan. "You're not supposed to use all your magic in one go! You can still say no!"

They'd been warned over and over again by teachers that using all of your magical reserves at once could kill you, and even if it didn't kill you, it would take something from you forever.

No one ever told you what that something was.

Ev decided it was worth the risk.

She concentrated on the meditation she'd been taught to build her magic. She could feel the lava in her brain and the throw in her stomach and the yellow in her heart, and she ignored all of them, digging deeper to the core of her being, from where her magic stemmed.

She found it, she held it.

She used it.

Without her permission, her mind suddenly filled with a jumble of nonsense.

Mother's laughter.

"Don't cry, I'm here."

"Evelyn, pay attention! What's 1 plus 2?"

"Give me a hug, my darling, it will be alright."

"Unacceptable!"

"Why are you so slow?"

"I love y- "

"You need to perform to standard because you know who will suffer if you don't? Don't you?

"Pay attention."

"Pay attention!"

Her eyes flew open. Mother. Not a single good memory, so why was she thinking about that woman now?

It probably wasn't important.

"By the power of the candle, this spell is come undone. By the power of the dragon, this spell is now broken. As water meets fire, you are free." As she said the last words, she added Claster's scale to the cauldron.

The cauldron exploded and Ev fell to the ground, unconscious.

18. Is this a Rescue?

The evil inherent in pixies can be easily seen in their physical appearance. They could look normal if they tried—it is a simple enchantment. The fact that they insist on continuing to look so alien is a clear indication that pixies have no interest in integrating with human society. The laws passed long before war was on the horizon were merely a reflection of this truth. It was apparent to all that it wasn't safe for humans to fraternize with pixies, and this remains the case to this day. Pixie magic is a very real threat, and those who claim that there are no real differences between pixie magic and human magic are very much mistaken.

Felix Granite

Ev's eyes fluttered open. Her head was pounding and her vision blurry. She tried to speak.

"Take it slow," said Siobhan.

Ev struggled to a sitting position.

"What happened?" she asked groggily.

"What happened?" said Stacey. "You want to know *what happened*? Well, for a start, you died. Was that the kind of thing you wanted to know?"

"She didn't die," said Lulerain, hovering nearby. "Although she did come close."

"Oh, my mistake. My friend coming *close* to dying is just fine, I shouldn't have overreacted, how silly of me!" Stacey's voice was getting louder and more hysterical with each passing moment.

"It's alright, Stacey," said Ev, holding her head.

"How can you say that? Look around!"

The ash was gone. The water was gone. The cauldron was a puddle of cooling metal on the ground. Lulerain, in her olive skin and clothes, was glowing faintly.

So far so good.

It was the penguins that really seemed out of place.

"Penguins," said Ev, groggily.

"Oh, didn't you know?" said Madison. "Freeing a pixie *always* leads to a plague of penguins. And don't forget the pink clouds. If you touch them, they feel like liquid soap, by the way. Maybe that's how clouds are supposed to feel? I've never met one before. They're almost interesting enough to distract you from how all the trees and grass and things are burnt to a crisp."

"Oh, good," said Ev. To be honest, she was just glad that everyone else could see the penguins and pink clouds too.

"I'm just testing my power, children," said Lulerain. "It's been a while since I was allowed to use it."

"But. . .*penguins*?" wailed Stacey.

"I like penguins," said Lulerain, with a shrug.

Stacey collapsed on the ground, her head in her hands.

"Relax, little girl," said Dropellet. "Lulerain is the strongest among us and her enslavement has been the hardest to bear. She is permitted some license to celebrate, albeit unconventionally. No one heard, and no one noticed."

"Of course," said Madison, cheerfully, "and tomorrow no one at all will think anything of the sudden appearance of hundreds of penguins."

Derek crouched next to Ev and whispered, "Do you still think we made the right decision?"

"Um. . .," said Ev.

"I was just 'playing around', as I think you children say," said Lulerain. She snapped her fingers, and everything immediately returned to normal.

"Hey! I was just getting to like them!" said Madison. "I'd already named six of them, you can't just let someone name something and then take it away with a snap of your fingers. You monster. Hey, do you think you could straighten my hair? I've never thought it was straight enough."

"I. . .what?" said Lulerain.

"Welcome to my life," said Stacey to the pixie. "Madison is the world's most self-focused person. Don't let her inability to be terrified or awed get you down. You really can't take these things personally."

Lulerain's lips were a thin line.

"Are you sure *we* made the right decision?" asked Dropellet.

"Unclear," said Lulerain. "But a promise is a promise, and we will help these children with whatever they need."

"That's nice," said Ev, helplessly.

"Boa, Drop, come forward my dear friends," said Lulerain. Boaclick and Dropellet drifted closer, and Lulerain placed a hand on each of their heads. "It is time for you to return to your full power. At last, we can right the many wrongs that have been done to us."

There was a brief glow from each of Lulerain's hands, and then she moved back.

"Finally," said Boaclick, flexing his fingers. "I'm going to explode every toilet in the building!"

"No, you're not. Perhaps another time, but not now."

"It's practically the only good reason to be free in the first place!"

"Boa," said Lulerain, a note of warning in her voice, and the gray pixie quietened down.

Lulerain turned to Ev. "We are at your service."

"Great," said Ev, groggily. "We're done then."

"What do you mean?"

"You can just snap your fingers and fix everything. Get on with it. I'm tired."

"Ev," said Lulerain gently, "that's not how it works."

"Why not?" she wailed. "Wake Amy up. Free Jonah. Get rid of Felix. Surely if you can create penguins out of nothing you can do those things too!"

"That was. . .superficial magic. It wasn't real, which is why they disappeared so easily. I'm not all powerful. I can't do those things."

"Of course, you can!"

"Healing magic does not come easily to us, especially when trying to heal humans. There are often. . .unfortunate side-effects. We can't always see ahead to the consequences of our actions. Once I tried to heal a girl's

528

finger, and my magic solved the problem by removing her entire arm. There are pixies who could wake Amy, but we are not them."

"What about Jonah?"

"What your grown-ups call 'detention' and what you children call the 'bad place' is a human spell. Human spells have built in protections against pixies. I cannot break it. Interrogation magic is very strong in any case. It can only be broken when certain conditions are met."

Ev's shoulders slumped and she lay back down.

"Getting rid of Felix is also harder than you think. Pixies are not morally opposed to the odd bit of assassination. It's just that The Seven are surrounded by anti-pixie enchantments as well. It's going to take a coordinated effort to overthrow that particular beast."

"So, what good are you, actually?" asked Madison.

"There are many things we can do, many things that we know. We are diplomatic when needed. . ."

Boaclick snorted.

"...most of us, anyway, and we can see the big picture. Bring people together who need to be brought together. Make things happen. Humans wouldn't follow us, anyway, even if we could muster a revolution, and there aren't enough pixies to just take over. But they might follow a human child with a pixie advisor at her side. Did you think it would be easy?"

Ev sighed. "No, I guess not."

"I am also sorry, Ev. Freeing me was a lot to ask of a small girl, and I will always regret what I made you give up."

"What do you mean? I didn't give anything up."

"Who is Harriet Acorn?" Lulerain asked.

"The worst woman to ever walk the earth. A cold and heartless monster. She was a terrible mother to me my whole life."

"You don't remember anything good?"

"There's nothing good to remember."

"That's what you sacrificed. Your ability to have a relationship with your mother as long as one of you is still alive."

Ev snorted.

"Like that was ever going to happen."

Lulerain just sighed, sadly.

"I'm sorry, Evelyn. I knew something like this would happen, and I asked you to do it anyway."

Ev shrugged.

"Nothing's changed. I feel the same way about my mother as I always did. Completely indifferent."

"Is this really the time to be discussing this?" Dropellet asked impatiently.

"You are probably right, my friend. Evelyn, it's time we continued, don't you think?"

"Continue with what?" demanded Stacey.

"The plan," said Ev, hollowly. "We have to get on with the rest of the plan."

"Right now?"

"Of course. We can't just go back to bed. Derek force-fed some children valerian, and now three pixies are free. Our days were numbered anyway, the moment we started working together. Let's be honest—none of us really thought we were just going to wake up and go to class tomorrow, did we?"

Her friends shook their heads.

"Exactly. We're doing this right now." She scrambled to her feet. "Firstly, let's let the pixies in on the plan."

"No," said Lulerain when Ev had finished explaining.

"What?"

"No, that won't work."

"Look, I've spent a lot of time. . ."

"And it's a great start. But it won't work. Not without a few modifications."

Lulerain explained what she had in mind to the listening children.

"That actually does sound a lot better," said Peter, begrudgingly.

"All right," said Ev. "We'll do it your way."

The first thing they had to do was leave Alerrawia. It would have been convenient if they could just fly away. Unfortunately, the anti-flight charms were up permanently since Ev's first escape. So, Ev thought that the only other option was to cut through the fence.

But Lulerain thought that flying out *was* the best option. Better yet, she knew exactly how to make it happen.

They couldn't draw too much attention to their escape. By the time anyone noticed they were missing, they had to be as far away as possible. They couldn't just blast through one of the gates and make a run for it.

"We have to fly over the perimeter fence," said Dropellet, whose job in the armed forces meant he knew a lot about how Alerrawia would respond to a breakout. "The only safe place to do that is just to the west of the third gate. That gate is never used, and the guards treat their rotations there as a night off. If we can distract them, flying away will be easy, especially if they *expect* to see activity in the air."

"Why would they expect that?" asked Derek.

"When the security system thinks that Alerrawia is under attack from within, three things happen: A huge number of guards are sent to the thirteenth floor to protect The Seven, most of the rest are sent to the main and kitchen gates to guard them, and air patrols are dispatched to gather more information, which means that the air barriers will be deactivated. The guards on the third gate will be distracted and confused. We'll get past them easily."

"Why wouldn't they increase security at the third gate?"

"The third gate can't open anymore, even if we wanted it to. It was welded permanently shut decades ago."

So, all the Withouters had to do was to make Alerrawia's security system think that it was under attack.

Easy.

Stacey and Siobhan would head to the IT nerve center on the tenth floor, where Stacey worked part time as an apprentice. It wasn't unusual for Stacey's parents to summon her there at all hours of the night to check on things. In fact, it happened quite often, because what was the point of apprentices if you couldn't make them do the jobs no one else wanted in the middle of the night? Siobhan would keep them both faded until they got to the nerve center. Once there, Stacey would be able to trip some alarms and cause a full-on panic, with Siobhan on hand to fade her and run, if needed.

The others were going to manually trip alarms all over Alerrawia, ones that Stacey couldn't access from the nerve center, so that the first thought *wouldn't* be that someone was messing around on the tenth floor.

Madison and Lulerain were going to trigger the alarm to the restricted section. All they had to do was try to get through the door. The moment the system realized they weren't members of The Seven, the alarm would sound. Lulerain would try to distract whichever member of The Seven was on guard with some legitimate library business.

By the time they figured out who tripped the alarm, Madison and Lulerain would be long gone.

Hopefully.

Derek and Peter, with Boaclick to hide and protect them, would head to the basement to steal the mass RDD that Shaun was so fond of using during PE class. Everyone knew where it was kept. There was a safe behind the desk in Shaun's tiny basement office. Derek would use his super strength to rip it open, after Boaclick deactivated any magical shields protecting the safe. Derek and Peter would use the RDD to disable all patrols that were out and about. The moment any of the patrol leaders didn't call in, another set of alarms would sound throughout the building, which would make things even more confusing.

That left Ev, Gavin and Dropellet.

To really throw the compound into disarray, they needed to launch a fake attack on the thirteenth floor. It was the riskiest part of the plan.

It was 1:45am. At 2am exactly, each of the four groups would put their plan into action, and Alerrawia would come alive. If even two of the four plans worked, their escape would be possible, but the more confusion they could cause, the better.

Dropellet shielded Ev until just before she reached the secure entrance to the thirteenth floor. With Dropellet and Gavin invisible at her side, Ev marched angrily up to the guard. She was vaguely relieved to see that it wasn't Charles, who she'd sort of started to like. This was the night shift guard, and Ev marked him down immediately as a pretty idiot.

"Hey! You shouldn't be here! Stand back!"

"Well, tell that to Robert!" said Ev, marching on. "All I know is that Madam woke me in the middle of the night and said I was late for Impulse Control. What was I supposed to do?"

She was nearly at the door now. The guard was perplexed. Children were not allowed out at night. That being said, this was exactly the sort of thing Madam and Robert would do to an Inner brat.

"Can we just ask him?" begged Ev. "I don't want to get in any more trouble. . ."

"I don't know," said the guard uncertainly.

Ev burst into tears. It was easy. Her nerves were so frazzled it was almost a relief.

"Stop that!" said the guard. He shifted uncomfortably. "Let me just call Christopher or one of the others. . ."

He reached for the intercom and hit a button. Nothing happened.

"What the. . ."

Ev let out a heart-rending wail, just to keep things moving.

"Stop it!" said the guard again. He hit a few more buttons, but the system was dead, courtesy of some light pixie magic.

Ev had asked why Dropellet couldn't just blow the door down instead of messing with the intercom, and Lulerain had said that it would draw the wrong kind of attention. Confuse and misdirect—that's what they had to do.

The guard stood, but still seemed uncertain. Ev flung herself on the floor and screamed.

"Just. . .just hold on!" said the guard. "Give me a second. . ." He entered his passcode and scanned his retinas. The door opened.

"Thank you," said Ev sweetly. "I wouldn't want Madam to RDD me again."

On the word 'RDD', the guard screamed, "My eyes!"

"Not that one. . ." muttered an invisible voice.

"My hearing!" shouted the guard. "You are in big trouble kid. . .Ah!"

This time, the guard fell to the floor.

Next moment, Gavin appeared. He was standing with his foot in the door, wedging it open. In his hand was Madam's RDD.

"It only took three tries find full body paralysis," he said.

Dropellet snapped his fingers, and the guard was immediately bound and gagged. Another snap of the fingers made the guard vanish altogether.

"Um," said Ev. "Have you. . .sent him somewhere. . .nice?"

"Storage closet," said Dropellet curtly. "Keep moving!"

The darted quickly through the door and closed it behind them.

"Hurry!" whispered Dropellet.

Attacking a member of The Seven would be wonderfully satisfying, but it would also have a relatively low impact, and it carried the highest risk of getting caught. So, instead, they headed south to the War Room, the place where all of Alerrawia's plots against the True Users were hatched.

As Ev, leading the way, rounded the spiral staircase, she heard voices.

". . .ridiculous rules! Children need disciplining."

"But you were obviously out of line, Gwyneth, or Felix wouldn't have summoned us. You must see. . ."

The conversation was cut short as Ev rounded the bend and she came face-to-face with Madam and Chloe.

"Hello!" she said loudly, to warn Gavin and Dropellet to hide.

"What are you doing here?" asked Madam, eyes narrow.

"You dragged me out of bed and said I had I had a catch-up class with Robert, don't you remember?"

For a wonderful moment, Madam was completely speechless.

"Oh, Gwyneth that really is going too far. . .," said Chloe.

"The brat is lying!"

"It says a lot, doesn't it *Gwyneth*, that Chloe believes me so easily."

"If I had my RDD. . ."

"*Gwyneth*! It's that sort of thing that got us in trouble in the first place!"

"I've really had enough of you," said Ev. "I don't have time for this. Can you just, I don't know, go away or something?"

"You are going to be sorry, you little Inner brat!" shrieked Madam, pouncing.

"Guards!" called Chloe in a panic.

"Leave us alone!"

Go away and never come back!

In her sudden panic, Ev unleashed the full force of her third ability straight at Madam and Chloe.

What happened next was this:

Chloe grabbed Madam, dragging her back with a force that surprised Ev. It surprised Chloe too, by the look on her face. Chloe threw Madam to the ground, pulled herself to her full height, and blasted the older woman with what looked like most of her magical reserves.

Around the same time that Chloe grabbed Madam, Dropellet grabbed Ev and pulled her back against the wall, invisible, just as guards arrived on the scene to see Chloe's attack.

They tackled Chloe to the ground.

"What. . .what did I do?" Chloe asked, eyes wide with shock.

Madam lay on the ground, unconscious.

"What's going on here?"

Eliza, rounded the corner in her day clothes, looking like she hadn't even contemplated sleep yet.

"I attacked her…" said Chloe, hardly believing her own words.

"Come with us," said one of the guards, pulling Chloe to her feet. "It's the sub-basement for you."

"Wait," Eliza ordered. "Why did you do it, Chloe?"

"I don't know. I just couldn't take it anymore. The girl. . ."

Ev's blood froze. Chloe was about to tell Eliza that she was there, somewhere, on the thirteenth floor.

"Yes," said Eliza gently. "What Madam did to that poor child was extreme. But she will heal, Chloe, while Madam might never come back from whatever you just did."

Chloe squared her shoulders.

"Well, maybe that's for the best."

Eliza waved her hand. Two guards led Chloe away, while a third picked Madam up and followed them.

Eliza sighed sadly to herself and went on her way.

"What's the time?" whispered Ev.

"1:56pm," said Dropellet.

Four more minutes.

"Let's keep moving."

Ev was still shaking from the encounter, but she would have to deal with that later. Right now, she had bigger things to worry about.

Gavin and Dropellet had the easy job. They would gently attack the door to the War Room until the alarms sounded.

Ev's job was harder, and to do it, she needed to look like someone else.

"Ready?" asked Dropellet.

"Ready," said Ev.

He snapped his fingers, and Ev shot up. Suddenly, she was towering over Gavin. Her hair was longer her eyes clearer, her chest. . .heavier.

And she was wearing a purple cloak.

"Hey, how do you know what my in-game avatar looks like?" she demanded.

"I don't. I just built from the picture you have of yourself in your head. I can't say I approve, particularly, but it should serve our purposes. Although, if we stand here chatting all night, the spell will wear off before you've actually done anything."

Ev nodded and strode down the corridor. It felt good to stride. She couldn't wait until she was grown up for real.

She stopped outside the scrying room and waited for Dropellet's signal.

The last few minutes felt like an eternity.

Then, suddenly, Dropellet flashed a red light at her, and she burst through the door, announcing, "Nobody panic. If you don't move, no one will be hurt."

The man closest to her looked shocked, and then his face cleared.

"Is. . .is this a rescue?" he asked.

Ev faltered, but only for a moment.

"Not yet. But soon."

Then, with abilities she had been honing for months, she found the bubbling pit of lava in her brain, welcomed the tingling sensation, and announced confidently, "Let there be light!"

Every crystal ball in the room burst into flame.

That set off the smoke alarms. In the distance, she could hear the War Room alarms blaring, and she hoped that there were others sounding all across Alerrawia.

"Hey!" yelled one of the scryers.

"Must dash!" said Ev. She could feel herself slowly starting to shrink. She fled, reaching Gavin and Dropellet just as the pixie turned them all invisible and a swarm of guards arrived on the scene, with Christopher and Ernouf close behind.

"What's going on?" yelled Christopher.

"We don't know, sir. . ."

"Then find out!"

He ran towards Felix's rooms.

Ev felt Dropellet's hand on her collar and heard the now familiar sound of him snapping his fingers. Instantly, things grew quieter, the alarms a distant ringing—Dropellet had teleported them back to the paddocks.

A moment later, Boaclick appeared with Peter and Derek.

"How did it go?" asked Ev.

"Fine," panted Peter. "That was terrifying. And fun. Should I be finding it fun?"

"Where are the others?" asked Derek.

"They'll be here soon!" hissed Ev.

Lulerain and Madison appeared.

"What took you so long?" hissed Ev. "I expected you to be back first!"

"Zara was on guard duty, which should have been easy," said Madison. "But she wouldn't just let Lulerain go with an 'I don't know'. She wanted a full report, and Lulerain had to pretend to obey. We didn't even get to touch the door, we had to leave. Sneaking around was fun, though. I need to find a way to be invisible more often." Madison was completely unconcerned that her part of the plan hadn't worked.

"It looks like we did enough anyway," said Dropellet, listening closely to the chatter on his hand-held radio. "The Gate 3 guards are distracted, and everyone else is exactly where we want them, more-or-less."

Ev nodded. "Good," she said. "I think. . .we have others to wait for, don't we?"

"Who?"

Ev glanced at her hand where she could see some hastily scribbled words.

"Siobhan and Stacey are faded, don't leave without them," she read out. Her brow furrowed. "Who?"

"Fading magic," said Dropellet. "I can just about remember. . .We can wait a short while, I suppose."

"Can you and Lulerain prepare for the next part of the plan, please?"

"But of course," said Dropellet, sardonically. He and Lulerain flew through the paddock wall.

"The next part being. . .?" Gavin asked nervously.

"We're going to fly away," said Ev.

"About that. . ."

"It'll be easy," said Ev. Gavin wasn't a flyer, and she had no idea how he'd find the experience, but she couldn't worry about that now.

Dropellet stuck his head through the wall.

"We're all set," he said.

"Have you done it already?" asked Ev.

"No, I decided to wait until the last moment, just in case."

"Good idea. Lulerain?"

"She's all set too."

In the distance, they could hear shouting and running. Lights were on across the compound. Several times, they had to keep very quiet because they could hear guards fetching griffins from the paddock. Even worse was when they had to duck behind the bushes because of a patrol passing between the two perimeter fences.

"We can't wait much longer, child," said Dropellet.

"Yes. Why are we waiting again? I can't quite put my finger on it. . ."

"You're waiting for us, and we're here," said Stacey. Abruptly, she and Siobhan faded into view.

"I was about to leave without you!" wailed Ev.

 "Sorry we took so long," said Siobhan.

"Even though it's entirely your fault?" demanded Stacey, who was livid.

"What are you talking about?" asked Ev. Dropellet tutted impatiently, but she ignored him.

"She disappeared for ages! Left me hiding under a desk while everyone responded to the alarms," said Stacey, angrily. "And I couldn't even remember *who* I was waiting for because she just faded away!"

"What were you doing, Siobhan?" asked Ev.

"Can this wait for later?" said Dropellet.

Ev looked at Siobhan for a moment and then turned away.

"You're right, this can wait," she said. She was too tired to think this through right now, and, anyway, Siobhan would have a good reason, and everyone would calm down.

"I hope you don't get seasick," said Boaclick conversationally to Gavin.

Gavin already looked green. "I wouldn't know," he said, miserably.

Lulerain appeared, leading a bedraggled griffin. Ev recognized her immediately—it was Vasagle, the rebellious griffin who had tried to lead an uprising. There were bare patches where her feathers had been unceremoniously ripped out.

"Good evening," said Vasagle, her voice hoarse. Ev almost jumped out of her skin. It was one thing to know that griffins could talk; it was quite another to actually hear one.

"How do you do?" said Stacey, politely.

"You can tell which of us had the most stable upbringing," muttered Derek, but only Ev heard him.

Vasagle turned to Gavin.

"You are the one who will ride me to freedom," she said. It wasn't a question. It was a statement of how things would be.

"Oh. . .All right," said Gavin, nervously.

The griffin turned to Lulerain. "When you are done, freeing my kin will be your top priority," she said. Again, it wasn't a question.

Ev wondered what Vasagle would do if whatever promises Lulerain had made her were broken.

"We can't hide with a griffin!" said Peter. "We need to leave now!"

"Any moment now, Peter," said Ev. Just then, they heard the unmistakable sound of Claster half flying, half scrambling to the roof of the paddock.

This was normal. In times of emergency, Claster was sent out on patrol, assuming they could convince him to wake up.

Dropellet was at Claster's head, commanding him. This was also normal. Dropellet's job was, after all, to manage Claster.

Dropellet darted down to the waiting Withouters.

"Stacey and Madison," he said. "Come with me, please."

"I thought you'd never ask," said Madison, cheerfully.

Stacey face was white but determined.

The girls scrambled up the ladders that leaned against the paddock, Dropellet turning them invisible the moment they touched the first rung.

Lulerain ushered Gavin onto Vasagle's back. He perched there miserably.

"I'm terribly sorry about this, ma'am," he said, nervously. Vasagle didn't answer.

"Ready when you are, Evelyn Acorn," said Lulerain.

Ev nodded, hoping she looked more confident than she felt. She turned to Dropellet, high above, and gave him a thumbs up.

Dropellet snapped his fingers, and Claster launched himself into the sky.

"Quickly!" hissed Lulerain. With surprising force for someone so tiny, Lulerain slapped Vasagle on the rump, making Ev wince. The griffin sprang into the air, Gavin in tow, flying just below Claster so they wouldn't be noticed by the guards at the nearby towers. Even if Vasagle was spotted, the guards would probably just assume that she was just another griffin out on patrol, but they wanted to take every precaution.

Lulerain, Boaclick, and the four remaining children launched themselves after the griffin.

For this part of the plan to work, they had to fly incredibly close to Claster's underbelly, almost touching it. Siobhan helped by casting her fading shield again, trying to hide them as best she could, but the effect was only partial—she was struggling to keep them shielded and stay in the air.

"You can relax now, dear," said Lulerain to Siobhan after a while. "They didn't see us."

The wonderful thing about flying was that, before you knew it, you were miles away from where you'd started, with very little effort. For a moment, Ev panicked.

"One, two, three pixies, one dragon, one griffin, one, two, three, four, five, six friends…" she muttered, over and over, until she felt better.

They'd done it. They'd escaped.

She flew to the head of the group. "This way," she called, turning slightly to lead her friends to where she thought the True Users would be.

19. Things are Bigger that the Three of You

And there shall be three tests, one to
ascertain divine right, one to ascertain
magical prowess, and one to ascertain ability
to govern.

True User Law

Ev was lost, but she wasn't ready to admit it. The last time she'd flown this way she hadn't exactly been paying attention. She didn't recognize a single thing.

She became gradually aware of a huge presence keeping pace with her and turned to see Claster's head looming next to hers.

"How's it going, Claster?" she asked, nervously. She had no idea how one was supposed to address a dragon, so she just spoke the same way she did with any of her friends.

"Going?" asked Claster. "I don't know where we are going. Do you?"

"Yes, of course!"

"It seems about time," said Claster, in a voice that was probably meant to be quiet but that boomed out across the sky, "that I thanked you for my unexpected freedom."

No one else was speaking. Claster had not spoken in decades, maybe centuries. Nobody wanted to miss a word.

"Dropellet freed you. . ."

"Perhaps, but you freed Lulerain, something you were taught never to do, and Lulerain freed Dropellet, so it is all down to you, human child."

"Then, you're welcome," said Ev.

"You are pleased with the decisions you have taken thus far?"

Lying to Claster didn't seem like a good idea, so she thought before she spoke.

"I think so," she said, eventually. "It's hard to tell for sure when we're still so far away from our goal."

"To save two other little children from the clutches of an evil man?" asked Claster.

"Yes. . ." said Ev, hesitantly.

"You seem unsure," said Claster. "Is that no longer your reason?"

"Well, yes, obviously I want my friends to be safe, but. . ."

"But things are bigger than the three of you," finished Claster.

"Things are bigger than the three of us."

They flew in thoughtful silence, except for Ev occasionally calling out directions at random.

"I am the only one, you know," said Claster, suddenly.

"Sorry?" said Ev.

"The only dragon inside the bubble. For centuries." He sounded sad.

"I am sorry," said Ev.

"It is not your doing," said Claster. "Although I believe that you are the one who can undo it."

"Undo what? The bubble?"

"Oh yes. I was here when it formed. It can be undone."

"That's impossible," interjected Peter. "They tried for years and then gave up because they couldn't do it!"

"They gave up because they didn't want to succeed!" snapped Claster.

"That doesn't make any sense. . ."

"Yes, it does, actually," said Madison from her seat atop Claster. "They want to have complete control of everyone. That's much easier when 'everyone' is a tiny little group."

"I'm not sure there's anything left out there. . ." said Ev, thinking about what she'd learned in the restricted section.

"How would anyone possibly know that?" boomed Claster.

"They said it's all gone, that we're all that's left."

"They also said to never free a pixie, and yet. . ."

The dragon let his words hang in the air. Ev sighed.

"I can't think about this right now."

"When you *are* ready to think about, human girl, come to me; I can tell you what must be done."

Ev nodded, looked away, and suddenly yelled, "Hey, I know where we are!".

"You mean, you didn't always?" asked Stacey.

"We can't just fly over the forest with a dragon," said Lulerain. "They'll shoot us down. We should land, find them on foot."

"Good point. . ."

The Withouters landed, and Gavin jumped off Vasagle, relief flooding his face. He hadn't said a word since take-off.

"Thank you, ma'am," he whispered, and then sat down hard on the ground.

"Make yourselves comfortable here," said Ev. "I'll be back as quick as I can."

"Oh, you don't think we're going to let you go alone, do you?" said Derek. "I'm coming too."

"So am I," said Siobhan.

"And I'm not sitting around like a damsel in distress either," said Madison, pouting.

"Fine, you can come," said Ev. Truthfully, she didn't want to go creeping through the forest by herself anyway.

The three children walked cautiously through the trees in the heavy morning heat, trying not to draw too much attention.

"What, exactly, are we looking for?" asked Madison in a voice that was much too loud.

"The True Users," hissed Ev.

"All right. So, why are we being so quiet?"

Ev stopped. Madison had a point. If they wanted to be found, what was the point of sneaking?

"Hello?" she called.

"Hello," was the immediate reply.

She jumped.

A man appeared from between the trees. He was one of the people Ev had met the last time she'd been there.

She swallowed.

"Hi," she said. "Maybe you remember me? I'm Mike's friend? We've fled Alerrawia and need your help."

"So, of course, you brought the dragon with you," said the man.

"He helped us escape. He's on our side. . ."

"And what side is that?" demanded the man.

"Whichever side Felix isn't on," said Derek.

"Well, I suppose you'd better come with us, then."

Menacing men, women and children materialized from among the trees.

They'd never been alone in the forest, not really.

"We're going to blindfold you, now," said the man, conversationally. "I'm also going to send another group to collect your friends."

"There's a griffin and three pixies with them, and of course, Claster," said Ev. "I'm not sure how they'll react. . ."

"We're not Alerrawians, little girl," said the man. "We don't hurt children."

"What about pixies, and griffins and dragons?"

"That really depends on what the pixies, and griffins, and dragons decide to do. They will of course need to submit to temporary restraints."

"Talk to the pixie Lulerain. She can persuade the others to do what you ask. Just don't sneak up on them, or anything, everyone's a little on edge."

The man handed them three blindfolds.

"Will you do this yourself or must I?" he asked.

"We'll do it," muttered Ev, taking them.

Last time, Ev hadn't made it as far as the camp itself, if that's even where they'd really planned to take her. The True Users camp was hidden by a set of complex spells, which was why Alerrawia hadn't just wiped it out already. No one could find it who didn't already know where it was. An entire army could march through the very heart of the camp and not notice a thing.

Even blindfolded, it was a big risk for them to take Ev and her friends there. She hoped it meant that they were inclined to trust them.

As they walked, the man spoke.

"My name is Jim Day. I'm a True User Lieutenant."

Ev said nothing.

"What made you leave that stinking pit of compromise?"

It took Ev a moment to realize that he was talking about Alerrawia.

"It wasn't working out for us," she said.

The man snorted.

"The entire place should be burned to the ground with everyone in it."

"You know that there are children living there, right? Kids like us who've had no say in how things work?"

"Irrelevant. You will become grown-ups like them and do what they do. As has happened for thousands of years."

"How does that square with your 'we don't hurt children' philosophy?"

Jim didn't answer.

After a long, slow walk, they were finally ordered to stop.

"Leader?" said Jim. "We have some Alerrawian kids here, claiming to be runaways. They brought a dragon, a griffin, and three pixies, currently being detained by Ray-Leigh and Taylor. What do you want us to do with them?"

Ev held her breath. Everything depended on the answer.

There was a whispered conversation.

"The Leader would like to know what in the bubble you're talking about?" said a man.

"I mean exactly what I said," said Jim. He didn't sound happy, and he didn't even try to speak with respect.

"You're supposed to shoot Alerrawian interlopers on sight," said the unknown man.

"I wasn't sure if that rule applied to children on first name terms with the Leader," said Jim. "So many rules have become negotiable of late, I thought it best to check."

There was movement, and a familiar voice said, "Remove their blindfolds, Jim."

Ev blinked against the sudden daylight.

"A bit more warning would be nice, next time," said Madison. "You practically blinded me!"

"Madison, no talking, please," said Ev.

"What's this about a dragon?" asked Mike. No hellos. No 'nice-to-see-you'. Just straight down to business.

"It's Claster, the dragon from Alerrawia. We freed him," said Ev.

"You did what now?" said the man Ev hadn't met before. He was dark skinned with curly hair. He looked skinny, but he held himself like someone who could take you out without even thinking about it.

"We freed the Alerrawian dragon. Also, a griffin named Vasagle and three pixies."

"Why?" asked Mike.

"What do you mean, why?" asked Ev. "Who needs a *reason* to free people?"

There was a pause.

"Why did you come here?" asked the man.

"Why are you asking questions?" demanded Jim. "You are just a Defender, and an Inner exile to boot; you have no place at meetings such as this. . ."

"Reuben is here at my request," said Mike. "He is to remain at my side at all times."

"That is a role reserved for Lieutenants. . ."

"And when I have Lieutenants I can trust, then maybe things can return to normal."

"Interesting," said Ev, interrupting Mike and Jim's staring contest. "So, this is what happens when you make a child a leader—the grown-ups fight over who gets to be closest to him. I suppose you thought a child would be easy to control, but this is Mike we're talking about here. He's been the designated adult of the universe since his very first day on this planet. Didn't you know? I'd say I felt sorry for you, but I don't, so. . ."

Mike laughed.

"Evelyn, I am overjoyed that you have returned. We have so much to discuss!"

"Yes, we do," said Ev.

"Leave us," said Mike. "I want to speak with Ev alone. Take her friends with you."

"So, we're prisoners, then?" demanded Derek.

"Think of yourselves as guests here at my pleasure. I will reassess your status once I have more information."

"Leave it be Derek. We knew it wouldn't be easy."

Derek gritted his teeth and nodded firmly, but Ev could see that he was fuming as the True Users led him away.

"Is that angry giant-in-training a friend of yours?" asked Mike quizzically, once they were alone.

"Yes," said Ev. "We met when he tried to break my arm, but we're good now."

"Strange that he listens to you."

"Why would *you* find that strange?"

"Fair point."

"I have a lot to tell you, and I need your help, and we can't delay, because they'll be looking for us by now, and. . ."

"Slow down! Things move at a more reasonable pace here in the forest. We don't just dive straight into negotiations. I will tell you my story, of how I became leader, you will tell me your story, of how you found yourself in Alerrawia, and then, perhaps, we will begin discussing your request."

"We don't have time. . ."

"Alternatively, we could simply turn you out of the forest or imprison you without hearing your petition."

Ev took a deep breath, trying to calm the pool of lava in her brain.

"As you wish," she said through gritted teeth.

"Excellent! Well, the system for selecting a leader is quaint, to say the least. . ."

Mike explained that the True Users selected new leaders using a simple test. If candidates didn't pass the test, they were never allowed to take it again. If no one passed the test, the True Users just went without a leader.

Mike didn't think much of the system.

"I wonder why your Lieutenant doesn't like you?" she said, with fake bewilderment.

"I really have no idea," said Mike, with complete seriousness. "All I want to do is update one or two of the sillier aspects of True User life, but so many here are far too unreasonable to see sense."

"Well, I suppose there are some things that could change. Sometimes the True Users seem to be just the same as the Alerrawians, because. . ."

"There are no similarities at all between the two groups!"

"No, I mean because the Alerrawians hate magic and want to use science for everything, and the True Users hate science and want to use magic for everything, when *I* think we should all just use both."

"I will not let you besmirch the good name of the people who have taken me in! Alerrawia is a pit of disease! The vast majority of Alerrawian systems rely on magic. They say that they allow it to exist in the service of science, but the truth is that they would be nothing without it! We live more. . .purely. I will not sit here and listen to your fatuous comparisons!"

"Sorry," muttered Ev. "I didn't mean to offend."

Mike calmed slightly. "Yes, well, perhaps the True Users *do* over-emphasize the old superstitions and beliefs a little more heavily than is strictly helpful, but their intentions are completely pure."

"I suppose that it was one of these older superstitions that let you become leader, huh?"

"Yes," he conceded. "I didn't even enter the leadership contest deliberately!"

Every year, on the anniversary of the formation of the bubble, anyone who performed a mighty feat of magic became eligible to be the next leader, whether there was an existing leader or not.

"The day that I was exiled *was* the anniversary! The True Users are always on the lookout for exiles from Inner so they can snap them up before Alerrawia gets to them, but I was the first in a long time, and the first child. I suppose my arrival seemed significant."

"They thought a scared little boy from under the ground would make a good leader?"

"No, strangely enough, I really don't think that they did, but rules are rules. The older the tradition, the harder it is to undo, it seems. I, of course, was thrilled to hear the news, and immediately began preparing to pass the subsequent tests."

Next, Mike had to demonstrate his magical superiority. He did this by burning down half of the True Users camp. In his sleep.

"I'd planned something a little more controlled, to be conducted in conditions of relative safety, but my accidental display turned out to be exactly the sort of thing they were looking for. I have no idea how I did it. I'm not even sure I could do it again, even if I wanted to."

"I have an idea about that. . ."

Ev told Mike about Hexteria, how it was in the food they ate in Inner, although in dwindling amounts.

"It sounds to me like you suddenly stopped eating Hexteria, and your built-up magic just exploded. It's basically the same thing that happened to me the first time I escaped.

"Interesting theory. I've heard about Hexteria, of course. Devilish stuff, isn't it?"

Ev could only nod.

"The final test was to prove that I knew how to govern. You know, the nuts and bolts of getting things done. I'd read all of those stories in Inner, and as you know I took every opportunity to read beyond the course materials provided. The content on socioeconomics, for example, turned out to be very useful during the oral examination, not to mention my extensive research into ancient political systems. There's nothing else I needed to know, really."

"Except, maybe, how people work?"

"What do you mean?"

"Jim isn't happy about you, and I'm sure he's not the only one. Haven't you noticed?"

"Any sensible person will be able to see that I mean nothing but the best for the True Users. I really don't know what you're talking about."

"Please just be careful, Mike. You're making people angry. I can tell, just by what *you've* told *me*!"

"There is absolutely nothing to worry about, Evelyn," said Mike. "Now, I have matters to attend to. . ."

"You haven't even heard my request yet!"

"All in good time. I will speak with you again soon. I promise."

*

The True Users' camp was a collection of tree houses laid out in more-or-less concentric rings. From what Ev had seen, there were more True Users than Alerrawians, but not by much. It took up a huge chunk of the forest. Now that Ev, Madison, and Derek had been invited in, they were able to see just how big it was.

Right in the middle stood a giant old redwood called Big Red. This was where Ev had had her completely unsatisfactory chat with Mike. He lived in and ruled from the redwood, and there were homes in the enormous tree for some of his more trusted advisors.

People gathered round Big Red when there was an announcement or important event. The most important people in the camp lived in the ring of tree houses closest to Big Red. The further away from Big Red you lived, the less important you were. In between the rings was where cooking, washing, and teaching took place, and the whole camp was surrounded on all sides by the magical force field that kept the Alerrawians from finding them.

"It's just like fading, but instead of for one person, it's for a whole village," said Ev, and for some reason the thought made her feel uneasy.

"What?" snapped Derek.

"Nothing," said Ev, irritably.

Ev, Madison, and Derek were in a treehouse about three rings from the center. All of their things had been

563

confiscated, including Madam's RDD. The only thing Ev still had was Granny's magically protected mirror, but she didn't want to risk losing it by using it, not until she had a plan. They couldn't leave the treehouse, anyway—their Suncharm had been confiscated too, and the sun was vicious. They were imposing on a family that wasn't exactly happy about them being there, but who were making the best of it.

"How long do you think you'll be staying, then?" asked Iris, for the fifteenth time that morning. She was a sweet, nervous woman. Her soft eyes and voice made her difficult to dislike.

"Leave the children be," said her wife, Viola. Viola was the motherly type. She'd been exiled from Inner six years ago. She and some others had tried to escape from Inner. It didn't work, and Vendavi killed her friends when they tried. Viola survived, but she was exiled, which ironically was exactly what she'd wanted in the first place. Iris had told them this story proudly on their very first evening in the camp, along with an apology about how they would be living closer to Big Red if not for the fact that Viola was from Inner.

"I'll say it again," said Ev, who was losing patience fast. "We're here for as long as *your* leader wants us to be. If he would just talk to me. . ."

"We have no control over that, Ev," said Viola. "He'll talk to you when he talks to you."

An argument was prevented by Ewan, Viola and Iris' twelve-year-old son, a wonderful kid who was far too clever to be a True User, in Ev's opinion. He bounced into the room.

"Mom, where are my shoes?"

Iris was already halfway down the ladder to attend to her cooking duties for the day. Viola ruffled Ewan's hair lovingly and went looking for her son's shoes.

"Ewan, any news for me?" whispered Ev.

Madison shifted slightly so to watch for Viola's return.

"The dragon is in the outermost ring on the eastern side of the camp. They're looking after him, but he's tied up. And he's only so far out because there's nowhere else for him to fit."

"And the others?"

"The pixies are in a cage in Big Red, but your griffin has been released to our griffins. They have their own laws—we're not allowed to keep her."

"What about the other Withouters?"

"Withouters?"

"The other children that came here with us."

"Same as you, about two rings out from where you are."

"Thank you, Ewan," she said. "You have been very helpful."

Ewan grinned and darted down the ladder, still without shoes.

"See you later!" he called.

"We'll be here. As always," said Madison. "Dying from boredom." She lolled back in her wicker chair dramatically.

Viola returned.

"Where has he gone?" she demanded.

"He just dashed out," said Ev. "I think he went to his lesson." Ewan was in training to be a Primary Spell Caster. It was a much sought-after profession among the True Users, and he was showing great promise.

Viola sighed heavily.

"I love that boy, and I wish he would be slightly less scatterbrained."

She sat down to sharpen her knives.

"Do you kids know the Enhancement Spell?" she asked, conversationally.

"Enhancement is quite a broad word. Spells get quite specific names in Alerrawia. . ."

"Oh, you'd know if you knew this one. It's the one that cancels out the effects of Hexteria. I've been meaning to ask you about it for days. It was one of the first things I learned when I got here."

"Of course, we don't!" said Derek. "They only teach that one to the teachers."

"Well, I was a teacher-in-training, and they never taught it to *me*," said Madison.

"Now you're just being difficult, Madison."

"Well, it's not such a hard spell, for the children who freed a dragon. You could learn, given time."

"I couldn't!" said Madison, petulantly.

"I had it, but they took it off me, along with all my other papers," said Ev.

"I have a copy here, somewhere," said Viola, shuffling through some yellowing pages on a wooden shelf. "Here it is! Take a look at this and see if you can figure it out."

Ev looked at Viola suspiciously.

"Are you trying to mom me, like out of a book?" she demanded.

"I'm not sure I understand you. . ."

"You're just giving us something to do so we won't be bored. . ."

"Oh, in that case, yes, I am 'momming' you. Is it really so bad?"

"Mom, I can't find my scrying mirror!" called Ewan from the bottom of the ladder.

Viola sighed again, picked the round mirror up from its usual place, in plain sight, and headed down the ladder.

"While I'm down, I may as well run a few errands, but I'll be back later," she told the children.

"Alone, at last," said Madison.

"Yes, except for the guards at the bottom of the ladder, of course," said Derek, peevishly.

True User guards were very different to Alerrawian guards. They were all, without exception, useful *and* deadly. Ev was even beginning to worry that they were also smart.

"And it's not like we can talk about anything that matters because they are *definitely* listening."

"No need to be like that," said Madison.

"And you," said Derek, turning to Ev. "Is *this* what you had in mind when you dragged us out of bed in the middle of the night?"

"Like I could have *made* you come if you didn't want to!"

"If I knew that it would mean sitting in a treehouse dying of boredom, then. . ."

"None of us knew!"

They lapsed into angry silence.

A short while later, Madison said, "Jim's coming," grumpily, and sure enough, his head appeared at the top of the ladder a few minutes later.

"You three are to come with me," he said.

"Where to?" demanded Derek.

"Oh, who cares as long as it's not here," said Madison. Derek's mouth snapped shut.

One of the guards waved his hands and muttered something that Ev didn't catch.

"What are you doing?"

"Sun protection," said the guard. "Unless you *want* to burn to death out there?"

The guards took them to the foot of Big Red.

"This is promising," whispered Madison. "Unless we're here to be publicly executed, of course."

"Shut up," hissed Ev through gritted teeth.

Off to one side, Ev saw Vasagle among several other griffins. She looked healthier than Ev had ever seen her, healthier than any griffin Ev had ever seen.

She looked how a griffin was supposed to look.

At the foot of Big Red, they were met by Peter, Gavin, and Stacey. Ray-Leigh, one of the women Ev had met the first time she'd run away, held a magically reinforced cage with three very unhappy pixies inside.

Next to Ray-Leigh stood Taylor, towering high above the other True Users.

"Giant," whispered Derek.

"Told you so," whispered Ev.

To Ev's surprise, two other pixies, one pink and one green, were also guarding the cage.

They even brought Claster to the center of the camp. The trees shook as he squeezed his huge body between them. A huge collar that glowed faintly teal hung around his neck, which was probably how they were keeping him captive.

A huge crowd was forming, even though this wasn't an official event. It would have been nice to think they were there to see her, but Ev knew that Claster, the only dragon in the bubble, was the real draw.

Mike descended from Big Red with Jim and Reuben either side.

"We can't decide what to do with you," began Mike, immediately, "so we thought we should hear what you have to say."

"Gee, thanks," said Ev.

"If you would like to waive this opportunity. . ."

"No, it's fine, we'll talk, it's only what we've been wanting to do for the last three days anyway," said Ev.

"Go ahead."

Ev took a moment to find the yellow in her heart, look straight at Mike, and thought:

You will listen to it all.

"I suppose it all started when Jonah was accused of attacking Amy," she began.

"What?"

"This is probably going to take a while. . ."

Ev told them the story of her life so far. She went back to explain how Alerrawians stole children from Inner. She spoke about all the prejudice she'd faced. She told the story of her disciplinary hearing and what had happened to her friends, and she explained why and how she was standing in front of Mike now.

Mike listened to every word.

"Fascinating," he said, when she was done.

"Um, thanks?"

"Quite difficult to swallow, however."

"What?"

"Put yourself in my shoes. No Alerrawian in the history of the bubble has ever arrived at these conclusions. No one has ever thought, 'Hey, maybe the True Users are just people like us, let's make friends.' No one has ever tried to escape. How do I know that this isn't part of some big plot?"

Ev was speechless, her mind blank.

"I'm not saying it's likely, but it does need to be considered. We'll investigate your claims and get back to you."

Mike stood, preparing to leave, when the yellow in Ev's heart jumped up her throat, into her brain, and thought:

Help me!

A strange noise came from the direction of the griffin contingent, a noise that Ev had never heard before.

Vasagle was clearing her throat.

"I will speak now," she said.

"As you wish," said Mike, a trifle irritably.

"I dislike the implication of my involvement in a plot," continued Vasagle. "This is unacceptable."

"Well, I didn't mean. . ."

"Wait your turn to speak," said Vasagle.

Mike stopped talking.

That's a first, thought Ev.

"Your concerns imply that not only me, but also the dragon and pixies, are all complicit in a scheme that would benefit no one but Felix Granite. That I would be somehow involved in a plot that would keep myself and my closest kin powerless. . .They pull our feathers, take our claws just before we die from overwork! Did you know that? And you say that I am involved in this? That I work for that demon? This, even when your own magic will tell you that we are free and clear of all restraints binding us to Alerrawia? How dare you!" Her voice became shriller and shriller as she spoke.

Go Vasagle, thought Ev.

"I, too, would like an explanation," boomed Claster, making Ev jump. She wasn't the only one. "At best, it is insulting."

"We have no information regarding your escape. . ." began Jim.

"Because you haven't asked!" said Claster. "Three days we have been prisoners, and not one attempt made to hear our story before today, and even now you only listen to the girl!"

"I, too, would like to speak," said Lulerain from her cage. "Ray-Leigh, when you apprehended myself and my friends, did you have any trouble? At all?"

Ray-Leigh snorted and looked away.

"No, we didn't," answered Taylor instead. "In fact, you were very helpful."

Ray-Leigh looked as if she was considering the pros and cons of attacking the giant there and then.

"If we had a nefarious purpose," said Lulerain, "there would be no point in any subterfuge. We wouldn't need to pretend anything. There isn't a pixie in this forest that would fight for you against their own kind. We hold all the cards. The only possible reason to do you no harm is because we mean you no harm."

There was a brief silence.

"I think," said a voice from the crowd, "that we should hear their plan. Three of the children have lived in my house for three days, and apart from mildly corrupting my son, they've been lovely."

The speaker was Viola, and the crowd parted as she walked to the front. She was highly respected, a top True User Defender, and Iris had told Ev more than once that

Viola would have been a Lieutenant if not for her Inner origin.

"The Leader called an end to this meeting. . ." began Jim.

"The Leader knows better than to undermine the will of his people. I, for one, would like to hear more."

"They're only children!" shouted someone from the back.

"Most of them are older than our own leader, who was chosen through our own methods," said Viola. "If we listen to him, we should listen to them."

"Yes!" shouted someone.

"Madness!" shouted someone else, and then the noise became too much to make out individual comments.

All around the clearing, True Users were muttering. Opinions were very much divided, not that anyone could really hear what their enemies were saying over the noise of their own shouting.

"I do not have time for this," Ev muttered.

"Then do something," said Derek by her ear. "I know that you can. I'm not sure what you've been doing, but a little thing like this shouldn't stand in your way."

"It's not that simple. . ."

"If they don't listen to us now, we may as well not have done any of it!"

Ev sighed.

"You're right."

She closed her eyes, let her mind empty, and just when the yellow in her heart started to bloom, she looked directly at Mike and his fellow leaders and thought:

You will listen to our request, and you will give it the consideration that it deserves.

Mike waved his hands for silence, waved impatiently at Jim and Reuben as they tried to talk to him, and said, "Evelyn Acorn, once of Inner, now of Alerrawia, we will hear your request."

"Now, what was so hard about that?" whispered Derek. "You and I are going to need to sit down and chat, sometime very soon. . ."

"Thank you, Mike. . .I mean Leader," said Ev, trying her best to ignore Derek's whispers. "I appreciate your willingness to hear us out." Ev tried her best to match Mike's overly formal tone, but it had never come as naturally to her as it had to him. "We've already told you of our story so far, of our trials and tribulations, and how we have, together, overcome enormous odds. Surely you must be wondering: *Why?* Why did these children take these risks? Trust me; we wouldn't be here if we thought we had a choice, if we thought that anyone else would care enough to do what needs to be done, and, yes, frankly it is ridiculous that it's come down to a bunch of kids, but that's not our fault, now is it?

"It's all quite simple really. Things in the bubble need to change. Alerrawians slaughter True Users and vice versa, for what? The people of Inner, who don't even know that the rest of us exist, are about to be wiped out, for no reason at all. . ."

"It's easy to demand change, harder to actually achieve it," said Jim.

Is it really as hard as you think?

"But. . .is it actually *impossible*?" asked Mike.

"Felix, the whole of Alerrawia as we know it, has to fall," said Ev.

"This is not a revelation to us, little girl," said Jim.

"Isn't it?" asked Ev. "Because you haven't exactly been trying, have you?"

"Watch your mouth. . ."

"Do you speak to your leader like that?" demanded Ev. "No? Then I would ask you to treat me with the same respect."

You will show me respect by being silent when I speak, Jim.

Jim shut his mouth, sullenly.

"If you knew what you were doing, you would have wiped Alerrawia out by now. I've seen what they call 'security' and I have escaped them *twice*, once *entirely* by accident. They are weak. True, they have guns, and you don't, but that shouldn't matter to powerful magicians. And you've completely ignored the one resource right at your fingertips, that could actually help you win."

"What resource?" asked Mike.

"A larger army."

"Yes, there are a few more of us than them, but that's not enough. . ."

This was the moment Ev had been waiting for and dreading. Their whole plan hinged on what came next.

"I'm talking about Inner. I'm talking about the generations of powerful magicians that have been left underground to rot. I'm talking about freeing them, joining forces, and defeating Felix."

The crowd erupted. Ev stood her ground, staring directly at Mike.

Reuben and Jim stood either side of Mike, each trying to yell over the other.

"Quiet!" shouted Mike. Ev could only just hear him over the noise of the crowd. Mike shook his head, closed his eyes for an instant, and then bellowed, "QUIET!"

The trees shook from the force of his command, and some of the smaller children in the crowd clamped their hands over their ears and shrieked, but then there was silence.

Ev held her breath.

"You have certainly given us a lot to think about, Evelyn," said Mike in his normal voice. "I'm sure you understand that this is something we have to think about before we make a final decision."

"Of course," said Ev, breathing out. It wasn't a yes, but it wasn't a no either.

"Good. I will send for you soon to discuss this further. For now, your continued cooperation is appreciated."

"Man, I would *love* to punch him in his little smug face," whispered Derek, "but of course, I've turned over a new leaf and wouldn't *dream* of doing a thing like that to a little git like him."

Ev was too relieved to say anything.

It was a step in the right direction, even if it was a small step, and for now she could relax, just a little, while she waited for Mike to make his decision.

"It seems like we might actually do it," said Gavin.

"We *will* do it," said Ev. "I know we will."

20. Six.

fade

/fād/

verb

gerund or present participle: **fading**

1. gradually grow faint and disappear
2. (with reference to magic) ability to fade not only from view but also temporarily from memory

New Alerrawian Dictionary

The six children and the three pixies, still in their cage, were taken to a large tree house in the first ring, where they were left to their own devices. Claster was taken back to a part of the camp where he could be more comfortable.

"We've been upgraded," noted Stacey.

"Yeah, hopefully that's a good sign," said Peter.

"It definitely is," said Lulerain. "You really got through to them today, Ev. I think they'll want to talk to us more tomorrow."

"I hope you're right," said Ev. "About them only wanting to talk again tomorrow, I mean. I'm exhausted!"

"Now does seem like a good time to rest," said the pixie. "Who knows when we'll get another chance?"

Ev curled up in a wicker chair and let her eyes slowly close. Her friends gave her some space, catching up quietly among themselves, and she was almost asleep when a voice said, "About that chat we need to have."

Her eyes sprang open to see Derek in the seat next to her.

"I know that eleven-year-olds can't do what you do, Ev," said Derek. "I don't like being manipulated, magically or otherwise, so I'm giving you this chance to come clean."

"Or what?"

Derek shrugged.

"I don't know," he said. "The thought that you're tricking us. . .it just makes me sad. It doesn't even make me angry. *Everything* makes me angry, but that thought. . .it makes me feel like nothing matters, at all, so I *really* need you to have a good explanation."

"It's not safe for me to talk about."

"Says who?"

"Say Granny Oakwood."

Derek nodded slowly.

"Granny is the one who told you not to say?"

"Yes."

"That makes me feel better. Assuming you're telling the truth."

"I will tell you everything, but we have to get rid of Felix first. For now, just know that it's *very* important to me that all my friends help me because they *want* to help me. If all I did was force you to do what I wanted, I would be no better than Felix."

Derek's eyes were narrow.

"You're saying you *could* force us, if you wanted to?"

Ev mentally kicked herself.

"Yes, I could. But I promise I never have, and I never will. Well, not on purpose, anyway. I'm a bit of an idiot, actually, but I've thought about my stupider decisions

and I don't think that I've caused any long-term damage. .
."

"Long-term damage? What the hell is it that you can do?"

"Quiet," whispered Ev urgently. "Please, I need you to keep this between us, okay? When it's safe, you will be one of the first to hear the whole story, I promise, but until then, can you trust me?"

"I can try to trust you."

Ev nodded. "I'll take it." She smiled weakly. Derek just nodded and went to sit near Madison.

She told herself that it wasn't safe, that she didn't know who else was listening, but if she was being honest with herself, she was scared of how her friends would react. If she was scared of herself, how could she blame them if they were too?

They spoke long into the night, and as the sky began to darken, Ev began to worry.

Another sunset meant another day that Alerrawia knew that they were missing, another day spent searching for them, another day for Felix to get angrier.

"At least they've relaxed security a bit," said Madison.

"Yeah," said Ev. The six of them were comfortable. The ladder to the treehouse was still being guarded, but the guards were friendlier, and there were fewer of them.

Something was nagging at the back of her mind.

The six of them. . .

Six.

"Where's Siobhan?" she asked, suddenly.

"Who?" Derek asked, sleepily.

"She went with us to look for the True Users. Didn't she? Or did she stay behind? Argh, my head hurts so much. . ."

"Whatever you're talking about, stop it," said Madison. "I'm trying to sleep."

What *had* she been talking about?

"Sorry," she muttered, confused.

The other children slowly drifted off, but Ev just couldn't settle. She got up and walked to the ladder and climbed halfway down.

"Excuse me?" she said to the guard.

"What?" he snapped.

"Something's. . .not right. I don't know what, exactly, but I think something's going to happen."

"Like what? All of the trouble *I* know of is safely locked away in this treehouse. Stop worrying and go back to bed."

Ev sighed and climbed back up. Maybe she *was* overreacting. Something had spooked her, that was all. Maybe she just felt uncomfortable in the new treehouse.

She curled up on the floor and dozed off soon after.

She was awoken by an explosion.

"What's happening?" yelled Peter.

"I don't know!" shouted Ev as another explosion shook the tree. "Let's get down! If the tree falls while we're in it. . ."

She didn't have to finish her thought. Moments later they were gathered at the foot of the ladder.

"Of course, if the tree falls while we're *under* it, the result will be much the same," said Lulerain from the cage under Derek's left arm.

"It's Alerrawia," said Ev. "It must be. Somehow, they've found us."

"What do we do?" asked Madison.

A treehouse on the other side of Big Red went up in flames. All around were the screams of families fleeing their homes.

"We fight," said Ev. "We need them to help us, which means we help them. We know how these people think. We can make a difference!"

Derek nodded. "She's right. It's probably our fault they're here, so we have to do something about it."

Another tree went up in flame.

"Come on!" yelled Ev, choosing a direction at random.

"Airstrike?" panted Peter.

"No, we'd hear the choppers," said Derek. "Long-range missiles."

Wherever they looked, True Users were casting protective shields over the camp. The air was practically glowing with their combined magic.

"Those won't work. . ." muttered Ev. She knew that Alerrawia had spell-piercing ammunition. It was probably one of the first magical innovations they'd come up with. Alerrawia had a way around nearly every spell known to man—the *only* thing protecting the True Users up until now was the powerful enchantment that had kept them hidden in the forest. Alerrawia had never been able to crack it, but somehow, here they were.

"They can't invent new spells," said Peter, his face white. "We've been inventing all of this new technology, but *they can't invent new spells*!"

It was one of the first things you learned—magic was stale and static, and there was absolutely no way to invent a new spell.

Except. . .

Alerrawia invented new spells every day. They called it magical innovation, and you were supposed to focus on how awesome the scientific part of it was, but the point was that children as young as six were encouraged to dream up new uses for magic all the time.

Everywhere she looked, the True Users were using the oldest spells in existence.

"We have to tell them," she said. "Does anyone know a tracking spell to find Mike?"

"No need, there he is!" shouted Madison.

Mike was tumbled down the last few rungs of Big Red's ladder. Jim caught him and Reuben hurried down after them.

Taylor was standing over the Leader and his friends, ready to take the worst of the blast, if they were attacked again.

Mike was visibly shaking, and he very quickly became the center of an ever-expanding throng of grown-ups.

"Everything will be fine," she heard him say. "Magic will always triumph over science."

"Oh dear," said Boaclick. "The little boy doesn't know the danger he's in. This *will* be fun!"

Ev ran straight for him, ducking low to push through the gathered crowd.

"Leader," she said, breathlessly, "your shield spells—they won't work!"

"Lies!" shouted Jim. "She's one of the ones that brought them here. We cannot trust a word she says!"

"Ev, these are the strongest protection spells in existence. Alerrawia cannot overcome them, because Alerrawia, like the rest of us, cannot invent new, stronger spells." Mike's voice was completely calm, like he was discussing the weather, or explaining something to a very stupid child.

Ev was impressed.

"Felix is *really* good, isn't he, if he's managed to make *you* believe the same lies he feeds us."

She lifted her hand in the air, closed her eyes for a moment to access the core of her magic, and blasted right through the protective layer of spells Jim and Reuben had so conscientiously cast around their dear leader.

It wasn't even a difficult spell. Emerson had spent five minutes showing it to her at the end of a spell work class and then sent her on her way.

"It's called 'Shield Piercer 94', because there are 93 that come before it, plus a bunch that come after."

"Impossible," muttered Taylor.

"We're doomed," said someone else.

"Not necessarily, not if you let us help," said Ev.

"Why should we listen to you?" demanded Jim.

"Do you have a better idea?"

"You're one of them!"

"One of who? One of the Alerrawians? They never wanted me in the first place, and if they're trying to get me back now, it is definitely *not* because they want to give me any awards. For the last time, I am not working for Alerrawia!"

"The problem," began Mike (Ev wished fervently that he would just shut up and let her deal with it), "is that Alerrawia can't have known the camp was without a signal from someone who was already here."

Ev went cold.

"It wasn't me," she said quickly.

"No, Jim assures me that you, Derek and Madison were properly blindfolded, and Ray-Leigh says the same about the others. But you agree that it must, somehow, be one of your party?" said Mike.

Her mind whirled.

"They've been quiet for a while. . ." muttered Rueben, just as two men ran towards them.

"Leader," panted one, "they've offered terms." He handed Mike a scroll.

"It seems that they will cease and desist if we return The Seven 'stolen' children," said Mike.

"*Seven* children?" said Reuben at the same time Jim said, "*Stolen?*"

Seven children.

Seven children.

One for Ev, two for Stacey, three for Madison, four for Derek, five for Peter, six for Gavin. . .

"Siobhan. . ." murmured Ev.

"You know who Siobhan Kenwood is?" asked Mike.

"Who? I. . .someone else. . .I think someone else was with us. . .fading. . .*argh*, my head hurts so much!"

"Get Ray-Leigh," said Jim to one of the men. "Viola as well. I don't like the sound of this. . ."

"The sound of what?" said Ev. She couldn't remember what she'd been saying, but at least the headache was gone.

"My point exactly," said Jim, grimly.

The rest of the Withouters had long since caught up with the group, and they were watching the exchange, eyes wide.

"But there *are* only six of us!" said Madison. "I know that because of counting. And math."

"Shut up, Madison," said Ev.

"If you could all stay exactly where I can see you until the others arrive, I would greatly appreciate it," said Jim.

"You're wasting time! If you don't respond their terms, they'll just start shooting again!"

"Now that they know where we are," said Jim, "there's nothing at all to stop them!"

Ev paused.

"But they have stopped," she said. "And they've offered terms. So, they must really want us for something.

If you give them what they want, then there will be *nothing* holding them back!"

"She has a point," said Taylor. "They're our only bargaining chips. We may have to hang onto them."

"We can help you defend against future attacks! We know the spells; we know how they think! We can help you stop them. If you send us back, they'll wipe you out without a second thought."

"What's going on," said Ray-Leigh, curtly, Viola at her side. "Why haven't we formed a defensive perimeter?"

"They've offered terms, and we're discussing them," said Mike. He handed Ray-Leigh the scroll.

"*Seven* children?" said Viola, squinting over Ray-Leigh's shoulder.

"It seems that there is a seventh child, who may or may not be a fader," said Jim.

Taylor whistled. "That's rare. We haven't had a fader here in decades."

"If they're here, can you see them?"

Viola nodded.

"Of course, but if it's all the same to you I won't discuss it out loud. The child could be standing right next to me, you know, and I don't want her doing anything to stop me. How old is she?"

"How old is Siobhan?" Mike asked Ev.

"Sixteen," said Ev, automatically. "I think. . .who. . .what?"

"The signs are certainly there. . .," said Taylor. "It doesn't affect us because we have no context for this Siobhan child—she's just a name on a piece of paper. But *they* know her, so the fading magic is strong. It fits."

"We'll make preparations," said Viola. "Leave it with us."

The two women stepped away from the group, surrounding themselves with privacy enchantments that put the Withouters' bumbling attempts behind the griffin paddock to shame.

"Where are they going?" Ev asked. "What are you 'leaving' with them?"

"Don't worry about that for now," said Reuben. "You're sure you can help us keep the Alerrawians at bay?"

"Yes! *And* we can teach you the principles of spell invention so you can do *more* than defend yourselves. I'm talking about *defeating the Alerrawians* here!"

"I'm not sure we can trust them. . .," said Reuben.

"For once, I agree with the rogue Defender," said Jim.

Ev sighed. "There isn't time for this!"

"We have to give these matters due consideration," said Mike. "You see, when you are the Leader, you. . ."

Ev let him drone on. She closed her eyes, calmed her mind, and found the yellow in her heart.

You will let us help you defeat the Alerrawians. In return, you will help us free Inner.

". . .but, at the end of the day, the fact remains that we do need help, and there isn't anyone else to give it," finished Mike.

"This is unacceptable!" shouted Jim.

"It is my final decision on the matter," said Mike. "In return I suppose you want help with your mad scheme to free Inner?"

"You guessed it," said Ev.

"Then we're in agreement. However, it seems you have a traitor problem, and to show us that you are on our side, I expect you to play your part in bringing the situation to a satisfactory conclusion."

He handed her the scroll to read for herself.

Ev read it, then read it again.

"I don't understand. . .there's a name here I can't quite make out. . ."

"It's the fading magic," said Jim to Mike. "They won't be able to remember until Viola breaks through. Assuming she can."

"If anyone can, it's Viola," said Reuben. "Especially if Ray-Leigh helps."

"Why, yes, thank you for that vote of confidence," said Viola, sticking her head out through her privacy charms. You could just make out that there were two people inside the magic bubble, but you couldn't hear what they said or see what they were doing.

"She won't be able to get away while you prepare?" asked Mike.

"No, I took the liberty of quietly blocking her exit the moment I read the scroll. Do you hear that, Siobhan?" Viola called into the darkness. "You can't leave. You may as well show yourself now, dear!" She pulled her head back into her bubble.

"Has she gone mad?" asked Derek.

"No. . ." said Dropellet from the pixie cage. "I think something's going on. . .Every time I get close to understanding what, it vanishes! My head is like a sieve."

"I'm having the same problem," said Lulerain. "I don't like it. We should do what they say until this is resolved, Ev."

"Thank you, Lulerain," said Jim, respectfully. "However, I was not planning to give any of you a choice."

He snapped his fingers and group of well-armed True Users surrounded the children.

"Put them in any tree that's still standing, and don't let them leave," said Jim. "Ev, you will stay with us."

Ev watched her friends being marched off, captives once more.

"We need to respond to Alerrawia's terms," said Reuben. "They're not the most patient people. . ."

Jim took Ev gently but firmly by the arm.

"This needs to be resolved first," he said. "Viola!"

Viola stuck her head out again and said, "One more moment, love, hang in there."

Jim tutted impatiently but said nothing.

"What is Viola doing?"

"You can just keep your mouth shut until spoken to," said Jim.

They waited in awkward silence, Jim, Ev, Taylor, Reuben, Mike, and a handful of Defenders.

Viola stuck her head out a third time.

"Ev, come here please," said Viola.

"Are you sure that's wise?" asked Jim.

"Don't ask me for my help if you're going to second guess me at every turn," said Viola severely.

"Yes, take her," said Mike. "Ev is right about one thing—we *are* wasting time!"

Jim thrust Ev towards Viola's bubble, and Viola grabbed her arm and dragged her through.

The moment Ev crossed the magical line, she was surrounded by silence. Ray-Leigh was busily reviewing some ancient scrolls covered in tiny writing.

"I've got it," said Ray-Leigh. "I think. I should be able to do enough to boost your magic, anyway."

"That will have to do," said Viola. She took Ev's chin in her hand and gently tilted it up. "I don't think it will hurt," she said, "but I *do* think it might come as a bit of a shock. One, two, three!"

Ev felt Viola's magic shoot through her, and she shuddered.

And then her mind cleared.

And then she remembered.

"*Siobhan*," she said, miserably. "Why?"

"Ray-Leigh, get Mike," said Viola, ignoring the question.

For a brief moment, Viola and Ev were alone.

"She didn't have much of a choice," said Viola. "I can see her mind, and she hates every moment that she spends betraying you. I think you should keep that in mind. She is only a child, like the rest of you. That grandfather of hers, Felix—he made her do it. Using magic, of course, because there is no hypocrite quite as bad as a Granite hypocrite. I think that she's even been fighting back, for the first time. There's some sort of competing magic that's trying to keep her loyal to *you* instead, but I can't quite work it out. . ."

Ev's mind filled with all the times she'd warped reality to keep Siobhan at her side.

"We have to stick together," she said.

"Yes! Exactly! Those words keep going round and round in her head, and they refer to you! Anyway, she didn't want to hurt your friends. . ."

"It was Siobhan who attacked Amy?" asked Mike. He and Ray-Leigh had entered the privacy barrier just in time to hear the last few words.

"Yes, it seems so, but under severe duress. I would bet good money that Felix made her attack your friend to keep control of her. A woman named Marcia is in on it too, and I think there are some others who know that Siobhan is Felix's granddaughter, but are keeping it secret."

"The Seven?"

"Could be. The only one's she is afraid of are Felix and Marcia, though. I'm not sure the others know about her role as your traitor. You have to understand that she feels awful, Ev. She hates herself right now. Everything she's done to you. . .she didn't want to reveal the location of the camp, she really didn't. She fought it for as long as she could, but in the end her grandfather's magic was stronger."

"Why didn't she just tell us?"

"She couldn't. She is under a spell of selective silence—she can't say anything about Felix being her grandfather or her role in what has befallen you. She's under several spells, actually, and I think she's been under them for most of her life."

"Do you understand now, Ev?" asked Mike.

"I do."

"Good. You know what needs to be done?"

"Yes. It won't be a problem," said Ev, sighing sadly.

"I'm tracking her," said Viola. "She's in one of the nearest treehouses, with her friends."

"Keeping an eye on them, looking for a way to use them to get out, I expect," said Ray-Leigh.

"That's not what I see in her mind," said Viola. "She is only a child, who wants to be around her friends one last time."

"Let's discuss our plan of action," said Mike, in a voice that was too grown-up for an eleven-year-old.

"Yes, let's," said Ev, trying to match his tone.

After some time, Ev joined the Withouters in their treehouse prison.

"What's going on?" demanded Peter.

Ev put up her hand for silence.

"I've made a deal with Mike," she said. "He's going to help us free Inner."

"Yes!" said Stacey.

"But what about the Alerrawian attack?" asked Gavin, frowning.

"Mike has made a deal with them too. . .," said Ev.

"That doesn't sound ominous at all," said Madison, sarcastically.

"They're not going to send any of us back, are they?" demanded Derek. "They'll send is to the bad place. . ."

"No. Not any of the six of us."

"Then what?"

"They counter-offered," said Ev to her friends, knowing that she was procrastinating.

"What's the counter-offer? Tell us already!"

"The thing is that no one can find the True User camp unless they already know where it is. That's why we were blindfolded. But the Alerrawians found it anyway, which means we have a traitor in our midst. . ."

"A traitor?" said Stacey confused. "One of us? I don't understand. . ."

"But we *were* all blindfolded," said Peter. "*I* didn't see anything, anyway. . ."

"Six of us were blindfolded," said Ev.

"Ev, what are you saying?" wailed Stacey.

"Now!" said a voice, and the next moment Viola and Ray-Leigh appeared. They were both pointing in the same direction. The air became heavy, and you could almost see the magic pouring from their fingertips.

Siobhan appeared, fading in and out of view as she tried to fight the magic, but in the end, she gave up and fell to the floor, sobbing.

"No use trying again," said Viola, gently. "We're blocking your magic now that we can see you. Don't tire yourself out."

"Siobhan?" said Madison. "But. . .where have you been?"

"She's been right here, with us, except that she *wasn't* blindfolded, and she's been sending messages back to Alerrawia since we left. That's how they found us—*she* told them."

Ev couldn't look at Siobhan. She was too angry and too sad.

"The counter-offer is that we return Siobhan, but the rest of us stay. That should give us enough time to mount a defense."

"No," whispered Siobhan. "Please don't send me back there! Not like this. . ."

"I'm sorry," said Ev, her back to Siobhan. "This is how it has to be."

"I tried to stick together, Ev. I really did. He *made* me. . .I. . .I. . ." Siobhan's face went blank as she tried to force out the words.

"What are you trying to say, Siobhan?" asked Peter.

"She looks like she'd trying to talk about the bad place. . .," said Derek.

"You're right! Something is keeping her from talking!"

"It doesn't matter," said Ev. "We're sending her back."

"He's going to be so angry with me," whispered Siobhan.

"Yes. He is. I'll see what I can do about that, I promise. Right now, it is what it is."

Viola and Ray-Leigh led Siobhan away. They would deliver her to the Alerrawian forces, and in return, the attack would end.

For now.

Jim arrived to free the pixies from the cage and to tell them that Claster was also free but choosing to remain on the outskirts. Then he left too, and the Withouters were alone again.

"I don't get it," said Madison. "Why would Siobhan help *them*?"

"Because she's Felix's granddaughter," said Ev. "They said so, in the scroll they sent. Didn't you think that it was weird that I was put in a room with you three? You're all so much older! It's because Siobhan was under orders to make friends with me. Apparently, she does that a lot."

"I did wonder why she was always being moved from room to room," said Madison, thoughtfully. "I mean, I didn't wonder *a lot*, because who really cares, but I *did* notice it."

"They hid that Felix is her grandfather so that she can keep tabs on the troublemakers. I was a troublemaker before I even got here, apparently. Too antagonistic toward Vendavi. So, they put me in with Siobhan."

"How do you know this?"

"The scroll they sent. Also, Viola, who's apparently some kind of super wizard, could find Siobhan *even while she was faded*, and was reading her mind since the first moment they knew she was here."

"What did the scroll say?"

"You're not going to like it, Stacey. You neither, Madison. Are you sure you want to see?"

"Yes!"

Reluctantly, Ev handed Stacey a copy.

To whom it may concern,

You have in your midst seven children who belong to Alerrawia, one of whom is the granddaughter of Felix Granite, leader of The Seven. If the children are returned to us, we will pause hostilities. Siobhan Kenwood, in particular, must not be harmed. Miss Kenwood is to be treated as an enemy officer. Any harm that comes to her will be treated as a deliberate act on your part to escalate the situation. It's a win-win situation, as I am certain you are desperate to rid yourselves of these troublesome children.

Please inform Madison Davis and Stacey Daniels that their parents have been taken into custody, for the good of Alerrawia, but will of course be released should the girls show the proper degree of remorse.

I await your response,

Marcia Breswick

P.S. Magic is a disease that should be eradicated. If you love your children, you will feed them Hexteria. It can't hurt to keep you safe from you!

"Stacey, Madison, I'd understand completely if. . ."

"Oh, I'm not going back for that," said Madison. "I mean, I don't want anything to happen to my mom, but this is just more big people pushing around little people stuff. She'll be fine. I feel sorry for her guards, though."

"Stacey?" she asked, tentatively.

"I don't think I can really do anything by going back. Do you know what I mean? They make it sound like my life will go back to normal, and so will theirs, if I do, but I don't think that can ever happen ever again."

She looked unbearably sad.

"I'm sorry, Stacey."

"Me too."

"What business does that Breswick woman have sending military missives?" asked Dropellet.

"I guess we've upset things. Maybe The Seven are taking charge of *everything*?"

They sat together in miserable silence.

"I just can't believe that Siobhan betrayed us like that. Was she working against us the whole time?"

"I don't know. . .," said Ev. "I really don't. She really seemed to be on our side, sometimes. Maybe she didn't have a choice. Remember when she froze, like she was trying to talk about *detention*? Maybe there's magic at work that we don't know about."

"Should we have sent her back?" asked Peter.

"I don't know. The True Users didn't really give me a choice."

"I'm sure you could have done something to keep her with us if you *really* wanted to," said Derek.

Ev shot him a look that said, 'Keep your theories to yourself,' but she knew he was right. She could have made the True Users do anything she wanted.

She told herself that she was still learning how to use her third ability safely, that she didn't know the right words to protect Siobhan without making something else worse, but she knew it was a lie.

The truth was that she was angry, angrier than she'd ever been. Her skull had been tingling since the moment Viola had released her from Siobhan's fading magic and allowed her to see the truth.

But if she wanted to be *really* honest with herself, she was feeling something else too. It was guilt. Guilt that she hadn't seen Siobhan for what she was, maybe, but also guilt that she'd sent the girl, who had even less choice than Ev did, back to an unimaginable fate.

Who was she angry with, anyway? Siobhan? Felix? Herself? *Everyone*?

"That must be where she went!" said Stacey suddenly. "When we were setting the alarms off—she must have gone to fetch a two-way radio or something so she could call them here."

"Yeah. Now that we know, it's obvious, isn't it?" said Ev. "When I was sent into Jonah's detention to interrogate him, she was waiting for me. Outside Felix's office. On the *thirteenth floor*. Why would she have been there? You can't just wander in, unless you have a good reason, and yet there she was, and I didn't even *question* it!"

"I always wondered why she was called 'Kenwood'," said Derek. "There aren't any other Kenwoods around. Names tend to repeat themselves around here. They must have given her that name ages ago because no one would talk to a Granite."

"But she's super good at magic," said Peter. "How can she be a Granite?"

"Even more reason for them to give her a different name—they hate magic," said Madison, choosing to forget that *she'd* hated magic until very recently herself.

"They don't hate it," said Lulerain. "If they really hated it, they wouldn't use it so much. They're scared of it, that's all."

"Well, I'm sure you've all heard that magic is, in fact, a disease that needs to be eradicated," said Madison. "Just joking!" she said as everyone turned to glare at her. "I, for one, *love* the instant meals prepared by the pixies.

Imagine if I had to waste all that time making food myself?" She pulled a face.

"Madison," said Ev with a sigh, "I know you're trying, but you're going to have to try harder. A lot harder."

Madison jumped out of her chair and grabbed Ev by her shoulders, eyes blazing.

"Do you really think that I don't know that the pixies are slaves, and that it sucks? Do you think I don't know that there's nothing wrong with magic? Do you think I don't wish that I had some fantastic innate ability? It's called camouflage, Ev. You have to blend in to be safe, and I've been doing it my whole entire life, and I can't just stop being fabulously sarcastic the moment you ask me to! Got it?"

"Yes, um, thanks for clarifying…"

"You're very welcome," said Madison, letting go of Ev and flopping back into her chair. "Now, correct me if I'm wrong, but we have some work to do, don't we? There are some people back at Alerrawia we want to help. I've heard the names 'Jonah' and 'Amy' floating around, plus there's the matter of my fabulously terrible mother. And, if we're serious about saving Siobhan, *again*, we should probably get moving for her sake too."

"You're right, Madison," said Ev. "The only way is up."

"What?"

"It's just something Jonah said to me the day I left Inner," said Ev.

"What do we do?"

"We've got to help the True Users defend themselves against Alerrawia, or else there will be no one left to help us."

"We're just kids!"

"Yeah, but we know how to mix science and magic. We know how to invent new spells. The True Users haven't tried anything new in centuries. We *can* help, and we must.

"Let's get on with it, shall we?"

21. You're Both Spectacularly Wrong in Uniquely Awful Ways

The six principles of scientific thinking are as follows:

1. Rule out rival hypotheses.
2. Remember that correlation does not equal causation.
3. Make claims that can be proven wrong.
4. Make claims that can be tested again or replicated.
5. Remember that extraordinary claims require extraordinary evidence.
6. Look for simple solutions, as they are more likely to be correct than complex ones.

Grown-ups find it harder than children to learn because their brains are already used to certain ways of thinking, but they *can* learn new things.

At least, Ev hoped they could.

It didn't help that most of the True Users refused to even think about scientific enhancements for their magical abilities. Viola and Taylor were among the few True Users who were willing to try anything new. Maybe, like Ev, they felt out of place in the forest. Viola lived in Inner until she was an adult, and Taylor. . .well, they were a giant, the *only* giant who lived with the True Users. They said that there were more giants in the bubble, but they lived on the outskirts, keeping to themselves, and the Alerrawians probably didn't even know they were there. Taylor lived with the True Users because the giants hadn't wanted them either, although Ev didn't understand why. Taylor was a wonderful person, and a great friend to anyone who gave them a chance.

"Their loss," said Ev with shrug when Taylor told her about the other giants. "They seem like weird people anyway—I'm glad you're here."

For some reason, tears came to Taylor's eyes, and they said, "Thank you, Ev. That means a lot," as they gently patted her on the head.

Viola and Taylor seemed happy enough to play along with the True Users' way of life, but they were both more than happy to speak up if they disagreed with something. For example, there seemed to be an unspoken rule that giants shouldn't be allowed to use magic, but Taylor and Viola both ignored this, and no one seemed to quite have the courage to argue with them.

It could be quite funny watching the two of them casually blast their way through all of the defenses their peers threw in their way. Funny, in an extremely terminal sort of way.

Ev decided that the easiest way to teach science to magical purists was to pretend that it wasn't science at all.

"It's just a slightly different way of thinking," she said to Jim. "Magic users *are* allowed to think, aren't they?"

"To find the right solution, you have to be all right with being wrong the first hundred times," she told a frustrated Ray-Leigh who'd been set the task of finding a new use for a basic search spell which was usually used to find things like lost pets and kitchen utensils.

"Try to think of another test," she said to Ewan, who was learning more quickly than she could teach. "There's no way to test if this idea is false; ideas always have to be falsifiable so that you know whether or not you're wasting your time. If you want to be sure that something is right, you have to put everything you have into proving it wrong."

"Don't be discouraged!" she told Reuben. "You've just learned another way not to do it. That's progress."

For the first time in her life, Ev was *glad* that the Alerrawians had pushed her to learn, learn, learn, even if they didn't leave her much time to actually think. They had

taught her a lot, and she was finally using some of it for
something useful.

Taylor and Viola weren't afraid of getting things
wrong. Ev mainly left them to figure things out on their
own—they learned more quickly that way. Which wasn't to
say that they wouldn't ask the Withouters for help if they
needed it; they were very good at *that* too.

Right now, they were huddling with Stacey, their
new favorite person. Stacey could tell them all about the
technology they'd lost out on over the years.

Stacey was teaching them how to build bombs.

You need a lot of different things to build a bomb,
most of which can't be found in a forest.

However, that wasn't really a problem for someone
who was *really* good at magic.

All Stacey had to do was think about something,
like dynamite, and Viola would sieve the knowledge
straight from her mind and use it to turn something
harmless, like a rock, into the material they needed.

Today they were hovering their bombs as high as
they could and letting them explode.

"Must they taint their magic like that?" muttered
Jim as yet another explosion rocked the clearing.

As usual, Ev ignored him, but it was getting harder.
He was so full of opinions, and so resistant to ideas from
other people, that it was almost impossible to have a
conversation with him. Ev wasn't surprised at all that Mike
preferred Reuben's company.

"Why not try combining that shield with a fire charm?" she asked a sharp-featured sixteen-year-old girl. The girl nodded, refocused her energy, and instantly produced a shield of flame.

"Huh. Neat," said Ev to herself.

The children were the easiest to teach because they hadn't spent as much time believing that things couldn't be done, like their parents. They just did what they were told. They didn't know they were trying something that no one had done before, so they just did it.

The grown-ups were having a harder time than the children because they still believed, despite what they were seeing, that no one could invent new magic.

"And this is why Alerrawia has gotten so much further. . ." said Ev to herself.

"Exactly what might you be insinuating with that statement?" She hadn't realized that Mike, who made a point of attending all training sessions, was within earshot.

She sighed. She already knew how this conversation was going to go, because they'd had it a dozen times before.

"The Alerrawians hate magic," she began, wearily, "but they also know that it is useful and choose to combine it with what they value most for better results. The True Users, on the other hand, hate science, and refuse to even consider it!"

"And in your limited view, this makes our way inferior?"

"It keeps you from defending yourself properly," she said. "We've been over this before! Look at you! You're living in the woods fighting for your lives against people that outmatch you in nearly every way! You can't deny that Alerrawia's attacks are getting better and better, can you?"

Over the last few weeks, Alerrawia had attacked the True User camp over and over again, with increasing success. Ev and the rest of the Withouters were working day and night to help defend against the worst of the attacks, but it was getting harder.

Some of the True Users, like Jim, were staunchly against accepting their help. He believed that the Alerrawians wanted to bomb the hell out of Ev and her friends before they had a chance to tell the True Users anything dangerous. Ev had explained that, yes, exactly, that was what anyone with sense would do in that situation, why was he surprised, so Jim had instigated a campaign to exile the Withouters, so Ev had had to explain that that wouldn't stop the attacks because 1) Alerrawia would have no way of knowing that they were gone, now that Siobhan wasn't there anymore, and 2) Alerrawia would have to assume that the Withouters had passed on sensitive information anyway, which still meant they had to destroy the camp and everyone in it.

And 3) it was only because of what the Withouters had taught them that the True Users hadn't yet been defeated, but she didn't mention that one out loud. The aim was to make friends, not enemies.

"You *do* think their way is vastly superior to ours," said Mike.

"No, I think you're both spectacularly wrong in uniquely awful ways. Look, can we just drop it? These conversations never go anywhere because *you* can't look past the fact that we're from Alerrawia."

She turned her attention to her students, calling out suggestions and pointers. When the class ended fifteen minutes later, she saw with irritation that Mike was still there.

"I want to show you something," he said. "It's been bothering me for a while now, and I think you'll find it most illuminating. You might be the only person who can understand my concern."

Despite herself, Ev was intrigued. Getting information out of Mike was like trying to milk an alligator, so she wasn't about to miss out on an opportunity to learn more.

It was a long and silent walk that led them straight to one of the bubble's three lakes.

"Look at it."

Ev looked.

"Very pretty," she said.

"No, look closer."

Ev looked until she thought she saw what Mike wanted her to see.

"It looks like the water has receded a bit. . ."

"Somewhat more than 'a bit,' I think you'll find. The lake looks big, but in reality, it's only at forty-three percent capacity. We should be standing under water right now."

"The lake is running dry?"

"All three of them are. It's an irreversible decline."

"No clouds," said Ev, softly.

"No clouds. No one else seems to grasp the significance. I don't think. . .I don't think people in the bubble are quite sane. They all ignore the truth in front of their eyes because they believe that, because the bubble has been here their whole lives, it will *always* be here. It gets hotter and hotter each year, our sun protection spells are not working as well as they once did, and *no one* seems to care!"

Ev, while relieved that the True Users had taught her the spell to shield herself and her non-magical friends from the sun, had to agree. The spell was far from perfect, and you could still get a serious sunburn if you stayed outdoors for too long.

"It's the same in Alerrawia. I actually found something. . ." She took her old school bag off her shoulder and rummaged through it, looking for the paper Alison Oakwood had written. "Here. It's one of the documents I stole from the restricted section. You've probably read it already, or someone has, it took Jim *ages* to give all this back to me. Alison talks about how we can't go on in the bubble, and she literally says, right there in black and white, that we *are* going mad. They locked her up for saying so! Or killed her, or something. No one knows what happened, just that she disappeared."

"Why does no one care?"

"Caring is hard work. It's easier to pretend that there's no problem, especially when it looks like you and your children will probably be okay. But what about your children's children? What about all the generations that come after? Why are we the only ones that see this?"

"We had a unique upbringing, I think. We were given things to read that other children were not. It's just an accident that I ended up in Alerrawia and you ended up here. If we hadn't read those stories, maybe we wouldn't be able to see the truth either. Or if you hadn't been exiled and I hadn't been chosen, the stories would never have mattered. It's chance that now, after all these years, you and I are in a place to make an actual difference."

"There are people in Inner who know how to think like us because they were given stories to read. . ."

". . .and there are people among the True Users and in Alerrawia who could learn to think like us if we gave them the right stories now."

They stared at the sorrowfully empty lake in thoughtful silence.

"I apologize for being a negative presence in your life," said Mike suddenly.

"Oh, um, it's all right. . ."

"No, it isn't. Communicating with others is not among my strongest skills. In Inner, I was able to get away with it, but out here. . ." He sat down heavily on a boulder.

Ev decided not to tell him that he had managed to be pretty annoying in Inner as well. She felt that it would ruin this unusual moment of self-awareness.

"Hey, it's all right. Really. None of us know how to be normal."

She sat down next to him.

"I have more in common with you than I do with the other Withouters," she said. "Except maybe for Gavin. He's from Inner too."

"I didn't know that."

"Yeah, well, he was adopted by a sensible family who managed to turn him into someone who can at least pretend to be well-adjusted."

"I'm glad that to know that others have escaped Inner in the past. I have found myself reminiscing of late, primarily about my time in Inner, and there is one thought that keeps presenting itself for my attention: They're still down there. My parents. Steve. Aren't they?"

"Yes. It's almost as bad as Jonah's detention and Amy's coma. We're the only ones. . ." She broke off, crying.

Mike patted her shoulder awkwardly. "I actually brought you all this way to tell you something else as well," he said. "I'm telling you because you're the only person who understands me out here, and it feels like a betrayal of friendship to keep it from you any longer. Many here would be deeply unhappy to find out I told you, but others, like Viola, have been threatening to tell you anyway, and I'd rather you heard it from me."

"What is it, Mike?"

"I don't think *anyone* in Alerrawia knows this, with the possible exception of Felix. Everyone. . ." he stopped, unsure how to continue. "Everyone possesses, to a greater or lesser degree, the capacity for magic. *Everyone.*"

Ev stared at him blankly while the information digested.

"You mean. . .?"

"If Felix is in possession of this knowledge, which seems likely, he probably also has access to his own innate abilities. A man like that would not lose a chance to enhance his power. Hexteria. . ."

". . .not only restricts magic-use, but it can also negate it altogether, in some people."

"Precisely!"

"Why would Hexteria affect people differently?"

"The True Users believe that it has something to do with personality."

"Like, only the pure of heart will be strong, kind of thing?" said Ev, skeptically.

"No, it seems to be more closely correlated with rebellious, fractious natures. Difficult or stubborn people are inherently less willing to be controlled, and their magic acts accordingly."

"Madison is one of the most difficult people I know, and she's never shown any magical ability! *I'm* difficult, and Hexteria blocks me. . ."

. . .except for my third skill. . .

". . .and Amy doesn't seem stubborn at all, but Hexteria doesn't stop her!"

"From what *I* remember of Amy, she could be very stubborn. If Amy said she wouldn't be around to chat, then she wouldn't be around to chat. You can be unobtrusive and still difficult, you know. As for you: there is *obviously* something going on with you. I don't know why you're pretending otherwise, but I'm choosing to respect your decision. As for Madison—yes, she is a tough one. It's possible she has one of the less obvious innate abilities and has been using it unknowingly her whole life. You see," he continued, "magic is the one true way. Perhaps if Madison spent less time watering down her abilities with man-made science. . ."

"Oh, not this again! Can't you see? You're so convinced that you're right that you can't do what needs to be done to make things better!"

"You are of the opinion that we are all wrong?" asked Mike.

"Yes!"

"So, if I may ask, what is the 'right' way?" asked Mike, an annoyingly condescending smile on his face.

"I don't know," said Ev, and before Mike could jump in with an "Aha!", she went on, "but not knowing is the first step in figuring out a better way. You have to admit that you don't know *before* you can start looking for the truth. You *have to* be willing to admit that you might be wrong, otherwise you could be passing on lies without even knowing it!"

"This is what they teach at Alerrawia? That ignorance is commendable?"

"Yes, in a way. If you think you already know the answer to a problem before you even look at it closely, you might miss a chance to solve it better."

They were still arguing, but they were arguing as friends, not enemies, and it was the best conversation they'd ever had.

"Viola and Taylor understand. So does Reuben, I think, and a lot of the others. They're ready to try something new."

"Many aren't."

"I know. We have to work with what we've got. Alerrawia is going to keep attacking. They're not going to stop."

"I know," said Mike.

"We need more people on our side if we're going to beat them. And we *have to* beat them. For the True Users to survive, for the Inners to survive, Alerrawia has to be stopped forever."

"And, to acquire these additional troops. . ." began Mike.

". . .we have to free the people of Inner," finished Ev.

And we have to do it now.

Ev had held off on warping reality for weeks. She was terrified of what would happen if she forced the True Users to help her. But sometimes, like now, it felt *right.*

Sometimes, the magic chose for her.

"Yes," said Mike, nodding decisively. "Yes, we have to get on with it, don't we?"

"We do, before Alerrawia destroys us *or* Inner."

"Or both. That Chronoburster you told us about is a nasty sounding device. Any idea on when they plan to use it?"

"No. If I knew *why* they wanted to destroy Inner. . ."

"Oh, that's simple. The magic users from Inner are the strongest, by far. You know that Viola was exiled for trying to escape? Apparently, she's not the only one who has tried. Their magic is getting stronger *and* they're learning how to think. Felix is getting paranoid."

"How would *you* know that? I mean, yes, the man is a complete lunatic, but you've never had the displeasure of meeting him."

"I have my spies," said Mike haughtily.

"You have spies in Alerrawia? How? *Who?*"

"I'm going to keep that to myself, for now. For their safety, you understand. What I will tell you is that this isn't the first time I've heard the name 'Oakwood.'" He waved Alison's paper at Ev. "There's an older woman with that name. . ."

"Granny!"

"What?"

"Never mind, go on."

"Well, whoever she is, she's tried a few times to make contact with us, offering help, but we decided it was too risky."

"I'm pretty sure you can trust her. Gavin is her grandson, and you trust *him*, don't you?"

"Noted. I will consider her request more closely, should she reach out in the future."

Ev thought of the mirror in her bag.

"If you ever want to reach out to her yourself, let me know. I might have a way."

"Good to know. Now, before we try to convince our people to stage a daring rescue, there are a few more things I would like to tell you. . ."

*

"So, you're telling me I could fly all along, but they *stopped* me?" said Madison. Ev had never seen her this angry before.

619

"Not necessarily *fly*—people have different abilities. . .," said Ev.

"Why would they do that?" asked Stacey.

"They are scared," boomed Claster, far above them. They were gathered in one of the camp's outer rings so that Claster could join them.

"Hey, wait a minute," said Stacey. She looked up at the dragon towering above them. "Did you know about this?"

"I know many things, tiny human."

"Why didn't you tell us?"

"If I spent all of my time telling you things that I know and you don't, there would be no time left for anything else."

"Claster is right," said Lulerain. "They're scared of magic, and they'll do anything to keep it at bay. Hexteria is supposed to be a *cure*, remember? Why would people who truly had no magic need a cure in the first place?"

"Why is the world like this?" wailed Peter miserably.

"The True Users know a bit about that too. They're descended from the people who were protesting Inner when the bubble formed, and they've passed on what they know through the generations. Mike explained it all, and he said our pixies would know about it as well."

Lulerain nodded.

"Our friends here in the forest have had plenty to tell us."

"The Granite Institute scared people into thinking that magic is bad," explained Ev. "By the time Hexteria was invented, people were *begging* them for a cure. You know those posters all over Alerrawia? 'It can't hurt to keep yourself safe from you', and the rest of them? Those were just one part of the Granites' campaign against magic. They wanted it gone completely!"

"That was around the same time people broke into clear groups," said Lulerain. "There were those who thought that science was the only way forward and that magic should be crushed completely; those who thought that science was an abomination that would kill everyone; and those who thought that both were fine if used well and depending on the situation. The last group were the original Withouters, you might be interested to hear. They didn't pick a side, and they had no place in the war. The first Withouters didn't last long. When war broke out, they either picked a side or died. 'Withouters' was a strange word, back then, because *both* sides used it to mean someone who didn't agree with them. To followers of science, it meant people who used magic for any reason. To magic users, Withouters were anyone who tainted their magic with science."

"Well, that's just mad, because it meant that *anyone* was a Withouter, depending on who you asked," said Stacey.

"Indeed," said Lulerain. "It's a very fitting name you chose for us, Ev, because it's the only one that fits us all."

"But Alerrawia *does* use magic," said Peter.

"Well, at some point during the war, the Granite Institute realized that no matter how advanced their technology, there were certain people whose magic was too strong to stifle with medications or anything else," said Ev. "That's why some of the posters say things like 'Even the evilest among us can be used for the greater good.' They hired or forced magic users to join their side. It's how pixie enslavement began, I think."

"One of the reasons," said Dropellet. "There was also the little matter of our power being far greater than theirs, but that story is perhaps for another time."

"So, the Granite Institute and its followers became Withouters?" asked Madison, brow furrowed.

"No, because they still believed that magic had to be wiped out," said Derek. "Not that magic and science can work together in harmony, like the Withouters. They just use it for the absolute necessities, like winning a war, or making breakfast."

"Remember when I told you that the bubble was created on purpose?" asked Ev. "I think that goes back to what Claster said—they're scared of us, even if they think we're useful."

"I just don't get why they did *this* on purpose," said Gavin, gesturing around.

"I don't think it went the way they wanted it to. I think it was supposed to be a temporary defense, and something went wrong. The memo Siobhan and I found in the restricted section said it was a mistake, that they'd destroyed the rest of the world in the process."

"They did not," said Claster.

"How can you be so sure?"

"Because I was there. I saw. I know."

"That's wonderful," said Madison, breaking the thoughtful silence, "but can we please focus on what's really important here: helping me learn how to fly?"

"It told you, Madison," said Ev irritably, "we have to figure out what your ability *is* first. . ."

"How?"

Ev had no idea. Apart from her, three of the other Withouter children had innate abilities. Peter and Derek could fly, and Derek also had super strength. Gavin's ability was healing, which had come in handy over the last few weeks.

"How did you first figure out what your innate abilities were?" she asked the boys.

"Same as you," said Gavin. "Five years ago, in a simulation in Inner."

"What's it like if you're born in Alerrawia?" she asked Peter and Derek.

Peter shrugged. "Round about age four, you just sort of start doing stuff, and your parents are all like, 'Aha! He can hypnotize butterflies!' or whatever, and life just kind of continues from there. I just sort of woke one morning closer to the ceiling than my bed. My parents were dead by then, and my uncle yelled at me to stop, but it's not like I could do anything about it. He had them put me on a special diet for a while, extra Hexteria, or something, but it just made me sick, so then I was floating uncontrollably *and* vomiting on him while I was up there, which I guess was pretty funny, but I don't really remember. In the end, he just decided to get me trained."

Ev was suddenly embarrassingly aware of how little she knew about Peter.

"Thanks," she muttered. "Derek?"

He shrugged. "I guess I was also around four-years-old when I dive-bombed my dad and shoved him through a wall," he said.

Everyone went quiet. With even fewer words than Peter, Derek had revealed more than they'd ever known about him.

"Thank you," said Ev. "That was. . .thank you for sharing. . ."

"He did deserve it, in case you were wondering," said Derek.

"I have no doubt at all that he did."

Derek sat back, arms crossed, looking straight ahead.

"Well, was there anything *you* seemed extra good at when you were little?" she asked Stacey and Madison, dreading the answer.

"No, apart from being generally fabulous and perfect, I can't think of anything that comes close to *their* stories," said Madison. "Although I'm *sure* that's just a sign that I'm extra good at everything."

"Stacey?" asked Ev through gritted teeth.

"Well, there was that Sunday when I was five that I built that radio from spare parts I stole from my parents that was so strong it messed with every radio in the bubble. I was transmitting across all frequencies simultaneously, or something, and no one could understand why they kept hearing kids playing all day. It was just because I'm good at electronics, but they questioned and tested me for ages anyway, just in case."

"Technopathy," said Lulerain. "It's hard to diagnose, because it looks like you're just good with machines, but that definitely sounds like technopathy to me."

"Or I'm just a really gifted engineer, who works hard. . ."

"No one is denying that you're excellent at what you do, but you almost definitely have technopathy," said Lulerain. "It just means that you can also understand technology and machines at a magical level. You've probably found that you can do things that other people in your classes think are impossible, correct?"

Stacey nodded, sullenly.

"Well, that means you're a gifted engineer *and* a technopath. Most technopaths go through life accidentally destroying any machine they touch because they have no idea what they're doing, but you've put your ability to good use."

This seemed to make Stacey feel a little better.

"What about me?" Madison wailed.

"Come with me, I'll try to help you figure it out," said Lulerain. "I might not be able to, mind. Some innate abilities are *very* difficult to identify, but I'll do my best."

A gong sounded in the distance.

"That would be for me," said Ev. "I have to help Mike persuade the True Users to help us. Be glad you're not invited—this is *not* going to be fun."

*

"Why are we even considering this mad plan?" asked Jim.

"Because our Leader has decreed it," said Taylor, calmly. "I, for one, am in full agreement."

And that exchange pretty much summed up the entire discussion so far. Ev sat in the middle of a ring of True Users, her head in her hands, listening to them start the fight all over again.

In an expertly cast privacy bubble at the foot of Big Red were Ev, Mike, Ray-Leigh, Viola, Jim, Reuben, and Taylor. As far as Jim was concerned, the Inners were as guilty as the Alerrawians for choosing science over magic. It didn't matter to him that no one in Inner had any choice. Ray-Leigh agreed with him.

The others were on Ev's side.

The only problem was that Jim and Ray-Leigh represented the views of most of the True Users, and they knew it. They even had a petition signed by well over half the camp stating that they wanted the Withouters gone.

"We're all people," said Ev, hopelessly from her seat on the ground. "No matter what side you're on, surely you can't just stand by and watch them die?"

"The Inners are like infants," said Mike. "Right now, they're in a dark womb, waiting to be born. The womb is their whole world. It's all they know. But babies don't stay babies forever. From the moment they are born, they learn. They can learn to exist in this world, with us, if we help them."

"We'll be freeing them to join our enemies!" said Ray-Leigh. "They will always be on the side of science. It's why they locked themselves away in the first place!"

"I've told you, Ray-Leigh," said Ev, looking up. "You have to consider *all* the facts when making a bold declaration like that. *I'm* from Inner. I didn't know about magic before I was collected by Alerrawia. Inner and Alerrawia put *everything* into it, and they still couldn't convince me that science was the only right way. Despite what you think, Inners are *not* indoctrinated against magic. They can't indoctrinate you against something that you don't know exists."

"And what about me?" asked Mike. "I became your leader within months, of leaving Inner. I didn't fight you or try to introduce science. I despise science as much as you do!"

"You are children," said Ray-Leigh. "You had no strong opinions about anything. The adults in Inner. . ."

"I am an adult from Inner," said Viola. "I would be very careful about how you choose to continue that sentence, Ray-Leigh."

"I will not get involved in this," said Jim. "Call it treason, but I *cannot* back this plan. . ."

"I understand your position, and that's why I am stepping down as Leader," said Mike.

"What?" Ev said.

"I've been thinking about it for some time. The entire camp is split in two, and it started long before the Withouters arrived. It was a mistake to elect a child in the first place, and I insist that you replace me."

"I. . .there is no process for this. . ."

"Then make one," snapped Mike. "Viola, I want to talk to everyone."

The privacy bubble dissolved around them to reveal the faces of every True User and Withouter in the camp.

"Jim Day has accepted my resignation as Leader," Mike announced to the shocked crowd.

"Yes, well, it seemed prudent," stumbled Jim, "and we will of course begin the search for a new Leader right away. . ."

"Fantastic," said Mike, "and I will begin my campaign to free the people of Inner. Any and all assistance is welcome."

And then he walked off, the stunned crowd parting to let him through. Ev, not knowing what else to do, followed him.

The other Withouters caught up with them quickly.

"Did that go well?" asked Derek.

"I'm not sure. . .," said Ev.

"It went about as well as could be expected," said Mike. "I can't make everyone help us, so I had to find a way for everyone to get what they wanted. As long as I was a political threat, people were going to oppose me. But no one can stop a regular True User from doing whatever they want—it's not our way."

He stopped when he reached Claster's clearing and turned.

So did Ev.

That was when she realized that they'd been followed.

"True Users *really* know how to move quietly," she said weakly as about a third of the True Users gathered around them.

Among the faces were many she recognized. She was surprised to see Ray-Leigh, less surprised to see Taylor. Reuben was there, as was Viola, with Ewan at her side, but Iris was conspicuously absent. Many of the people Ev had trained were in the crowd, although she was sorry to see that it was far from all of them.

"Well, it was unlikely to ever be unanimous," said Mike with satisfaction, "but this isn't bad."

He turned to Ev. "What do we do now?"

22. She Has Her Own Ideas

The griffin, part lion, part eagle, ruled over all the creatures that lived on land or flew among the clouds. One day, a new animal appeared.

"I want to rule myself," it said.

"You cannot," said the griffin. "You walk on the land and fly in the air; I am your ruler."

"You rule everything that walks on the land and flies in the air?" asked the new animal. "You must be very powerful."

The griffin shook his feathers proudly. "I am, indeed!"

The new animal had a devilish streak.

"Oh, what it must be like to rule everything that walks and flies and swims," it said.

"Everything that walks and flies," said the griffin.

"But not swims?" asked the animal.

"I have no dominion over the seas and lakes and rivers," conceded the griffin.

So, the new animal jumped into the water and taught itself to swim.

"I command you to get out!" shouted the griffin.

"You cannot command me!" said the animal. "I am of land and air and water. I am better than you."

"What do you call yourself?" demanded the griffin.

"I am a man."

That is why to this day there are two ruling species living side-by-side; the griffin to rule the creatures of land and air, and the human to rule itself.

The Story of the Griffin

True User Campfire Story

"…so, if you agree with *this* version of the plan, raise your hands," said Ev.

One hand, two hands, three hands. . .

"We seem to have a majority, Evelyn," said Lulerain, breaking Ev's concentration.

"Good," said Ev with a relieved sigh. It hadn't been easy, finding a plan that even half the Withouters would agree to, but they'd finally managed it. "Well, you all know what to do to. Those of you who aren't needed right away should rest."

"Might I have a word, Evelyn?" asked Claster, his voice shaking the nearby trees.

The Withouters, a now much larger group than ever before, were gathered in a clearing a little way from the True Users camp. Viola had cast a lighter version of the enchantment that had once protected the True Users from Alerrawia.

"Um, in private? Because, no offense, but I don't know where we can go that's safe *and* where no one can hear you. You have quite a loud voice."

"It matters not to *me* who hears us speak. I merely wished to indicate that there is very little help I can offer. Dragons cannot squeeze through human-sized tunnels, and those of you who need to fly, can."

"There could be fighting! We might need you in a fight!"

"Alerrawia has known how to 'handle' me for centuries. They will have no difficulty turning me against you in combat. I cannot risk it."

"What are you going to do? Leave?"

"It is probably safer if I do, but I do think that there may remain one way in which I could be useful to you."

"What way is that?"

"The bubble can be escaped. The world outside was *not* destroyed, although I have no idea what state it is in now. I know how to undo the magic, but there is something else that I must do first.

"I must go north, and I must speak to the giants."

Taylor, who like everyone else had been listening to every word, gasped.

"You can't. . ."

"I must. You know that."

"But they won't listen!"

"Not to me, but perhaps if you. . ."

"They will *never* listen to me!"

Ev watched the exchange taking place above her, mouth open.

"What are you talking about?" demanded Ray-Leigh. "Taylor, is there something you know that you haven't told us?"

"It wouldn't have made a difference to anything," said Taylor. "Or else I would have told you as soon as I first arrived!"

"We can end it where it began," said Claster, looking only at Taylor. "We know how, which means we *must*!"

Taylor's shoulders sagged and they nodded miserably. "You are right, of course. I will join you."

"Hold on," said Ev. "You can't *both* just leave!"

"I am sorry, Ev," said Taylor. "We have to."

"What are you even going to do?"

"Claster is right—it's not something you should be worrying about right now. You can manage without us; I know you can. This is something that only we can do."

"But I thought the other giants hated you. . ."

"They do. But I've been gone a while. Maybe things have changed." They smiled sadly, and Ev hoped they were right.

"Oh, let them go," said Madison. "They wouldn't make much of a difference if they stayed, and what they're talking about sounds *super* intriguing and important, so just say goodbye already."

"You're always *so* sure that you're right and everybody else is wrong!" said Stacey. "You have *no idea* when to shut up, do you?"

"I *always* say and do exactly the right thing at exactly the right time," said Madison, nose in the air.

"Goodbye, Ev," said Taylor. With one bound, they leapt onto Claster's back, and the next moment they were both just a dot on the horizon, heading north.

"They'll be caught," said Gavin.

"Maybe not," said Viola. "There's nothing north, just wilderness until you hit the bubble. The Alerrawians haven't ventured out that far in decades."

Ev's hands were clenched in frustration.

"We don't need them though," said Madison, firmly. "Trust me on this. We'll do just fine without them."

"Madison is right," said Lulerain. "Our plan doesn't need to change at all. We've come this far, and we *will* succeed."

She was talking to Ev, but it was the gathered Withouters who seemed to find comfort in her words.

"Yes," said Ev. "Of course, we will succeed. This changes nothing." She smiled, hiding the crushing disappointment she felt. The Withouters visibly relaxed, and some even smiled back. "Now, like I said, you should either be preparing or resting—I don't want to see anyone doing *anything* else."

The group dissolved.

"On the topic of preparing, I think you and I should have a chat with Stacey," said Lulerain, quietly.

Ev, Stacey and Lulerain huddled inside a small privacy bubble conjured by Ev. It was the first one she'd ever made, and she wasn't sure that it would hold for very long, but they weren't going to be discussing anything too secret, and anyway, she needed to practice.

"I was wondering if you fully understood the full ramifications of everything you discovered in the restricted section," said Lulerain to Ev. "I think there's one thing you missed, another one of their lies."

"Which lie, specifically, are you referring to this time?"

"I think they're lying about how vulnerable Vendavi is. I don't think we should assume that Inner will self-destruct if we try to get in. I think it's just another one of those things Alerrawia tells us to keep us in line."

"But shouldn't we play it safe?" asked Stacey.

"Maybe we don't have to," said Ev slowly. "We already know that Alerrawia hacks into Vendavi all the time to steal kids, and *that* doesn't cause a self-destruct."

"Indeed," said Lulerain. "I've suspected this for some time, actually. Think back to the day you arrived in Alerrawia, Ev."

"I crawled through the tunnel, all alone, and then Jonah came to get me. . ."

"*Yes*! Jonah came to *get you*!"

Ev's eyes widened.

"I'm such an idiot!"

"No, you're not, at least not more so that anyone else in Alerrawia. If they can *send a child* down the tunnel to fetch another child, then obviously the system is not as vulnerable as they want us to think it is."

"I see," said Stacey. "So, what you're saying is, I might be able to be a little more aggressive with my hacks, when the time comes?"

"I think so," said Ev. "This might also explain the words on the back of the door a bit more. . ."

"What words?"

"The door I came through when I first arrived in Alerrawia has words written on it. Lots of them. Only stupid Inner kids see them, so no one thought it mattered much, but *Amy* knew what they meant, she just didn't know how to tell me!"

"What are the words, Ev?" asked Lulerain.

"There's an old sign with the usual nonsense about how magic is bad and how we should all be thankful that the Granites are trying to do something about it, and all that, but there was a much newer sign as well. . ." She dug through her papers, looking for the note Amy had written for her a lifetime ago. "Here it is."

Entry to and from Inner and Alerrawia is restricted to approved observers and the Granite family.

Trespassers will be punished to the fullest extent of the law.

Alerting the denizens of Inner to your existence will result in death.

"This sign is *much* newer. Why would they have to warn people not to let the people of Inner know you're there if it were impossible to visit? I think people *can* crawl around those tunnels without Vendavi noticing. I don't think Vendavi ever went into a complete lockdown, like we were told."

"Pity *we* can't use the door from Alerrawia," said Stacey. "We'd get caught instantly."

"Yes, but I still think this bodes well for our plan in general," said Lulerain. "We can worry a little less about Inner self-destructing and a little more about getting as many people out as possible."

"So, we're still using the exile door?" asked Stacey.

"Yes. Can you do it?"

"With the right equipment…"

"Can't Viola create what you need from your brain?"

"She's tried! Dozens of times! It's too complicated for her to understand. . ."

"Never mind," said Ev. "Our plan accounts for that, we'll get you what you need."

The Withouters had long since realized that their only way into Inner was through the exile hatch.

The problem was that the hatch couldn't just be opened with magic. It couldn't be opened from the outside at all, and even if you managed to open it, it would eventually close again, no matter what.

It had to open from the inside, which meant that Vendavi needed to exile someone. Once it was open, Stacey could keep it open, just not for very long.

Unfortunately, exiles were rare. Mike was the first exile in years, and Alerrawia might try to destroy Inner again at any minute.

So, somebody had to override the system and convince Vendavi to exile someone.

Stacey could do it. Easily. She could probably do it in her sleep.

The problem was that she didn't have the technology she needed.

Which meant that they had to go back to Alerrawia to get it.

"I should have just stolen it on my way out!" wailed Stacey. "Why wasn't I thinking?"

"Because you're not a natural thief, and so it didn't occur to you," said Lulerain, soothingly. "You were under a lot of pressure, worried about being caught, hiding when Siobhan left you. . .It is what it is."

"We have a plan, Stacey, don't worry. We'll get what you need."

Ev let her privacy bubble dissolve and was surprised to see Vasagle waiting for her.

"How did you find us?" she asked. No one should have been able to find the Withouters, not with the magical barrier they'd erected.

"I invited her," said Lulerain.

"You are returning to Alerrawia," announced the griffin.

"Lulerain, you can't just tell anyone you feel like where we are. . ."

"We owe Vasagle a place at the table for the role she played in our escape," said Lulerain. "*I* owe her. She is aware of everything we intend to do."

"I will assist in this endeavor on one condition," said Vasagle.

"I'm not sure we *need* your assistance. . ." said Ev through gritted teeth.

"We will free the remaining griffin slaves in Alerrawia on our return. This will be the primary objective of the mission."

"No, it won't," said Ev. "We *will* free the griffins, and everyone else in Alerrawia, but there are things that must happen first!"

Vasagle ruffled her feathers and stomped her feet, angrily.

"I have decreed otherwise!"

"You have no right to decree anything when it comes to humans!"

"I have all the right!"

"You will *not* join us!"

Ev had to shout, because Vasagle was screaming wordlessly, her wings spread wide. It was one of the most painful things Ev had ever heard.

Vasagle flapped her wings, and a blast of griffin exploded outwards, knocking everyone to the ground.

By the time Ev had scrambled to her feet, Vasagle was gone.

"Where did she go?" she demanded.

"She flew, we'll never catch her!" said Mike.

"And what, pray, would we even *do* if we did catch her?" asked Ray-Leigh. "Griffins have their own laws—*we* can't control her."

"She attacked Ev!"

"She attacked all of us," said Ev, weakly. "She's hurting. She's sad. She lives in a world that doesn't do what she tells it to, not anymore. Just let her go. I will speak to her after we get back from Inner."

"She might do something stupid," said Madison. "Add to the general chaos of everything that's about to happen."

"I don't think she will," said Ev. "We can't command the griffins, but she knows that she can't command us either. It's a two-way deal. She won't interfere."

"She will, but no need to listen to me!" said Madison. "I'm happy with extra chaos, anyway. I'm told it suits my temperament."

"Madison. . ."

"I know, I know, I'm shutting up now, boss kid."

"That being said," said Ev, "I see no reason why we should wait any longer. Prepare to move out."

Throughout the clearing, Withouters sprang to their feet, ready to do whatever Ev wanted.

"Do you find it weird that everyone listens to you?" asked Derek, quietly.

"Yup," said Ev. "I'll never get used to it."

"You could just warp reality so that it isn't weird anymore."

Ev's heart stopped.

"How do you know?"

"I didn't know, I was just guessing, but it looks like I got it in one."

"I don't use it, it's for emergencies only, except for when I used it accidentally, before I knew what I was doing, but I can fix that, I'm working on it, and. . ."

"Relax. I'm not going to tell anyone, for now at least. It's pretty obvious that you're not using it much, otherwise you wouldn't get stuck in the middle of so many arguments. But it's not right that you keep that from us. You have to tell the others, the moment we get through this mad plan. *If* we get through this mad plan."

"Thanks, Derek. . ."

"Don't thank me until we're sure I'm doing the right thing."

"Does anyone else suspect?"

"No idea, but probably not. The whole 'you can't have more than two abilities and still be a powerful magician' thing is obviously another lie, but it's one that most of them still believe. I, personally, don't believe anything anymore. I save a lot of time that way."

Ev watched Derek as he went to show Gavin the correct way to pack a backpack.

"What are you thinking about, Ev?" asked Lulerain, popping into existence next to her ear.

"I'm thinking that Derek is a completely different person to who he pretends to be."

"Nearly everyone is. We're ready to go, just waiting for your word."

They set off for Alerrawia, the pixies carefully keeping them shielded as they moved, which was not an easy task. Cloaking a huge group of people when they were standing still was one thing, keeping it up while they were on the move was another. Lulerain, Boaclick, Dropellet, and the True User pixies had their work cut out for them, and they had to move slowly to prevent detection.

When they were just out of sight of Alerrawia, but still hidden among the trees, they split into two groups. Mike, Dropellet, and the True Users-turned-Withouters in one, Ev, Boaclick, Lulerain, and the rest of the original Withouters in the other.

The pixies were used to communicating with each other both telepathically and holographically, so it was essential that they were in different groups.

They'd decided that only people who knew how Alerrawia worked would be in Ev's group, but Ev had been thinking a lot about the scryers lately.

"Viola, I think it would be helpful if Ewan joined my team."

"What do you need him for?"

"Just surveillance. He's a great scryer, and we won't let him get anywhere close, I promise" said Ev, and, because the yellow in her heart demanded it, she thought: *Don't you think Ewan is more than capable of looking after himself?*

"Please, mom!" said Ewan.

"I will personally take responsibility for his well-being," said Lulerain. "I will not leave his side."

"All right," said Viola, "but you do what this pixie says, not the other children."

Ewan's head nearly fell off he nodded it so hard.

"And don't tell your mother," said Viola. "I'm in as much trouble as it is for bringing you in the first place."

"I won't tell mother, mom! I promise!"

"All right, fine," said Viola. She turned to Ev. "If I have any reason to regret this decision, any reason at all, you will wish you'd never been born."

"Yes, Ma'am," said Ev.

That was how it came to be that seven children and two pixies found themselves tiptoeing cautiously toward the one place they didn't want to be.

Ewan had a piece of magically created glass that he used for scrying. Ev explained how Alerrawia used scrying for surveillance by looking only a few seconds into the future. Moments later, Ewan he had a perfect picture of Alerrawia's perimeter.

"I can't see inside," he said. "There are wards, but we can keep an eye on the gates, at least."

What they could see was this: the main gate and the kitchen gate both opened at regular intervals to let soldiers, hunters, gatherers, and fishermen in an out. Each of the two gates had guards with weapons and identity scanners.

They would never get past the scanners, even if the guards didn't recognize them on sight.

"Are you sure we'll be able to get in?" whispered Peter.

"Oh, only Boaclick needs to get in," said Madison, much too loudly. "He'll sneak in in Siobhan's bag, of course."

"I shall do nothing of the sort!" said Boaclick, hand clasped dramatically to his chest. "I never hide in children's bags, unless I absolutely have to, or I have a little gift to leave them. Like a dead rat."

"Ignore her, she's talking nonsense," said Ev.

Madison's brow furrowed in confusion for a moment, but then it cleared.

"I am not talking nonsense! I agree, it sounds a little strange, but I *am* right. I'm *always* right."

"How can *Siobhan* be part of this plan? You're making absolutely no sense. . ."

"Who's that?" asked Stacey, suddenly.

"Ewan, can you zoom in on that section?" asked Ev, pointing at the puddle, but Ewan just looked at her in confusion.

"I mean, make that bit bigger so we can see what's happening more clearly."

"Oh sure, that's easy," he said.

"It's Siobhan!" said Ev.

"You were saying?" said Madison, gleefully. "I am *always* right. Always."

"Always?" asked Peter nervously.

Madison's face darkened.

"Yes, always. Sorry, Peter. . ."

Ev was about to ask Madison what she meant when Stacey said, "Why does she look like that?"

It was definitely Siobhan, but she was walking strangely. She was with a group of gatherers, the people whose job it was to harvest any useful plants that grew in the wild.

"She should be in class," said Ev. "Alerrawian children are *always* in class. . ."

"And why would Felix's granddaughter be gathering, anyway?" asked Lulerain. "This doesn't make any sense."

"She's walking weird," said Peter.

"She's shackled," said Gavin. "Look at her feet!"

"What are the grown-ups doing?" asked Peter.

They watched as one of the gatherers said something that made the rest laugh, and another pushed Siobhan to the ground. It was hard to hear what was going on, but it looked like they were yelling at her to get up again.

"Why?" whispered Stacey.

"That's what you get for being a good little girl," said Madison. "Didn't you know? That's why I'm not good."

"Lulerain," said Ev, "tell Dropellet that we have a slight change in plan and to stand by for further instructions."

"I will Ev, but he's going to want to know details."

"All in good time," said Ev. She turned to Madison. "Let's hear more about this little idea of yours?"

"It's not an *idea*. It's how things are going to be. I'm very clever, you know, the cleverest person here, anyway. I always know what's going to happen next."

"She's right," said Stacey, miserably. "She makes these crazy assertions, and then they *happen*! It's awful. I'd love it she was wrong, ever, but she just isn't."

For a fraction of a moment, Ev thought that Madison was a reality warper, a truly terrifying idea, but then Lulerain said, "Oh, I understand now! You're a seer!"

"Say what now?" said Stacey.

"Madison can see the future, *without* needing a crystal ball, or puddle, or mirror. It's her innate ability."

"I just remembered that you were going to tell me that," said Madison. "Huh. Well, that does explain a lot." She bit into an apple with a crunch.

"Madison, I don't think you understand," said Stacey. "*You* can *see* the *future*! This is huge!"

"Not to me, because I've already taken a look at this conversation, and it's not that surprising. Hey, how far into the future do you think I can see?"

"Better test that another time," said Lulerain. "You don't want to tire yourself out now, not when we're so close to Alerrawia."

"Oh, it comes and goes when it wants to, anyway," said Madison. "*I* don't know what I'll see or when, otherwise I would never have ended up here. I don't think I can make it do anything."

"It comes with practice," said Lulerain. "We'll work on it another time, I promise."

"Suits me," said Madison, taking another bite.

"They're coming closer," said Ewan. "What do you want me to do?"

"Just keep tracking them, especially Siobhan," said Ev. "Madison, what do we *do*?"

"I don't think I can tell you, because it's your idea, you have to have it yourself, and if I tell you what your idea was before you've had it, the world might explode, or, worse, I might get a headache, so just get on with the idea-having, so we can get out of this gross forest."

"I was just going to explain all that," said Lulerain. "Although, not in *quite* the same words."

"I know," said Madison.

"Argh!" said Ev in frustration.

"Calm down, Ev. You'll think of something," said Lulerain.

Ev took some deep breaths, slowing her heart and clearing her mind. Her head was tingling like crazy because of her frustration, but fire wasn't going to help her now.

A tiny bit of yellow leapt in her heart.

I am going to think of a plan to get us into Alerrawia. Siobhan's bag and Boaclick may or may not be involved.

Neither listening to Madison nor relying on the trickster pixie seemed like a good idea, but if Madison could see the future. . .

With a crash, the idea landed in her mind.

"Got it," she said, opening her eyes. "Lulerain, I have a message for Dropellet. Peter, you can help me with this one."

She told them her plan.

"Insane, as always, but at least it makes more sense than rushing the main gate," said Derek.

They had planned to use a supposed True User attack as a distraction so that a cloaked pixie or child could sneak in and get what Stacey needed, but Ev had never felt good about the plan. There were too many unknowns. This new idea was far safer.

For them, anyway.

Once she was sure that everyone understood the plan, Ev, Boaclick, and Peter set off, sneaking closer and closer to Siobhan and her captors. Boaclick whispered directions, passed on to him from Ewan, who was carefully surveying the scene, via Lulerain. When they were close enough to see and hear that gatherers, they stopped, shielded by Boaclick.

"So. Hot," said one of the gatherers.

"Really? I hadn't noticed," said another, her voice heavy with sarcasm.

"No need to be like that. . ."

"Oi! You!" This was at Siobhan. "Quickly, we can't stay out here all day."

"Stupid curfews. . ."

"Well, if you *want* to burn to death. . ."

"That's dissenting talk, that is."

"So? Who's going to hear us?"

"They could just give us more Suncharm. . ."

"Not when every single brat in the bubble needs some to go play on the swings." This comment was accompanied with a sneer.

"Right! We should get top priority. . ."

"What was that?" said a third gatherer.

"It came from over there," said a fourth, pointing in the opposite direction from where Ev and her friends were hidden.

"Bobcat?"

"Maybe. Could be raccoons."

"Regulations say we've got to investigate."

"And leave the little worm to her own devices?"

'Little worm' was Siobhan.

"We should have never sent her back," whispered Peter.

"Shush!" hissed Ev. "Boaclick, now!"

Boaclick closed his eyes to send a message to the other pixies.

The gatherers were still arguing about who would stay with Siobhan and who would investigate the noise when an arrow flew through the air and hit a tree right next to their heads.

"Battle stations!" yelled the man who'd called Siobhan a worm, and for a moment Ev wished she'd told the True Users that it was okay to kill them.

A bolt of lightning ripped through the air, setting part of the forest on fire and separating Siobhan from most of her captors, but the gatherers were too busy to notice, because at that moment, the True Users attacked.

It wasn't a real fight. There was a lot of shouting and fire, but also a lot of avoiding and running away.

"I hope they don't notice how fake this all is. . ." muttered Ev.

One gatherer was still on Siobhan's side of the blaze, trying to find a way through the flames to help his friends.

"What do we do about him?" hissed Peter.

"I think I can knock him out. . .What's that?"

There was a movement in the trees, a little way behind the gatherer. Ev tensed, ready to attack. The bushes rustled. Ev raised her hand, found the lava in her brain, and prepared to fire.

A tiny, black masked face emerged.

"It's just a raccoon!" said Peter, in relief.

The raccoon glanced at them, looked away, and then quickly looked back.

"Did that raccoon just do a double take?" asked Peter.

The raccoon grinned and waved. Because it seemed polite, Ev waved back.

"A friend of yours?" hissed Peter.

"I think I may have met that particular raccoon before," Ev whispered back.

With surprisingly human movements, the raccoon pointed at the stranded gatherer and gave Ev a questioning look.

"Go for it," she whispered with a nod. "It can't hurt to try."

The raccoon jumped on the gatherer's back, used the man's ears as handles, and swung round until they were looking each other in the eye. Then, with its legs wrapped around the man's head and the man's ears still firmly in its paws, it head butted him. The crack rang out across the clearing.

"They've evolved very strong skulls, I hear," said Ev, weakly.

With another little wave, the raccoon disappeared into the undergrowth, leaving the unconscious gatherer behind.

Siobhan watched all of this, whimpering. She was now completely alone.

Shielded by Boaclick, Ev and Peter snuck up behind her. Siobhan had no idea they were there until Peter clamped a hand over her mouth and Boaclick wrapped her in the privacy shield.

"Don't you dare say anything," said Ev quietly.

Siobhan nodded. Her eyes were wide with fear.

"Let me tell you what's going to happen," said Ev. "You're going to help us with something, and in return, we'll help you."

Siobhan's eyes filled with tears.

"You can let her go, Peter."

"What if she tries something?"

"She won't. Will you, Siobhan?"

Siobhan shook her head, and Peter let her go.

"All right, listen carefully," said Ev. "We need you to get something for us from inside Alerrawia. Can you do that?"

"I. . .I. . .don't know, they keep me in the sub-basement when I'm not out here. . ."

"Why would they do that?" demanded Ev, shocked.

"It's my punishment," said Siobhan, hollowly.

"Your punishment? But you helped them!" said Peter. "You betrayed us!"

"It wasn't enough. It's *never* enough! I. . .I. . ." Siobhan was crying now, struggling to speak.

"We can talk about this another time," said Ev. "Will you help us?"

The sounds of fighting in the distance started to fade and the fire from the lightning strike had almost died down.

"Listen Siobhan," said Ev. "Boaclick is going with you, in your bag. You are not to reveal that he's there. Just act normally. Once you're back, he'll tell you what to do."

"I just want you all to know that I don't like this, and I think things are going to go spectacularly wrong," said Boaclick, grinning. Then, before Siobhan could say anything, he dove into her overloaded satchel. "Of course, spectacular is how I like to roll, so let's get on with it!"

"Will you help us?" said Ev, urgently.

"Yes, Ev," said Siobhan. "We have to stick together."

"Ev!" hissed Peter, dragging her back. Now that Boaclick was in Siobhan's bag, they would have to shield themselves, and neither of them were particularly good at it.

They darted back into the trees just as the gatherers returned. They were in good spirits. After all, they'd just triumphed over a True User raiding party.

"Cowards didn't even try!" crowed one.

"Yes, I noticed that too," said another, "and I don't like it. We better head back. Where's the worm?" He grabbed Siobhan by the hair and shoved her toward the others. "Don't dawdle, you useless waste of space! And you!" he added, prodding the unconscious gatherer with his foot. "Get up! What happened, anyway?"

"Raccoon," said the man, groggily, as he pulled himself to his feet.

"Damn pests. . .Come on! Let's get going!"

When the gatherers were out of earshot, Peter said, "She'll turn us in the moment she gets a chance!"

"She already had a chance. She didn't take it. Lulerain and Dropellet have a direct link to Boaclick— they'll know the moment something goes wrong."

"She must hate us so much. . .," said Peter. "We sent her back to this!"

"We didn't know! I thought she might be sent to *detention* for a while, but this. . .I had no idea."

"We'll help her, then?"

"I think we have to. Don't you?"

"Yeah, I think we do. . ."

Without Boaclick at their side, it took Ev and Peter a while to find their way back to the others, but they knew where they were going.

"Ev, can I ask you about something."

"Go for it."

"*Is* Madison always right?"

"Sadly, yes."

"So, I'm not going to survive all this then. . ."

"What are you talking about?"

"She told me, the day we first all teamed up. Remember? She said that I'm not going to make it."

"She probably just made a mistake. . ."

"I don't think so. I've been feeling something. In my magic. Like it knows it's not going to be around much longer. . ."

"There you are!" said Lulerain, appearing in front of them. "They're already at the gate! What took you so long?" The pixie was tense, and Ev didn't blame her. This was the crucial moment. Boaclick was strong enough to prevent the scanners spotting him on the way in, but not strong enough to keep himself invisible at the same time. Ev just hoped that they didn't decide to search Siobhan's bag manually, because then it would be over before it began.

"Show me the kitchen gate," said Ev to Ewan.

Ewan focused on the gate and zoomed in without being asked.

Now they could see Siobhan enter Alerrawia, as well as listen to Dropellet and Lulerain's updates directly from Boaclick's mind.

"What's he thinking?" asked Ev.

"That it smells just as bad as when he was last here," said Dropellet, dryly. "I'll tell you if he happens to have any important thoughts."

Siobhan's group inched closer and closer to the gate. Everyone held their breath. Then, Siobhan was pushed roughly through, and they could see her no longer.

"He's in," said Dropellet. "Everything's fine."

They breathed out.

"Now what?" asked Stacey.

"We wait for dark," said Ev. She beckoned to Lulerain, and the two of them stepped away from the group.

"Where are Mike and the others?" asked Ev.

"They've gone to keep watch on the exile tunnel."

"Alright, I'd feel better if you or Dropellet went to join them. I know you have the forest pixies to communicate with. . ."

"I understand. It's better if it's someone you know you can trust. I can take Ewan back to his mom. Madison can keep the scrying pool going if you need it—that sort of thing comes pretty naturally to seers."

"That's a good idea," said Ev, grateful that the pixie hadn't decided to argue. "Be careful."

"I will be. Ewan, time to go!"

"But I can be so much more useful here!"

"Your mom said to listen to me, didn't she?"

"Yes, Lulerain."

"Then listen!"

Ev watched the pixie and the unhappy boy disappear among the trees.

One of the things Boaclick had told Dropellet was that Siobhan was under a spell that blocked her magic completely. Once it was dark and Alerrawia had gone to sleep, Boaclick, invisible and constantly at Siobhan's side, would break the spell, Siobhan would fade, and they would both head to the IT Nerve Center on the tenth floor. There they would find the advanced tablet computer Stacey needed to hack into Vendavi.

It sounded so simple in her head. So why was she so worried?

The children tried to sleep, knowing that they wouldn't get much of a chance later, but it was difficult, so, when Dropellet said, "It's show time," they were all awake.

"Can I see what Boaclick is seeing, please?" Ev asked Dropellet. The pixie nodded, and a holographic image sprang to life from Boaclick's perspective.

This is what Ev saw.

Siobhan was in the sub-basement, locked in a cell. Boaclick had just freed her and was encouraging her to fade as quickly as possible. The cell door was nothing to a pixie. The moment that Siobhan faded from Boaclick's view, the door sprung open.

It was difficult for Ev and the others to follow what happened next. When Siobhan was faded, they forgot all about her. It was only because Boaclick had taken precautions and cast a few preventive spells of his own that *any* of them could keep track of her.

With difficulty they watched Boaclick sneak through the corridors of Alerrawia, ducking and diving to avoid the patrols. They couldn't see. . .who was it? Siobhan. They couldn't see Siobhan at all.

"There are a lot of guards out and about. . .," said Ev.

"That's probably down to you and your friends," said Dropellet. "They're making sure that no one else gets any brave ideas."

Boaclick's journey to the tenth floor was painfully slow and completely excruciating.

"Ev," said Madison, making Ev jump. "Something's wrong."

"What is it now?"

"I'm not sure, not quite yet, but something is going to go horribly, fantastically wrong."

As always, Madison was completely confident and entirely unconcerned.

"She's *always* right, Ev," said Stacey. "Always."

"Madison, can you give us any details? There's not much we can do if you. . ."

"I don't have any details! It doesn't work like that! Something is going to go wrong, and I thought you'd like to know!"

"Here," said Gavin. "Let me show you how to clear your mind and access your magic. You might see more if you do."

Ev nodded gratefully at Gavin as he and Madison took a couple of steps away from the group. Madison might know something important, but until she could tell them what it was, she would just be a distraction.

"They've made it to the tenth floor," said Dropellet. "Does the. . .girl know what she's looking for?"

"Boaclick has a note from Stacey. She said it would be enough for. . .Siobhan? Yes, Siobhan, because she showed Siobhan where the tablets were the last time they were there."

"Boaclick says they have it," said Dropellet.

"Good," said Ev. "Now to get back to the cell. . ."

Boaclick would leave the same way he arrived—in Siobhan's bag. It seemed like the safest way. The Withouters didn't want the missing tablet to be noticed until it was far too late.

"Ev," said Gavin urgently. "Ev, something's happening!"

Ev turned to see Madison's eyes were wide open, but slightly glazed like she wasn't really seeing what was in front of her.

"Madison. Madison! Can you hear me?"

"She has her own ideas. . ." said Madison in a voice that wasn't entirely her own.

"What the. . ." said Dropellet. "The little fool is running!"

"Where's she going?" asked Stacey.

"I don't know! Boaclick is struggling to keep up, she took him by surprise. . ."

"Do you mean that Siobhan has her own plans?" Ev asked Madison.

"Yes, her too," said Madison, looking past Ev's shoulder.

"Stupid girl!" said Dropellet. "She's heading for a window; she's going to try to fly away!"

"She'll never make it!" said Derek. "The sky barrier is up! It's suicide!"

"Here they come," said Madison.

"Who, Madison? Who?" shouted Ev.

Just at that moment, Siobhan, unable to fade and fly at the same time, appeared.

"There she is!" said Dropellet. "Boaclick can see her now. . ."

At almost exactly the same moment, Vasagle and a band of forest griffins shrieked right through the magical barriers protecting Alerrawia. Boaclick turned to watch them, distracted by the noise.

"She didn't want to wait for you," said Madison, sleepily. "She has her own ideas."

Alarms sounded, and moments later Vasagle and her troop were surrounded by captive Alerrawian griffins and deadly guards of all sizes. Vasagle blasted them with her magic, as did her friends, but they were no match for Felix's well-trained forces. One by one, they crashed to the ground.

"Ask Boaclick where Siobhan is!"

The hologram's perspective changed as Boaclick spun around, searching for Siobhan.

"The barrier will kill her if she tries to fly out!" said Peter.

"Maybe we can break the barrier for her? If we *all* try?" said Derek. At least, that's what he said with his voice. His eyes said, '*You* can break the barrier, Ev. You and I both know you can.'

"Yes," said Ev. "The three of us fly. Now."

NOW!

She grabbed Peter and Derek's hands and jumped into the air, dragging them with her. She turned to Gavin and said, "Get Madison and Stacey back to the other Withouters. Dropellet, you go with them, keep them safe."

"Come back, you idiots!" shouted Dropellet, but Ev ignored him.

They flew as quickly as they could, but it wasn't quick enough. In the distance, they saw a flash and heard a faint scream.

"She hit the barrier," muttered Ev.

"That wasn't the barrier," said Derek. "Trust me, we would know if it was. That was a stunning spell—maybe more than one. They've knocked her out of the air."

"Then we can still help her! Fly!"

FLY!

With renewed strength, the three children dashed through the sky. Alerrawia loomed closer and closer, and suddenly they were right at its walls.

It was probably only because of Vasagle's distracting antics that they were able to get even that far.

Alerrawia has no barrier that can stop Evelyn Acorn, Peter Rayner, and Derek Black.

Seconds later, they were soaring over the familiar grounds of the Alerrawian compound.

"Hands up!" said someone, a man. Without looking, Ev turned her fire on him.

"Let there be light!" The man screamed, but Ev ignored him.

Where was Siobhan?

"Get them!" shouted someone else. Moments later, Ev, Peter and Derek were surrounded by flying guards, all with hands pointed in their direction.

"Attack!" screamed Ev.

Her command came too late. Darkness engulfed her and she knew no more.

23. . . .We Have to Stick Together . . .

Detention will now take two forms: the
usual form, where students are temporarily
sucked into a parallel dimension to suffer
the consequences of their actions; and a new
form, where students will be required to take
part in arduous, real world punishments with
real-world consequences. This new form
will be known as Trial by Fire.

*Extract: Memorandum sent by Marcia
Breswick to all carers, teachers, and parents*

"Wakey, wakey."

Ev recognized the voice immediately.

She opened her bleary eyes to see Marcia standing
over her with a look of utter contempt on her face.

"You probably thought you were being very clever,
but magic will *never* get you what you want," said Marcia,
scathingly. "I have some *very* interesting ideas about what
to do with you."

"Do you?" said Ev. "Then I must congratulate you;
I didn't think you had the imagination."

"You insolent little. . ."

Oh, someone deal with her, won't you?

"That's enough, Marcia."

Ev sat up to see who had spoken and spotted Christopher sitting just next to the door of her cell, Ernouf at his side.

"How dare you speak to me like that!"

"I just open my mouth and words pour out," said Christopher. "Stop trying to scare the girl. You're not good at it, and, anyway, we have our orders. The children are to be taken to Felix, and *he* will decide what happens to them."

Marcia was livid, her mouth was a thin line, but she would never go against Felix's wishes.

"Well, at least the brat can't do any magic," she said. "Not with all the Hexteria pumping through her veins."

"*That* explains why a feel like someone scooped my brain out with a shovel," said Ev. "Thanks for letting me know."

She did a quick inventory of her magic, and, while she could feel the leap in her stomach and the lava in her brain, she couldn't *do* anything with it, but it didn't matter. The yellow in her heart was still alive and well and, if she wasn't careful, it would make *all* her decisions for her.

"Marcia, tell Felix that they're starting to wake up, there's a good girl," said Christopher. "I think it's best that I keep an eye on this one—she's *very* good at getting under your skin."

With a huff Marcia stomped out of the cell, slamming the door behind her.

Ev was alone with Cristopher. She'd never known what to think about him, and she certainly didn't understand why he did even half of what she'd see him do. Sometimes, he seemed to be helping her. Other times, he was as much an obstacle as any other member of The Seven.

To be safe, Ev focused her full attention on Christopher, and was about to make him help her when he said, "You're really in trouble this time."

"Thank you for telling me, I would never have known otherwise."

"When you're called in front of Felix, one of two things will happen—either you'll be sentenced to perpetual detention, or you'll be outright murdered."

"Wonderful," said Ev. "I'll pencil it into my calendar."

"Which means," continued Christopher, "that if you're going to escape, *again*, you'll have to it now."

Ev's mind went blank. "Um," she said. "I think I've lost track of this conversation. . ."

"Well, I can't waste time explaining every little thing to you," said Christopher, "so, just follow me and try to keep up. Oh, and I think you need *this* for something."

He handed her the tablet Siobhan had tried to steal and then made straight for the door. "Don't dawdle." He walked out, leaving Ev sitting speechlessly on her hard bed.

Ernouf gently tugged at her pants and whined.

Christopher stuck his head back in the room. "What are you waiting for? A gold-embossed invitation?"

Numbly Ev stood and stumbled after Christopher.

"I assume you want me to rescue your little friends too, correct? It's not too late to free yourself of them, you know."

"Ah, yes, *now* I remember why I don't like you very much," said Ev. "Of course, I want you to free my friends too, assuming that's what you're actually doing."

"Suit yourself," said Christopher. "It's riskier and stupider, but if that's what the great Evelyn Acorn wants, then that's what she'll get."

"Why are you helping me?"

"I'm not helping *you*, I'm helping *me*," said Christopher as he glanced through the little window in the door to another cell. "I would have thought that was obvious, by now. *I* think my best chance at fixing the mess affectionately referred to as the bubble is by freeing you. You've done things no one else ever has. I don't know how, and I don't really care, but I can spot the winning side when I see it. So, we're going to get your friends, and then *we're* going to leave."

He glanced through the window of another cell.

"Do you even know where they are?"

"It's a process of elimination. I know where they *aren't*, and I can find them from there."

"Why should I trust you?"

"Because I've been helping you and your friends from the beginning. More-or-less. Mike has been keeping me and Eliza updated when he can, but my most recent information comes from Boaclick. He couldn't get out after your little scheme went awry, and he came straight to me."

"You're Mike's spy? *Eliza* is Mike's spy?"

"Yes. Boaclick has known for years. He's always sticking his nose where it's not wanted—he spotted me more than once sending illegal magical transmissions from the grounds. I never fully understood why he didn't report me, it's just the sort of thing he loves to do, but when he came to me for help tonight, I knew that he'd just been biding his time. He's not as stupid as he pretends. . ."

Magical transmissions?

"You're a magic user," said Ev.

"Everyone is. Surely you know that by now?"

"Yes, but I didn't know if *you* knew," muttered Ev.

"Everyone on The Seven knows. It's a difficult secret to keep, but we seem to get away with it."

"*Everyone* on The Seven uses magic?"

"Well, not Robert and Shaun, they hate it too much and, between you and me, they are terrible at it. Felix and Marcia use it all the time, but only in secret, and they think that nobody knows. Eliza uses it strategically, and Zara is the only openly magical person on The Seven, which means, strangely enough, that she has the hardest time using *any* magic at all."

"And you?"

"I use it whenever it suits me."

"I feel like I'm meeting you for the very first time."

"Actually, you and I have known each other longer than you think. If it's easier, you can call me Vendavi."

Ev stopped in her tracks.

"It was you? *You* were the one who hurt us?" she whispered.

"What? No, that was the actual system, I was just your helpful guide during those extremely entertaining simulations you did so badly in."

Ev had a big problem with words like 'just' and 'helpful' in that context.

"You have *no idea* what it's like!" she hissed. "No idea! Those simulations. . ."

"Can we talk about this some other time? We really do need to get a move on."

Ernouf gently nudged the back of Ev's knees.

For a moment, Ev watched Christopher walk away. Then, silently, she followed him.

This wasn't the last that Christopher would hear about it, but he was right—it would have to wait for another time.

While they walked, she quietly performed the Hexteria cancellation spell on herself. Viola had known exactly what she was doing when she'd given it to them—it was easy enough to do once you knew how. If Christopher tried anything, she would be ready.

"We have a winner," Christopher finally said. He opened a cell door to reveal Derek.

"I have nothing to say to you," said Derek immediately, "And that's the end of it. . .Ev, what are you doing here?"

"Evelyn and I are collaborating on her third escape from Alerrawia," said Christopher. "If she was any good, she would have stayed gone the first time, of course, but here we are. Are you coming?"

"Ev?" said Derek uncertainly.

"It's okay," said Ev. "Just be ready to shove him through a wall if necessary."

"Very amusing," said Christopher, turning his attention to the next cell. "Here's the other one."

As soon as Christopher looked away, Derek gently took his cell door between his thumb and forefinger and squeezed. The metal gave way easily under his grip. He winked at Ev, and she winked back.

"Out you come, we've wasted enough time as it is," said Christopher to a quivering Peter in the next cell.

"It's okay, Peter," said Ev, "I'll explain later, but long story short, Christopher is helping us escape, and apparently there's a time limit."

"How long do *you* think it would normally take Marcia to run to Felix with news?" asked Christopher. "It's a miracle we haven't been caught already. . ."

"Where are all the guards?" demanded Derek as he gently took Peter by the arm and dragged him out of the cell.

"Officially, the sub-basement and everything that happens here is a secret, insofar as *anything* is really a secret in this place," said Christopher. "The guards guard the entrance, but most of them spend very little time down here."

He glanced through another window.

"Her too?" he asked.

Ev stood on tiptoes to see into the cell.

"Yes, definitely," she said firmly. "Let her out now."

Christopher raised an eyebrow, but he unlocked Siobhan's cell without a word.

"She did betray us. Twice. In case you forgot," said Derek.

"The first time she was forced and the second time she was just scared. We're not leaving her here."

"And I would say she's sorry," added Christopher, "if the unhealable scar on Felix's face is anything to go by."

A trembling Siobhan stepped out of her cell. Her face was bruised where she'd hit the ground, and she walked with a limp.

"Come now," said Ev, placing a gentle arm around Siobhan's shoulders. "I'm sorry I let this happen, but I'm not going to leave you again. You and I are going to stick together properly this time, okay?"

"The spell is broken," whispered Siobhan. "He said I wasn't useful to him anymore."

"He's an idiot who has never been useful to anyone in his entire life. We don't need him. *Nobody* needs him."

"Very touching, I'm sure Felix's heart will just melt when he catches us, which will happen any moment now if we don't *hurry up*!"

The children hurried after Christopher as he led them from the sub-basement to more familiar ground.

"Where is everyone?" asked Derek.

"Thanks to you, there's a curfew now," whispered Christopher. "Everyone's in bed, under guard, but that doesn't mean there won't be *someone* wandering around, so kindly shut up."

Ev was tense. Silently she released Peter from his Hexteria prison just in case he needed to fly away. She thought about doing the same for Siobhan, but she was worried that she would get scared and fade.

Ev didn't want to lose her again.

They followed Christopher in silence, sneaking up the ramp from the basement and into the grounds.

"Wait!" hissed Siobhan. It was the first word she'd said since they'd found her.

"What is it?"

"He's taking us to the main gate! I knew it. . .this is just another Trial by Fire, *I knew it*!"

"Quiet!" hissed Christopher.

Ev took Siobhan's shoulders in her hands. "What's a Trial by Fire?" she whispered. "Tell me quickly and quietly."

"It's a new punishment," said Siobhan between terrified sobs. "They want to hurt us now; detention isn't enough anymore. Now they send us to do dangerous things, grown-up things, and it's *horrible*! He's taking us to the main gate! It's a trial!"

Siobhan was becoming hysterical, her voice getting louder and louder.

"Calm down!"

Calm down!

Siobhan stilled, chest still heaving.

"What is she talking about?"

"She thinks I'm taking her out for another dangerous gathering mission," said Christopher, beckoning them to crouch behind a helicopter. "It's Marcia's latest idea. Felix has given her free reign since your escape, and she's using it to make life as miserable for everyone as possible."

"So, you're *not* marching us to the main gate?"

"I am, actually. It's the easiest way for us to leave. Oh, I almost forgot." He rummaged in his backpack. "You're going to need to put these on."

Siobhan whimpered.

"Those are shackles," said Derek.

"Your powers of observation are outstanding. Think of them as a costume so you can play the part of scared little children being taken outside for your punishment a little more convincingly."

Derek and Ev exchanged looks. If the shackles got them out of Alerrawia, it didn't really matter if Christopher were lying or not, because they could get rid of him and his shackles easily enough once they were safe.

"Alright," said Ev. "We'll do it."

"We will?" asked Peter, shakily.

"Yes, idiot," said Derek.

"Yes, idiot," repeated Boaclick, appearing with a pop. "Which specific idiot are we referring to at this exact moment in time?"

"Where have *you* been?" demanded Christopher.

"Watching *your* back if you must know. You're all terribly noisy, I had to disable an entire patrol. What, did you think you'd made it this far through pure skill and luck?"

The pixie watched as the children shackled themselves. "It occurs to me that if this is all just a trick, then Christopher should be the one we follow to certain death, don't you think?" he said. "If he can make you do this, he can probably make anyone do any. . ."

Boaclick was cut short by a blur of fur that sprung from the shadows and pinned him to the ground.

"Let there be light!" said Ev, and a fireball appeared instantly in her hand, but then she hesitated.

Boaclick was cackling his head off.

"Not play time now!" he gasped.

Then Ev saw that his attacker was Mr. Snugglebottom.

With impossible strength for someone so small, Boaclick pushed the bobcat off and patted him on the head.

"What can we do for you, Mr. S?"

"Maybe he wants to come too?" said Peter.

"He won't come with us," said Boaclick. "He always stays where there are the most children to protect."

"What's that around his neck?" asked Derek.

"Something for us, most likely," said Boaclick. He unfastened the strap around the bobcat's neck. "It's a note." He handed it to Ev. It read:

For: The Withouters

Permission to overthrow the government.

Validity: Forever

Signed: Granny Oakwood

On the back it said:

Keep me informed. It seems that it's finally the right time.

As soon as Boaclick had the note, Mr. Snugglebottom stretched, yawned, and wandered off.

"*Now* can we leave?" asked Christopher.

"Oh, relax, we have plenty of time," said Boaclick. "Last I heard, Marcia and Felix were arguing about how bad your punishment should be. They can't quite decide what they prefer: detention forever, or a slow and painful death."

"Nevertheless. . ."

"We're ready, let's go," said Ev.

Boaclick dived into Ev's bag, and they set off for the main gate, this time walking openly. As they got closer, Christopher started speaking loudly.

"Keep moving, worms," he said.

There was a guard on the gate. With a sinking feeling, Ev saw that he was a useful idiot, the worst kind of guard to encounter now, of all times.

For some reason, he looked familiar.

"Halt, who goes there," he said in a bored, uninterested voice.

"It's me, Frank, taking this lot out for a trial," said Christopher.

"I don't see any paperwork for this. . ."

"Last minute decision, you know how it is."

The guard's eyes narrowed, and Ev knew that it wasn't working. She searched for the yellow in her heart, but it evaded her.

Then she remembered where she'd seen the guard before. He'd been in the library what felt like a hundred years ago when she'd warped reality and told Siobhan that. . .

"Whatever happens out there, we need to *stick together*," she said loudly, interrupting her own thoughts.

"Yes, Ev," said Siobhan immediately. Peter and Derek just looked confused.

The guard's eyes crossed for a moment and then cleared.

"Fine, take them, but make sure you get that paperwork to me as soon as possible, or *I'll* be the one in trouble."

He waved them through.

"Oh, you're going to be in trouble, alright," muttered Christopher the moment they were out of earshot. "I told you, Ev—they're all idiots in one way or another."

Ev knew differently, but she couldn't say anything.

"Can we take these shackles off yet?"

"Once we're among the trees."

"How long will it take them to notice?" asked Derek.

"They may have already noticed, but if we start running, we'll be spotted. We *do* have to move as quickly as we can."

"Walk, don't run!" said Ev in a sing-song voice.

"That guard will tell them which way we went the moment he gets a chance, so just keep moving."

No, he won't, thought Ev. He and I have to stick together.

Once they were among the trees, Cristopher removed their shackles and Boaclick cast a privacy charm around them to keep them hidden from the many eyes of Alerrawia.

"Boaclick, inform the others of our situation and request advice on further movements, given our new. . .friend. Don't forget to tell them Siobhan is with us too."

"Already done. Lulerain recommends proceeding as planned on the advice of Mike who recognizes *his* name," said Boaclick, nodding at Christopher.

"Good, thank you. Tell them we're on our way and that they should proceed with the necessary preparations."

"My, you really have taken to your role as Savior of Everyone *very* well, haven't you?" said Christopher. "And everyone else seems quite happy with it too."

"Where is your wolf going?" demanded Ev as Ernouf vanished into the undergrowth.

"He's scouting ahead, checking for trouble."

"Keep him by your side, please."

"Very well. Ernouf! Here!"

Ernouf completely failed to appear.

"Oh, I forgot for a moment that I have absolutely no control over Ernouf's decisions whatsoever, he just sometimes lets me pretend that I do for the sake of being allowed to stay in Alerrawia, where his meals are caught for him. He's somewhere close. Probably."

"I don't like it."

"Neither do I, much, but there's nothing *I* can do about it. I've tried, trust me."

"I do not trust you. That's the main problem we have here."

"Very good! I don't trust anyone either. It's the only sensible way to live. However, in this case, as your friend Mike trusts me, shouldn't you do the same?"

"That rather depends on *why* Mike trusts you."

"I keep him updated on what's happening in Alerrawia. At least, I did until you lot escaped, and then it became impossible to send messages. You see, little girls are not the only people capable of seeing that Alerrawia is sick and needs help. We've been working against the Granites for generations, but we had to be careful. There were always too few of us, and Felix is good at keeping people distracted. When Eliza recruited me, I could see right away that the resistance hadn't achieved anything worth doing in *years*. Do you know where we're going, by the way?"

"Eliza recruited you?" asked Ev, ignoring the question. "I thought her judgement was a little better than that. . ."

"The Faradays were against the Granite Institute from the beginning. So were the Oakwoods. Granny is old and looking for others to follow in her footsteps. Eliza is old too. She has no one to pick up her mantle once she is gone. Felix will choose someone *he* can rely on to fill her position on The Seven."

"How did *you* get your position on The Seven?"

"Felix chose me, of course. I'm very good at playing both sides."

"That's *exactly* what we need to hear from you right now. . ." muttered Derek.

"Eliza and I have known about Felix's plan to annihilate Inner for ages, but we couldn't do anything about it. The best we could hope for was to distract Felix. You were *very* helpful with that, Ev. I would thank you, but I don't want to. I saw right away in your simulations that you were just the sort of troublemaker that would keep Felix on his toes, although it took some effort to convince him to accept you. He wanted to stick with Amy and Jonah, a girl too traumatized to speak, and a boy too traumatized to use his abilities, because they would be easier to control. It took all our best efforts to convince him. Eliza argued that someone like you would definitely be exiled from Inner, and then the True Users would have you on *their* side. It was a very compelling argument, but even then, you were almost turned away at the door, although what we would have done with you, I have no idea.

"We didn't predict just exactly how disruptive you would be, of course. Eliza started thinking that you might be the answer to all of our problems. I just think she was spending too much time with Granny—I'm too old to believe in heroes. But then, when Felix nearly died from shock at your disciplinary hearing, I began to see what they were seeing. I didn't understand what I was seeing, but there's definitely more to you than meets the eye."

Ev and Derek exchanged a quick, furtive glance. If Christopher noticed, he didn't say anything.

"We started to think of our distraction as a possible solution, a way to save Inner from destruction for a little bit longer, but we didn't really know how. Felix isn't great at focusing on more than one threat at a time, so *I* just decided to make you as threatening as possible. Not that you needed much help. When Eliza and I messed up so badly with the restricted section. . .well, you know about that. There were a few things I could do to help. When I searched your bag, for instance, I saw that you had an RDD, so I just left it there. Then we realized that you had your own plans. . ."

"When did you realize?"

"When you freed three pixies, a griffin, and a dragon and left," said Christopher. "I'm not sure what Felix thinks—he and Marcia locked the rest of us out when you escaped. The Seven are now The Two, for all intents and purposes. But Eliza figured out what you were doing very quickly. She's in charge of the scryers on thirteenth, you see. It's down to her that the scryers have been mysteriously unable to track your movements each time you leave. Did you ever think about that? Thanks to Eliza, Felix thinks that scrying magic is unreliable. At Eliza's request, the scryers looked into your future, and it was a confusing mess, as these things often are with longer-term predictions, but she saw enough to know that you plan to free Inner and overthrow Felix."

"Do I succeed?"

"It's hard to say. It's like looking through a keyhole and then trying to draw a picture of the whole room. It's difficult to pick moments in the future that give you an accurate idea of what will happen, even if you leave aside the fact that futures change all the time. If the scryers looked again now, they would see something completely different, but just as confusing, all because of this conversation. That's why the scryers only look a few minutes ahead, as a sort of live surveillance system. It's the most useful they can be."

"Do you expect us to believe that *you* care about Inner?"

"Not at all. I care about is surviving, which none of us will do for much longer with Felix in charge. He gets crazier every day. He thought that removing your closest friends would make you less of a threat, but instead, it drove you to heights none of us thought possible."

"Whose idea was it, exactly, to hurt Amy and Jonah?"

"Felix's, of course."

"You mean nobody put the thought in his head? Like, maybe a member of The Seven who thinks that friends hold you back?"

"I have no idea what you're talking about," said Christopher, his face a mask. "Siobhan was the one who hurt your friends."

Siobhan whimpered. Ev put a comforting arm around her shoulders.

"Let's clear the air," said Ev. "I know you were forced, and I know you tried to fight it. . ."

". . .we have to stick together. . ."

". . .exactly. Anyway, it sounds like you've more than made up for it! What's this I hear about Felix's face?"

"At my disciplinary hearing I just kept thinking about you and how you had to go through all that because you accidentally flew away, and how *I* was going through it because I'd done exactly what I was told. I just got angrier and angrier. I thought I couldn't do anything because of the Hexteria, but I was there when you were practicing the spell Viola gave you. I released myself, I faded, I headed straight for him, and then. . .well, I didn't have a plan, did I, so I just grabbed a knife from his dinner plate, because he *was eating* while deciding how to destroy me, and I stabbed at his face, and I put all of my magic behind the blow so I couldn't stay faded, and Zara took me down, and then I was thrown in the sub-basement, and later they just started

taking me out on those *horrible* gathering missions, and. .
."

She was crying too much to continue, but Ev had
already heard her say more than she'd ever done at one
time before.

"I knew I was done when I realized I wasn't under
his spell anymore," she whispered. "As long as I was
useful, I was safe, but. . ."

"But you did *everything* he asked you to!" said
Peter.

"He's not good at magic, even if he wants you to
think he is. He could only make me tell him the answers to
questions he asked; he couldn't just make me repeat
everything I learned from Ev and the rest of you, and he
didn't know what was going on or what questions to ask, so
he never got the full story, and I wouldn't tell him myself. I
still said too much. . .he asked me why I was struggling to
be your friend, Ev, and I *had* to tell him that it was because
I didn't want to hurt you after you saved me in flying class,
and anyway, you had Amy and Jonah, so he made me get
rid of them both!"

Siobhan's eyes were wide with horror.

"That spell that hurt Amy. . .it nearly killed me, but
he didn't care, just made Marcia fix me up, badly, because
she also sucks at magic, and sent me back to you. He
thought if he got rid of them you would be demotivated,
that you would be my friend and let me make you into a
model student, but it didn't work, and he blamed *me*. I hate
him!"

"I knew that man was using you for something," muttered Christopher. "If I'd known what, I'd have taken steps to keep you away from Ev, but who knows if that would have worked, what with our little leader girl's love for surrounding herself with useless hangers-on."

"Christopher, no talking," said Ev. She turned back to Siobhan. "Is it thanks to you that we didn't get into more trouble after breaking into the restricted section?"

"Maybe. Felix didn't know what questions to ask me to find out what you discovered, and anyway, I didn't really understand what you discovered, and he decided that you hadn't found anything at all. I didn't tell him you took stuff when we left. The library search was just normal procedure, to scare the pixies into paying closer attention. He still doesn't know what you found."

Siobhan took a huge, shaky breath. "This is the first time in my entire life I can speak without magic stopping me. The very first time." She sobbed inconsolably.

"Because of you, Amy is alive instead of dead," said Derek. "So, like, look on the bright side, or something."

"I fought it," whispered Siobhan through her tears. "I didn't want to do it, so I fought it, and it went wrong. . ."

"It's alright," said Ev, patting her gently. "Everything will be alright."

"You say that," said Christopher. "But I don't see how, unless you have some amazing plan up your sleeve. We've been doing nothing but scrambling together last-minute plans for weeks. Eliza might not even know that I've let yet."

"This is all *terribly* interesting," said Boaclick, who'd been too busy keeping them hidden to be his usual annoying self, "but you should probably know that we've nearly reached our destination."

Boaclick led them to a small clearing where the rest of the Withouters were huddled.

"What took you so long?" demanded Madison the moment she saw them. "I knew it would all be alright, so why did you take your time? Stop to chat with old friends, did you?"

"Hello, Madison," said Ev, wearily. "Viola, Ray-Leigh, could you please keep an eye on these two?" She nodded towards Siobhan and Christopher. "*Especially* him. He helped us, but we can never trust him."

"Beautifully put," said Christopher.

"Come this way, dear," said Viola to Siobhan. "Everything will be just fine." She turned to Ev and Mike and said, "That man's spells are gone, by the way, I noticed the moment she arrived. Siobhan is free to make her own decisions now."

"Wonderful," muttered Ray-Leigh as she begrudgingly grabbed Christopher and dragged him away from the main group. "*Another* child doing what *they* think is best. . ."

Viola took Siobhan to a quieter part of the clearing, talking to her gently every step of the way.

"Mike, we need to talk," said Ev. Without waiting for an answer, she threw up a privacy barrier. It was getting easier and easier to do.

"Christopher and Eliza are your spies," she said.

"Ah. I see he told you. His usefulness as a spy diminishes exponentially the further he is from Alerrawia, but never mind."

"If you'd told me when I'd asked who your spies were, it would have saved me a lot of time, but *never mind*. They've got Vasagle and all of her friends."

"And you brought the traitor as well."

"She had no choice. She's here under my protection."

"Very well."

"She's not really the one I'm worried about. . ."

"Christopher *has* been a very useful spy, if somewhat self-serving," said Mike. "I am unable to think of a reason why he might betray us."

"I can't either. I also can't trust him. Oh, and there's an enormous wolf running around somewhere who technically belongs to Christopher but mostly seems to belong to himself."

"We spotted the wolf just before you arrived. It's keeping its distance. Should I tell my people not to shoot it?"

"That's probably a good idea. Let's not look for reasons for Christopher to turn on us, shall we?"

"We can have him around without trusting him. Ray-Leigh is more than capable of keeping him under control."

"Okay. You tell her to watch Christopher at all times. I'll take responsibility for Siobhan, maybe get Viola to help. As for the rest: we have the tablet, we have our people.

"It's finally time to free Inner."

24. I Saw a Mouse the Other Day

It was bad for you, dear child of Inner. There is no denying this. But let us not forget that exiling an adult from Inner is one of the most horrendous punishments ever devised. To take someone who, for their entire life, has been told that there is nothing beyond the walls of their home and then throw them out into a world that isn't supposed to be there is worse than simply killing them. On the rare occasion that an adult is exiled from Inner, it takes all of the skills of those who find them to keep them from going mad, a task that would be difficult even if we weren't all a little mad already. To convince someone to leave of their own accord may well be impossible. In a way, you are the lucky one.

Alison Oakwood

Inner: How and Why?

Mike led them to the exile tunnel, which was little more than a hatch embedded in the side of a crumbling rocky outcrop.

"Stacey, over to you," said Ev, but the older girl already had her new toy in her hand and was tapping at the screen furiously.

"Almost connected," she said, seconds later.

"What? Already?"

"Lulerain has been helping me access my ability. It's *amazing* what I can do now that I know what I'm capable of. Almost there, and. . .yes, I'm connected to Vendavi, and I've disabled those bug robots you told me about. The system has no idea that I'm here. Do you want me to do it now?"

"Sure, why not," said Ev, weakly.

"A little bit daunted, now that the big moment has finally arrived?" asked Christopher.

"Christopher, shut up," said Ray-Leigh. "If you speak again, I'll stop you myself."

Ray-Leigh was never too far from Christopher.

"I better be careful; my guard is watching. . ." muttered Christopher.

"Christopher," said Ev, sweetly. "I've explained that you are *not* a prisoner. Ray-Leigh is simply keeping an eye on you for your own good."

"Just trying to help," he snapped, irritably. "I. . ." His mouth opened and closed, but no sound came out.

"If we need your advice, I'll let you speak again," said Ray-Leigh.

Christopher glared at her, but that was all he could do, and he knew it.

"Lovely. It's suddenly so peaceful," said Ev. "You need to show us how to do that sometime."

"As you wish," said Ray-Leigh, stiffly.

"Are we doing this or not?" asked Stacey, impatiently.

"Yes, go ahead and exile someone."

"Anyone in particular, or should I just close my eyes and pick at random?"

"You can choose?"

Stacey showed her the screen. "*This* is an alphabetical list of all of the people living in Inner, and *this* column shows where they live, and *these* controls here let me mess up their lives in whatever way I see fit."

"Is there someone called Steve Rosebud anywhere on the list?" asked Mike.

Stacey swiped up.

"Yup, here he is."

Mike and Ev exchanged a glance.

"Him," said Ev, firmly. The word 'selfish' sprang to mind, and she stamped down on it, hard.

"Why don't we just exile *everyone*?" asked Peter.

"That is something that Vendavi *would* notice," said Stacey. "Self-destruct or no self-destruct, I don't think we should take the chance."

Stacey tapped her screen.

Nothing happened.

"Did it work?" asked Mike.

"Yup, sorry it's not more dramatic, but computing isn't really a spectator sport. Look here. See this blinking red light? See this red text? He's been ordered to leave. Ah, and now he's in the tunnels. This is going to be a pretty weird day for him."

"How long until he gets here?" asked Ev.

"It depends how fast he crawls."

Ev watched the tiny blinking dot on Stacey's screen that represented Steve stumbling unknowingly to freedom.

"He's moving more rapidly than I did. . .," said Mike.

"But still *quite* slowly," said Derek.

"What's that?" said Viola. Ev's head snapped round, and then she heard it too. There was something in the undergrowth, something moving, *chittering*. . .

A raccoon emerged. It waved. She waved back.

"It's just the raccoons," called Viola. "False alarm."

"How did they find us?" asked Ev.

"They've mutated. We don't how, exactly, but we've never been able to use magic to hide from them. It would be nice to study them in more detail, but that assumes that you can catch and keep one without dying."

"Have you tried asking them instead?"

Viola looked at Ev appraisingly, one eyebrow raised.

"It's not the stupidest idea I've heard. Then again, I have heard *a lot* of ideas in my time."

Ev took a step towards the raccoon. Siobhan grabbed her sleeve to stop her, but she shook the older girl off.

"Hi," she said.

The raccoon stood on its hind legs and cocked its head.

"Are you here to help?"

Ev could have sworn that the raccoon nodded, but it was hard to tell, and before she could ask the others what they thought, the raccoon lifted its face to the sky and screeched.

Raccoons poured in from every direction.

"I don't like this," said Ray-Leigh. She was on her feet and ready to fight, as was Viola and most of the other grown-ups.

"Leave them!" said Ev.

Leave them!

She watched as the raccoons formed a perimeter around the Withouters, just inside their enchantment of protection, facing outward.

"They're here to provide an extra layer of safety," said Ev. "They *do* want to help. While we're in there, they'll be out here, keeping us safe."

One of the raccoons turned, gave her a brief thumbs up, and then went back to its post.

"Well," said Viola. "You learn something new every day."

"Steve Rosebud is about fifteen minutes away," said Stacey.

"Ev, may I have a quick word before we attempt our rescue?" said Lulerain.

With a sigh, Ev cast a privacy spell that enclosed just the two of them.

"What now? We've gone over the plan, and. . ."

"It's about your mother."

"What about her?"

"You have a chance to free her. . ."

"Why would I *ever* do that?"

"Ev, I'm trying to make you understand. Before you released me from my enchantment, you *did* care about your mother and what would happen to her. You really did. You sacrificed your relationship with her to help me. I'm telling you now; if you get a chance to get her out of there, you *must* take it."

"There are plenty of other Inners, far more worthy of rescue."

"Do it for me. Please? Give me a chance to right this great wrong."

"Fine," said Ev reluctantly. "If possible, we will free my mother from Inner."

"Thank you, Ev. I *will* make it right. I promise."

"There are *tons* of other, better things for you to be focused on right now, but I can see this is important to you, so I'll do my best, even if I think it's a terrible use of my time."

With a wave of her hand, the privacy barrier dissolved.

"Ev!" called Stacey.

Ev darted back to Stacey's side.

"This is it?"

"This is it."

Mike joined them and, without thinking, Ev grabbed his hand. He didn't say anything, just squeezed her hand tightly.

Steve was their friend, the only one of their friends that had never left Inner. They both remembered how they'd felt when they'd been made to leave.

Without speaking, Ev and Mike stepped closer to the hatch so that they would be the first people Steve saw.

The hatch opened. A head appeared, followed quickly by a body that tumbled to the forest floor.

"Who's that?" asked Mike.

The person who had appeared was a fully-grown man.

"What the. . ." said the man, then he lunged at the nearest Withouter, shoving her aside. "Where am I?" he demanded.

Ray-Leigh sprang into action, pinning the stranger to the ground.

"I think you may have the wrong person, Stacey," said Ev, her voice shaking.

"Nope, that's Steve Rosebud," said Stacey, confidently.

"Who are you people?" demanded the man. His shaggy black hair flopped over piercing blue eyes.

"Are you Steve?" asked Mike.

"Who are you people? Where am I? What is this?"

Ev heard a low growl and turned to see Ernouf, crouched at Christopher's side.

"No, Ernouf," she said. "He's not for eating."

Ernouf stopped growling and relaxed, slightly, but he was still loaded to spring.

"Good boy," said Ev, mainly because she'd never seen Christopher looking so surprised, and she wanted to see how far she could push it.

The strange man from Inner was staring at Ernouf in shock.

"What's that?" he whispered. "What's happening?"

"There, there, calm down," said Viola in a warm voice.

The man froze.

"What have you done to him?" asked Ev.

"I've shut him down for a moment. He's in shock, his brain needs a break. And, anyway, he'll be more open to questioning like this."

Ray-Leigh crouched in front of the man.

"What's your name?" she asked.

"Steve Rosebud," said the man in a monotone, staring blankly into space.

"He can't be," said Mike. "Steve is our age. He was our friend!"

"Steve Rosebud is a child," said Ray-Leigh to the man.

"No. I'm a monitor," answered Steve.

"What is a monitor?"

"I monitor chats."

"What chats?"

"Between the children. It's for their own good. They're good children. Nice children. They sometimes think badly about Inner, but they're good children. I don't let Vendavi take them."

The man, Steve, was shaking from head to toe.

"He's not used to magic," said Viola. "We shouldn't question him for too long."

"Put him to sleep for a while," said Ev, her voice breaking. "We'll figure out what to do with him later."

"Go to sleep, friend," said Viola. Steve lay down, closed his eyes, and began to snore.

"You know," said Ev, "I used to think I was paranoid for thinking that they watched everything we did. How silly of me."

"What did he mean when he said he wouldn't let Vendavi take us?" asked Mike.

"I think he meant he tried to protect us from Vendavi. I think maybe he didn't tell on us when he could have done."

"But he lied to us about who he was!"

"He thought he was doing the right thing, Mike. He didn't know any better. Just like us."

"What will we do with him?"

"Viola, can you watch him?"

"I'm watching her." Viola nodded toward Siobhan. "Not that she needs watching—she just needs friends."

"I'm fine now," said Siobhan, with a smile. "I'm fine for the first time ever."

"Alright, then I can watch your 'friend'."

"I don't want to interrupt what seems to be a very important moment," said Stacey, "but are we still doing this? The hatch isn't going to stay open forever, you know, and I'm wasting a lot of effort keeping it ajar as it is. . ."

"Yeah," said Ev. "We're still doing this. It doesn't change the plan. Stacey, you'll tell us, via the pixies, where to go. We get those closest to the exit out first and work our way in. If we can make them crawl out on their own, good. If they're confused or don't want to, we try our best to make them, but we do *not* hurt them. Make sure they know there's a time limit." She paused and took a deep breath. "We probably won't be able to get everyone out. We need to accept that right now. We'll do our best to get as many people as possible, but we will not be able to get them all, and that's okay. Do you understand?"

Nods all around.

"Good. If they don't want to come, and if you can't safely make them, leave them, and move on. Peter, a word, please."

They stepped away from the group.

"You don't have to go in if you don't want to."

Peter smiled. "It's alright. I'm cool with it. Really. If I don't make it, I don't make it. This still feels like the most important thing for me to be doing with my time."

"It's your choice."

Peter laughed and said, "Thanks. I'm good," and Ev realized, for a brief moment, that her friend didn't really think that he could die.

"I think. . ."

"Ev, we should get going," said Ray-Leigh, impatiently. "We can't wait around all day."

And that put an end to her chat with Peter.

Ev would go through the hatch first, followed by her team: Lulerain, Madison, Derek, and ten or so True Users. Stacey would lead the second group, which included a handful of True Users, Boaclick, Gavin, and Peter, and Ray-Leigh would lead the last, including the rest of the True Users as well as Dropellet and Mike. Ray-Leigh made Christopher join her group, and Ev took Siobhan. They left Viola behind to keep an eye on Steve.

"Ewan is staying behind with me, and the wolf doesn't look interested in joining you either," said Viola. "All on my own, with just you, a crazy man, a giant wolf, and a ring of raccoons for company," she added to Ewan.

"Why can't I go?" asked Ewan.

"Because I say so," said Viola.

"Sometimes I'm glad that I don't have any parents around to tell me what to do," said Derek, quietly.

"I don't know," said Ev. "It must be kind of nice to have someone who cares if you live or die. Everyone ready? Then let's go."

Using pixie telepathy and some hastily scribbled maps, the three teams crawled into Inner, one at a time.

Ev's team started with the cluster of junior cell groups where she had lived for six years. She knew she was going the right way when she spotted:

It can't hurt to keep yourself safe from you! Begin Hexteria today!

She tore the poster from the wall.

"If convenient, take down the posters. They don't need to see them."

She kept crawling, leaving the posters she passed for the others to deal with. The tunnels were too narrow to pass someone else—if Ev stopped, *everyone* stopped, so she had to keep crawling. Her team was responsible for freeing Inner children, and they didn't want to leave anyone behind.

She looked at the map Stacey had given her.

"Almost there," she called over her shoulder.

Almost home.

Ev sped up. She exactly who she would free first—the other children in her group. She hadn't had much time for them, but at least she knew their names.

"Do you want us to check all these cells you've dashed right past?" called Lulerain.

"Yes," said Ev, without looking back.

"Ev, slow down!" said Siobhan, and then she bumped straight into her when Ev suddenly stopped. "Ouch!"

"This is where I used to live, Siobhan," said Ev, pointing at a cell door. "Want to take a look?"

"Do we have time?" asked Siobhan nervously.

"There might be a new child in there. We should check."

She knew there wasn't, not if Stacey's maps were anything to go by, but she had to see. She grabbed the hatch handle and slid the panel aside.

"Behold," she said. "The life of an Inner child, aged five to eleven."

It was as if she'd never left. Her screen array stared at her, mutely, her bed was in the same unmade state she'd left it in. The only difference was the layer of dust that covered it all.

"It's so small," said Siobhan.

"Yes. I didn't really notice that when I lived here, though."

She closed the hatch, her face carefully turned so her team couldn't see her tears. "No one in there," she said, loudly. "Derek, you check the first room on this side, and then go back and turn left. See if any of the cells on the other side of this block are occupied."

They knew from Stacey's maps that the cells were arranged in blocks of ten, each cell with a hatch leading into the crawl spaces that surrounded them. It made more sense for teams to split up, because they couldn't do much crowded one behind the other anyway. Some of the grown-ups went with Derek, and Ev hurriedly crawled on so that the rest of her team could start being useful.

"Stacey's group has started freeing older kids," reported Lulerain. "They're facing a bit of resistance. . ."

"Just let me know if anything goes wrong."

She didn't expect Derek to find much, because the first two cells he would open would be Amy and Jonah's, but she wanted him to check them anyway, just in case.

Next to her cell on the other side, however, there *would* be a child to free, and she wanted to be the one to do it.

She opened the hatch and a frizzy-haired, buck-toothed girl of about ten looked back at her.

"Hi, Jill," said Ev, lamely. She squeezed herself into the cell so that the others could pass behind her.

Jill just stared.

"So, this may be a bit of a shock, I realize, but I'm Ev. You may remember me? I used to live here and then I moved away?"

Still nothing.

"The trick is not to panic," said Ev, desperately, although Jill didn't look like she was about to. "Anyway, everything is a lie, and you really need to come with us, now."

"This seems most irregular," said Jill, finally. "Is this an exam?"

"Would it help if you pretended it was?" asked Ev.

"I saw a mouse the other day," said Jill.

"That's nice. . ."

"Vendavi told me I hadn't, but I did. I saw it. Mice are supposed to be dead, even if they are sometimes in those strange stories Vendavi lets me read."

"Well, they're not dead, and neither are a lot of other things. . ."

"Are there more mice out there?" asked Jill.

"Yes, lots," said Ev.

"I like them. They're cute."

"Good, now, if you don't mind, we have a lot of people to rescue. . ."

"I come with you now?"

"Yes, you come with us."

"All right."

Jill had spent her whole life allowing people to tell her what to do. This was just more of the same.

"There's an awful lot of you!" she said when she'd crawled out. "Where are your jumpsuits?"

"Just follow us," said Ev. "I'll try to explain it all later."

Obediently, Jill climbed through the hatch.

Further along the tunnel, True Users were coaxing two other girls out of their cells.

"Larissa and Cathy," said Ev to herself.

Larissa was crying and had to be pushed along the tunnel. Cathy looked a little dazed, but far calmer. She waved at Ev and Jill. "More people!" she shouted, happily.

Derek rounded the far corner nearest Larissa's cell with two frightened boys in tow.

"Found two," called Derek. "The rest of the cells were empty, one quite recently."

Those were Mike and Steve's cells. Which meant that these boys were. . .

"Hello Kyle, Shawn," said Ev, hoping she sounded cheerful and not demented.

The tunnel was getting really crowded. She turned to the nearest True User.

"Do you think you can get them outside?"

"We've dealt with many frightened Inner refugees over the years. We'll be fine."

"Good. You two, take the kids we've already found outside, and help Viola keep an eye on them. Don't come back in. You'll probably just lose track of us and get lost."

Ev and the others who were staying squeezed into cells to let the rescued children and their rescuers crawl past.

"It's going well, Ev," said Lulerain, quietly.

"Jonah's in detention, and Amy is in a coma, and Steve is. . .something else, but, yes, I suppose it's going fine."

"It really is. Although, word from Stacey is that the faster we can move the better."

Ev nodded. "That went well," she said, loudly. "So, we're going to keep working in two groups."

There were four more groups of five- to eleven-year-olds to rescue. She split her team up into two groups, putting Derek in charge of the second.

"You handle the two closest groups, we'll head to the other two," she said to Derek. "Once you clear a group, send the rescued out with one or two grown-ups and move on."

They moved much faster through the rest of the junior groups. If everyone took a cell, they could clear a group in fifteen minutes, as long as none of the children were too stubborn about leaving.

Ev herself freed a boy named Frank, about nine, who started speaking the moment he saw her and didn't stop until she sent him outside with a grown-up.

"All these people!" he said. "It's not right, there being all these people, and nobody telling *me*!"

He was extremely happy to join them and didn't seem the slightest bit worried.

Mostly, the children were just glad to see other people. They cried, or they laughed, or they said nothing and clung to them desperately.

"Almost done," said Ev. "I'll do the last one."

Ev opened the last cell door in the last junior cluster. Inside was a very small boy with blonde hair and huge blue eyes. His face was tear stained.

"Hello," said Ev, gently. "What's your name?"

"Brian," said the boy, eyes wide. "They sent me away from mommy and daddy!"

"I know, Brian. Do you want to come with us?"

"Are we going home?"

"Yes. But it's a new home."

"Will mommy and daddy be there?"

Ev's eyes teared up. "I don't know. But I hope so."

She put one grown-up in charge of Brian all on his own, because he looked like he needed some one-on-one attention.

"We've finished here, Ev. The kids were the easiest—the other teams are having a slightly harder time."

"Tell my team we're going to head in further and try to free some family and grown-up groups. Coordinate with the other teams and figure out the best direction for us to pick."

"The other teams have pretty good coverage, Ev. We'd only get in their way. Although. . ."

"What?"

"There's the section we were going to leave until last because of the damage caused in the Chronoburster attack. Vendavi cordoned parts of it off, according to Stacey, but there are still some intact cells with grown-ups scattered throughout the area."

"If there are people there, we should rescue them. . ."

"Your mother is there."

Ev groaned.

"Then maybe we should just leave."

"Ev, you promised you'd let me fix this, if there was a chance, and there *is* a chance. You and I can go alone, maybe with Derek, and everyone else can get out. We won't just free her, either—we'll see who else is around too."

"Fine. Siobhan comes with us too. We don't know who we'll run into down there."

Ev sent some of her team out and some of them to help Ray-Leigh and Stacey wrap up their sections, then she, Lulerain, Derek and Siobhan, using Stacey's maps, went to explore the damaged part of Inner.

"It will be different with grown-ups," said Lulerain. "Children are more open to change, and they're far more likely to do what they're told. The grown-ups have lived here their whole lives. Tread carefully, and let Derek handle them if they seem chaotic. Siobhan, please be ready to fade us all if needed."

Siobhan nodded.

"You can go outside if you prefer," said Ev.

"No, I'm happy here. Don't worry about me."

"I *am* worried about you, and nothing is going to change that."

Siobhan smiled, and for the first time it looked real. "I'm really okay, Ev. Really. I'm happy for the first time in my life. I wouldn't be in here if I didn't want to be—I don't *have to* do anything anymore!"

The words 'we have to stick together' flooded Ev's mind, and she felt a stab of guilt, but she told herself quickly that it wasn't the same as what Felix had done, not really.

"Stacey says we don't have much time left," said Lulerain.

"Okay, we'll spend no more than twenty minutes looking, and then we head back. Lulerain, tell the other teams to start wrapping things up as well. It's time we started thinking about getting out of here."

"Already done."

"We can't get everyone, so, we're going to try rescue Mike's dad and Jonah's mum, because they're around here somewhere too, and any family groups with really young kids as well."

"And your mother, of course," said Lulerain.

"Yes, fine."

Ev examined the map Stacey had made closely as they crawled.

"This one," she said, stopping suddenly. "This is Jonah's mom. Derek, you go three doors down and get Mike's dad."

Siobhan was at Ev's side as she opened the hatch, and Lulerain hovered just behind them. She opened the hatch and what she saw was this:

A middle-aged woman, sitting in front of a computer screen, watching rows of figures scroll by. A 'working adult', as she would be called in Inner.

She turned in surprise when the hatch opened, probably expecting to see a bug bot.

"Hi," she said. "My name is Evelyn Acorn. I'm from the outside, where everything is better. I don't have much time to explain, but I need you to come with me."

"I'm not sure I understand," said the woman, whose name was Deirdre according to Stacey's notes. Deidre Tulip, mother of Jonah Tulip. She stared at them blankly.

"Your son needs you," said Ev. "Jonah."

"Jonah is dead," said Deirdre. "As good as, anyway. He is gone from me, and therefore he is dead."

"He isn't dead, but he *is* in trouble," said Ev, desperately. "He needs you. . ."

In truth, Ev couldn't think of someone who'd be less help to Jonah then this colorless, gray statue, but she didn't know what else to say.

"Time is ticking, Evelyn," whispered Lulerain.

"What is that?" demanded Deirdre, suddenly. "Floating at your shoulder? Is it a bot?"

"It's a pixie," said Ev, relieved by the sudden show of interest. "She's. . ."

"Pixies are not real," said Deirdre, dismissively. "It isn't really there."

Ev gave a huge, sad sigh.

"I could have been you," she said.

Deirdre ignored her and turned back to her work.

Carefully, Ev found the yellow in her heart, and let it do the rest.

You'll come with us, now. No complaints. No whining. No saying things aren't there that are. Come with us NOW.

"Come with us now, please."

"Alright," said Deidre, instantly, she swung round in her office chair, stood up, and headed for the hatch so quickly that Ev and Siobhan had to scramble to get out of her way.

"Just stay close to us until we get out of the tunnel, Deidre."

"Ev, we really should get your mother next. . ."

Before Ev could answer, an older man, with dark, graying hair and a white beard came scurrying down the tunnel.

"Yeah, so I may have a problem!" called Derek, who was a little way behind the man with two other grown-ups slung over his shoulders. "I thought I should just release as many people as possible, give them a chance, you know, but this one is crazy! He's running around telling everyone that there's nothing to worry about and they should return to their 'regularly scheduled activities'. Hey! You!"

Derek tried to make a grab for the man, but he missed.

"For the good of Inner," said the man, eyes wild, "please return to your cells and your assigned tasks! This is merely a glitch that will be overcome shortly."

Ev could see his face clearly now.

"Janian! Janian Granite!"

"You know who I am! Then you know you must obey me in everything!"

"Tried that. It didn't work out. Listen to me. Everything we've been told about Inner and the world—it isn't true. You should come with us. We're going outside."

Come with us.

"You must go back to your cells," he said again, eyes vacant.

"We're not going back to our cells, Janian," said Ev. "We're going outside. Would you like to come?"

Come with us!

"There is no 'outside'! To suggest otherwise is Withouter thinking!"

"Yes. We're Withouters, and we're going outside now. You can follow us if you like."

COME!

Janian paused, and then scurried back the way he'd come.

"Leave him, Derek," called Ev. "Let him go."

Derek ducked into the door of an open cell to let Janian past. In the distance they heard him yelling, "Go back to your cells!"

"Who's he even talking to?" asked Derek. "There's no one down there!"

"I don't know," said Ev, but to be honest, what she was really worried about was why she hadn't been able to make Janian come with them. The yellow was there, burning strong. She'd *felt* the magic work. So, why hadn't he listened?

"You can't save everyone, Ev," said Lulerain.

"Yes, yes. . ."

The thing was, she *could* save everyone, if only she could figure out how reality warping actually worked.

"Why didn't he come with us?" she asked herself.

Derek gave her a look. "Maybe it's better that he didn't. Or maybe you didn't really want him to. Or something. Anyway, he's gone now, what are we doing next?"

"Derek, get those people out of here—we're running out of time. Deidre, go with him."

"I'm not sure I should. . ."

Go with him!

". . .but I will, if that's what you want."

"I do. Lulerain, it says here that Amy's parents are both together with her little sister. Can you get them?"

"I can," said the pixie, "but what about your promise?"

"I haven't forgotten. Siobhan and I are going to get my mother. Happy?"

"Yes, Ev," said Siobhan, obediently.

"Not really," said Lulerain. "Perhaps I should get your mother and you. . ."

"This is how it will be. I want to see her, decide for myself if she gets to leave this place or not. *You'll* free her even if she's dangerous."

"Ev. . ."

"You have a task to complete."

You have a task to complete.

Lulerain sighed, sadly, but she flew down the tunnel to find Amy's family. Derek, Deirdre following close behind, started making his way back to the exit with the other men he'd rescued.

She was tempted to just leave, to tell Lulerain that they'd tried, but her mother hadn't wanted to come.

But that's why Siobhan was with her. To keep her honest.

"Leading by example means keeping my promises," said Ev. It felt like something Granny would have told her. Maybe it *was* something Granny had told her, and she'd just forgotten.

Ev knew exactly where her mother's cell was. She memorized it from Stacey's map, but when they found themselves at the hatch, she still said, "Is this the right one?"

Siobhan checked the map and nodded. "Definitely."

"All right, here goes. . ."

She grabbed the handle and pulled the hatch open.

Inside, she could see a plump, dark-haired woman that she vaguely recognized, older now than when they'd last seen each other. Older and somehow. . .smaller, like she'd shrunk with time.

Or perhaps it was Ev who had grown.

The woman turned around in surprise. Her face formed a comical trio of o's as she stared in shock at the intruders.

"Mother? Mother, it's me. Ev."

"What are you talking about?"

"Mother, I've come to get you out. It's much better outside. . ." Her heart wasn't in it. She wanted nothing more than for her mother to stay exactly where she was.

But she'd promised Lulerain.

COME!

Her magic had no effect at all. It often felt weak when she was trying to create a reality that she didn't actually want, but this time there wasn't even a faint spark.

"Is this a test?" asked her mother suspiciously. "Vendavi? Is this a test?"

Harriet Acorn, we are experiencing some anomalies in the system.

Please stand by for further instructions.

That didn't sound good.

"Thanks, Vendavi," muttered Ev's mother, also known as 'Harriet'.

"You have to come with us now!"

"Vendavi says to stand by, so that's what I'm going to do," said Harriet. She turned back to her keyboard and started typing.

"Mother. . ." She was interrupted by an explosion.

"What was that?" demanded Harriet.

Dropellet popped into existence in front of Ev's nose.

"Chronoburster. Get out," he said, and vanished again.

"Inner is going to be destroyed! You *must* come with us!"

"That's impossible," said Harriet, her back still turned. "Inner is impregnable, nothing can destroy it."

"Mother!"

"You should leave."

Now the ground was shaking. Harriet's possessions tumbled all around her cell, but the woman just calmly kept typing, even when her displays flickered and died.

"We should just leave her," said Ev.

"What? But we came all this way! We *must* take her with us!"

"She won't come!"

"There must be a way we can do it without hurting her..."

"Oh, who cares if we hurt her!" Ev gathered all of her magical reserves, concentrated, and blasted everything she had directly at her mother.

Harriet fell to the ground, unconscious.

"Help me get her out. . ." panted Ev, exhausted.

"You're not supposed to use all of your magic like that!" said Siobhan, crawling into the cell. "I can't lift her!"

"So? You're a magic user, aren't you?"

"Yes, of course. . ." Siobhan closed her eyes for a moment and then carefully levitated the still form of Ev's mother toward the hatch. Ev backed out of their way and then followed them down the tunnel.

"Let me help you with the levitation."

"No! You can't, anyway, you've used up all your magic because you're an idiot."

The tunnel shook from another explosion.

"This way!" shouted Siobhan, shoving Harriet ahead of her down the narrow tunnel with all the magic she had.

Ev scrambled after her, but something made her pause.

"What was that?"

"What?"

In the distance, a sound. . .

"Wait for me!"

"Who was that?" asked Ev.

"I didn't hear anything!" said Siobhan.

"Someone's calling for help!"

"Wait for me!"

Ev turned to see Peter, crawling awkwardly down an adjoining tunnel.

"What are you doing here?"

"I got separated, things got confused, I think I'm hurt. . ."

"Just crawl, we have to get out. Keep up! Don't fall behind!"

She could hear Peter panting behind them.

"Keep going," she called, but without looking back—looking back gets you killed.

She didn't know where she was going, but every time she had to choose a direction, she picked the quietest one.

They had to get outside.

They crawled for ages. Ev was exhausted. She could barely keep moving, but every time she stopped or even slowed down, the tunnel they were in would begin to crumble, forcing her to go on.

"I. . .can't. . .keep going. . ." panted Peter.

"You can and you will," said Ev. Her heart was full of terror, because she'd been here before, she'd done this before, only this time it was a *real* friend, not just something from her mind.

"This way!" shouted Siobhan. "We're almost there!"

Ev followed Siobhan closely and watched her disappear through an opening. She scrambled her and pulled herself out. Fresh air! Sunlight! She could see her friends and the forest.

She turned and called to Peter.

"Come on!"

But Peter didn't move, just lay in the tunnel, exhausted.

"Come on!" she said again, starting to panic. "It's all right, you can do it, just a little further, trust me."

Come on!

Nothing happened—she had no magic left.

"Come on, Peter!"

Peter did his best to pull himself to his knees and crawl for the hatch.

"That's good! Keep crawling!"

"Madison said. . ." The ground shook, cutting Peter off, and what was left of the tunnel collapsed on top of him.

"Peter!" screamed Ev.

"Run!" screamed Siobhan.

Ev felt the panic building up. The thick dust was already too much for her lungs. They began to close, and she felt dizzy.

Siobhan grabbed her. "We have to go!"

Now Siobhan was dragging Ev *and* trying to levitate her mother at the same time. The stumbled away from the hatch.

"I'll take her!" shouted someone, it sounded like Gavin, and next thing Siobhan was pulling Ev with all her strength.

"Gavin has your mom; you need to move!"

With a final shudder, the ground behind them caved in, and it was only because Siobhan jumped two feet in the air and flew the last few paces that they weren't swallowed up with it.

Ev turned to look for Peter, but it was too late.

Peter was gone.

25. They Knew

I once wrote a paper about this phenomenon, and I was punished most severely for it, although not nearly as severely as I will be when this book comes to light. Know that you are only permitted to read this because they have no choice—the magic that protects these words is old and deep and they have no idea how to stop it.

In that paper I explained how living in a closed system can lead to madness. I will not write more here, as this book is about helping you survive the transition from Inner, but I cannot end without warning you to be careful. The people around you may not be thinking rationally. Their decisions may not be based in reality. More importantly, be careful of yourself—are *you* thinking rationally? Are *you* living in reality? We are all part of this system and therefore we are all at risk.

Alison Oakwood

Inner: How and Why?

Epilogue

Ev and Siobhan crashed to the ground in a flurry of debris. People were shouting and running. Someone grabbed Ev and pulled her to her feet, but she fell again, crying.

"What happened?" she heard Stacey ask.

"Peter is dead," said Madison. "He didn't make it out. I told him he wouldn't, but that didn't stop him. . ." For the first time since Ev had known her, Madison sounded shaken, even sad.

Her tears doubled.

"Ev? Are you alright?" asked Stacey.

"How could I be?" she shouted. "I saved the wrong person! I should have helped him. . .If I'd still had my magic left, but I had to save *her*. . .where's Lulerain?"

"Ev, calm down!"

"It's her fault! This was her idea!"

"Ev! Stop it!" This was Siobhan. "Please, stop it!"

"It was an accident." Gavin. "No one's fault. Try to breathe."

"Don't tell me to breathe!"

"Don't blame yourself, Ev," said Stacey.

"I don't!"

But who else was there?

"Where's Lulerain? Lulerain!"

"I'm right here, Ev," said the pixie, quietly. "I know it must be difficult. . ."

"Oh, you *know,* do you? You know what it's like for a bunch of other kids to follow you into danger and then *die*, do you?"

"Ev. . ."

"I wasted time saving *her*. I did it for you, and when the time came, I couldn't help Peter. This is your fault!"

"What do you mean you couldn't help him?" Derek asked, quietly. "You can do anything."

Ev's heart clenched.

"Derek, I tried everything, I promise. . ."

"You can do anything you like. You always do. So why *didn't* you save him?" His voice was a shout by the end.

"Derek. . ."

"Don't talk to me! I don't want to hear a word that *you* have to say!" Derek leapt into the air and darted into the forest.

"He crossed the threshold!" shouted Viola. "He's no longer hidden, no longer protected. . ."

"He'll have to look after himself," said Ray-Leigh. "They'll find us now. We have to go!"

"She's right," said Madison, quietly. "Derek won't come back. For anyone." She stared blankly at the mess that had once been Inner.

"Evelyn!" Ray-Leigh, again. "Keep it together! We're waiting on your word!"

Christopher just stared at her mutely, still restricted from speaking by Ray-Leigh's spell, but his eyes said, "Get on with it, wonder girl."

Ev took a deep breath. She surveyed her people.

All around the edge of their shielded bubble were the raccoons, watching and waiting for any sign of enemy intrusion. Just inside the raccoon ring, forward-thinking True-User grown-ups had informally spread themselves out, just in case any of the Inners tried to make a run for it.

Next were the Inner children, terrified, intrigued, tired, and the Inner grown-ups in varying states of consciousness, most of them too dazed to do anything.

And in the middle was Ev, with her closest friends all around, ready to defend her at all costs.

"They're your responsibility now," said Lulerain quietly by Ev's ear. "All of them."

"Do not speak to me," said Ev, through gritted teeth.

The younger Inner kids were asking for their parents, but not all of them had made it. It was hard to tell which was worse: seeing the children search for their parents in vain or seeing them find them and be ignored. Some of the parents held their children, comforted them, sang to them, but they were few and far between.

"They'll come around," said Viola. "They weren't supposed to ever see their children again. They need time to adjust."

Ev's mother had awoken. She was looking around, skeptically, analyzing the situation so she could decide who to blame. Ev already knew who *that* would be. She looked away before she was seen.

"Mike are you sure the True Users will let us all into the camp?" she asked.

"Yes. They'll grumble and they'll moan, and they'll try to make us feel guilty about the burden, but they'll take us back. They'll raise the orphans. They'll keep them safe."

"For a given definition of safe. . ." muttered Madison.

"Madison, not now," said Ev, but she knew exactly what her friend meant. The True Users were only slightly better than the Alerrawians, but unfortunately, they were the only other option.

"There is *one* problem, however," said Mike.

"Yes?"

"The camp has moved. It had to—the Alerrawians knew where it was. Jim used us as a distraction to relocate and recast the spell of protection. I don't know where it is, is what I'm saying."

Ev looked at the ring of raccoons, still standing guard. The one she'd come to think of as the leader turned and waved.

"I think we'll be fine," she said, "with a little bit of help from our new friends."

She cleared her throat. "Friends," she said, trying to ignore how small and stupid she sounded. "Friends, you need to follow us to safety. We can't stay here—the people who destroyed Inner will find us."

"What is going on?" demanded a man who looked equal parts dazed and angry.

"It's all right, dad," said Mike. "Everything is going to be all right."

"Who are you? What is this?" asked another man, and that started them all up.

"This is treason, you know," said Mother.

"Only from your perspective," said Viola.

The children started to cry. Inner grown-ups tried to run and were stopped, either by the True Users or the raccoons. There were nearly three hundred people in front of her, not a big number in the world from before, but an unstoppable force by bubble standards.

If they could be reasoned with.

She hadn't had much time to recover, but a tiny spark of magic had returned to her heart. She could feel it, sitting there, biding its time.

But there was no time. She grabbed on to it and used it.

Calm down and listen to me.

The chaos stilled and every eye turned to look at Ev.

"We are leaving now," said Ev to the group. "If you are from Inner, find someone who isn't and follow them. If you need help moving, wait and someone will come get you. If you are a child, find another child and take their hand. Every child needs to be in a pair, and every child is responsible for making sure their partner follows a grown-up to safety."

Everyone sprang into action the moment Ev stopped speaking.

There was a moment when it seemed like one of the Inner kids wasn't going to find a partner, but Madison quietly stepped in and took her hand. She turned to Ev and said, "Goodbye. I still mostly think you're too weird to live, but I'm glad that I got to know you. I think this is the last time you'll get to speak to me, by the way, so if you have anything to say. . ."

"What are you talking about?"

"I can't see past the journey to the camp. That doesn't seem like a good sign."

"Evelyn, we need to move," said Ray-Leigh.

Madison took her young charge by the hand and joined the other kids before Ev could say another word.

"Thank you, everyone," said Ev. "Just remember the rules: children follow grown-ups. Inner grown-ups follow Withouter grown-ups. Withouter grown-ups follow the raccoons."

"Say what now?" said Ray-Leigh.

"You heard me."

The raccoons were already on the move. Without waiting to see if anyone was following her, Ev took off after them.

After a while, the grown-ups started passing her. Eventually, even the children were walking more quickly than she was.

She was just so tired. Very soon, she was at the back of the pack with Gavin, Stacey, and Siobhan.

Ev's eyes were heavy. Any moment, she would tumble to the ground. She shook her head and focused on putting one foot in front of the other.

One step, two steps, three steps, four steps. . .

. . .four-hundred-and-thirty-seven steps, four-hundred-and-. . .

With a pop, Lulerain appeared in front of her. "Madison says, 'Something's coming'," said the pixie, and then she disappeared again.

"Listen," hissed Stacey. The three children stopped and strained their ears.

"Those are screams," said Gavin.

"Children's screams," said Stacey, who was already running.

"And helicopters!" shouted Gavin.

Then Ev was in the air, flying as quickly as she could towards the sounds of gunfire and helicopter rotors.

Moments later, she could see the helicopters, but her dwindling magic was threatening to let her down.

One of the helicopters turned slightly, and its pilot looked Ev dead in the eye. Without thinking, Ev flew full speed towards him, blasting the helicopter with all the magic she had left in her.

"Let there be light!" she screamed. The last few drops of lava sprang from her brain and down her arms.

She knew it wouldn't work, and, anyway, helicopters were protected against fire magic, but she had to do *something*.

The helicopter wobbled for a moment, righted itself, and then turned back to its mission.

Ev, out of magic, fell to the ground with a scream, but someone caught her with a levitation spell, and she landed gently.

"Get up!" shouted Christopher—Ray-Leigh must have released him from his spell of silence.

All around was chaos, people running, people shooting, people screaming. Ev's mind was numb with fear and panic.

One, two, three helicopters, one, two, three, four bodies. . .

One soldier, coming straight for me.

One wolf, tackling him to the ground.

One raccoon, grabbing my ears. . .

"Hey!" she shouted as the raccoon head-butted her, gently.

With a tiny paw, the raccoon patted her on the head as if to say, "Never mind, all better now," and then it sprang at an Alerrawian soldier about to fire on a group of Inner children who were clustered around Christopher.

"Ev, hold still!" said Viola. She closed her eyes and concentrated, and the next moment Ev felt her magic flow back, stronger than before.

"It's temporary. Be sensible."

Then she heard Christopher, with all the authority of Vendavi, telling the children, "I don't have time to get into the details, and, honestly, neither do you. You have magical abilities. Your new friends have released you from the poison that keeps magic locked away. It would be rude not to use it now, don't you think?"

The children looked at him, blankly, and Ev knew it wouldn't work. There wasn't time to teach them. . .

"If you don't do something, you will die, and so will everyone else," she said, edging closer to the group which was now being protected by some of the original True Users. "Close your eyes. Look for your magic. It might feel like a color in your stomach or a sound in your heart. It could feel like anything, but you'll know it when you find it."

Find your abilities.

"Now, grab ahold of it. Keep it steady."

Use it!

There was a sizzling sound as Shawn set the grass around his feet on fire. He grinned. "Nice. What else can I do?"

"You won't know until you try," said Ev. "Right now, we all need protection. Ask your magic how best to do it, then do it!"

With a nonchalant shrug, Shawn created a ring of fire around the younger children and the grown-ups who were protecting them.

"Nice!" said Ev, just as Jill and Larissa raised shaky shields around their cluster. "That is *very* good!"

They'd never used magic before, and yet here they were doing things that were supposed to take you months to learn. Just because Ev had told them to.

No wonder Felix thought they were a threat.

Use your abilities for the protection of our group. You are confident. You are sure. You know exactly what you are doing on this day and in this battle.

"Do what you think is best," she said out loud.

Kyle turned to an approaching soldier, clasped his hands to his chest, then *pushed* outwards. Ev could almost see the magic flowing from him.

The soldier rose a few inches in the air, then collapsed to the ground in a confused heap.

"Who am I? Where am I? he asked.

"Good," said Ev. "I'm impressed." Above her, Cathy was hovering, aiming unrefined bursts of raw magic at anyone they could reach.

"You've certainly managed to add a bit of chaos to the proceedings," said Christopher.

"Shut up and fight!"

Shut up and fight!

To his surprise, Christopher's lips slammed shut and he spun around to punch an oncoming soldier in the face.

The raccoons were also fighting, biting, and slashing. Throughout the forest, Ev heard the sound of skulls cracking together as the raccoons executed their signature move.

The Inner children fought alongside the Withouters. Even the younger ones were joining in, spurred by the actions of the others. The grown-ups from Inner were huddled in a confused mass, many unconscious either from the shock of being rescued or the battle. Viola and Reuben were defending them, while Ray-Leigh darted between groups, fending off the aerial attack as best she could.

Which was pretty damn well. Ray-Leigh might have hated the changes that Ev had brought to the forest, but that hadn't stopped her from learning.

"Keep the helicopters distracted!" shouted Ray-Leigh.

"Fire on the helicopters, if you can!" Ev yelled at the children.

Mike was whispering frantically to Dropellet. Moments later, the pixie grabbed the attention of a raccoon, and then they both vanished with a pop.

Gavin and Stacey emerged from the trees, panting—they'd only just caught up. Gavin shielded them both and they ran to a child who was on the ground, unconscious. Ev watched as Gavin touched the girl's forehead and her eyes fluttered open.

Everyone else was fighting the best they could.

"Where's Madison?" asked Ev, but no one heard her.

She looked around desperately.

"Where's Madison?"

"Oh, for Pete's sake!" shouted Christopher. "This is a battle! You can't go thinking about one person!"

"Where is she?"

"Over there!" shouted Christopher. Ev followed his pointing hand to see Madison and a small child surrounded by soldiers. They were completely cut off. Madison was doing what she could with the little bit of magic she had, but it wasn't enough.

Ev took a step towards Madison, but there was too much battle between her and her friend.

"You, big kids! Take the little ones to the tree line. Keep them together so you have less space to defend."

She sent a burst of uncoordinated magic at some approaching soldiers which kept them back long enough for the kids to move to relative safety, but only for a moment. They shook their heads, started advancing again, and Ev realized that whatever Viola had done to her was wearing off.

A blast of brilliant raw magic hit the soldiers. Two fell to their knees, screaming, and the others ran to find a safer bit of battlefield. Ev turned to see Jill Holly at her side.

"Thanks."

"Don't mention it."

"Jill, I need you to help me. We have to keep the kids safe. When I say now, blast everything you have into the sky. All right?"

Jill nodded.

"Now!" she screamed.

Covered by Jill's blinding blast, Ev ran for the tree line where the kids were hiding. Viola joined her.

"I can see what's on your mind, and I can do it better than you."

Ev nodded and left Viola to cast the hiding spell, the one that had protected the True Users for centuries, over the children.

Ev returned to the battle to see who else needed her help.

At that moment, the rest of the True Users appeared.

"Finally, reinforcements," she heard Mike mutter as he bashed a distracted guard over the head with a rock. "They probably stopped to debate it first."

"Let there be light!" shouted Ev, blasting the guard that was about to attack Mike with just enough fire to send him screaming. Then she had to jump clear of a burning helicopter as it fell from the sky.

"Glad *some* of your lessons stuck in their heads," said Christopher. "Better late than never, I suppose. I see they remembered how to bring down Alerrawian helicopters."

"I didn't teach them *that*."

"No. You just taught them how to think it up on their own."

The raccoons rounded up the last few Alerrawian survivors, and then the battle was over.

"Did any of them escape?" called Ev.

Ray-Leigh shook her head. "Not as far as I can tell. My magic doesn't detect any escapees. Anyway, the raccoons were watching the outskirts of the fight—I think they caught the stragglers."

"Good. Ray-Leigh, I'm putting you in charge of dealing with prisoners. Gently, please."

"Sure. For a given definition of gently. As defined my me."

"Dropellet, tell Viola that the children are hers to care for. Find a raccoon to tell you where she and the children have gotten to, and make sure they head for the new camp. Gavin, you need to help the wounded. I don't care who they are or where they were born—Alerrawian, True User, Inner, Withouter. . .help them all. Christopher— you can start dealing with the dead. Everyone needs to be moved to the True User's new camp so we're not stretching our defenses so thin, and the four of you are responsible for getting them there. Now, please!"

You have things to do!

Without arguing, the Withouters went about their tasks.

"Am I bringing the dead to the camp too?" asked Christopher.

"Yes. We need to bury them."

"Even the Alerrawians?"

"Even the Alerrawians."

"And especially Madison, I assume. . ."

Ev looked at Christopher blankly, her mind unable to comprehend what he was saying.

"Your friend, Madison," he continued. "She's among the dead. I thought you might like to know. That little kid that she put all of her effort into saving is okay, though, so there's that, even if this habit of you and your friends to only think about individuals and not the group as a whole is. . ."

"Shut up."

"I'm only saying that, had she left the child and contributed to the bigger efforts. . ."

"Shut up!"

Shut up!

Christopher's mouth slammed shut.

"Gather the dead, Christopher. Do it quickly. Do it with respect. And do it quietly. I will deal with you later."

Jim Day approached, Dropellet and some other pixies at his side.

"Well," said Jim gruffly. "You did it, I suppose. I am surprised, to say the least, but. . ."

"Thank you for your assistance and your ongoing support of our efforts," said Ev. "Please ask your people to help with relocation."

Madison is dead.

"Of course, I just wanted to say. . ."

"Thank you for your time."

She had to find Gavin and Stacey because Madison was dead.

"Evelyn," said Dropellet, keeping pace, "Lulerain wants to know. . ."

"Lulerain can go on wanting. I am not taking on any advice or questions from pixies at this time, but I will let you know if and when that changes."

With a shrug, Dropellet vanished.

Madison is dead.

Stacey was helping Gavin by keeping things organized, making people form lines.

"Madison is dead," said Ev when she reached her friends.

"I know," said Stacey.

"What do we do?"

"I don't want to talk about this. Not with you."

She turned her back on Ev, maybe to help an older True User, maybe to make a point.

"I'm sorry, Stacey."

"I'm sure you are. But sorry doesn't help anyone."

"Stacey. . ."

"I don't blame you. I'm just angry and sad, and I can't talk about it right now. Okay? Please go somewhere else and do something important, otherwise what was the point of any of it."

Stacey walked away to help someone else, leaving Ev with Gavin.

"She'll be okay."

"Will she?"

"Oh yes. But will you?"

"I don't even know what 'okay' means anymore. . ."

"You're needed," said Gavin, and Ev turned to see Jim coming at her again.

"What does he *want*. . ."

"Probably to plan. Or talk about what comes next. Your people and his people are in this together, and as much as he doesn't like it, he has to talk to you. He's 'being a grown-up about it'. I think that's the phrase. I don't think it matters that you're eleven or that your friends are dead. You have to get on with it anyway."

"I didn't ask for this," she hissed as Jim got closer.

"That's probably why you're so good at it."

Ev gritted her teeth and turned to Jim.

"How can I help you?"

"We need to figure out what we're doing. . ."

"Indeed. I was just getting on to that. Do you have any information that would be helpful?"

Jim opened his bag and removed a document.

"It's another ultimatum from the Alerrawians. They delivered it to the old camp—we've had someone keeping watch, just in case."

"What does it say?"

Jim handed her the document.

"It's slightly insane," he said.

Alright, listen up, you worms. We've given you every opportunity to let go of your backwards ways and join us in pursuing a life of scientific purity, but you have turned us down at every opportunity. How DARE you thwart the will of centuries of Granites by freeing the denizens of Inner? How DARE you attack OUR people? How DARE you side with that BRAT to destabilize the entire bubble?

We have tried being reasonable, but you have made the wrong choices over and over again. NO MORE CHANCES! We destroyed Inner—we can destroy you.

Felix Granite

"Well. . ."

"Yes. We've received a lot of little notes from Felix over the years. They *have* been getting progressively. . .stranger. . .but now. . ."

"Everyone in the bubble is going mad," said Ev. "Didn't you know?"

"Come on, now. . ."

"It's true. It's a little more obvious with some than others, but we are all going mad."

"Perhaps by pre-bubble standards, but. . ."

"Anyway, *Felix* is definitely losing it, even if you don't believe me about the rest of us. We need to take him down before he finds a way to destroy us."

"It's not that easy. . ."

"That's what you said about freeing Inner. Stop being scared of things that aren't easy and start doing the things that need doing."

"There is so much to consider, and. . ."

"Yes, there is. Luckily, you won't be considering them alone, but as part of a leadership council. Led by me, naturally, but I will listen to the advice of my grown-ups. When it suits me."

"You're Alerrawian! How *dare* you declare that you will lead True Users!"

"I will not be leading True Users. Nor will I be leading Alerrawians or Inners. I will only be leading Withouters."

Jim paused.

"Unification?"

"Yes. Because, when we leave the bubble, I suspect we'll have bigger problems to face, and it won't help if we're also fighting each other."

"*Leave the bubble?* Perhaps you *are* going mad. . ."

"I am not going to waste my time trying to explain things to you that you already know. We're cooking in here. The water is running out, which I'm sure is impacting the food. And, yes, we're going mad, thank you for noticing. We are leaving."

"This is. . ."

"Of course, there is nothing keeping you here. If you want to stay away from the Withouter camp, you are welcome to do so. You can even take others with you if they feel the same. We wish you all the best."

"The *Withouter* camp?"

"Yes. Withouters outnumber True Users now. We claim the new camp as ours. If you have a problem with that, you can take it up with Viola. Or you can stay and be a part of the change. It's up to you."

"There's a lot to think about. . ."

"Stop delaying! Stop sticking to what you know just so you don't have to think about the big questions! Choose!"

CHOOSE!

"I'll stay! I'll be on your council."

"That's wonderful news, and we're very excited to have you on board. Now, get our people moving. I want us all under the protection of the new camp by sundown."

As Jim marched off, Dropellet appeared again.

"If I may have a moment of your precious time," he asked dryly.

"Yes?"

"Ray-Leigh is ready to move the prisoners. Viola has already relocated the children to the new camp with the help of the raccoons, which is the strangest sentence I've ever said, and Christopher is ready to move the dead, although Lulerain had to educate him on the meaning of the word 'respectful.' Gavin says they're ready to go too, if they can get two more healthy magic-users to help them move the wounded."

"You two," Ev called to a couple of teenagers who were lunging against a tree, giggling. "What are your innate abilities?"

"What are your innate abilities?" mimicked one of the youths in a high-pitched tone. The other laughed.

"Out of Inner for two minutes, and already they've learned that being human means being cruel," muttered Dropellet.

Ev ignored him and said, "You are addressing your leader. Answer the question."

Answer the question.

"I don't understand the question. . ." said one desperately, his eyes crossed in an attempt to perform an impossible task.

"That's fine. . ."

That's fine.

". . .what about you?"

"I think. . .well. . .I think it's something to do with floating?"

"You can fly," said Ev. "Good. You felt your magic during the battle. I want both of you to access the core of your magic, and then do whatever Gavin Oakwood, he's the one over there with the injured, tells you to do."

Access your magic. Obey Gavin Oakwood until the injured are safe in the camp.

"Yes, ma'am."

Ev turned to see Dropellet looking at her, quizzically.

"There is more to than meets the eye."

"It has been said."

"Lulerain wants to speak to you."

"Lulerain can wait her turn. Tell everyone to follow the racoons to the Withouter Camp."

"Have you let the racoons in on that plan."

"They know what needs to be done."

It was true. The racoons would know what needed to be done. They would lead them to the new camp, and Ev wouldn't have to say a word to them. She didn't know how she knew, but she knew.

"Very well."

In fits and starts at first, and then altogether, the Withouters moved out, the pixies keeping them shielded as they stumbled after the racoons.

Ev trudged along with them. Her mind was a mess.

Jonah in detention. Amy in a coma. Peter and Madison dead.

Was it *really* worth it?

"Hello, Ev!" said a cheerful voice.

"Hello," said Ev, automatically.

"I think there might be more than mice out here."

"That's right, Jill."

Jill, who hadn't been around a real person for years and who didn't know when someone needed to be left alone, kept on talking.

"I like the racoons. They are racoons, aren't they? Only, I read a story about them. I read lots of stories. I'm glad I did—all this would have been even stranger if I hadn't!"

"I read those stories too. Not everyone was allowed to, though."

Jill's eyes were wide. "Really? So, we were special?"

"Not special. Just lucky."

"We are *very* lucky, aren't we? Stories and racoons and mice!"

Jill ran on ahead, perhaps to see the racoons better.

"I am lucky," said Ev out loud. "I *am* lucky. *I* am lucky. I am *lucky*."

"Are you alright, Ev?" asked Mike, catching up with her just in time to hear her mantra.

"Just trying to see if I can make it feel true."

"Maybe it doesn't feel true because 'lucky' isn't quite the right word. 'Luck' implies that something outside of your control is calling all the shots, as if there were some big Luck God snapping her fingers and deciding your future. But that's not how it works. You're here because of the decisions you made. Some things were luck, like the stories, and ending up with just the right combination of genetics to make you the person you are, but it was still *you* who decided. *You* made the decision to run away, *three times*. *You* made the decision to break Lulerain's spell. *You* made the decision to free Inner. *You* decided that it didn't matter where people lived in the bubble, that it didn't matter what they believed, *you* decided that you would help all of them anyway. If you'd let 'luck' stay at the wheel, you would still be at Alerrawia, quietly being a model student, but instead you're here, trying to save everyone, and the fact that you couldn't save us all is just because you're human, and it's not like that's *your* fault!"

"Peter and Madison are dead. . ."

"Peter and Madison *knew* they would die! Madison saw it! And they played their part anyway, because they *knew* that what we did today was more important than anything else. They *knew*!"

"They knew. . ."

"Yes. It was their decision. They didn't let 'luck' control their lives either. They decided, they acted, and they took the consequences that they knew were coming. Just like you."

Ev straightened her spine, raised her head, and took a deep breath.

"They knew. They *knew*. *They* knew!"

"That's better," said Mike, with a satisfied nod. "Now, let's get these people home. It's not over yet."

26. When Do We Begin?

Myth #18: Giants continue to walk among us.

While it is true that giants did once exist, there are none living in the bubble. They are not fully human, and therefore would not have been able to survive. Giants no longer exist.

Felix Granite

Alerrawia: To the Future

Volume 4, Page 54

Head down to avoid attention, Ev strode as quickly as she could through the Withouter Camp.

"Ev!" someone called.

Ev sighed. She knew she should have shielded herself, but she was trying not to waste her magic.

She put a smile on her face and turned to see who had called her *this* time. It was Gavin.

"I think we're out of the woods with the last couple of patients. We only lost two! I'm very relieved."

"Excellent news, Gavin!" said Ev, wishing he would go away. "You're doing a great job as head healer. After we've defeated Alerrawia, you'll have more help and equipment and you'll be able to do even more."

Gavin grinned and went about his business with a wave. Two steps later. . .

"Ev! Ev, I have a question."

Viola.

"I was wondering—do you think we should start getting these kids ready for a long-term place in the camp? I know right now we're all about battle training, but once the fighting is over, they're going to need something else to keep them busy. . ."

"Wonderful idea! That's why you're in charge of the children. I leave it in your hands to decide on the best way forward."

"Thank you, I'll think something up and bring it to you for approval."

"I look forward to seeing it," said Ev, her face aching from the fake smile.

This time she was almost at the door to the den before she heard her name.

"Evelyn, can I talk to you about the prisoners?"

"Certainly, Ray-Leigh. What's the problem this time?"

"I just think we need a long-term plan. Right now, it's working out fine, but what about when the real fighting begins? We can't leave them here alone, and we can't afford to leave anyone behind to watch them, not anyone who's actually any good. . ."

"I've been thinking about offering some of them them opportunity to join our ranks. What are your thoughts on that?"

Ray-Leigh's face hardened automatically, and Ev could actually see her mentally reminding herself that Ev was in charge now, and that she had to at least listen.

"Interesting," said Ray-Leigh, slowly. "There are one or two who show promise as allies, I suppose. But it's a very small number."

"I would be very interested to hear more about them. Please bring a proposal to the next council meeting. Also, I would like you to start thinking about our magical imprisonment options. Something temporary, for now, at least until we see how things play out on a larger scale. Nothing as cruel as *detention*, of course, but something where we can safely leave them for short periods of time."

Ray-Leigh nodded. "Thanks for taking my request seriously," she said. "I'll put something together and get back to you."

"Excellent."

The moment Ray-Leigh turned away, Ev pulled open the hatch in the ground and slid into the cool, underground den.

'Den' was the cheerful word that everyone was using because 'morgue' was too. . .accurate.

"Christopher. Good morning," she said, wondering what she'd have to do to get rid of him this time.

"Evelyn," he said, with a nod. "As you requested, I have finalized the funeral arrangements. There will be three services: one traditional True User Service, one newly invented Inner service, and one traditional Alerrawian service for the enemy dead, although you know my thoughts on bothering with that last one. It looks like most people want to attend all three, so we're just going to have them back-to-back. Burial for the True Users, cremation for everyone else."

"Except for Madison."

Christopher raised an eyebrow, sending Ev, not for the first time, into a daydream about what he would look like if she shaved both of his sarcastic eyebrows off.

"Burial, then? With the True Users?"

"She'll be staying down here, for now."

"Evelyn," said Christopher, in the voice he reserved for particularly stubborn children. "Madison is dead. They're all dead. There is nothing you can do about it. Preserving her corpse in this freezing hole is not going to change that. Better to let her go, don't you think?"

"No. Madison will be staying, down here, until further notice. Understood?"

Christopher sighed. "Fine, but I hope you come to your senses sooner rather than later."

"If that is all. . .?"

"I'm being dismissed, am I?"

"Indeed."

"I'll go make myself useful, then. Have fun with the dead!"

Ev waited until she heard the hatch slam shut above her before she took her usual place at Madison's side.

"I've been awake for two hours," she began, "and already I've dealt with seven problems. Seven! What's the point of putting people in charge of things if they still have to ask your advice every step of the way?"

You're the one who wanted to be in charge. . .

. . .was Madison's imagined reply. Ev knew it was unhealthy to be having imaginary conversations with a dead friend, but she didn't care.

"I didn't though! It just happened. . ."

Tough.

"You're no help."

Of course not. I'm dead.

"I've been thinking. About the other thing."

752

No answer. Of course, there was never an answer, but Ev just couldn't figure out what Madison's response would be to what she was about to do.

"I've decided. It *is* worth the risk. Think of what it means if it works? It would give us an edge in battle, we could take greater risks. . ."

Who are you trying to convince? Me or you?

Ev ignored Madison's reply, which was difficult because it was entirely in her own head.

"I'm going to do it, Madison. I'm sure it will be fine."

If you were sure, you wouldn't need to say so as often as you do, but that's just my opinion.

"Madison," she said, "it's time to come back.

Madison—come back.

Nothing.

"Madison. Come back."

Madison, come back. . .

Madison just lay there.

Ev shook her head, squared her shoulder, shut her eyes, and searched for the yellow in her heart, the little spark of magic that let her alter reality.

"Madison! Come back now!"

Come back NOW!

Madison drew a huge, rattling breath, sending Ev stumbling backwards.

"Evelyn! What have you done?"

Lulerain had popped into view.

"I. . .I. . ."

"Oh, Ev. . ."

Madison's chest was rhythmically rising and falling, but her eyes were closed.

"Madison?" whispered Ev.

No response.

"Madison, you can wake up now."

Lulerain flew to Madison and examined her carefully.

"She's breathing. Her heart is beating. Everything seems fine, except. . .let me show you."

The pixie waved her hands. A dark cloud of. . .something—Ev couldn't quite make it out—hovered above Madison's head. It swirled menacingly, a thundercloud with blotches of purple and flashes of green, glimpses of many-tentacled monstrosities and blood-covered loved ones. It was completely silent, but something about it made Ev think that that the cloud was trying to howl.

"What is it?"

"It's an approximation of what's going in Madison's head," said Lulerain. "Truthfully, I don't know

754

what it is. Something has happened to her mind. I'm not sure she can wake up from this. . .sleep? Is that what it is?"

"I don't know!"

"Maybe you should! You're the one who did this!"

"I just wanted her back. . ."

"I know, Ev," said Lulerain, with a sigh. "I know. Sometimes I forget that you are only a child. I have asked too much of you, time and time again. . ."

They looked at Madison.

"What do I do?"

"What *did* you do? Let's start there, shall we?"

"I'm not sure I should tell you."

"That's up to you. But if you don't tell me, I cannot help."

"Granny said that if people knew, they wouldn't understand, that they would be afraid, and that it would make things harder for me."

"I can keep a secret."

Ev took a deep breath.

"I'm a reality warper. I have a third innate ability and it's reality warping and I'm strong in *all three* and that's what I did to bring Madison back."

Silence.

"Granny was right. Does anyone else know?"

"Derek worked it out, but I think he's the only one."

Lulerain nodded. "I knew he was smarter than he let on. If he's the only one, then it's probably a good thing that he's disappeared. You can't tell anyone, understand?"

"Of course, I understand!"

"This is unfamiliar territory for me. I don't know how to undo reality warping. I'm not even sure I can. I'll do some research, once we're back in Alerrawia, but it will have to wait. You understand, don't you?"

"Yes."

"She'll have to stay like this until the fighting is over."

"Yes."

"And you *must not* try to fix it with more reality warping. Do you understand *that*?"

"Yes."

"And you *absolutely must not* try again!"

"Yes."

"Peter is also gone, and. . ."

"I said 'yes', didn't I?"

Lulerain sank onto the slab where Madison lay, her head in her hands. Ev had never seen a pixie do anything other than fly, but now Lulerain's wings were still, and her shoulders hunched.

"I am sorry, Ev."

"I'm really tired of hearing that from you."

"This time I'm sorry for not seeing that you were struggling. You're *good* at being a leader, you know. Really good. So sometimes I forget that you are only eleven."

"Eleven-and-a-half, actually."

"The next time you want to try something like this, please talk to me first. Talk to *someone*! You're not as alone as you think."

"Yes, Lulerain."

"At least we're talking again. . ."

"What are we going to do?"

"I told you—I can't do anything until we get back to Alerrawia. Maybe there's something in the restricted section. . ."

"I mean, what do we do right now? Tell everyone what I did? Say we made a mistake and she's not dead after all? What?"

Lulerain grabbed her ears in frustration. "I don't know!"

"I need your help!"

The pixie took a deep breath. "Alright, how about this. I've already heard from Christopher that you don't want Madison cremated with the other Alerrawian dead. It's why I came down here to look for you, actually. We'll say that you want to start a memorial graveyard back at Alerrawia for the heroes we've lost. Madison will be one of them, and so will Peter, although that will be an empty grave. Open up applications for others to be buried there too. The leadership committee can debate and select *after* the fighting is over, but for now all applicants will be kept on ice. Sound good?"

"Good enough."

"And you can cast a protection spell around Madison. They'll just think that you're being extra protective, and no one should try break through—who wants a kid's corpse, anyway? Hopefully, that will be enough to keep people from noticing that *this* corpse breathes."

"I'll make the announcement later."

"You'll need to leave a pathway open for me in your spell so I can check on her whenever necessary."

"No one has taught me how to do that yet."

"No one taught you to wake the dead, either, yet here we are."

Ev looked at her feet.

Lulerain waved her hands and the dark cloud above Madison's head vanished.

"Cast your spell now, Evelyn. Our secret-keeping begins immediately. Keep it better than you did your secret about your third innate ability. We can't stay here much longer—we have to get back to work, or people will know something is wrong."

"I just need one more moment."

"Ev. . ."

"I'm not going to do anything! I just need to. . .apologize."

"Alright, but don't take too long."

Lulerain popped out of existence and Ev was alone except for all the dead people and Madison.

"I'm sorry, Madison. But I will make it right. I will fix it."

She buried her head in her hands and cried as hard as she could, because it was the last time for a while that she'd be able to do it. Then, when she was done, she raised her head, dried her face, and took a deep breath.

She took one last look at Madison and was about to cast the protective spell when she saw something lying on her friend's chest that hadn't been there before.

She bent down to look more closely.

"A cinquefoil flower?"

A lifetime ago they'd used cinquefoil to free a pixie, but how it gotten here?

For a split-second, a memory surfaced. . .

"Siobhan?" Ev asked.

. . .and then it was gone, but for some reason, Ev felt better, like she wasn't alone after all.

"Perhaps it's a good omen, Madison," said Ev. She tucked the flower into Madison's hand. "You keep it. I have to go now, but I will always be nearby."

She finished casting the spell of protection over her friend and turned to leave.

No one will notice that I've been crying.

She knew that was a safe thing to ask from the yellow in her heart, just as she'd known, deep down, that waking Madison *wasn't*.

But she'd done it anyway, and now she had to live with the consequences.

She re-emerged, blinking in the sunlight, and was almost immediately accosted by Dropellet.

"We need. . ." he began.

"We need to gather the council, and then later I have an announcement to make," said Ev.

"The entire council?"

"Yes. Get them immediately."

The council had initially consisted of Ev, Dropellet, Lulerain, Ray-Leigh, Viola, Christopher, Gavin, Stacey, Mike, and Jim, but then Dropellet had pointed out that they needed some freed Inners on board too, so she'd added Steve Rosebud, Sally and Arthur Ox (Amy's parents), and

Jill. After a long argument, Harriet Acorn was also added on the basis that the biggest troublemakers should be kept the closest.

There were too many people on the council, if she was being honest, and it was very difficult to get anything done, but it was a decision that *she* had made, and there was no way to undo it now.

"Ev!"

Instinctively, Ev looked around to see who needed her *this* time, but the voice was coming from the mirror hanging around her neck.

"Granny!" she said, relief flooding her mind. "I haven't heard from you in ages. . ."

"It's a war, Ev. They've blocked most communications. I've had to really get creative to find a way to get through. We don't have much time, so please listen."

"I'm listening!"

"Whatever you're planning to do, you *must* do it soon! They've got Eliza and Zara in the sub-basement, along with dozens of others, whether they're part of the resistance or not. With Eliza gone, we've lost the scryers! We're blind out here. We've got control of the grounds, but the compound is impregnable, and they're going to start killing hostages if we don't end the siege. Do you understand?"

"I do! We're working on a plan, we. . ."

"Whatever you're going to do, do it soon."

"I will, we were just about to make the final plan, we're. . ."

The ground shook. The mirror fell from Ev's hand and hit a rock, shattering.

"No!"

The ground shook again. And again. And again. Ev grabbed a tree to keep her feet.

"What's happening?" she shouted.

"No idea!" said Dropellet, but she could barely hear him over the thundering thuds that now filled the air.

A shadow passed overhead, and Ev glanced up to see Claster circling above.

Another thud shook her grasp and she stumbled to the ground, bruising the palms of her hands as she broke her fall.

The camp was in chaos. Those who were able to keep their feet were casting protective spells in all directions, trying desperately to see and understand the threat.

There was a rustling in the undergrowth, and Ev turned to see a sea of raccoons pour into the camp.

Behind them, huge pairs of hands parted the tree branches.

I giant emerged, bigger than Taylor, stronger than Taylor.

It might have been her imagination, but to Ev the giant also seemed *angrier* than Taylor.

The giant looked around dismissively.

"Where is the one they call Evelyn Acorn?" they demanded.

Ev looked up at the enormous person who could end her life with one squeeze, took a deep breath, and stepped forward.

"I am Evelyn," she said, her voice only cracking slightly.

The giant bent low to get a better view. Ev's heartbeat frantically in her chest, and she could feel her reality warping magic trying to get her attention, trying to protect her.

"A dragon and a renegade will have us believe that some humans are better than others."

"I'm not sure 'better' is the word," she said, hoping she sounded more confident than she felt. "'Trying to be better' might be more accurate."

"You want to rid us of the Granites and free us from this dying bubble."

"I do."

"All of us?"

"All of us."

The giant nodded and straightened.

"Very well. When do we begin?"